Praise for
Mind Catcher

"John Darnton has delivered a medical sci-fi thriller that . . . hurtles along like an ambulance, hightailing it nimbly around every sharp corner of technical knowledge and scientific research." —*Chicago Tribune*

"The settings are cinematic . . . the characters are just complex enough to encourage our sympathy or loathing; the technical bits—brain surgery, bizarre neurological syndromes, sinister computer devices—ring authentic. *Mind Catcher* fully discharges its obligation to generate suspense." —*The New York Times*

"What really scares us about science and technology isn't that they will be perverted by mad researchers or abused by dictators. It's that their progress is unstoppable, irreversible. John Darnton taps into that fear in his latest 'science adventure' thriller." —*Los Angeles Times*

"Bridging the spiritual and the technological with a yarn of dastardly doings, Darnton pulls the reader in. . . . *Mind Catcher* does what it sets out to do, which is catch the reader's interest and speculate about the progress of science in the context of real human life. It is a science fiction book in the true sense of the term. That it actually contains soul is what makes it worthwhile."
—*The Detroit News*

"The pacing is downright cinematic."
—*The Seattle Times*

"Darnton . . . knows how to generate anxiety in the reader." —*The New York Times Book Review*

"This is a dazzling, fast-paced novel that taps into issues about mind-body duality, cyberspace, artificial intelligence, and stem cell research. Well-drawn characters, tense emotions, and philosophical debates provide additional depth to this exciting scientific thriller." —*Booklist*

continued . . .

Praise for
The Experiment

"Thrills and haunts. . . . John Darnton's vivid prose, intriguing characters, and scientific precision . . . hold you hostage from the first page."   —Patricia Cornwell

"As compelling as Robert B. Parker's Spenser or Patricia Cornwell's Kay Scarpetta . . . complex and original . . . absorbing."   —*The New York Times*

"A chilling genetic mystery . . . [a] sizzling technocaper."
—*People*

"It is easy to get swept up in the narrative, which culminates in a satisfying finale."
—*Entertainment Weekly*

"Full of cutting-edge mystery, suspense, and controversy."
—Liz Smith, *New York Post*

"The plot spirals into a double helix of intrigue . . . a galloping tale. . . . The central anxieties of *The Experiment* strongly reflect the velocity of our technologies and the godlike desires of our nature, which, we know, are set to collide in the new century."
—*The New York Times Book Review*

"A first-rate thriller. . . . As with [Michael] Crichton, it's not the science per se that the book is interested in but the metaphysical and moral questions that lie in the wake of humanity's recent innovations. . . . Packed with delicious twists. . . . Darnton has written a gripping, at times harrowing, cautionary tale."
—*Rocky Mountain News*

Also by John Darnton

The Experiment
Neanderthal

JOHN DARNTON

MIND CATCHER

AN ONYX BOOK

ONYX
Published by New American Library, a division of
Penguin Group (USA) Inc., 375 Hudson Street,
New York, New York 10014, U.S.A.
Penguin Books Ltd, 80 Strand, London WC2R 0RL, England
Penguin Books Australia Ltd, 250 Camberwell Road,
Camberwell, Victoria 3124, Australia
Penguin Books Canada Ltd, 10 Alcorn Avenue,
Toronto, Ontario, Canada M4V 3B2
Penguin Books (N.Z.) Ltd, Cnr Rosedale and Airborne Roads,
Albany, Auckland 1310, New Zealand

Penguin Books Ltd, Registered Offices: 80 Strand, London WC2R 0RL, England

Published by Onyx, an imprint of New American Library, a division of
Penguin Group (USA) Inc. Previously published in a Dutton edition.

First Onyx Printing, October 2003
10 9 8 7 6 5 4 3 2 1

PUBLISHER'S NOTE
This is a work of fiction. Names, characters, places, and incidents either are the
product of the author's imagination or are used fictitiously, and any resemblance to actual persons, living or dead, business establishments, events, or
locales is entirely coincidental.

BOOKS ARE AVAILABLE AT QUANTITY DISCOUNTS WHEN USED TO PROMOTE PROD-
UCTS OR SERVICES. FOR INFORMATION PLEASE WRITE TO PREMIUM MARKETING
DIVISION, PENGUIN GROUP (USA) INC., 375 HUDSON STREET, NEW YORK, NEW YORK
10014.

To the memory of my father, Byron Darnton,
who died in New Guinea in World War II

And to the memory of my mother,
Eleanor Choate Darnton,
who said she knew of his death
the moment it occurred

Prologue

Tyler pulled the blanket up to his chin, like a bib, and tried snuggling deeper into the mattress. He turned onto his side, then his stomach, then his side again. Nothing helped; he still felt antsy. His nerves jangled. He was hot. His legs tangled up in the sheets and he kicked them free. The blanket was too heavy, and he turned onto his back and threw it down below his knees and lay there, sweating, exasperated, and, as ever, taut with fear.

To him, six years old, sleep was a monster. It lay in wait for him every night and ambushed him. It always caught him off guard, even though he had long ago learned to expect it—and the expecting brought its own kind of dreadful anticipation and made everything worse. He and the monster wrestled, and the monster always won, dragging him down into a sea of darkness and fear. Moments later, he would awake, bursting to the surface and gasping for air as if he had been held underwater by a giant hand. Cold water, cruel hand.

His parents called it "night terrors"—he had heard them talking about it once in the living room—and they assured him it would pass. They stayed in his room, read to him until their voices were hoarse, put in a night-light that was supposed to alleviate his fears but whose ghostly glow cast frightening shadows and changed the horses on the wallpaper into beasts. Nothing helped. Every night, in the darkness under his bed, the monster waited.

And tonight was worse. Tonight his mother was away on a *business trip*. He didn't know where she was going, only that she was going to take an airplane. It felt horrible, her being away from home—the universe was out of kilter. It created an emptiness so large that he took it inside himself and felt it as if something were physically wrong, a painful bloating. He clutched his koala bear, which she had bought him on her last trip, and rubbed his cheek upon the soft fur, already wearing off in patches, and smelled the warm musky smell.

At least his father was there. That helped a bit, a comforting thought. Earlier, his father had tucked him in and, like every night, sitting on the edge of the bed had told him a Jingo story. They always began the same way. Jingo, a little boy "very much like you," felt bored. So he reached under his bed, and there he found his magic pebble. He rubbed it:

And then something very strange happened. At first he felt hot, and then he felt cold. And then he felt warm, and then he felt cool. And finally he felt just right. Then he opened his eyes and he was standing before a huge white mansion. He went up the front steps and opened the front door and before him was a long corridor, stretching as far as he could see. And on both sides there were door after door after door. It was the house of a thousand rooms. *So Jingo walked down the corridor and opened one of the doors....*

Each night a new room, a new adventure. Lions and tigers and jungle gyms and tree houses and circuses and dodgem cars and hurricanes and sandstorms. Sometimes Jingo shrank down to the size of an ant, and other times he grew up to the height of a house, and sometimes he was a knight or an Indian, and other times he was an astronaut or a caveman. But always, the stories ended the same way: Just as the situation became impossible, as the danger became too threatening or the excitement became too much to bear, he spotted a small white door. He opened it and, magically, there he was, back in bed.

Tyler loved the ritual. He loved it so much that he didn't tell his father that he made up his own stories and that some of these scared him. There was one that scared him more than all the others. Jingo was lying down on a bed and he couldn't move, and people were around, grown-ups who whispered and were worried. Everything was white. And then he felt himself rising up and leaving his own body except that the other people didn't notice it, and when he reached the ceiling he looked down and he saw himself lying there, with the people crowding around him. And at last he spotted the emergency door, but it wasn't white. It was dark, grayish, almost black. And he knew that whatever was on the other side was the most frightening thing in the world. He knew he shouldn't open it, but he couldn't help himself. He put his hand on the knob and began to turn it, and suddenly he heard an awful sound: a loud, roaring, frightening sound, as if the whole room was collapsing behind him and everything was being sucked out through the narrow opening. And the door began to open wider and wider. At that moment, something always happened—he gave a start or, if he had been sleeping, he awoke quickly, just in time. And so he never saw what was on the other side of the door, except that he knew deep down that it was horrible.

Tyler tried to think of other things.

His mother was away. That was bad; it filled him with emptiness. Still, the thought of a plane excited him. He had been on a plane last year, flying to Florida. He blushed when he remembered how scared he had been when his father told him they were "flying," because he didn't know how to fly, and how when the suitcases were brought to the hall he had hidden behind the couch. Then his mother found him, and when he finally admitted the reason for his fear, his father laughed and Tyler felt ashamed. But she hugged him so tightly it almost hurt; she wrapped her hands around his face with her palms holding his cheeks and kissed the hot tears that streamed down them. And he smelled her smell, that indescribable fragrance that always shot him in the heart because it meant that everything was fine, it was all going to be all right because she was right there with him.

The plane, it turned out, had been fun—crayons and coloring books, white cotton clouds out the window as far as he could see, and the pilot in a crisp uniform walking down the aisle and putting a hand on his shoulder.

Tyler was an only child, but he didn't feel lonely. His world was a snug clapboard house and trim backyard in Westport, Connecticut, and he peopled it with all kinds of imaginary creatures. A wall in his room contained shelves that were piled high with toys; his dresser had decals of Disney characters. Outside, underneath a bush that hugged the house, in a space where he alone could fit, he had created a miniature town; he cut roads in the earth with the heel of his hand, stacked twigs as woodpiles next to the doors of the small houses his father made, and sometimes maneuvered the metal Matchbox cars into sensational wrecks. He loved climbing trees— especially a friendly old pine tree in the center of the yard—and sitting high on the swooping branches, watching the neighborhood and swaying in the breeze.

Then there was school and the friends he had already made: Johnny, tall, scrawny, with a perpetually runny nose; Tim and Craig, the redheaded twins; and Lovett, a quiet boy who had a comic book collection two feet high. Tyler was striking-looking, with his olive complexion and shock of dark hair and bright, burning eyes under long black lashes. At recess, quick to devise games and fleet as a jackrabbit, he was at the center of things. Other children took to him, fell naturally under his spell. Mrs. Spangler, the first-grade teacher, often called upon him to read the words in large print under the pictures splashed in color.

His life—if he had ever stopped to think about it in such terms—was perfect . . . except for the nights, the horrible nights.

Tyler pulled the blanket up again and flopped over onto his stomach. His face sank into the pillow so that it was hard to breathe. He bunched the pillow under his right cheek. He could hear his father puttering around in the bedroom next door and a snatch of music. That made him feel better, less alone. Still, it wasn't the same with his mother gone. He had no idea where she was or when she would be coming back or even—and this was the fear that cut into him—*if* she would be coming back. When she had knelt down to hug him good-bye in her gray suit, her long hair sweeping over her shoulders as she gathered him into her arms and the smell of her perfume covering every pore of him, she had said she would be back "before you know it." But he had known, as he watched her through the front window, stepping briskly down the walkway, that that was just one of those meaningless things adults say.

Suddenly, he froze. He lifted his head off the pillow. *Something* was there. He heard *something*.

He didn't know what it was. But this was not falling asleep, not dreaming. *Something* was in his room.

Tyler held his breath. He could feel a presence. He could feel it feeling him. His ears were flooded with no sound, and his heart jumped around in his chest. Did he dare to turn around? Slowly, he pressed his arms into the bed and raised his chest up and rotated his head. He faced the door and opened his eyes—wide, in the dimly lighted room.

There she was!

Standing in the doorway, still in the gray suit. *Mother!*

The light came from behind her, covered her in an aura so that it was hard to see her. But he knew instantly that it was she. And she was looking down at him, longingly, with an expression so intense he had never seen it before. It was love and pain mixed together.

The lower portion of her face was covered in shadow. He couldn't tell if she was smiling at him. Something about her, her posture framed in the light, slightly slumped, made her seem different . . . distant, sad.

He was scared. He was ecstatic. He wanted to hide from her and to get up and run to her. He felt so many things all at once.

And then the figure in the doorway moved a bit, shifted to one side. Slowly she raised her right arm. Her fingers were extended. They were moving. Tyler knew the movement was important. Was she motioning to him to follow her? Or was she waving good-bye?

The moment was frozen in time, forever. Then slowly she turned, took a step away, looked back over her shoulder. And then she was gone.

Tyler blinked. He closed his eyes firmly, held them closed for a second, and then opened them. There was nothing there, no remnant, not even a shadow. He looked around the room. Nothing had changed; nothing had moved. And the door—the door was firmly closed!

The next morning passed in slow motion. He stayed in his room much of the time. The phone rang often and neighbors came to the house, speaking in low voices. He heard a newscaster speaking solemnly on television. He heard his father talking—a choked sob, so low he couldn't believe it came from him.

And then, after a while, when he heard his father's footsteps in the hallway, moving toward his room heavily, he already knew somewhere inside what his father was coming to tell him. He knew that his life was about to change forever. He wondered in the welter of emotions why it was that he was able to keep standing, why his mind was still working, why he was able to make out the patterns on the wallpaper. And he wondered, as he clutched his koala bear and saw the doorknob turn, exactly how his father was going to tell him, and for some reason he didn't know he prepared himself to feign surprise.

I

The Accident

Chapter 1

Cleaver leaned over the hospital bed to straighten the sheets on the old man's bed and reached out to touch the back of his hand. He thought of mopping the old man's brow, but there was no point. He was too far gone—he probably wouldn't even feel it. And besides, with the helmet stuck on his head and the wires and cords running out of it and feeding into the apparatus that stood behind the bed, there was precious little brow showing. Only a thin band of skin, wrinkled and hoary, gray as a fish.

He checked the breathing. It was labored and raspy, as if his chest were filled with marbles.

Now that the moment was at hand, Cleaver was barely able to suppress his excitement. He felt pleasantly, surprisingly, boyish. Who knows what he would have done if he'd been alone—spun around in his doctor's cloak? Clicked his heels in midair?

"Shouldn't be long now."

That was Felix, his young assistant, taking the old man's pulse across the bed, holding two fingers on the limp wrist in a tableau that looked posed—*doctor at the bedside of a dying patient*. It was pointless to take the old man's pulse with the heart monitor blipping away in the corner.

Cleaver grunted in reply. "Think I'll go check on his wife," he said, turning on one heel and walking toward the door.

He felt like being alone. A time like this called for something special, a bit of introspection—*a sense of history*.

In the hallway, Cleaver detoured off the corridor to the old smoking veranda. It was dimly lighted, but he knew the furnishings by heart: two battered sofas, half a dozen metal folding chairs, a bridge table whose brown coverlet had a ten-inch gash. The linoleum was pock-marked with cigarette burns, and in one spot the tiles were missing, dark squares with snakelike squiggles of dried glue.

It never ceased to amaze Cleaver how the state had let Pinegrove slide into ruin. Here it was smack in the middle of New York City, stuck on the southernmost peninsula of Roosevelt Island in the East River. Tug-boats and barges passed within fifty feet of it, and hundreds of thousands of windows peered down upon it; yet few people could tell you what the building was. For all that it mattered, he could be working in a lunatic asylum from the Middle Ages.

Pinegrove had been built in the 1930s, a time when people still used that word—*lunatic*—and contemporary literature spoke of it as a progressive institution. But times changed; treatment of patients gave way to warehousing them, and then, with the advent of psychoactive drugs, to releasing them. In the 1960s, it emptied three entire wards of confused schizophrenics onto the streets. The hospital workers' union exerted sufficient muscle in Albany to keep two floors open, thereby requiring staff, but the legislature provided scant money for upkeep.

Over the years, the place fell apart. The English garden that had been the pride of an early administration choked with weeds. Trees that needed pruning sometimes dropped leafless limbs on the roof, and twice slabs of lethal slate fell to the ground. On the deserted top floor, Cleaver had found water stains in the ceiling.

Now Pinegrove was a last redoubt. Its forty beds were for the most severe and hopeless cases of mental derangement and brain impairment. "If you can walk, talk, or lift a fork without killing someone, you don't belong here," the chief attendant used to joke.

But at the same time neglect had conferred a cloak of

anonymity for Cleaver's work, which suited him fine. No bureaucrats to tangle with.

He walked over to the wall of thick glass planes threaded with wire loops, protected by a metal grille running from floor to ceiling, and looked out on the Manhattan evening. The cars rushing by on the FDR Drive already had their headlights on, and the lights in the residential towers above, gleaming in the dusk, made them seem closer.

His eye caught his own reflection. The white lab coat gleamed back at him in the dark glass like a ghost, and he could see his face: the large brow, the bald pate, the longish hair on the sides only beginning to show flecks of gray. He was forty-two, and ready for fame.

He knew the experiment with the elderly couple would work. He had been touched by them—a husband and wife, together for some thirty or forty years, down on their luck, no place to live. But he had had to put his compassion to one side. The old man was ready to die, and now waiting for him to expire was like waiting for the sun to set. No more personal than that.

Cleaver looked outside. Tiny waves lapped at the shore; the rocks were shiny with slime that gleamed gold in the reflected light. An old sewage pipe ran down to the water's edge. He almost shook his head. Pinegrove! What a place for an experiment that would smash the frontiers of neuroscience. Why did Science put so little stake in the surroundings for her chosen moments? All those humble backdrops: the Manhattan Project—the basement of a Chicago football stadium. The A-bomb—a cottage in the Nevada desert. And now here, this place ...

He stared across at the Manhattan skyline and found St. Catherine's Hospital and frowned. Saramaggio was there—the world-famous Leopoldo Saramaggio, chief of neurosurgery. Those talented enough to be on the surgeon's team basked in the glory that he brought, and the adulation bothered Cleaver. He worked side by side with the man; his expertise with computers was essential to his operating room. Saramaggio needed him more

than he needed Saramaggio. Saramaggio hadn't realized
that yet—but someday he would.

He brushed the thought aside. At Pinegrove, he was
the top dog. It might be run-down and partially abandoned, but it was all his. And look what he had done
with it! He had begged and cajoled six million dollars
from medical foundations and installed a modern laboratory. All the equipment he required was tucked away
out of sight in the basement. And most important, he
had a steady supply of patients to study. They were the
hard core, the lost and rejected who had no hope of seeing daylight—the paranoid who would never recover,
the dysfunctional man with a syndrome so bizarre it had
no name, the boy born with the left hemisphere of his
brain missing. Some had been abandoned on the streets,
others sent by parents who were at their wits' end. If
they once had had caring families, those families visited
for a while and then usually stopped coming. Because—
face it—the place was depressing.

All this meant that Cleaver had a certain necessary
latitude in his work. It was part of a long and venerable
tradition in neuroanatomy: Paul Broca's work with
epileptics at the Bicêtre Hospital in Paris in the 1860s,
Carl Wernicke's probings of the brain's receptive language center in Germany in the 1870s, Wilder Penfield
performing brain surgeries under local anesthetic to
draw his map of bodily sensations in the 1940s and '50s.
None of them had been constrained from their work.

And after all, there was nothing to be gained by
studying normal people. Advances were made through
the injured and the freakish, as cruel as that sounded.
Great strides came from great men who did not shrink
from operating: They cut through flesh and sawed
through skulls; they split the brains of monkeys and
planted electrodes deep into the cerebra of cats. He
thought of Friedrich Goltz, the young professor of physiology, making a point about the localization of brain
function at the Seventh International Medical Congress
in London in 1881—of how he had opened his suitcase
to pull out the bloody head of a dog that had undergone

four major brain operations. Now *he* had been a true scientist.

Someday, perhaps, Cleaver's name would be joined with theirs. He would finish what they had started. For he was trying to do nothing less than delineate and measure the most elusive of theoretical concepts: the mind itself. Call it what you will: human consciousness, psyche, reason, what the ancients called "the seat of the Soul," or theologians called the soul itself. It constituted the first and last great riddle. For how could the human mind examine itself? That would be like an eye trying to view itself without the aid of a mirror.

But we know that it exists. We know it intuitively because we experience it from within. Socrates, who didn't even know that the brain was the center of mental functioning, who believed that the heart was the organ that did the thinking, still knew that something ruled us that could not be explained only in physical terms.

Cleaver called it *anima,* the quintessence of consciousness, that bit of us that makes us aware of ourselves and separates us from everything else. Derived from the Latin, the feminine of *animus,* the mind or spirit; a word with a long and honorable lineage, including Carl Jung, who'd depicted it as the true inner self. But Jung had merely theorized that it existed. Cleaver was out to prove it. He was going to do so this very night by setting a trap. If the anima exists in life, then it must be released in death. And if it is released in death—and as folklore has it, travels through space to make contact with a loved one at the precise moment of expiring—then why not try to record it through neuroimaging? And record it not just in the person dying—you'd expect to see dislocations in brain activity there—but in the living person, the receiver. Why not see if the living person registers extraordinary brain activity at the exact moment the dying one gives up the ghost?

Cleaver broke his reverie and walked back down the corridor. He passed the ward and peered through the thick glass window of the door. He could see a dozen or so patients, some lying immobile in bed, others shuffling around the room, and he could hear the muffled hubbub of monologues and ranting and pitched discourse. He continued on past the nurses' station and the bisecting corridor until he came to the room he was seeking.

Like the old man's room, it too looked out upon the river. He'd done that on purpose when he set up the experiment: Why not at least give them a pleasant view, he had thought—something ethereal, something transcendent. He entered without knocking and fixed his eyes upon the old woman. She wasn't looking at the view. She was propped up in bed, pillows behind her, the helmet fixed in place from above, so that in the dim light for a minute she gave the appearance of a hydrocephalic. Her eyes were closed as if she were dozing. Felicity, the other assistant, was fussing with the machines, checking the dials and taking readings.

"How's it going?" asked Cleaver.

Felicity startled at his voice. She had not heard him approach.

"Fine," she said, all businesslike. She had a clipboard close at hand, though it was superfluous. The data on the machines were being recorded.

"And the TMR?" he asked, looking at the helmet that fit snugly around the old woman's skull. The acronym was short for *transcranial magnetic receiver,* a device that recorded the electrical impulses of brain activity. It was almost as efficient at picking them up as a positron-emission tomography scan and had the advantage of being portable. The information was sent into a computer, and the turn of a knob could bring the cross section of any part of the brain onto a two-foot-wide screen.

"Seems to be okay. It's quiet at the moment."

"Of course it's quiet," came a rasping voice from the bed, surprisingly assertive. "You told me to rest."

Cleaver was amused by the old woman's spunk. She had always seemed stronger than her husband. He walked over and put a hand on her shoulder, the way long ago he had once seen a professor at NYU Medical School do it during rounds with his students. In response, the woman sat up straight, so that a pillow fell into the crevice behind her back. She looked up at Cleaver.

"Elmore," she said, in a plaintive voice, her face crinkled with worry. "How is he?"

Cleaver debated his answer. It wouldn't do to let her know too much. He didn't want to alert her—it could throw everything off. But that was unlikely. Besides, there was no point in lying to her.

"He's close to the end. He's not in any pain, and he's lying there quietly. But I don't think he has much more to go."

The woman bit her lip and turned away, facing the river. Cleaver walked over to the machine and twirled a knob. The screen filled with an exterior view of her brain, rising up like a twisted fist at the wrist's end—the folds of the cortex, the tight little knot of the cerebellum, the nub of the brain stem. He turned two more knobs and pulled up cross sections, thin slices cut along the sagittal, coronal, and axial planes.

Right away he could read her state. Her emotions were causing little bursts of activity that registered in glowing colors from the dye she had ingested. It always reminded him of storms, heat lightning illuminating clouds over the ocean.

That was good. That was just what he wanted to see. Any time now, surely within an hour or two, the moment would come.

As it turned out, Cleaver had to wait considerably longer. Time enough for him to have slipped into his office, taken off his shoes, and grabbed a catnap on the old leather couch, had he not been too excited to sleep. Even time enough to have walked up to the Queensboro Bridge and caught the aerial tramway to Manhattan for a solitary dinner, had not the prospect of being so far away filled him with anxiety. As it was, Cleaver tried to read but couldn't concentrate. He watched television alone in the lounge and then went out for a nighttime stroll.

He was walking on the Queens side of the island when the call came. He had been negotiating the crumbling promenade, a whiff of river muck in the air. A salt-tinged breeze blew past the red Pepsi-Cola sign, and he could hear it whistle faintly as it passed under the bridge to the north. Then, with a shrillness that startled him, his beeper went off. He raced back to the building, slipping on the lower step and banging his left shin, which caused him to curse loudly.

He arrived on the third floor, breathless.

"Well," he said to Felix in an accusatory tone, as if his assistant had been the one wandering around outside in the dark.

"His vitals are falling fast. He's circling the drain."

"All right. I'm going to the other room. You know what to do—remember, watch the brain activity and send a signal at the exact moment of death as near as you can determine it, not a moment before and not a moment later."

Felix nodded.

Cleaver dashed down the corridor, the tails of his lab coat flapping behind him. When he got there, he could scarcely believe his eyes: *The old woman was asleep*.

"Wake her up," he said, more sharply than he intended.

Felicity jumped up from a chair and ran over to the bed, but the old lady had already opened one beady eye.

"No need to shout," she said. "I'm up."

Cleaver was tempted to apologize, but he held his silence, for already he had noticed something. The old lady's other eye had opened, and now both of her eyes were suddenly widening with alarm and she was looking over into a far corner as if she were seeing a terrible vision. Her bottom lip was trembling.

He looked behind her bed. The small light, behind her and out of her sight, was illuminated. Felix had sent the signal. Cleaver turned his head slightly and saw that the screen was registering all of the electrical impulses that she was firing off, explosions of color here and there; they were bouncing around like fireworks, but he could already see that they were concentrated deep below the cortex, close to the hypothalamus. The switch Felix had thrown had also registered in a wavy line on the screen; now there would be a chronological record of the activities of both brains, perfectly synchronized. The video cameras in both rooms were also operational.

The old woman's lips trembled more and formed themselves into a tight, dark hole. She began to speak— a low, almost guttural sound of amazement.

"Elmore," she said. "Elmore." She repeated the name over and over. She was now staring at the corner, leaning toward it as if she were being pulled by a strong magnetic force.

"I see you, I see you," she said. "What is it? What is it, darling?" She was oblivious to them, totally absorbed in the vision, lost in another world.

Cleaver felt his own pulse racing. Everything was going perfectly. He was getting it all down, a record to be scrutinized and analyzed and made sense of.

The old woman stared at the corner for several minutes, but stopped talking, only nodding. Then she sank back against the pillow, her eyes still wide but no longer focused on the apparition. Her features were hard to read—upset but also close to rapturous. Whatever secret she had learned, she was keeping it to herself. Cleaver could see on the screen that Elmore was brain-dead.

It was over.

He collected himself and puffed himself up and looked portentously across at Felicity, who appeared dumbstruck. She coughed lightly, as if to bring herself back to earth.

"Well," Cleaver said, "you have just witnessed something extraordinary. Do you know what you saw?"

She stared at him and shook her head mutely.

"Psychic contact at the moment of death, fully recorded for the first time. What do you say to that?"

"Gosh," said Felicity, leaving her mouth open.

Cleaver looked away. *Gosh,* he repeated to himself. He shook it off.

It had been a great experiment, he thought. And like all great experiments, deceptively simple. It was like a nut inside a shell. People had talked about the phenomena of death visitations for centuries, probably for millennia—all those old wives' tales about seeing a loved one at the stroke of dying, about people separated by vast distances who come together at the final instant, about near-death experiences in which people rise up from their own bodies and move toward a blinding light. There had to be something to them. But only Cleaver had thought to try to measure the phenomenon—the neurobiology of the soul—and devised a means to do so.

For as long as Cleaver could remember, his intellectual life had been driven by two concepts. One was the idea that the mind could exist outside the body; that the thoughts, fears, dreams, nightmares, and emotions had an independent existence. He had just proved that. The other was the idea that machines and man could merge—*through* that disembodied mind—to create the new man of the future. For if the mind could be measured—if it existed as something that traveled from one point to another—then it could be captured. And if it could be captured, it could be yoked to the endless potential that machines provided—a sort of divine spark of guiding intelligence that would make the Creation look like child's play.

He looked over at Felicity and sighed. Too bad he didn't have a lab assistant befitting the moment.

No *Mr. Watson, come here, I want you.* No *What hath God wrought?* Instead—what did he get?

Gosh.

Chapter 2

Kate Willet had resisted putting the name-tag sticker on the breast pocket of her new pin-striped suit. The truth was, she was not big on guided tours, had never been one of the crowd.

Certainly, she was not one of *this* crowd. She looked around as they filed onto the bus—mostly women with frizzy hair who were too old for the short skirts they wore and men whose meticulous grooming (one had a black goatee with not a single hair out of place) suggested self-satisfaction. Practicing members of the American Psychological Association.

A lanky young man her age, in his mid-thirties, sat down beside her. She flashed him a smile, more of a half-smile, just to be friendly. It was her small-town upbringing.

"Some trip, huh?" he said, pointing out the window with his chin.

She took it as a reference to the earlier tour of the South Bronx. The day was hot and the fire hydrants were opened; small dark bodies ran through the gushing water, screaming.

Kate nodded noncommittally. She had lived in the city for only three weeks and was trying hard to adjust. What she liked most so far was the street life. Besides, children made her homesick for normalcy—when you looked at them, they looked back.

A large hand came across her lap, open and eager.

"Butterworth," he said. "Fred Butterworth."

She had to turn toward him to shake it.

"Kate Willet."

There was a slight pause.

"So, Kate. Where's your practice?"

"Afraid I don't have one," she replied. "I'm not a psychologist. Or a psychiatrist. I'm only along for the ride."

"Oh, and what do you do?"

"I'm a neurosurgeon."

"Oh."

She could recognize the disappointment. Her profession tended to stop people in their tracks, especially men. It made them defensive.

"I've transferred to New York only recently, after residency in California. I'm at St. Catherine's."

He perked up.

"Under the famous Saramaggio, I presume."

"That's right."

He actually whistled, softly.

"What do you think of him?" he asked.

"Well, he's certainly brilliant. Good hands, as they say. If I can be half as good someday, I'll be happy."

Her seatmate nodded, and she fell silent. The truth was, she was nervous about meeting Saramaggio again. The one interview had gone well enough—in fact, he had been charming—but his reputation as an implacable perfectionist was scary. She loved medicine and wanted nothing more than to excel at it. That was why she had come east to work with one of the best neurosurgical teams in the country. But something about him was off-putting, a whiff of the god complex that afflicted so many neurosurgeons. She had come to dislike her previous head of surgery in San Francisco, a man who was technically superb, but had had an ego the size of a beach ball. When all was said and done, he didn't really seem to care about his patients. He rarely saw them after the operation, and they in turn rarely sent in snapshots after their recovery. It was disillusioning to think that genius might be a question of manual dexterity.

She shared none of this, of course, with Mr. Butterworth. She stole a sideways glance at him. He wasn't bad-looking, but his eyes looked dull. Like a number of women, including her Shakespearean namesake, Kate was choosy: She could be interested only in a man who matched her intelligence. She needed him to have that hard edge, a playful acuity that could race alongside her so that not everything had to be spelled out. It was the flint that sparked flirtation in her.

Her standards were high, but not, she believed, unreasonable. She had come close to love once or twice, close enough to feel something but without going down in flames, and she was beginning to despair that she would find the right person. Her loneliness was accentuated by New York, which overwhelmed her. On the sidewalks, people walked so fast they seemed to leave her standing still, and once or twice in the evenings, rubbing her sore feet after a day of exploring, she worried that she had made a mistake in coming here. She had left behind a good man in San Francisco—Harry. He was witty and kind, so presentable that her girlfriends joked that they wanted to be notified the moment a breakup was imminent. But she had begun to suspect he wasn't for her, and now the separation told her she was right.

"This next place we're going—Pinegrove—it's really supposed to be something," said Butterworth. "Like some kind of horror show."

His face clouded over.

"Oh, I'm sorry," he continued. "Your place—St. Catherine's. Isn't that affiliated with Pinegrove?"

"Yes," she said. "That's the reason I'm here. I want to see it."

"Good. That makes sense. Say, here, let me give you this."

He lurched up, half standing, and fished into a pocket, brought out a card and handed it to her. She looked at it:

Frederick Butterworth
The Hospital Supply Corporation
Flushing, Queens, NY

*From ambulances to X-ray machines,
If we don't have it, we know where to get it.*

"Thanks," she said. She put the card in her purse and turned to look out the window, trying to figure out the route. When she turned back to talk some more, she had to smile. Mr. Butterworth was asleep, and he didn't awaken for half an hour, not until the bus turned a corner around a warehouse in Queens and ground down to second gear to cross the tiny bridge onto Roosevelt Island.

After the tour, the visitors filed into a large room painted in institutional green, with chairs arranged in ragged rows. They were as quiet as children at a hanging. Perhaps they were shocked by the wards they had just visited—the antiseptic smell that assaulted the nostrils, the jabberings and harsh sounds of chairs scraping against the floor, the patients wandering aimlessly around or sitting and rocking on their beds. One patient, a man in a crew cut with an empty grin and darting eyes, had open sores on his head.

As psychologists and psychiatrists, they had spent time in wards that housed the mentally ill and were hardened to the sight of people babbling back at their own hallucinations. And many of these patients were like those in state institutions anywhere. But it was the whole package that was hard to take—the old stone building, the vacant floors echoing with the sound of their footsteps, and finally the wards themselves.

Kate sat near the back on a wooden chair whose right arm spread before her, a test-taking chair. She was angry at what she had seen. It wasn't that the patients looked as if they were being mistreated, just that they had been so clearly shunted off to a place where they could be forgotten. She imagined them living their lives out one long day at a time in these dreary surroundings, meaninglessly and endlessly, without respite.

Butterworth sat on her right, and she could see that the brief tour had had a sobering effect on him. They exchanged looks, and he raised his eyebrows and slowly shook his head from side to side.

A man in a doctor's coat was introduced, Dr. Warren Cleaver. Kate recognized the name. He worked with Saramaggio and was said to be brilliant, with degrees in both artificial intelligence and neurology. Rumors dogged him—that he was more of an automaton than his computers—but she had put some of that down to envy because he was clearly going places. What was he doing working with mental patients? she wondered. She examined him—a short stocky man with a large head and a bald dome, like Lenin, she thought.

The administrative assistant, a gray-haired woman with thick spectacles, did most of the talking. She described Pinegrove's history, talked about the budget and how hard it was to wring more money out of the state and to find competent nurses and attendants. Money was hard to come by; clearly the administration was working against formidable odds. Her recitation of complaint came in a passionless monotone.

She mentioned that Pinegrove had received a research grant. A hand shot up in the front, and a man stood to ask a question: "What research do you do here? Do you specialize?"

She glanced over at Cleaver. "I think it's fair to say that our program is drawn up by Dr. Cleaver and it closely parallels his interests."

"And what are you interested in, Dr. Cleaver?" asked the man.

Cleaver walked over and stood before the group, his hands resting behind his back.

"First, let me say that I sense some of you are a bit shocked by what you've seen here today. I hope so. That is why I want visitors to come here. I want them to see what happens to an institution when the only ones who care for it are those who work there. What you've see here today is the emblem of society's negligence."

He looked around at their faces.

"Now let me try to address the question. What am I interested in? I am interested in the human mind, pure and simple, in all aspects of it—how it grows, how it develops, how it thrives, and how it breaks down. Especially how it breaks down. Disease and misfortune are great teachers."

What an odd thing to say, thought Kate. But it was true.

Cleaver looked around again and continued.

"That's my reason for being here, to help some of these poor souls and by working with them to help others. So far, my work has taught me two things. One: The study of the abnormal is the path that will lead us to understand the normal. By looking at something that is broken, we can understand how it functions when it is whole. Two: The mind is truly a marvel. It is capable of more things than we can ever imagine."

A woman in the back row raised her hand.

"Can you tell us what part of the brain you're working on now?"

"No, no, not the *brain*," he said. "I never said the *brain*."

She looked quizzical.

He walked over to a wall and pulled down a chart that depicted a cross section of the brain. So the room *was* a classroom after all, thought Kate. Cleaver looked around, apparently for a pointer, and, failing to find one, turned to the chart and tapped it with a forefinger. When he spoke, the words came out in a rush.

"This is the *brain*. The limbic system, the brain stem, the upper brain, the cortex, the cerebellum—everyone here knows it all; you can see it, name it, talk about it. It is something you can put on a piece of paper, something you can cut into. That is not what I do."

He tugged a cord and sent the chart flying back into its case.

"What I examine is the *mind*. And I examine the difference between them—the brain and the mind. That's the whole point—the difference. People speak of the mind-body problem, but that misses the boat. Think of the mind-*brain* problem. Where does one stop and the other begin?" He looked searchingly at them. "What makes consciousness? What makes us conscious?"

He was speaking like a college professor now.

"Descartes. *Cogito ergo sum,* I think therefore I am. What does that mean? Most people misconstrue it. It doesn't mean that thinking is in itself proof that I exist. It means that the *knowledge* that I am thinking is proof that I exist.

"The riddle is not that we think. The riddle is that we *know* we are thinking. Animals think, up to a point. Put a piece of meat on a table, leave the room, and a dog will conceive of a way to get it. A rat can negotiate a maze. That is thought—a crude form of thought, but thought nonetheless. Yet it's limited. When a human hatches a plan or engages in some activity, he is not only thinking, he is simultaneously aware of the fact that he is thinking. Do you see?"

The woman who had asked the question nodded. Cleaver began pacing back and forth at the front of the room.

"The brain is no big deal. We can figure out how it works. Blood bringing nutrition to cells, neurotransmitters firing across synapses. But what does that tell you? Not much. How does all this activity give rise to a uniform collection of higher thought that can step aside and examine itself? How does it give rise to consciousness? How—in other words—does the mind come into being? For the mind is built of consciousness. And the existence of consciousness is not derivable from physical laws."

He was clearly getting carried away by his own thoughts.

"It is that sense of consciousness—or whatever you want to call it—that creates a sentient being. It's what makes you realize that you are you and nobody else, and that when you wake up tomorrow you'll still be you. Because otherwise you'd be nothing, only a shadow. You'd live in the exact moment, the precise present. There'd be no past, no future. There would be thousands of yous, hundreds of thousands of yous, each one for a different moment. What links you from one moment to the next is consciousness. It's our mode of existence. It's the shell that keeps us intact. Without it, we'd last about as long as a naked snail on a beach."

He came back to earth. The woman in the back row persisted.

"I thought your interest was artificial intelligence," she said. "Why do you work to make machines intelligent if you believe that only humans are capable of conscious thought?"

He didn't reply instantly, then said, "I didn't say that only humans were capable of it. I said humans are the only ones with that capability *now*."

"So are you working to provide it to machines? Do you think machines will be as smart as we are someday—or smarter?"

"As smart as we are? Hard to say. I don't think so. Do you?" It was a rhetorical question, and he didn't wait for an answer.

"Any other questions?"

Kate raised her hand.

"I was wondering about the patients here. Do you have any programs to help them? Can you do anything to ease their suffering?"

Cleaver hesitated, then shook his head regretfully.

"I wish we could do something. But if there's anything we've learned as scientists, it's that we have to choose our priorities. We have to accomplish what we can, what's realistic. These people can't be helped—not with our current state of knowledge. That's the painful truth. So what we have to do is think about the ones in the future, and how we can help them. Now, then. We promised you earlier that we'd be taking a closer look at some of the more unusual cases here. Let's do that now."

He sat down, and there followed a parade of patients with bizarre symptoms. They were ushered in by the administrative assistant, who seated them one by one in front of the group. She had the timing of a ringmaster—and the sensitivity as well, thought Kate. Some of the patients appeared heavily drugged, and others were clearly confused by the ordeal.

The first was a mousy-looking man in his fifties with long stringy hair and darting eyes. He was presented as a classic paranoid. He had, it turned out, killed his family—a wife, a seven-year-old son and a three-year-old daughter. It was, he said, "the voices" that had told him to do it.

The assistant questioned him. When did the voices begin? Many, many years ago. And had they stopped? He hesitated, then nodded yes. Bits of spittle formed around his mouth.

"Really? Totally stopped?" she pressed.

"Yes. Almost always. Except . . . except when I wear the goggles."

Cleaver took the floor and expanded on "the closed system" of paranoid reasoning—how the mind searched for an explanation, no matter how far-fetched, to account for something deeply unsettling like auditory hallucinations. Once the outrageous premise was accepted and accounted for, then everything else followed in logical order. The house was solid; it was the foundation that was cockeyed.

"In this instance, we have a disruption in the auditory center of the cortex. The paranoid incorporates that into a larger scheme of rationalization, attributing it to nonexistent goggles, and proceeds to act as if that were an unshakable truth. He follows the delusion wherever it leads him, even to murder."

Kate didn't like that they were discussing the patient in front of him, as if he didn't exist. She looked at the man, but when he gazed back at her, he rapidly dropped his eyes and she looked away.

There followed half a dozen others—patients with severe memory loss, multiple personalities, frontal lobotomies, and various personality disorders.

One woman in her thirties with long blond hair would have been beautiful but for the fact that her face registered no feeling whatsoever. She did not respond to questions and sat in the chair immobile, but her eyes moved and slowly surveyed the audience.

"Akinetic mutism," said Cleaver. "A rare disorder, sometimes misdiagnosed as catatonia. You see how her eyes can track movement. She is alert, in the sense of being aware of her surroundings, but she does not react to them. She is sluggish and will lie without moving for hours. She is in what we call a coma vigil.

"Patients who recover—which is extremely rare—describe the state as one of unending eternal listlessness. Nothing reaches them. Free will does not exist. Life goes by like a movie."

The woman was led slowly away, and a garrulous young man took her place. He introduced himself as Bruce, and to all intents and purposes appeared to be normal. Then the questioning began. He was raised, he said, in a small town in Michigan, but he didn't miss it particularly and he didn't want to return because "both of my parents are missing."

"But, Bruce, how can they be missing?" asked the administrative assistant. "Both of your parents came with you to check you in last year. They visited you two months ago."

"No, those weren't my parents," he replied matter-of-factly. "They're perfectly nice people. But they're not my parents. They're impostors."

Cleaver stepped forward and addressed the visitors.

"*Impostors* is the key word," he said. "It occurs over and over in patients with Capgras's syndrome. Bruce here is not being paranoid. In many respects, he is a normal young adult. He is simply convinced that the people who are closest to him have been taken away and replaced by people who look just like them.

"It's my contention that this disorder resides in a malfunctioning of the amygdala. When Bruce looks upon a loved one, he lacks an emotional response. He literally feels nothing whatsoever. The seat of his emotional attachments has been short-circuited. And yet he knows on an intellectual level that he *should* be feeling something. How is it possible to look at your father and mother and feel absolutely nothing? The mind has to come up with an explanation. So the explanation is they are not really your parents—they are stand-ins, impostors."

"What you are looking at is a pathology of the emotional self. I believe it is caused by damage in the limbic system. How else could the abnormality be so minutely specialized? Bruce only spots an impostor when he is actually looking at a human face. If he talks to his father on the telephone, he has no doubt that he is talking to his real father. To me, that indicates a disruption in the pathways between the visual area of the cortex and the amygdala."

The man who had asked the first question interrupted.

"Freud would disagree with such a mechanistic interpretation," he said. "He had a view of the human personality that based it in social relationships. It was—if I may say so—a more complicated approach. More sophisticated."

"Occam's razor," Cleaver replied. "In science, the more complicated the theory, the less correct it tends to be. I wonder what Freud would make of Phineas Gage."

The questioner looked chastened. Kate knew the name; it was one of the most famous cases of personality transformation. In 1848, Gage, a Vermont railroad worker, had been caught in a dynamite accident that sent an iron bar through his left cheek and out the top of his head. He'd survived, but with his prefrontal cortex damaged, causing him to undergo a mysterious metamorphosis from a law-abiding, churchgoing family man to a lying, drinking, cheating reprobate.

"May I ask," continued Cleaver, fixing the questioner with his dark eyes, "do you believe in God?"

"Well, yes, I do."

"I would be willing to bet that if I could get you on my operating table, I could seek out a certain tiny portion of your left frontal lobe and remove it, and when you woke up, you would find that your belief had deserted you. And who knows—perhaps even your belief in Freud."

There was a ripple of laughter at that.

He looked around and added, "And now, if there are no further questions . . ."

So saying, Cleaver thanked everyone and walked out the door.

After a few minutes, the administrative assistant led the tour toward the exit, but along the way, a small group clustered around the window of a door, peering inside the room. Kate joined them and gave a small gasp.

"My God," said the man next to her, shocked. "What's wrong with him?"

The room was dimly lit and she could not see very well, but she did not care to get a better view. There was one bed in the room and a young man supine on it. His wrists and ankles were tied to the sides of the bed with thick white straps, and he was lying totally stiff, as if he were a piece of wood. His eyes were open and staring straight up at the ceiling; they did not move. Nor did he seem to blink. His skin was ashen gray. His shirt was off, and when Kate looked closely, she saw that his upper torso and his arms and his ankles and his face were covered with wounds—deep angry red gouges running in parallel lines. He had evidently inflicted them upon himself with his fingernails.

The administrative assistant came up behind them. When she spoke, Kate almost jumped out of her skin.

"That is a most unfortunate man," the woman said. "He has an extremely rare illness called Cotard's syndrome. It is, Dr. Cleaver believes, closely related to the Capgras's syndrome that you saw earlier, only a much more severe form. In this case, the patient has no emotions whatsoever. He is totally without affect.

"The patient is stripped of all signs of life. In fact, he becomes convinced that he is actually dead, and it is impossible to rid him of this peculiar delusion. At times he will smell his own flesh rotting. And at other times he becomes convinced that worms are crawling over his rotting corpse, and he scratches himself without ceasing. For that reason, he must from time to time be restrained."

Kate couldn't wait to leave. Butterworth was waiting for her at the nurses' station.

"Pretty grim, huh?" he said.

She nodded, preoccupied. She was looking over his shoulder, searching for someone.

"Excuse me," she said. "I won't be a minute."

She went over to the administrative assistant and pulled her to one side. They talked briefly, and the woman frowned; then Kate came back, and the group gathered in the lobby to leave.

"What was that all about?" asked Butterworth.

"Nothing, really," said Kate. "I noticed that the man back there had a sore that looked infected. I told the administrator, and she said they'd look into it."

"She didn't look too happy about it."

"No," agreed Kate. She seemed preoccupied again.

Chapter 3

All the way down the corridor, even through the heavy door that sealed with a tiny sucking sound when it closed, Saramaggio could hear the craniotome. High-pitched and piercing, it drew a distinctive hollow sound from the material that was being cut by its rotating bit—the resistant bone of the human skull. The sound was unmistakable—oddly enough, even to people who had never heard it before.

Saramaggio was infamous for having his business calls switched to the operating room during surgery. A nurse would hold the receiver to his ear while he held arms encased in sterile gloves in front of him like a sleepwalker. Meanwhile, ten feet away, the assisting surgeon would be opening a bone flap in the skull, standing above the patient, whose head was draped in green sterile cloths that tented the face. He would pin the square flap of skin from the brainpan to the Layla bar. Then his foot would strike the pedal, he would raise the long black drill, lower it gingerly, and that earsplitting sound would come screaming off the walls. Sooner or later, the caller—a credit card representative or a bank loan officer or stockbroker—would ask, with that telltale hint of dread in the voice, "By the way, what *is* that sound in the background?"

"You don't want to know," he delighted in answering.

Leopoldo Saramaggio—Leo to his friends—was nothing if not dramatic. He liked being talked about, being at the center of things, and being in charge. From the start, he had been blessed with the ease of privilege. The scion of a family who owned a ranch in Nebraska, which he called "a farm" to give an up-from-the-bootstraps arc to the narrative of his life, he'd gone to Yale undergrad and Harvard Medical School and Johns Hopkins for residency without so much as a blink. He was a good surgeon, very good, and probably would have risen quickly even if he hadn't been in all the good clubs, from Skull and Bones to the Knickerbocker. Now middle-aged, he was in danger of becoming a cliché, the high-living, fast-talking, dashing brain surgeon. He drove a black Ferrari, though without vanity plates, which he judged to be tacky. He had a pilot's license, and a plane was his to use at any time, courtesy of a CEO whose aneurysm he had repaired. Any number of places in New York happily threw open their doors to him—restaurants where he was not permitted to pay the check, grand-tier boxes at the Met, courtside seats at Knicks' games.

It was amazing how many of the wealthy and well-connected sooner or later required the intervention of a top brain man in some medical emergency. Leopoldo—please, you can call me Leo, he would say right off the bat—accepted these tributes as his due. They were not graft but tokens of esteem. The difference was important to understand, for what motivated Leo Saramaggio was not money, though he did not lack for it, but the look in the eye of a person whose life he had saved. Or the way the husband or wife bolted upright in the waiting room and practically ran to him, anxious but hopeful. There was no experience like it; Zeus himself couldn't have felt a deeper pleasure.

At St. Catherine's, it was an open secret that Saramaggio was the power. If there were ever to be a showdown between him and Calvin Brewster, the hospital administrator, there was no doubt who would come out on top. But a showdown was the last thing likely to happen; Brewster wouldn't let it come to that, no matter what Saramaggio did. And the chief neurosurgeon could be imperious and demanding. He wanted only the best equipment to work with, hang the cost, and the best assisting surgeons to work under him, salaries to be

commensurate with talent. He thought nothing of barg-
ing into Brewster's office to complain if the paper towel
dispenser in the residents' bathroom was empty.

In Saramaggio's life, there was only a single dark
cloud. At the moment, it was on the far horizon and no
bigger than a man's hand, but he knew it was going to
be growing larger. He had hit fifty-five two weeks ago,
and though he was fit and played tennis (twice a week,
with a savage competitive edge), he was beginning to
feel his age. Not so much physically as psychologically.
It took the form of a quiet desperation, like someone's
footsteps at his heels. Yes, he was an accomplished and
well-known surgeon, but what he needed, what he
craved, was something that people would remember
him for—a feat of medical greatness. And he was working toward this with every fiber of his being. He had the
idea. With Cleaver's help, he had the equipment. Now
all he needed was time for research and experimentation, and then, one day, the right patient.

Zeus was born immortal; the rest of us have to work
at it.

"You'll learn your way around here in no time," said
Saramaggio, talking over his shoulder. He was speaking
to the new resident surgeon, Kate Willet, showing her
around.

They entered his office, the walls covered in diplomas, plaques, awards, and VIP photographs.

He knew all about her, of course. Her file, at least an
inch thick and bursting with excellent reports, had been
sitting on a corner of his desk for weeks, and he had interviewed her himself after she'd won the resident of
the year award at Moffitt Hospital in San Francisco. But
when she'd reported for work this morning, he had been
uncharacteristically reserved and standoffish, almost as
if they had never met. Perhaps he acted that way because she was so young and attractive. Having her
around would be pleasing but also distracting.

Saramaggio had a reputation as a Lothario. He was
married to a long-suffering woman named Joy, and their

hundred-year-old Colonial on Round Hill Road in the back country of Greenwich, Connecticut, was home to them and their three children. Still, someone at his level and of his creative temperament could hardly be expected to be a slave to monogamy. He slept with many of the nurses and interns but rarely carried on long-term affairs. As soon as he'd seen Kate, when she'd walked into his office for that initial interview, he'd known he would hire her, and that sooner or later he would have to make a pass at her. But in truth, he didn't feel up for it just at the moment. He was beginning to wonder if affairs of the heart, with all the attendant emotion and Sturm und Drang, didn't drag you down. He was starting to think that women took away more than they brought.

"Today, of course, you can just observe. I like my team to get accustomed to my rhythm. If you have any questions, just shout them out—provided of course that you pick your moment."

She nodded.

"I'll let you choose the music for the OR today," he said, raising a hand, palm upward. "As long as you don't choose any of those California mantras. They drive me crazy."

How about rap? she thought subversively. Instead, she asked, "What operation are you doing?"

"A lobectomy."

"Epilepsy?"

"Yes."

"Severe?"

"Well, we're doing surgery—aren't we?"

She blushed. The question had sounded stupid to her the moment she'd said it. She asked it largely to keep the conversation going; she wanted to impress him and show that he had been right to hire her. Now she felt nothing but awkward. He was definitely no longer the charming man who had interviewed her.

Saramaggio excused himself—he had to make a phone call—and so she slipped out of his office. Waiting in the hallway with nothing to do made her feel twice as uncomfortable. She pretended to study a large map of Manhattan and parts of Queens tacked up on a bulletin board. It was covered with red pins and white pins. She noted that the pins were clustered around the housing projects of East Harlem.

"Looking for an apartment?"

The voice startled her, and when she turned around she saw a young, thick-shouldered man in green scrubs. His skin was light dark; he was Indian or Pakistani, and black chest hair grew in the V neck of his jersey—like a little garden of shrubbery in a vest-pocket park, she found herself thinking.

"No . . . I . . ." She felt flustered again. "I was just wondering . . ."

"It's a map of our emergency cases. The information is called up from ER. The red pins are for penetrating trauma, and the white pins are for blunt trauma."

"I see."

"God knows why we keep it. I guess it'll make for a doctorate in public health someday."

"And it tells you what neighborhoods to avoid."

"Yes. That could be."

He smiled and stuck out his hand with warmth that seemed genuine. He had the slightest singsong of an accent.

"Singh. Gulchaman Singh. Call me Gully."

"I'm Kate Willet."

"I know. Word travels fast. Welcome to our team. I'm assisting today."

Finally—a friendly face, she thought.

He led her to a large board partitioned off by operating rooms; it listed a dozen operations: the time, patient, procedure, surgeon, anesthetist, scrub nurse, and circulating nurse. They found the one for Dr. Saramaggio. Room 7.

"We might as well go in," said Gully. "He likes to come in at the last moment, just when the patient is fully opened and his expert touch is required. Sometimes he's gone again before you know it."

She listened to detect a tone of criticism, but didn't find it.

They suited up and entered the OR. The scrub nurse was already there and had lain out the sterile instruments on the Gerhardt table, high above the operating bed. She stepped down from the platform to help Singh on with his sterile gown and gloves and did the same for another man. The anesthesiologist came and checked the array of gadgets that kept tabs on the vital signs. Finally, the patient, a Hispanic-looking woman in her thirties, was wheeled in on a gurney. She had been drugged with Valium, but her eyes looked scared as she was transferred to the operating bed under the powerful overhead lights. An intravenous line was started, and she was sedated by an infusion of propofol, or "milk of amnesia," as the residents called it. She was placed on a ventilator and taped down on her back with one shoulder raised by padding.

The music, chosen by someone else, was Vivaldi—*The Four Seasons*.

The assisting surgeons worked quickly. They sterilized her shaved head with iodine, turning the skin bright orange, then placed green sterile cloths across a retainer bar surrounding her forehead; her face disappeared within a three-sided tent, open to the anesthesiologist. They cut through the skin. There was a smell of burning as they cauterized the frontalis muscle and separated it from the skull, then used the screaming drill to cut a rectangular piece of skull that was lifted off and handed to the scrub nurse, who placed it on the sterile pads of her table. They extended the bone window, gnawing away at the edges with sharp-edged pliers and then cut through the dura, exposing the brain, a mass of blue-and-red bumps and blood vessels, slightly pulsating. The monitor showed three lines: heartbeat, respiratory rate, and temperature. One surgeon cut deep inside while the other suctioned off the blood and rinsed the tissue every so often with saline.

Kate stayed to one side. Soon she was joined by two other observers, a boy and a college-aged woman, who looked about wide-eyed and talked softly, as if they were in church. She gathered that they were guests of

Dr. Saramaggio, and she took their presence in the OR as another sign of his ability to run roughshod over the rules.

After two hours, the surgeons began to map a portion of the cortex. The anesthetist brought the patient up to consciousness, and Gully fixed a sterilized coronet with sixteen electrodes suspended on thin, coated wires onto her skull. He inserted one depth electrode into her amygdala and another into her hippocampus, and the other assistant asked her to count. A halting voice came from within the tent. She reached twelve and then stopped for several seconds before going on to twenty. The assistant held up a picture of a farm and asked her to name the animals one by one. Several times, she opened her mouth, but no sound came out; they stopped and made a notation.

"This is to preserve her language center," Gully explained to the puzzled young visitors. "You know, she's an epileptic, so we'll be removing the part of her brain that kindles the seizures. If the electrode stimulates the spot and she can't talk, we know that we must save it."

Saramaggio entered with a flurry, looking somehow dashing with a thick microscopic lens over one eye. He acknowledged the visitors with a princely nod, was helped into his gown, and peered into the brain. Then he stood up and examined the MRIs pinned to an electronic board.

"The area of seizures is interesting in this case," he announced, speaking to his young guests. "She has what we call *absence* seizures, which means a total suspension of consciousness. She had one in my office two weeks ago. She sat there and suddenly went blank—her face was a mask, no emotion whatsoever. Then she stood up, opened the door, walked out into the corridor, and sat in the waiting room. All without any idea of what she was doing. Totally unconscious. When she awoke several minutes later, she had no memory of any of it."

"Uncle Leo," said the boy. "She's awake now. How can she stand the pain?"

"She doesn't feel any pain. There are no nerve endings in the brain. That makes sense, the way things in the body usually make sense: Nerves exist to warn the brain of danger elsewhere. There's no reason for them up here—anything gets this far, and the jig is up."

"But will she be okay? Missing all that brain that you're taking out?"

"I can't promise that she won't show any difference. But we try to minimize it. That's what all that mapping was about. Above all, we try to preserve language. Now in this case, she is a Latina and Spanish is her primary language. We've decided to preserve English, which is her secondary language. It's located in a different area, farther back in the cortex."

"Why the English and not the Spanish?"

"She needs it for work," Saramaggio answered. "Naturally, we consulted with her."

"What's she do?" asked the young woman.

Saramaggio looked over at Gully, who answered for him.

"She's an assistant computer programmer up in White Plains."

"But will she be any different? Will she be able to function just as well?"

"You never know," replied Saramaggio sententiously. "I've seen amazing things. I've seen patients who lose half of the temporal lobe and if you sat next to them at a dinner party, you wouldn't notice a thing. Others . . . just a little piece and they're permanently changed."

Kate found it disconcerting that he was talking like that at the precise moment that he was using a Penfield #4 to probe the soft brain tissue, with its milkshake consistency. He was searching for a pathway to go deeper. She could tell how dexterous his hands were; they moved not quickly, but continually and efficiently.

"We used to do a lot of split-brains. When the epilepsy is so severe and widespread, you have to separate the two hemispheres—you do it by severing the corpus callosum, the bundle of nerve fibers that connects them. The left brain, you know, specializes in language and the right in certain perceptual tasks, but it's not always so cut-and-dried. Sometimes—and this is really strange—the two hemispheres fight. I had one patient whose left and right arms would hit each other."

"No kidding," said the girl, suddenly interested. "What happened to him?"

"Luckily for her, it didn't last too long. The right hand won. Usually the brain works it out—one of them becomes dominant. But sometimes they still battle on in little ways, like one hand will always turn the faucet on, and afterward the other turns it off—that sort of thing. A tug of war."

He said something to Gully and pointed into the brain with his other hand. Then he stepped back and watched while Gully cut out small slabs, which were placed inside a sterilized dish and handed to the scrub nurse. "You know, it's not really such an elegant piece of engineering," he continued. "It's jerry-built—billions of neurons thrown together and trillions of synaptic connections, just trying to muddle through. Pathways fire and misfire; electrical malfunctions occur; small strokes happen. Parts spill over into other parts. Areas turn soggy or short-circuit and no longer function, and other areas carry on. Sometimes they do it well enough, and other times they don't—they get overloaded and crash. And then all of a sudden you're hearing voices out of radiators. And another part of your brain will tell you that it's perfectly normal to hear the voices, and before you know it, the radiators are telling you to do something; you're on a mission to perform a heroic task—like assassinate the president."

Kate was impressed by his eloquence and decided to forgive him for his rudeness to her earlier.

The OR was silent for a moment, except for the steady bleeping of the monitors, until Gully said quietly, "Dr. Saramaggio, we're ready."

At that, the surgeon stepped into position, pulled his glasses down, and was handed instruments. Now his hands were moving quickly, but still with that same sense of certainty.

At one point, the probe dug deeply and the woman

reacted with a quick intake of breath. Then she gave a little sob.

"I don't want to go on," she cried out abruptly. Her voice, coming from under the tent, startled everyone.

Saramaggio moved his hand slightly, and instantly she fell quiet.

"That reaction," he said calmly, "was caused by me. You see what a little stimulation can do. I touched the amygdala. It's the gateway to the emotions. Fight or flight. All of the senses—sight, taste, touch, hearing—feed into the limbic system. But smell is the most powerful of them all, the one that triggers aggression and sexuality and territorial defense. And smell is hardwired straight into the amygdala." He paused, then pointed to a plastic hose. "Ms. Willet, would you mind?"

Kate swabbed the brain with saline solution. She was working so intently that she didn't pay attention to the new figure, decked out in scrubs, who slipped into the room and stood to one side. Only when he took up a position directly across from her and she looked into the eyes above the mask did she realize who it was: Cleaver.

He wheeled over a bank of machines that she had never seen before.

What was he doing?

Saramaggio stepped aside, sat down, and lowered his mask. It lay under his chin like a tiny hammock. He ushered his guests out of the OR.

Cleaver attached another coronet, this one with twenty-four electrodes, and began to place them methodically at key points on the patient's brain.

"What's going on?" asked Kate.

"Just a little detour," said Saramaggio from his chair. "It's routine experimentation."

She watched, disbelieving, as Cleaver finished attaching the electrodes and turned to the bank of machines, adjusting knobs and reading dials. A computer screen flashed on. The second assisting surgeon gave the patient an injection.

"What's that?" Kate asked.

Cleaver remained silent, so Saramaggio answered for him.

"Two-deoxyglucose. It's like glucose, but it can't be broken down by metabolic activity."

Kate thought for a moment, then pieced it together. "And since cells consume glucose for energy, they'll absorb it. The more active the cell, the more it takes in. And if it can't be broken down, it'll accumulate. And that way you can read it."

"Precisely," said Saramaggio, with a hint of admiration in his voice. "Advanced autoradiography. You're a quick study."

"But it's only used on animals—and you have to kill them to read it."

"No, we have a sensor we can use."

"But what do you want to read it for?"

"For this," cut in Cleaver, holding up a thin stimulator.

He sank the stimulator deep beneath the cortex. Then another and another, until seven were in place. He checked the machines and signaled to the second attending surgeon, who gave another injection. The computer screen danced to life, a cascade of throbbing pulses. Cleaver and Saramaggio stared at it, spellbound.

Two minutes passed.

"Enough," said Saramaggio.

"Give me one more minute."

Saramaggio sighed.

The minute passed, and Cleaver signaled to the nurse, who lifted up the shock pads, placed them on the woman's chest, and yelled "Clear!" With the jolt, the patient's body twitched. The screen cleared.

"Perfect," pronounced Cleaver, who began removing the stimulators.

"Right," said Saramaggio. He stood up, examined the open skull, then turned to Kate and said, "Close her up."

Five minutes later, the two men left the room.

Kate moved into position and worked quickly to stanch the wound, slowly sewing it up. Gully helped her.

"Okay," she said. "I want you to tell me exactly what happened here."

Gully smiled uncertainly. "As he said, experimentation," he said. "They do it fairly often on cases like this where the probes go deep and the lower brain is laid out."

"But what's the point of the experiment?"

"Oh, that—I thought you knew. It's big."

"Big what?"

"That injection, the second one, it stopped her heart for ever so short a time. And the computer, the one that was attached directly to the limbic system, it took over for her. It was sending the signals that made her breathe and her heart beat. When they turned it off and administered the shock, that was to restart her own system."

"I've never heard of such a thing!"

"Yes, it's amazing. They've done it a dozen times now. They haven't published it yet."

He could see that she looked disturbed.

"It's all legal," he said. "The patients all sign papers giving them the right to do it."

"But what if something happens—the risk, if something goes wrong?"

Now he smiled.

"But it doesn't. It hasn't yet, not once."

"And why do it? What's it for?"

"It's Dr. Saramaggio's dream. Someday he will perform an operation that's so very complicated he will need help keeping the patient alive while he does it." Gully smiled. "And that is what the computers will do."

Long after she left the OR, Kate wondered about what Gully had told her. What kind of operation could Saramaggio possibly have in mind?

Chapter 4

Tyler was having a great day so far—the kind of day he used to dream about on those dreary winter afternoons in school in New York City. It was early July, which meant that most of the summer still lay ahead, a prospect that filled his thirteen-year-old body with a glow of well-being. He didn't hate school exactly, and he knew he should appreciate the fact that his father worked so hard to send him to Horace Mann. It was just that he dreaded getting up in the half-light of morning to take the subway up to the Bronx and that he felt so confined in a classroom—at times his legs ached under the desk and he would daydream himself out the window and imagine running across a field as fast as he could, with the wind ruffling his hair, or lying on his belly and watching an ant crawl up a blade of grass. And now he could do that for real.

He was with Johnny, still his best friend from the early years in Connecticut before Scott had sold the house and moved into the loft in midtown Manhattan. Johnny's parents had moved into the city, too, and they loved to go on excursions and often brought Tyler along. Now they were spending a perfect weekend in the Catskills.

Tyler knew somewhere inside that they felt sorry for him because he was motherless. *Motherless.* How he detested that word! It made him feel as if he had some kind of illness. He had come to recognize a certain look that people, especially women, cast in his direction when they thought he was busy doing something and wouldn't see it. The look was sad and pensive, with a moistness in the eyes that made them glisten. He didn't like it at all—and Johnny's mom specialized in it. More than once, he and Johnny had talked about how she seemed to be always trying to mother him.

They were staying at a hotel called the Balfour, a wonderful ramshackle old place made half of wood and half of stone, on the rim of a crystal-clear glacial lake on top of a mountain. The hotel hadn't been built according to a thought-out plan; it had simply expanded over the years, adding on new wings in a helter-skelter way, the way a boy would have built it. So it had dozens of hidden passageways and secret compartments and dumbwaiters to hide in. Outside there was swimming in a roped-off area of the lake with a small gray sandy beach, miniature golf on a manicured lawn, a garden with a hedge maze, and scores of paths that wound up to a stone tower that crowned the mountain summit. From there you could look for miles in every direction over a blanket of pine forests.

From the moment they had woken up, Tyler and Johnny had been racing around. They had the run of the place, wrestling on the beach, dunking each other in the cold water, and rolling down the hill like logs, giggling. To get them out from underfoot, Johnny's mother had ordered some sandwiches for lunch, put them in a backpack with some Cokes, and sent the boys hiking.

They came to the trail that was nicknamed "the Teardrop," a scramble that eventually wound its way to the top up and over giant boulders. A notice at the bottom warned that it was risky, but also held out the lure of adventure with names like "Skinny Man's Squeeze" and "the Pancake" and "Don't Look Down Bridge."

They looked at each other.

"My dad said we shouldn't take this one," said Johnny.

"Mine would say the same thing if he were here. He can't stand for me to take chances."

"What d'ya think?"

"I dunno. It looks good."

"Maybe we should flip," Johnny offered, pulling a quarter out of his jeans.

"Heads we go, tails we don't."

The coin caught a sliver of sunlight and glinted in midair before landing on the dirt path. They bent over it. Tails.

"Shoot."

They decided to go anyway.

Halfway up, they stopped to rest. The climb was as advertised, if anything even more difficult. Tyler had gone first, climbing up boulders five feet wide, slipping into crevices and caves where he had to crawl on his belly, and crossing ravines on narrow wooden ladders. Just when he'd see an obstacle that convinced him he must have strayed from the path he'd see another red arrow painted on a rock, pointing the way.

It had been exciting. When he negotiated a particularly arduous passage—as when he'd squeezed through two boulders and then stepped across a crack that ran down fifty feet—Tyler would yell back, "You're not going to believe this!" Sometimes his echo would carry.

And a few minutes later, Johnny would reach that spot and Tyler would hear him cry with delight from deep within the rock: "You're right! I *don't* believe it." And then *his* voice would echo.

Tyler sat on a boulder and put his feet up on a facing one. He leaned back and spread his arms behind him and faced the hot sun. The warmth bathed him. Johnny sat nearby, took off his pack, and reached in for a bottle of water. He took three or four long swigs and handed it to Tyler, who drank some and poured a little into his cupped hand and wiped it on his forehead. It dripped down the front of his T-shirt, feeling cool.

"This is great," Johnny observed.

Tyler thought of how his dad always worried about him and wouldn't let him do anything that even hinted of danger. And those were the very things that were fun. Only two weeks ago, they had had a fight about rock climbing; a long time ago his father had promised that he could try it, and now he was changing his mind. It wasn't fair.

Still, he said to himself, there's nothing dangerous about this. He looked down at the jumble of rocks spreading below them, getting smaller as they receded into the distance and disappearing below the treetops. He could see the hotel, which looked suddenly small and oddly artificial from this height, like a photograph. Except that he could see things moving—on the lake there were miniature boats and even tiny figures bent over, rowing. He suddenly had a flash of memory: the little houses he used to play with under the bush near the back door of his home.

"It's more than great," he said quietly. "It's perfect."

Something in his tone made Johnny turn toward him. "You sound weird."

Tyler smiled.

If Johnny only knew what he was thinking sometimes, if he could get inside his head and see the thoughts that lodged there—not thoughts exactly, but feelings, sometimes scary ones, but other times comforting—then he would know just how weird he was. The feelings were impossible to describe. They came at the strangest times, usually at night when he was looking up at the star-studded sky. Something took hold of him; it seemed to grasp him around the chest—he didn't know how to describe it except to say he felt time breaking up into small pieces, to open the way for something big and everlasting, and then something inside him was soaring upward and outward and he was floating magically, so that he was a part of everything and everything was a part of him. That was the only way to describe it. A merging with something, something huge and cosmic. The feeling didn't last long, a couple of seconds, but it had an after-glow that he could hold on to, sometimes for hours.

He didn't quite feel it now, but he almost did. He knew it was close, and that was comforting; for it had been a long time since he had experienced it, and he was beginning to fear that as he was growing older, he was losing the gift for it.

The cicadas were making a din that rose up from the trees below.

"Do you wanna eat now or go on?" asked Johnny.

Tyler looked behind them at the almost sheer cliff that disappeared out of sight far above. The path looked as if it ducked inside the rock somehow. Maybe there was a chimney that they would have to climb. That would be fun.

"Let's go on," he said. "We can have lunch at the top."

They stood up, and Tyler could already feel the soreness in his thighs and his calves. His sweat had dried on his shirt, and it felt cool against his back. Again he led the way, and he clambered over the rocks for scarcely ten feet before he saw another red arrow painted on the grainy surface of a boulder. He was right: It was pointing directly toward a crevice that split the cliff and ran all the way up to the top. He could see that it was dark inside, and that made it even more inviting, like Aladdin's cave.

He stepped inside between the two sheer sheets of rock and looked up. They twisted and bulged and slanted so much that he couldn't see daylight. He walked along the base, and as he stepped across a muddy puddle he felt water dripping down on his head and shoulders. About twenty feet in, he came to a ledge where the outcroppings of rock formed a natural staircase, which he climbed until in the half-light he came upon a slender ladder. The worn wood felt cool to the touch. He went up the ladder and felt it twist gradually to the left as the rungs narrowed and it squeezed behind a boulder that was wedged between the two giant slabs of rock. He came to a ledge and walked across it sideways and then came to another ladder. He could hear Johnny underneath him, breathing excitedly. He dropped a pebble down upon him.

"Hey, cut it out."

"You're lucky that's all I drop."

"Knew I should have gone first."

"You ever seen anything like this?"

"Never. It's great . . . unbelievable."

There were two more ladders ahead, and Tyler climbed them. At one point the rocks verged so close together that he could feel the rough unyielding surfaces in front and behind. *This must be Skinny Man's Squeeze,* he thought.

He didn't feel claustrophobic. On the contrary, he felt snug and secure in the dank darkness.

Then, finally, he saw a stab of daylight. Five more steps and a final bend and he was suddenly outside, blinking in the sun and lifting his head to a breeze. Before he knew it, Johnny stood beside him and gave a little gasp.

They were standing on a giant dome of rock, and on three sides the view fell away as far as they could see. There were valleys of forests, and farms with tiny white houses and red barns, and twisting little ribbons of road, and purple ponds and lakes. Way off to the north, they could see a cluster of buildings gleaming in the sun, a town, and beyond that a river flanked by trees. Off in the distances on all three sides were mountains that sat frozen in green humps and marched off in waves that got dimmer and dimmer and then disappeared altogether in the hazy horizon. Above, against the light blue sky, white clouds rose up in billowing luminous towers. They changed shape in slow motion and cast shadows upon the land, large dark puddles.

The rock they were standing upon sloped down on all sides so they couldn't see the edge. Standing upon the crest of it was like standing on some huge creature, the brow of a whale maybe, and it made them feel giddy. The sun was at its height now, and it beat down relentlessly. They could hear a chorus of cicadas coming from the underbrush on the mountain behind them.

They found a small indentation in the rock where they could sit and dangle their legs. Johnny took his knapsack off and set it down. He began unbuckling it to bring out lunch.

Tyler rose and walked down the slope. It was scary because the rock just kept curving downward toward nothingness. If he stumbled, he would roll until he hit the air, and then he would drop straight down like a stone.

"Hey, be careful," yelled Johnny. "Come on back."

Tyler stood where he was for a few seconds, enough to save face, and then turned and walked back.

He looked up ahead. Johnny had pulled out a sandwich and was eating it, holding it by the wax paper. Behind him the mountain rose up another fifty feet or so. To the right side, Tyler could see the beginning of a path, half-hidden by wild grass. It headed up a gentle slope and disappeared; it looked like an easy walk all the way to the top. But on the other side, on the left side, was a rocky ledge about four feet wide at the base of the rock face. It seemed to be a miracle of nature, it was so perfectly carved, like a balcony set in the mountain for a view of the valley.

He felt himself drawn to it.

His eyes moved up the rock face above the ledge. It ran up sheer and solid for about twelve feet, and then it jutted out into a thin overhang. There was a dash of color. He focused. It was one of those devices that climbers stuck into the rock. It trailed yellow-and-blue bits of rope that swung in the breeze, and white powder—rosin, he thought—caked the edge of a nearby crevice. For traction, he had been told, so they can grip with their fingertips or cling with the tips of their shoes.

He felt the exhilaration of knowing that someday soon, maybe sometime this year, he would be joining them.

He looked higher. A flicker of movement suddenly caught his eye. A climber, splayed against the rock face. Then another higher up. And another. Once he saw them, he couldn't miss them. They were apart from the rock but also seemed to belong to it, hardly moving, then bursting in midair like some magnificent creatures, like gods. The three figures were moving slowly and carefully, like spiders hanging from gossamer threads, with equipment dangling from their belts. They wove their web assiduously, from crevice to ledge to crevice again. The sun abruptly peeked out from behind a cloud and reflected so brilliantly off the rock it was hard to make them out. They seemed suspended in slow motion, utterly silent.

Tyler walked over to the rock face near the ledge and leaned against it, feeling the hardness and the rough surface on his fingers. He leaned into it and began to move sideways, crablike, toward the ledge.

"Hey, c'mon," yelled Johnny.

Tyler ignored him.

He moved more quickly now, without thinking. And before he knew it, he was all the way out on the ledge. He turned his head slowly, and the view took his breath away—a green carpet stretching off into forests and fields and mountains. He could no longer hear the cicadas; instead, he heard wind whipping by at his feet. He felt the sun directly on him, like a spotlight. The climbers were far above him.

Slowly, Tyler crouched into a squat and turned toward the nothingness, and then stood up. Now he could see everything, facing it all; it was spread before him as if it had been tossed at his feet. His arms behind him were still touching the rock. Out of a corner of his eye, he could see Johnny, standing now, staring over at him.

He dropped his arms to his sides. Then he stepped forward a foot. He was standing in the middle of the ledge. Looking down his nose, he could see past the edge into the chasm. He was perfectly balanced, solid and fearless.

He heard something, a sharp smack near his foot. Then another. The ground moved a bit, and it took him a while to realize what it was: pebbles, rocks, dropping down.

There was a shout, a yell. He was confused. Things were happening quickly. He looked over at Johnny, who was waving his arms. More rocks, a big one now.

He touched the rock face behind and looked up. One of the climbers was dangling by a rope, groping at the cliffside awkwardly and then turning slowly away from it, suspended in midair, so that his hands were pawing the emptiness helplessly.

"Look out!" yelled Johnny.

He heard a clang of metal bouncing off rock. But it was too late. The thing came out of nowhere and struck him. He barely registered it, a crash on his head. A darkening. Then his knees began to buckle.

Johnny saw it all—the climber suddenly plummeting down, falling backward with his arms flailing until the rope caught him and he bounced a bit. The rocks raining down, the metal device bounding down the rock face and turning as it hit, looking like a beast running for its life, falling and leaping up again. He saw it crash into Tyler, actually into him, his head, so that when Tyler turned slowly to begin his long fall, he was frozen for a second in silhouette and it was sticking out of him. He looked like someone shot by an arrow right in his skull.

Johnny scrambled frantically down the mountainside, tripping, jumping, half running, half falling in stretches. He was bruising his shins and elbows and ripping the skin on his fingers and his nose was running and his legs were bleeding, but he didn't feel any of that. He had to reach Tyler.

He had looked down and seen him lying on another ledge about twenty or thirty feet below. He couldn't determine if he was still alive. He looked hard to see if he was still breathing, if there was any movement at all under the red T-shirt, but it was too far to be able to tell. The more he looked without being sure, and the longer Tyler lay there without moving, the more he feared for the worst. It was all so unreal—one moment Tyler was standing there, full of life, and the next he was lying on the rocks below. His body seemed crumpled up, collapsed in on itself in some unnatural way. He was on his left side, his face turned away into the rock, and his right arm was pinned behind and twisted up into the air. Johnny hadn't been quick to decide what to do—whether to go straight to him or to run down the path to the hotel. And then he had heard the voice from up above, one of the climbers, a woman. She shouted that she would go for help, that he should try to reach his friend.

At that he'd sprung into action. But getting there was taking forever.

His heart was racing. Without quite realizing it, he was having the spooky thought that if he didn't reach him soon, Tyler would die, that it was up to him somehow. He didn't know what he would do to help him exactly, just that he had to get there right away and do *something*. Comfort him in some way and make him feel better. Make him feel not so alone. But getting there was not easy. Finding him in the tangle of boulders and scrub pine, getting to the right level, was infuriatingly difficult. Twice Johnny was sure he was at the right spot and saw a ledge, but when he reached there, it was empty. The second time he looked down and saw that he was standing only about eight feet above him. He climbed straight down, falling part of the way and smashing his knee, but he didn't feel it at all. Instead he walked over to the body, taking his time now, and peered down. Tyler's T-shirt was pulled halfway up; his back had been bleeding from gashes, but the blood had stopped and was caking against his skin. Johnny half closed his eyes and looked at the head. The piece of metal was still there, sticking out of one side, embedded. His skull seemed closed in around the wound. A thin trickle of blood had fallen on the rock, following the grain and collecting in a tiny crevice a few inches away.

Johnny knelt down and lifted the arm that was twisted—it fell limply back into a normal position—and felt for a pulse. But he didn't know if he was doing it right, and before he could even try, Tyler shifted a little, shuddering and bending his top leg so that he gently kicked Johnny on the thigh. Then Johnny could see that he was breathing. He knew that he should somehow keep him warm, so he took off his own shirt and draped it over one shoulder. It looked pathetically small. Then he took Tyler's hand in his and squeezed it tightly and told him, over and over, that it would be all right and that people were coming to get him and that he should just hang on. He had no idea if Tyler could hear him, but he didn't know what else to do. Johnny looked up. There was a breeze now—the tree branches were waving.

The emergency workers didn't come for a long, long time. Johnny saw them first up above, on the ledge where Tyler had been standing when he had been struck—ages ago, it seemed—and when the two men arrived, he saw they were wearing climbing gear and realized they were not rescue workers but two of the climbers. They didn't know what to do either, and after looking closely at Tyler's wound—one of them grimaced and looked away—they just stood around nervously without saying much. Johnny knelt over Tyler and felt protective of him. Then another group came from below. It included two men wearing white jackets and a third who wore a jacket with the words *The Balfour* stitched on a front pocket. He was lugging a large first-aid kit.

He opened the lid of the kit, and they looked inside.

"We better wait," said one. "We need more than this. His bleeding has stopped."

"What's that in his head?" asked one.

They looked over at the two climbers, who looked away.

"It's a camming device," said one quietly. "It's a . . . it's called a Camalot number two."

"I dropped it," said the other, after a while. "It just slipped. I . . . I was taking it off my belt and with my other hand, I was holding on. I lost my grip. So I just . . . I fell and as I fell I just let it go."

He was crying, but not making any sound.

No one spoke for a while.

"Is he going to be all right?" the climber asked.

"It's hard to say," said one of the emergency workers. "We have to clean him up before we can get a good look. He's breathing okay, which is good. But I don't want to even try to remove this—we'll leave that to the hospital." He pointed at the piece of metal.

After a short while, two more people came, a man and a woman, and they were carrying all kinds of equipment. They arrived out of breath. One of them unpacked a neck brace that he slid under Tyler, straightening his head and binding it in place with a roll of adhesive, carefully avoiding touching the head wound.

"Jesus Christ," said one. "What the hell is that?"

"Equipment," said a climber. "It fell from up there." He pointed, and the man and woman both looked up.

"Heavy?" asked the man.

"Yes," said the climber.

"Heavy enough to smash his skull," said the emergency worker, a tone of anger in his voice. "What do you think?" he asked his partner, nodding at it.

"I think we bind it, just to hold everything in place. Until we get him down the mountain. We have to get some blood in him."

Meanwhile, the other two men pieced together a stretcher. They pushed it under Tyler, gently shifted him onto it, and bound him to it with straps. Then they hoisted it up into the air, lightly, as if it didn't weigh much, and started off across the boulders. They made slow progress, taking pains to keep the stretcher level. Every so often, the one in front would stumble a little and that end would dip down.

"For Christ's sake, be careful," said the man in the back. His voice sounded suddenly strained, and he was sweating.

Johnny realized that he hadn't seen Tyler move since that one time.

Chapter 5

Scott was home when the call came. It was four p.m. on a Saturday, and usually he would be out somewhere in the city, doing something with Tyler. But Tyler was off in the Catskills, and the day was muggy. He was feeling lethargic, so he stayed at home lounging about and reading.

He did not have a premonition. Sometimes when Tyler went away, even with Johnny's parents, whom Scott trusted, he had vague feelings of anxiety. If they persisted, he was apt to pace around, and even from time to time look into Tyler's bedroom, staring at the unmade bed and everything else. He always knew he was being neurotic, but he actually did feel better looking around at the room with all its familiar objects—the bookshelves jammed with books, the computer, the desk with drawers hanging open and papers lunging out, the posters for *Trainspotting* and *Reservoir Dogs* on the wall, and the koala bear sitting in a place of honor on the easy chair. Surely if anything had happened they wouldn't just be resting in place.

But this time he did none of that. This time he scarcely even thought of Tyler. He knew he was in good hands and that he would be having a good time. Instead, he thought vaguely that when his son came back, Sunday night, he would take him out for a pizza and maybe a movie. He knew that Tyler preferred seeing movies with his friends now, but his son was too considerate to object when his father offered, and they usually ended up having fun.

So Scott was not at all prepared when the call came.

At first he didn't even know who was calling. It was Johnny's father, but his voice was so strange, low and with a trembling to it, that it took him some time to recognize it.

"Scott, listen . . . listen. . . . There's been an accident. . . ."

He couldn't hear anything else, although he was listening and paid attention to every word. His mind got in the way. He felt it darken over, like a curtain descending, so that he couldn't hear anything or see anything or think anything, not right away. That was probably his body, shutting down to protect him.

Only two weeks before, Scott and Tyler had gone camping in an ideal spot in the shadow of the Shawangunks an hour and a half north of the city. For Scott, it had been a perfect night, one of the best in years.

Not another soul was around. The cliffs rose up about 150 feet behind them and made the campsite feel secure, tucked into the base of the escarpment. Looking up, they could see clumps of twigs sticking over the outcroppings, the nests of hawks that were slowly circling in the evening air currents. Down a slope ahead was a small lake. Scott had checked the map and thought it was probably Goose Pond, though he couldn't be certain. The paths had twisted and doubled back so often that he wasn't exactly sure where they were. But that didn't bother him—being a little bit lost was part of the fun of camping in the wild.

Tyler collected wood for the fire, and Scott could see his red T-shirt in the distance, appearing and disappearing through the slender trunks of the cedars. His heart soared at the sight—his boy looked so big to him.

Comet, their dog—years ago, Tyler had provided the name, one only a boy would come up with—traipsed at his heels, a happy mongrel.

Scott dropped a slab of bacon in the skillet and then cut up Irish potatoes and added them. They sizzled in the grease. He put on a can of baked beans and set out the hot dogs and rolls. Tyler liked to cook his own.

Tyler came back, lugging an armful of wood, excited.

"Dad, I saw four deer," he said, dropping the logs. He pointed back toward the lake.

"Good."

"One was right there on the shore, drinking. Two of them were fawns. They had little white spots on their fur."

"Deer are one thing. Let me know if you see a bear."

"I wish you'd told me. I've seen dozens. They were following us all the way in here."

"Ha ha."

"They looked hungry."

"Well, then, you better eat your hot dogs before they get here."

The next day was to be Tyler's thirteenth birthday. Scott had wrapped his present—a Swiss Army knife, the jumbo model with four different blades and eight pull-out tools—and hidden it inside the knapsack. He planned to get up first and cook scrambled eggs with onions—Tyler's favorite. He'd place the knife on the log next to where he'd sit. He had a tape of three of Tyler's best friends from school singing "Happy Birthday"; he'd use it to wake him up.

Gone were the days when Tyler jumped out of bed right away. Now he grunted and groaned and curled back up in that posture that said, *Please, just a little bit longer.* Adolescents—why did they need so much sleep? Was it because they were growing so much? Or because of all those hormones pouring into their systems. Or maybe, he thought with a little smile, it's exhaustion from all that scheming and plotting to get around their dads.

They ate hungrily and mostly in silence. Tyler wolfed down three hot dogs and was still hungry and cooked two more. Scott always underestimated his appetite.

In the store on Forty-second Street, he had hesitated a moment before buying the knife—was Tyler old enough to use it safely? He had caught himself. *Old enough? He's practically four years older than I was when I got my first knife.* Still, he would have to make a point of teaching Tyler how to hold it, how to keep his fingers on the edges of the handle and open the blades outward.

"Dad, what was that you were saying about the trees?"

"These are cedars. You see how they rise up straight and tall and their branches form a canopy way up there. Nothing else grows beneath, and it's quiet with the blanket of needles on the ground. That's why the Indians thought this area was so special. It was sacred ground to them."

Tyler peered around, taking it all in.

"Cool."

Scott looked across at his son. The fire cast a glow on his face, so that his features, which lately seemed to sprout out of all proportion, swam about. Still, he was striking, He would make a handsome adult. His brown eyes burned with intelligence, and when he smiled he could charm a snake. His lips were full and sensual— like his mother's.

Scott was proud of the boy Tyler had become. So many times these days, he had to fight down the impulse to be overprotective, to swaddle him in layers of cotton. So much was at stake. He felt it selfishly sometimes: So much of his own world resided in that one little—now, not so little—body. He would be devastated if anything happened to him. So he had to hold himself in check sometimes, difficult as that was, because he wanted Tyler to grow up to be a strong and capable man, ready to take on the world. He knew Tyler was at an age when he needed to build self-confidence by meeting challenges, and that challenges inevitably carried risk. But it was hard on a parent. The world struck him as such a dangerous place—and with good reason. It was filled with storms and earthquakes and poisonous animals and cars that crashed and germs that spread disease. *And planes that fell from the sky.*

If only, he thought to himself, there were some way

for a father to control the risk, to dole out the risk in acceptable doses—like spoonfuls of medicine.

He searched in his pack for the old beat-up coffee percolator, filled the top with fresh grounds, and set it over the embers. While he was waiting for it to brew, he opened up his second beer. He had wanted to bring along some scotch, but had dismissed the idea; he knew the dangers of strong drink—it was a curse that ran way back in his family. His father had died in a car crash when he was young, and his mother, who had never remarried and had raised him alone on a leafy street in Washington, D.C., had been an alcoholic for much of his childhood. She had been sober twelve years, with the help of AA, by the time she died, and so he knew the lore. He knew one of the first signs of trouble was drinking alone.

They sat back and watched the trail of smoke wend its way through the tops of the trees. It was beginning to get dark, and they could see bits of sky where red streaks were lingering in the clouds.

They fed their scraps to Comet, who devoured them greedily.

Tyler looked contented, which made Scott happy. Nothing in the world, he thought, could make him happier than seeing his son at peace. He was glad that they had gone camping when Tyler was young. For years they had explored the outdoors together—skiing in Vermont, sailing on the Sound, hot summer nights sleeping in the craters of dunes along Cape Cod. It didn't make up for a mother's love—nothing could replace that—but it was a bond of male kinship. It was something they could hold on to during the years of conflict that were now upon them. Already, there were unaccountable spells of distance, times when Tyler came home from school moody, remote, and wrapped in a shield of inarticulate anger and went straight to his room to blast himself with music. And there were times when they were awkward in each other's company and didn't have much to say to each other.

The coffee was ready. He poured some into a metal cup and felt the heat travel up through the handle.

"Dad," said Tyler, looking up at the escarpment. "Don't forget your promise."

"What's that?"

"You said that when I was thirteen, I could take up rock climbing. Right here is the best spot in the country."

Scott felt a slight sense of panic rise up from his stomach.

"Don't be crazy. We don't have the equipment or anything. We don't even know the first thing about it."

"I don't mean tomorrow. I mean sometime soon. I've been talking it over with Johnny. He wants to do it, too. There's a place up here where they teach you."

Scott felt his pulse quieting down. It wasn't a problem for right away.

"Well, we'll see," he said.

"Dad"—the word had a nagging tone to it now— "you *promised*."

"I said we'll see. Now that's enough."

He knew his admonition carried less weight that it had only a short while ago. Time was, when he'd said "that's enough," it *was* enough.

"And you said I could get my learner's permit when I was sixteen, and go skydiving when I was eighteen."

"Maybe."

"You didn't say *maybe*. You said *definitely*."

"We'll see. That's enough now."

Tyler sulked.

Scott took the burdens of single parenthood seriously. He tried to have a normal home, though that was difficult with just the two of them. He had moved into New York City to cut out the commuting time. Those additional hours were precious. They had a spacious loft crammed with bikes, baseball bats, sneakers, male paraphernalia of all sorts. Doing double time as a parent, Scott had let his career slide. To become a top photographer, as he had wanted years ago, you had to be a globe-trotter—you had to have that packed suitcase waiting by the door. He had learned to ratchet down his ambition. He turned down out-of-town assignments, took on the occasional fashion shoot, even, God help him, actor portfolios. Anything to pay the rent. He was good enough for some of the top magazine editors to turn to him when their backs were to the wall.

He and Tyler. A twosome against the world. It almost tickled him how he scrambled to construct a world of almost bourgeois comfort for his son, but without a mother it wasn't complete. Every time he saw Tyler watching some TV show about some suburban family of five, he felt his heart sink. He went alone to teachers' meetings, school plays, baseball games in Central Park, feeling out of place as a "singleton." The others all seemed to come in pairs—just like the animals walking up the plank to Noah's ark, he used to think. How his heart soared when Tyler's friends came over just to hang around—it made everything seem, for a while, so blessedly normal.

When he'd gotten the phone call that said Lydia's plane had gone down, he'd felt his life snap in two, just like that. He'd carried his grief everywhere, like a sack of stones, and had overcome it only out of sheer will for his son's sake. At first he refused even to consider remarrying. It seemed disloyal. They had been married such a short while and they had formed such a partnership, such a strong unit. She had loved to plan their future together, talking about everything, from the coat of paint for the house of their dreams (pale yellow, clapboard Colonial) to the number of children (four, maybe five). She had drawn it so vividly, it was hard to turn his back on it. And then when he was ready for other women, they never quite worked out. He'd had a number of girlfriends, some of them serious, but none seemed to fit just right. He took care to have them sleep in the small walled-off room at the rear of the loft, so that Tyler, when he came in to snuggle as he did every morning, would find him alone in the huge bed. It was funny, this insistence upon a strict moral code; he was certain that if Lydia had remained alive, the two of them would have been much more liberal in their childrearing. Sooner or later, the girlfriends stopped trying to compete.

He finished the coffee and set the metal cup down.

Seven years, he thought, since the phone call. Seven long years. He had muddled through somehow. He had done the best he could. And sometimes, like now, when he looked across at Tyler, he thought he had done pretty goddamned well.

"Ready for sleep?" he asked.

Tyler nodded.

They moved away from the fire and found a small clearing to unroll their sleeping bags in. They could feel the hay underneath. Their feet, in socks, inside the bags, were warm. Comet lay down with a grunt, four feet away.

There was a half-moon, enough light to see a straggly cloud go by. Then it cleared and they were looking straight up at the stars.

"Dad, could you point them out again?"

It was an outdoors ritual. Tyler wanted to spot the constellations, but in reality he wanted something else, something that came at the end.

Scott ran through them, guiding his son from one to the other. The North Star. The Big Dipper. The Little Dipper. Cassiopeia. He covered the whole dome spread above them. And then he came to the one they were waiting for—Orion.

"And there, see his belt. And look, hanging from his belt are the three little stars that make up his knife. Now follow that down to where it's pointing."

Tyler did. He saw a trim little star, all on its own, sparkling.

"See it?"

"Yes," he replied.

"That's it."

Scott remembered the first time he had found the star for Tyler and told him it was hers, and he remembered telling him about the corny rhyme he and Lydia had made up years ago, on their honeymoon: *By the stars of Orion, I swear you are mine.*

He remembered checking into the hotel, signing in for the first time, Mr. and Mrs.

It touched him how the boy loved to hear stories about the two of them.

"You remember, Dad, how you used to tell me Jingo stories."

"Of course."

"Every night a different one. Jingo would end up fighting alley cats or falling down an old well or eating a funny leaf and shrinking to the size of a grasshopper."

"But he always got home safe and sound, in bed."

"Once he went through the small white door."

Scott had a sudden image of Tyler lying in his bed under the carved wooden headboard years ago, the blanket tucked under his chin, listening with his brown eyes opened wide. How Tyler had loved the ritual. And when he got a little older, he loved to hear just the opening line—the rest he recited back himself, never missing so much as a single word. Jingo rubbed the magic pebble:

And then something very strange happened. At first he felt hot, and then he felt cold. And then he felt warm, and then he felt cool. And finally he felt just right.

And when he opened his eyes he was standing before a huge white mansion, "the house of a thousand rooms."

As he turned over to sleep, Scott had wished that real life could be like that, always assured of a happy ending, even one that was tacked on for convenience—a little exit door to make sure that everything turned out okay.

⌒

Scott drove up the New York Thruway at breakneck speed. He tried to slow down once or twice so that he wouldn't get stopped for speeding, not for fear of the ticket but because he didn't think he could abide the delay while a patrolman wrote it out. But his mind was racing off in so many directions that he couldn't concentrate on driving. Whenever he looked at the speedometer it had climbed back up to eighty.

He heard a voice—his own—murmuring the same phrases over and over: *Oh God, please don't let him die. Just don't let him die. I'll do anything. Just don't let him die.* Ordinarily he didn't think of God at all, but he didn't find it strange that he was now pleading with Him. He prayed for a number of things, and he set them down in order: First, that Tyler live. Then, that he not be hurt too badly and make a complete recovery. And pain—please let him feel no pain. Put that high on the list. And please make sure the hospital is a good one and that there is a good doctor on hand who knows what he's doing, and if they have to operate—please don't let that happen, but if it does—then make sure the surgeon is really good and doesn't make any mistakes.

He didn't have much to go on—just that there had been an *accident*. How his heart seemed just to stop at that instant; his whole body went rigid when he heard the dreaded word, and he knew right away that it was about Tyler. Johnny's father was calling, and Scott hoped for a brief second that it was Johnny who had had the accident. But of course he knew that wasn't the case—because why would Johnny's father be calling him, and why else would he have that quivering, guilty tone in his voice? All this went through his head before he even heard the next sentence. And then Johnny's father told him what had happened and said it had occurred while they were climbing—*climbing*. He told Scott that it might be serious, but that it was too soon to tell. He was probably lying, hedging it—he probably knew it was serious and thought he was doing the decent thing by breaking it to him gently.

Scott had told Tyler over and over that he couldn't go climbing until he was fully prepared and had taken courses and knew what he was doing, for God's sake. But Tyler hadn't listened. He had wanted to do it anyway; he couldn't wait. He was so eager for adventure, for life—he was so impatient. And why should that thought make Scott love him more? Because he did—

not love him more exactly, because that would be impossible, but connect to the love so strongly that all this was doubly unbearable. He pictured Tyler thinking the decision through, on the threshold of disobedience, wondering whether he should go climbing or not and finally deciding to go ahead. Thinking about it just drove home how unique Tyler was, how so very precious. And without meaning to, Scott started thinking all kinds of things about Tyler—how smart and good-natured and funny he was, and how he had a dear little laugh that jumped out when he was telling a joke, and how he was open in his love and gifted in so many ways, and even—superficial though it might be—how handsome he was. He had his mother's long dark eyelashes.

Lately he even seemed to be looking out for me, Scott thought. *That was so touching, so typical of his generosity. Like how he got so good at Ping-Pong and before, when he was little, I used to try to throw a couple of points his way to save his pride, but carefully so as not to get caught, and the last time we played—where was that? Oh yes, the basement of that kid's house— suddenly he was way ahead and I started catching up and I looked across the net at him and when I saw his face I knew:* He *was intentionally missing some shots and trying to do it sneakily, just like me.*

And out of nowhere, an image ran through Scott's mind: Tyler running along the beach on Cape Cod, Comet yapping behind him and Tyler veering off into the surf and grabbing Comet and the two of them rolling around in the water, laughing. So much life—so much love for life—in those little bones.

Scott started to cry. Tears streamed down his face so that it was almost hard to see the road, and he didn't bother wiping them away but just let them come and fly back in the wind. Please God—*please, please, please*—just don't let him die.

And he remembered Johnny's father had mentioned something about a wound to the head and that he had fallen a bit. The *head*—that was scary; that could mean something really serious. He couldn't think about that.

And falling *a bit*? What does it mean exactly to fall *a bit*? What kind of euphemism was that?

He got angry thinking about it, and he held on to his anger as long as he could because that felt better in some weird way.

Scott arrived at Kingston Hospital not long after the ambulance. He went straight into the emergency ward, and as soon as he saw Johnny and his parents in the waiting room, the look on their faces, he knew that the news was not good. He walked over to them, but couldn't look them in the eye. Johnny hung back, looking guilty.

They said that Tyler was inside and that the doctors seemed to be really competent and that they were waiting for one to come out and report.

Scott spun on his heels and walked right through the swinging doors into the emergency area. There were four or five separate rooms, but he could tell instantly which was the right one by a kind of invisible commotion inside and he went straight for it, and if anyone got in his way he was going to push that person aside. He stopped for just a moment at the threshold and saw a wall of people in white, their backs to him, bending over a table. And then one of them moved slightly and he caught a glimpse of the body covered in a sheet— *his son, for Christ's sake*—and then he saw the head, which was turned away, some blood. He walked over, and they parted and let him stand there. He took his son's hand.

He stood for some time just looking, examining him, taking in everything intently, every speck of blood.

What is that sticking out of his head?

He tried talking to him, softly first, calling out his name, then more loudly. There was no response.

A doctor came over and introduced himself—Scott didn't hear the name—and the doctor began to put his arm around his shoulder, but then thought better of it.

"Can we step outside for a minute?"

Scott was about to say no, he didn't want to leave his son, but then he thought that maybe on some level Tyler

could hear them talking and so perhaps it made sense
after all. They went two steps beyond the door.

"I wish I could tell you more, but everything is still
preliminary. We don't know how extensive the damage
is. He has some broken bones, his left shoulder and his
right arm. It was some fall. I think he twisted in midair
and tried to right himself."

The doctor attempted a half-smile. He was young.
Scott looked at his upper lip, where there was a bead of
sweat, and tried to concentrate on what he was saying.
He knew that the man was avoiding the main issue.

"His vital signs are good, surprisingly good. His heart
is strong. His pulse is okay. He lost a lot of blood and
we've given him extensive transfusions and he's accepted it all just fine. That's all to the good."

He paused, choosing his words.

"What we don't know—what we can't tell—is how severe the head wound is. We're freezing it to hold down
the swelling. We've taken X rays. They show some damage to the cortex and perhaps deeper. They're a bit difficult to read. We can't . . . It's hard to tell the extent of
the trauma with the implement still embedded."

"What is it?"

Scott's words sounded hollow.

"It's called a Camalot number two. Rock climbers use
them to hold their ropes. They insert one into a crevice
and it expands. It fell and struck your son—apparently
from fairly high up." The doctor furrowed his brow.
"Didn't anyone tell you what happened?"

Scott shook his head. "Not in detail."

"That other family . . . outside in the waiting room.
Friends of yours, I'm told. They can tell you everything.
Their little boy was there. He saw it."

Scott didn't want to leave Tyler.

"But in any case, I've seen enough to know that we're
not really equipped here to deal with it. He requires a
level of expertise that . . . we don't really have. He needs
the best—the best neurosurgeon, the best equipment,
the best care. I'm sure you agree."

Scott did. No question about it.

"So I'm arranging for an immediate transfer. To St. Catherine's in New York. It's the hospital with the foremost neurological center in the country, maybe the world. Dr. Leopoldo Saramaggio. There's no one better anywhere. If I had to have someone operate on my son, he'd be the one."

"But how—?"

"How do you go? Emergency evacuation. Helicopter. It's already on the way."

Scott didn't even ask if he could go on the aircraft. Nothing could have kept him off.

He met briefly with Johnny's parents, who told him everything they knew about the accident. Johnny himself remained quiet, and so at the end, Scott put his arm around the boy.

"Scott," began Johnny's father. "I don't know how to say this. . . . I feel so bad. I'm so sorry that—"

Scott waved him off. He didn't want to hear it, not now. There was too much to do.

He made arrangements for them to drive his car back. They offered to wait with him, but he said no, that wasn't necessary. They left, stricken, without looking back.

Scott went back into the emergency room. After a while, he heard the chopper approaching, the odd pounding sound of the blades. Outside, the bushes waved wildly in the dust.

He was surprised not to see it—it landed on the roof.

Tyler was transferred to a stretcher that was wheeled into an elevator and carried to the helicopter because the roof was lined with pebbles stuck into the tar. The aircraft had landed on a square of tarmac, right inside a painted white circle. The stretcher was loaded from the rear, and Scott went with it.

He managed to do the whole trip, from the emergency room to the inside of the shaking noisy behemoth, without once letting go of Tyler's hand. His son's head was wrapped in plastic tubing filled with ice. Still, Scott could see the handle of that hated metal thing.

He had to force himself to look at it.

Chapter 6

Saramaggio was stuck in a traffic jam downtown when he got the call on his cell phone. His car was inching down lower Broadway in SoHo, and he was heading for his favorite gallery on Prince Street for an exhibition of German Expressionists. He had been hoping to add another Schiele to his collection; he already had two hanging on the walls of his beamed living room in Greenwich. He hated paying the extra insurance premiums, but Schiele's paintings, which had doubled in value ever since the controversy over ownership of Nazi-seized art in the late nineties, were well worth it.

His phone had an unmistakable Nietzschean ring, the opening bar of *Also sprach Zarathustra*. He had chosen it as a joke at first—after a colleague in the OR had called him an *Übermensch*—but he had gotten accustomed to it and even thought of it as something of a personal theme song.

He reached into his coat pocket.

"Yes, I'm here."

His driver, provided by St. Catherine's as one of numerous perks to ensure that he would never dream of going to another hospital, heard him groan.

"What hospital is he coming from? And what is it exactly that's stuck?"

A pause.

"How the hell did *that* get there?"

Another pause.

"Uh-huh. And how old is the boy?"

A third pause.

In the rearview mirror, the driver saw him look at his Rolex.

"You say they just left? They should be there in half an hour—maximum." He sighed. "Get everyone lined up. I'd like Gully. And that new surgeon, Ms. Willet. I want room seven. And of course Betsy."

Betsy was his scrub nurse, who knew the procedure so well—which instrument he wanted and when he wanted it, almost like a top golfer's caddy at the U.S. Open—that he rarely had to speak to her. He would work with no one else for the moment, at least until he found her wanting in some way and took on someone new. That was—literally—his standard operating procedure.

He punched the *off* button.

"Turn around, Harry. We have to go back to St. Cat's."

He sighed again and looked out the window. He disliked emergency surgery, especially when it was done on the fly, when the patient arrived just as he got there himself and he didn't have time to prepare. When an operation was scheduled, he usually began thinking about it hours before, sometimes even the day before, running through all the possibilities, playing it out like a film. That way, when he stepped up to the table, he found that he was working almost on a subconscious level; sometimes his mind wandered and his fingers seemed to move on their own. That was when he was at his best. And of course he couldn't do that when he didn't have any idea of what he would find. That was pure improvisation, and improvisation involved a certain amount of chance. He didn't like chance.

Oh well, at least it sounded like an interesting case. And there was always the distant possibility—he didn't want to anticipate it because that would be too providential—that the wound would fit the profile he was looking for, would finally allow him to cap the myriad of experiments in the OR. That, of course, would be the final coup de théâtre. All that time in rehearsal—could it really be the moment to step out on the stage?

And the boy was young. That was good. His brain was still growing. It was malleable.

He punched out a number on the phone and reached the gallery manager and commanded him to hold the Schiele for him.

"Of course, I'll take it," he said. "And if I don't like it, I'll return it and you can sell it to someone else."

⌐⎯⎯⌐

On the trip down, Scott didn't stop talking to Tyler once, even with the thumping roar of the helicopter's motor threatening to drown him out. Sitting on a thin cushion on a fold-down metal bench and leaning over the stretcher and holding his son's hand, he filled Tyler's ear with a steady stream of encouragement.

"Everything's going to be all right. Don't worry. You'll see. We're getting you to the best doctor there is. You'll be fine."

He repeated it over and over like a mantra, as much for himself as for his son. But after a while, the words seemed to lose meaning, and then he just started saying whatever came into his head. He began recounting Tyler's favorite stories, like the one about how he had met his mother (at a lecture hall in college—she arrived late and breathless). And how ecstatic his mother had been in the maternity room when she pushed and pushed with all her might and finally he emerged all slippery and bloody and she learned that her newborn was a boy.

"She leaned up exhausted and sweating and still panting and told the doctor to bring you over to her. And then she counted all your fingers and all your toes, twice, and looked between your skinny legs—at your penis and your testicles—and finally when she was satisfied that everything was as it should be, then and only then did she lay back with a huge smile and hold you on her chest. I don't think I've ever seen her happier."

At one point he found himself singing lullabies:

"Hush, little baby, don't say a word. Daddy's gonna buy you a mockingbird . . ." And reciting nursery rhymes.

> *Jack Sprat could eat no fat*
> *His wife could eat no lean. . . .*

> *Little Jack Horner sat in a corner*
> *Eating his Christmas pie. . . .*

Scott suddenly remembered the Jingo stories; it was their own private world, the "house of a thousand rooms." A thousand rooms, a thousand adventures. It was their way of communicating, Scott's way of telling his son about the world and how to live in it and dominate it and how even though unspeakable things could happen (like the death of a mother), it was not really a bad place after all.

Except that it is a bad place. You are never safe. His boy lay before him, smashed, his beautiful brain, his mind, scrambled like an egg.

Memories and half thoughts flooded into Scott's mind, and he opened the sluice gates and let them out and said everything he was thinking—except, of course, for the one thought that wouldn't go away, the thought that he kept trying to push back into whatever cave it came from. It was like trying to slam a door on a monster that could change shape and size and shrink down to slip in over the transom or turn into smoke to squeeze through the keyhole. The monster was the fear that Tyler was going to die. And behind that monster was another one: the fear that he would survive, but that he would be brain-damaged—a *vegetable,* as that horrible word summed it up.

Scott kept looking for signs of life—fingers moving, the chest rising, a sound from deep within his throat. He could not bring himself to look closely at the white bandage that protruded out of Tyler's head like some grotesque appendage. It was packed with ice that was melting and dripping onto the metal. He wanted to reach over with both hands and grip the bandage and the piece of metal underneath it and rip them out.

He looked up at the interior of the helicopter—the backs of the seats of the pilots, the attendant sitting by so quietly he was scarcely there, the ribbing and rivets that held the green metal skin, the plasma and glucose bags dangling madly from their metal perches leading into plastic tubes that fed into his son's arms. The invisible blades above, making a thudding sound. Everything so unreal. So terribly, terribly unreal. How to believe that all this was actually happening?

He realized with near panic that he had stopped talking. So he leaned over the stretcher and started up again.

> There was a little boy named Jingo,
> A boy very much like you.
> One day he was feeling bored . . .

Kate went to the top floor to watch through the plate glass window as the helicopter landed. She liked to know as much as possible about her patients, especially in cases like this when there was so little to go on. Saramaggio hadn't returned yet, and short of prepping the patient, they couldn't do much until he was suited up and ready to go. At least she could make sure that everything was prepared.

The report had mentioned a passenger on the helicopter, a distraught father. As soon as the stretcher was carried out, with a young man about her own age hovering beside it, she saw that the report was not exaggerated. She felt moved by the sight of the man, his face tight and numb, stumbling a step or two to keep up with the stretcher and refusing to let go of the boy's hand, clutching it as if he wanted to pour his own life into him.

The thought struck her instantly: We've got to be able to do something. *There are two lives at stake here.*

She met them on the floor of the OR. The boy was wheeled into a preop room and worked on by three nurses. Kate supervised. They gave him morphine, took his pants off and cut his T-shirt away, and washed his upper torso in strong disinfecting cleanser. Finally, they fixed him tightly to the gurney with a strap across his chin and another across the lower forehead, and removed the bandage and the ice packs and began disinfecting the wound and cutting his hair away and then shaving his head carefully with a sterilized razor.

Kate went to check on the father. He was in a small office near the waiting room, sitting across a desk from a nurse's aide, a woman with short-cropped hair who was taking down information on a clipboard. She was running down a list of diseases and ailments and allergies, and he was shaking his head in response to each one. He stopped the litany only once: to report measles, at age five. The aide wrote this down, laboriously. Kate could tell that this was exasperating the father. He was looking at the wall and responding in a monotone. He seemed younger up close and looked incomparably, inconsolably anguished. She could see tear streaks on his cheeks, and she felt that same rush of empathy she had felt when she saw him leave the helicopter.

She looked over at the form and read his name: Scott Jessup.

"You say you're the father?" asked the aide.

He nodded.

"And the mother—where is she?"

"Dead."

The aide stopped writing and looked up.

"Cause?"

"Pardon?"

"Cause of death?"

"Accident."

She looked at him questioningly.

"Plane crash."

"Was she in good health?"

The father nodded.

"Did she have any of the following diseases? Arthritis, rheumatism—"

"Look," he snapped. "How does any of that matter? I mean—for Christ's sake."

"I'm sorry, but we're supposed to ask."

Kate cut in.

"Susan," she said gently but firmly. "Why not let me finish up?"

The aide got up and left.

"I'm sorry," she said. "She's just—"

"—doing her job."

"Well, sort of. We can skip all that. The only thing that's important for us to know is whether he's allergic to anything, whether he's had general anesthesia before, and what kind of medication he takes, if any."

"No, no, and none."

"*Good.* And is he right-handed or left-?"

"Right," Scott replied, looking puzzled.

"That's so we know if the injury occurred on the dominant side."

She made the notations on the form, and looked on the desk and saw a Xeroxed copy of his health plan card: Blue Cross Blue Shield.

"Don't even think about this," she said.

He nodded.

"Good. Now, you should know that you have one of the best neurosurgeons in the country—maybe *the* best. Leopoldo Saramaggio. He will be here any minute, and he will start right away. At first, I expect it will be exploratory. It will probably take at least two hours and maybe more. You can wait right here and one of us will come out as soon as we have anything to say. And we can take it from there."

"Will you be in the operating room?" He paid attention to her for the first time.

"Yes. I'll be assisting. Do you have any questions?"

He shook his head no.

"Now there is one important thing left to do." She reached into a drawer and pulled out three pages of printed material and handed it to him, along with a pen. "This is a consent form. Please read it carefully, and if you agree, then initial the first two pages and sign and date the last page."

He signed it without even looking at it and tossed down the pen and left.

⌒

Tyler was given a CT scan. The operation began as soon as Saramaggio arrived. Scott caught only a glimpse of him, a lanky figure in a surgical gown moving quickly down the hallway. Then he watched through a small rectangular window in the door as Tyler's gurney was wheeled out of the prep room to the OR. He saw him clearly. His head was gleaming in the light—it was totally shaven, which rendered his facial features smaller and made him look vulnerable, as if he were being carted away to be sacrificed. The hated piece of metal was visible, sticking up into the air. Now that some of the blood was gone, Scott could see the wound that it had made, an indentation at the base that was frighteningly large. It looked as if it had been sucked into the skull. The metal base had some sort of wires and gears red with blood.

The operation lasted three hours.

Scott didn't know how to interpret the time. Was it better if it took longer? Did that mean they were somehow patching him up? Or was it a bad sign—did it mean that the damage was so severe that every step of the way was dangerous?

While he waited, he paced around the dreary waiting room with its mix of nonmatching hard-backed chairs and aging couches and a wall with prints of English landscapes. From time to time, he walked over to the window and looked vacantly out at the cars moving along York Avenue and watched a traffic light change. Twice he sat down and picked up a dog-eared magazine; he read the first three paragraphs of an article over and over and then threw it back on the wooden coffee table.

At last, the woman—what was her name?—came out.

He rushed over, and she led him into the side office again, away from the other people.

"Dr. Saramaggio is on his way out to talk with you. Please sit down."

She knew that he needed to know something right away.

"Basically, as I said, it was exploratory. We got a good look. Your son—Tyler—is holding up well."

"Will he live?"

She looked at him directly. His eyes were blazing.

"Yes. For now. He does not seem to be under immediate threat. But that is what Dr. Saramaggio wants to speak to you about."

They did not have long to wait. Saramaggio came in, and his long frame seemed to fill up the room. His shoes and the cuffs of his green pants had brown streaks of blood on them. Kate saw Scott stare at them. Saramaggio extended his right arm and shook hands a bit too vigorously and then asked the two of them to accompany him to his office.

The walk, down a flight of stairs and along two corridors and through three pairs of swinging doors, seemed to take forever. Kate thought it unconscionable. Why couldn't he just have talked to him up there?

Saramaggio settled behind his desk with a little sigh that connoted exhaustion. The framed plaques and diplomas and certificates behind him filled the walls.

"Mr. Jessup," he began, propping both elbows on the desk and leaning across it. "I don't have to tell you that your son's case is ominous—extremely ominous. It is life-threatening, and the sooner that we all accept that and come to grips with it, the sooner we will be able to proceed."

Scott was sitting on the edge of his chair, immobile.

"In fact, I don't mind saying I haven't seen anything quite like it. The foreign object—what is it called . . . ?" He looked over at Kate.

"A Camalot number two."

"Camalot. We've left it in place—as I said, this was an exploratory operation. It must have fallen from a great height. It has penetrated the brain to a distance of 10.2 centimeters. That is substantial." He held up a thumb and forefinger in a C, to demonstrate.

"It has bisected the cortex and reached the lower portions of the brain."

He paused, looking grave.

"However—and this is the part that is so very unusual—the implement appears to have missed the vital life centers. It does not appear to have irreparably harmed the thalamus, the hypothalamus, the hippocampus, or the brain stem. As a result, the autonomic nervous system appears to be still working, and as you undoubtedly know, that is what keeps all of our necessary and involuntary functions going—the lungs, the heart, the circulating system, and so on."

"So he's not in immediate danger?"

"For the moment, apparently not, no. But only for the moment. The situation is very unstable. It could change at any moment and everything I've said so far could be nonapplicable. And so far I've told you only the good news."

"What's the bad?"

"The bad. Well, even though he is relatively stable in this odd way, he is completely unresponsive to external stimuli. His brain is registering activity, but it is doing so randomly. He is not responsive to sounds or sight or touch. It is almost as if he is in some state of shock or deep coma.

"And in the meantime he still has that damn piece of metal in there. Why it hasn't yet brought about some virulent infection, I don't know. It must be removed, but it's difficult to imagine doing that without causing extensive damage. The effect could be traumatic and instantaneous—it could shut down his system in a second. Or it could be something more subtle and long-term—it could change him in ways that are impossible to predict. Change his whole personality."

Kate was worried for a moment that Saramaggio was going to tell the tale of Phineas Gage—who eventually died in the OR when a neurosurgeon persuaded him to have an operation—but he continued on. His mind had darted ahead to something else.

"So what is to be done?" asked Scott.

Saramaggio leaned back in his swivel chair and linked his hands behind his head so that his bony arms stuck out on either side. They looked like the wings of a giant pelican.

"Well," he said. "If we're all agreed that the situation is desperate—and it is, I assure you—then perhaps desperate measures are called for."

"Like what?"

"There are certain experimental procedures. They are highly unusual. In fact, I am compelled to say that they have never been attempted—at least, not on humans. But as I say, we are presented with a highly unusual case.

"It will be your decision, and I warn you: It won't be an easy one to make."

Kate looked at Scott, lost and alone in his nightmare. Saramaggio was peering up at the ceiling, a kind of suppressed energy in his casual pose, almost as if he were afraid that if he looked at them, they would read his mind.

Chapter 7

In the cafeteria line, Scott pushed the brown tray slowly along the metal rails without realizing that he was holding up the line. He went to a cashier's station and put his money down, but it was closed; then he found the right one and paid for the coffee. He sat down at a table in a corner and stared at the Styrofoam cup, the river-brown liquid inside. He looked out the window at the gathering dusk.

He didn't know what to do. He was drained and blank—unable to react, unable to think. He couldn't make even the simplest of decisions: Should he stay at the hospital or leave? He hated it here, and yet he wanted to be nowhere else.

Some time and space away from here to think, that's what he needed. What to do about Saramaggio's proposition? But how could he go? Tyler was up in the intensive care recovery room on the sixth floor, and Scott had to be near him. He had to be near him even though he couldn't actually see him because he was not allowed inside. Saramaggio had told him Tyler would spend the night there, in an isolated room off to one side that was germ-free. At this stage, infection was the enemy, he had said. *Enemy*. Saramaggio had used a number of battlefield metaphors when he was presenting the case for the operation. Words like *attack* and *retreat* and *surrender*. He was not a likable man, but Scott didn't care about that. All he wanted was for him to be the best surgeon in the world. *I don't care if he's the biggest son of a bitch around. I don't care if he thinks he's a goddamned general as long as he's the best man for the job.*

Scott knew that Saramaggio was pushing for him to give his permission for the operation, despite his attempts to appear casual. He'd admitted that it had never been attempted before. He was probably itching to do it. Maybe he was lusting after fame—an operation like this one would surely bring him a lot of publicity. What was the word he'd used? *Procedures.* That was a laugh—how could something that had never been done before be relegated to a *procedure*?

He fought back a rising tide of anger and reviewed what the surgeon had told him. Because the piece of metal had extended so deep, into the subcortical portion of the brain, it had already caused extensive damage. Who knew how much exactly? Impossible to say. Under normal circumstances, damage of that sort would be irreversible—*and it might well still be irreversible.* Those were his words, and they hit Scott like a splay of machine-gun bullets. *But . . .* A slender ray of hope, a thin reed on the riverbank to grab at. . . . *But recently—* and here Saramaggio had measured his words carefully, like a jeweler placing weights on a scale—*recently there had been significant new discoveries in the field of neurobiology.* Discoveries so astounding that the full implications weren't yet understood. Among other things, they might make possible radical treatment of spinal and brain injuries.

The discovery, Saramaggio had said, was neural stem cells. The basic building-block cells—cells that had not yet differentiated into becoming skin cells or liver cells or stomach cells. He explained that these were not the stem cells from embryos that had been in newspaper headlines; these stem cells had been discovered deep inside the central nervous systems of animals and then of humans. In laboratory dishes, they had done wonderful things: They had been coaxed into developing into neurons, the basic brain cells, and glial cells, cells that are the "glue" of the brain. Because they came directly from the patient, they were a perfect match.

"What we're proposing here," Saramaggio had said, "is a twofold procedure. We extract stem cells from the brain, which will then be cultivated in the lab. When they are fully developed, we will reimplant them. We re-populate the damaged area with functioning cells."

"Has this ever been done before?" Scott had asked.

"As I said, only with animals—specifically mice. But we've had good results."

Mice! Scott had thought to himself. *Mice!* He sup-pressed a desire to strike out. "What happens to him in the meantime? How can you assure that he stays alive?"

Saramaggio had paused for the first time.

"That's the tricky part," he had replied. "We're count-ing on his own system to keep him going. But we have a backup if that fails. One of my associates—Dr. Cleaver—has been developing a computer that can as-sist the brain. It monitors activity in the hindbrain—specifically in the medulla, which regulates vital body functions including respiration, heart rate, and gastroin-testinal functioning. If there is a problem, it can actually send electrical impulses to the specific nuclei—which are clusters of neurons—to get things going again."

Scott couldn't believe what Saramaggio said next. The hubris of it.

"The medulla, incidentally, was where the bullet from the assassin of President Kennedy struck. That's why there was not a sliver of hope for him. But today—or maybe in a few years—we'd be able to save him. Pro-vided, of course, that he had the good fortune to be transported to St. Catherine's."

Good fortune. Scott had felt anger rising up like bile in the throat. But he knew he had to contain himself for the sake of his son; he was more interested in coming to the right decision about him. He had asked the question foremost in his mind: Was Tyler suffering? "Not one iota," Saramaggio replied. "Believe me—he has no idea what's happening. It's like he's sleeping on a rubber raft in the middle of a lake on a windless day." For once, the surgeon's hearty enthusiasm was comforting.

Saramaggio had said that the Institutional Review Board would convene the following morning to approve the operation and that it would take him a day or two to prepare. Scott had the night to think it over and come to a decision about giving permission.

The cafeteria was almost empty. He took a sip of coffee. He had never missed Lydia as much as he did at that moment.

A shadow crossed the table, engulfed his cup.

"Do you mind if I join you—or would you prefer to be alone? I understand if you do."

He looked up. It was that surgeon, the woman who had appeared empathetic. She was standing before him with a cup in her hand.

He gestured at the empty chair across from him. He acted out of some vestigial sense of politeness—to be honest, he *did* want to be alone.

She sat down, settled into her chair, and looked over at his cup.

"It's pretty dreadful, I'm afraid."

He nodded solemnly.

She blushed.

"I meant the coffee. So weak."

Distracted, he gave a little sign of comprehension by lifting his chin.

"Ah, Dr. . . ."

"Willet. Kate Willet."

"Dr. Willet. Let me ask you something."

"Go ahead."

"This review board, the one that's meeting tomorrow. How often do they do that—get together to decide if an operation can be done?"

"Rarely. Very rarely. I've only been here a few weeks, so it's hard to say. But at the previous hospital where I was—in San Francisco—it happened only five times in ten years. Once for a heart transplant that was special—it involved a new kind of temporary valve—and another time for a new method of repairing aneurysms. The board has to give its approval. It happens whenever there is something that is new in any of three areas—procedure or equipment or technique."

"And in this case?"

She looked at him directly.

"In this case, it's all three that are new."

He nodded and looked down at his coffee. They were silent for a while. Finally, she spoke.

"I think you should know—I hope that Dr. Saramaggio made it clear—that this operation is revolutionary. It's never been attempted before—nothing like it has. So we are literally stepping into unknown territory. I know you are trying to compute the odds, but it's impossible in a situation like this."

"It's not a poker game. It's the life of my son."

"I know." And she added softly, "I can see how much you love him."

He turned away, his eyes welling up with tears.

"If you only knew. . . ." he said, and he stared out the window.

They fell silent again.

"If only there were some way to get him back," he said. His words sounded stupid to him, but he didn't care—it was what he felt.

She nodded.

"I know how you must feel."

"Do you?" he replied.

"Well, not exactly. I think it's different for everyone."

He looked directly at her. Then out the window, then back at her.

"So what happened in your case?"

"It was my mother. She raised me—alone. My father was killed in Vietnam when I was a baby, and she never remarried. The love of her life and all that. She was a teacher in a small town in Washington, and some years back she had an accident. She fell off a ladder—she was cleaning out the gutters of our house, if you can believe it—and she struck her head. She never really fully recovered. It was hard, of course. I remember what one doctor told me. . . ."

"What?"

"One day the doctor took me aside, and she said that I had to stop thinking of the way my mother was, that I had to stop measuring her against what she used to be.

That I shouldn't think: She can do sixty percent of what she used to do, she knows half the words she used to know. Instead, I should regard her as someone different in a basic way. She had closed a chapter and was now off on a new life. And what was important was the new person she was becoming and whether she could become one hundred percent of that new person.

"I don't know if I ever really believed it, but it seemed to help when I thought of it in those terms. And she recovered gradually, almost one hundred percent. But as I said, everyone is different."

"And—now? She's still alive?"

"No. She died last year. Cancer."

"I'm sorry."

"No—I'm sorry." She lowered her voice, ashamed. "I shouldn't be talking about myself."

"Don't be sorry. It helps."

That was being truthful. It did help—for just one moment.

He pushed the cup aside and stood up. So did she.

"You really can go home, you know. There's nothing you can do here. You might as well try to get some sleep. Tomorrow's going to be grueling, no matter what you decide."

"I hate to leave. I just wish I could see him."

She didn't hesitate a second.

"Come with me," she said, turning on her heels. She took him up in the elevator to the sixth floor, then unlocked a storeroom and turned on the light. He saw stacks of surgical gowns, neatly pressed, on a shelf.

"Put on one of those and a mask and a cap. I'll meet you down the hall."

She escorted him through the double doors into the operating area, down a hallway and through another pair of doors on the left. They entered the intensive care recovery room and passed by half a dozen patients, most of them lying motionless with their eyes closed, surrounded by an array of equipment that hummed and bleeped every few seconds. Three nurses bustled around the beds. One elderly woman, her gray hair frizzed around her head like a halo and a tube extending out of her mouth, watched them with an eagle eye.

Kate opened a door and motioned him into a dimly lit room.

"Just try not to breathe too near him." She walked away.

Tyler was lying on a bed that was partially raised, so that his back was reclining upon a pillow. Another pillow was under his legs. It took a moment for Scott's eyes to get accustomed to the dark, so that he didn't immediately notice that his son's upper torso was strapped tightly to the bed. Tyler's head was held in a brace so that he couldn't move at all. It was bandaged thoroughly so that it was gigantic, a large white balloon. The tip of the camming device, also under the bandage, was only a slight bump. A night-light over the bed shone down and cast a glow upon the sheer whiteness of the bandages.

Scott moved closer quietly, as if he feared waking him. He leaned over the bed and looked down at Tyler's face, which seemed compressed under the bandage. He was surprised at how the bandage threw everything off. It was shocking—his boy looked freakish, a swollen mummy. Then Scott concentrated on the individual features—the long lashes, tightly closed. Why did he have bruises around the eyes? The strong nose, the full lips that used to be so expressive—they always betrayed a joke ahead of time. That part was still there, so familiar—so . . . so inexpressibly beloved.

He held his son's hand and squeezed it hard and thought for a moment that he felt a slight pressure: *Was he squeezing back?* No. And then Scott realized something—that as he was standing there he was crying. He realized that it had been happening for some time but that he hadn't been aware of it, as if it had been happening to someone else. He could feel the tears streaming down his cheeks and his body quivering with sobs. He stood there a long, long time, holding his son's hand and crying.

When he left, he didn't see Kate. He dropped the gown in a laundry basket and pushed the down button on the elevator and walked through the lobby out into the street.

He was surprised, outside, to find that it was already pitch dark.

Scott walked home, all the way down the East Side and then across town to his loft on West Twenty-eighth Street. It was Sunday night. The streets were filling with cars returning from the weekend, and the restaurants were booming; but he didn't notice any of that, and he couldn't have even said what day of the week it was. He passed by the store in his building that sold used furniture—once a thriving fur shop, the name LIEBERMAN BROTHERS still visible in outline on the plate glass window—and turned into the long entryway. At the end was the large elevator, originally used for freight. He felt a stab of memory—years ago, he had instructed Tyler on its use, and he had a vision of the little boy standing there, stretching to his full height to try to reach the button for the fourth floor.

It felt odd to be home. Comet lunged at him, her paws scraping his thighs, the tail thrashing back and forth. Scott petted her, then sat down on the floor and hugged her. The dog was suddenly important to him in a way she hadn't been before. He stood up and found the dog's bowl and filled it. He looked around; everything was in place—the dishes from breakfast in the sink, the newspaper where he had tossed it on the floor next to the sofa, the crammed bookshelves lining a brick wall. In the back, he could see his lab; the door was open and a stack of prints lay upon the enlargement table, and behind it was a shelf of chemicals with the names neatly printed in his own hand. How many times had he warned Tyler not to touch them?

He felt a gnawing in his stomach, probably hunger, but he didn't want to eat anything. Instead he went to the wooden cabinet under his CD and record player and pulled out a bottle of J&B and poured himself half a glass of scotch. He took a long swig. He remembered something: A sometime girlfriend had kept a pack of cigarettes in the bedside table. He went rummaging and found them, a crumpled pack of True Blue. He went back to the living room and lit up, pulling the smoke deep into his lungs the way he used to. He coughed and felt dizzy and had to sit down. It had been more than five years since he had smoked.

He took another sip of scotch. He looked around. How strange that everything seemed undisturbed, all the artifacts and remnants of a normal life—the chairs, the books, the lamps—as if it were not true that the entire universe had just sucked itself into a black hole and blown itself to smithereens.

In one corner, a light was glowing, the readout light of the video machine. He looked at it, disregarded it, and took another sip of scotch and another drag on the cigarette. Now he could keep the smoke down, and he felt it actually cut into his lungs. His blood was racing through his veins, tickling.

He was alone, totally alone, the last man in a dying ember of a world.

Then he did what he had known he would do. He stood up and went to the door of Tyler's room and opened it and stepped inside. It was dim, but he didn't want it to be brightly lit; he didn't want to see the objects but just to stand in their presence, to feel them. He smelled the smell of his son. He saw the *Trainspotting* poster, a pile of homework and reports and letters and a copy of *Huck Finn* lying on the floor beside the unmade bed—how Tyler had loved that book, filling his father with such pride. There was a pile of dirty clothes. He picked up a shirt and put it to his face and inhaled deeply.

He left, closing the door behind him. Then he took Comet for a walk around the block. The dog pulled at the leash, eager for a romp.

He came back to his room, undressed, and sat on the edge of his bed. Think of Tyler as someone else, she had said. Think of him having to become one hundred percent of a new person. He tried. He couldn't. It was impossible. Tyler was Tyler. He wanted him back—all of him.

He fell asleep quickly, but woke up after only an hour. The red numbers on the clock gleamed at him from two feet away. He got up, finished the scotch, and walked around the vast room. As he walked, he began touching things—the edge of the bookcase, the top of the easy chair, the doorknob of the kitchen. He retraced the circle over and over, touching the same objects in the same places. He did this for a long time.

Then he went back to his bedroom and tried to sleep again, but couldn't. The sheet twisted and turned around his legs; the blanket felt too heavy. The red numbers gleamed some more. He felt a weight, as if the ceiling were pressing down upon him.

Finally, when the numbers read 5:00, he nodded off to sleep again. He had nightmares, one after another—murderers chasing him, rabid dogs jumping out from behind trees, his own mother trying to kill him, a manor house of ghosts living in thousands of empty rooms. He awoke sweating.

Right away, as soon as he opened his eyes, he felt the weight again and the presence that had taken over his mind—the knowledge of the accident. It rushed in at him like water rushing into a sinking vessel.

But somewhere in the long night, at least, he had come to a decision. He would let Saramaggio perform the operation. In the dawn light, he saw it clearly. There was no other choice.

II

The Operation

Chapter 8

The next morning, Cleaver drove across the George Washington Bridge into the hazy suburbs of New Jersey. The traffic was heavy, so to pass the time he occupied himself with one of his favorite sexual fantasies. He was undressing a woman in a white room with stainless steel tables—except that she was not exactly a woman. She was a cyborg. And she was beautiful. Her flesh, or what passed for it, gleamed and had a slight plasticky feeling, though it contained a fine mesh of wiring that made it pleasantly warm to the touch. She had sense receptors implanted so that she could respond with heavy breathing when he removed her blouse and placed his hands on her perfect upright hard breasts. The breathing turned into soft moans when he reached under her skirt.

Cleaver was excited. He looked up—the car was drifting into the bumper of the car ahead of him, and he hit the brake. *Damn.* He had better concentrate on the driving. He wiped the cyborg out of his mind, sorry to see her go. No matter how many times he allowed himself to slip into this fantasy, it never ceased to arouse him. At first he had been a little embarrassed, even to himself. But he had never had luck with women, so he'd decided to build himself one in his mind. Over the years, he had honed it down, polishing the details—the jut of her chin, the glint of the metal table, how her sharply cut hair, purplish black, brushed against her shoulder. What made it so titillating, he admitted, was that she *was* a machine and that she had been designed to service him, submissively and without choice.

After inching his way over the final stretch of the bridge, he turned onto the Palisades Parkway, then took the first exit, turned right at the light, and eased the car along the depressing boulevards of Englewood Cliffs. The afternoon was warm, and from time to time the sun cut through the smog to dapple the roadside. He knew the way, and soon he found himself in a development of look-alike houses and gracefully curving driveways. The layout buoyed him: slight dips and rises in the road, bosky groves, clumps of pines hugging the shoulder—all created to fit some developer's vision of rustic living. He liked the artificiality of it.

He stopped in front of the one house that stood out because of signs of neglect. There was nothing major— the ranch house was of indestructible brick—but instead an accumulation of small insults: rank leaves overflowing the gutters, water stains on the white plastic shutters, an unmowed lawn sprinkled with ghostly crowns of dandelions. How all this must rankle the neighbors, mused Cleaver, as he walked up a pathway of cracked flagstones. He had to knock a long time before the door opened. A young man in a tie-dyed T-shirt and dirty chinos looked him over uncertainly and then retreated without a word.

Cleaver entered the living room. The wall-to-wall carpeting was cluttered with empty furniture and papers and books. A TV set was on—a film clip of a car careering around a street, its tires screaming—and from a corner came the sound of a CD playing techno. He could feel the repetitive throbbing in his feet and mounting his legs. It bothered him. He crossed the room and stepped into a long hallway. To the right was a bedroom filled with young people. A cloud of smoke hung over them. He looked in: six or seven men and women sitting on two beds and chairs. Only one looked up, his face blank. Cleaver didn't recognize any of them. He walked down the hallway until he came to a door and pushed it open. Inside was the master bedroom. The curtains were drawn, but the room wasn't dark. A halogen lamp sent a harsh light onto one wall and part of the ceiling, and three computer screens were lit, casting a glow outward. He could see two bare mattresses lying on the floor, gray with blue stripes and large brown stains. The room's corners were lost in shadows.

He found Quincy seated before one of the computers, his face reflecting the ghostly iridescence. Quincy looked up, mumbled something, and went back to the screen. It was hard to read his expression in the half-light, but he seemed irritated by the interruption.

"I told you I was coming."

"Yeah, right."

Cleaver waited a moment. Quincy continued typing.

"I didn't come all the way out here to watch you hack," he said.

Quincy looked at him again, hit a few keys, and shut down the program.

"Shit."

Cleaver wondered whether he was destroying a virus or creating one.

"What's the matter?"

Quincy waved him off.

"I got a lot to do," he said, almost pugnaciously. "This is work, too. You're not the only one."

The young man had a hatchet-blade sharpness to his face and a sunken chest that made him look frail. Long strands of hair fell down from a widow's peak and bounced along his cheekbones when he turned his head, which he did frequently, in quick sharp movements like a bird. He had a lingering case of acne that reddened his cheeks and made him look dyspeptic.

"But I want to see how it's coming along."

"And I told you I'd prefer to wait. It's not finished."

"It'd better be finished soon. Anyway, I want to see it."

Quincy sighed, stood up, and attached a ring of keys on a long chain to his belt. He left the terminals running, walked out the door without a word, and reached back to turn out the lights, leaving Cleaver to stumble after him in the dimly lit room.

He went into the room down the hall, and Cleaver

followed him. Now he could see: There were four boys and two girls, spread out on facing beds and pillows. Two of them lay flat on their backs, with their heads propped against the wall. The others were sipping beer from cans and passing around a joint. Cleaver noticed the pungent smell of marijuana. They barely looked at him, too engrossed in conversation to care. Or too high.

"Moravec is the thinker of the age," said one who looked like a skinhead. "He'll be recognized years from now when people look back. Darwin and Einstein all rolled into one."

The boy who had looked up before was seated to his right, working a computer that was sitting on a bridge table. He had his shirt off, and his back was covered with a body-ripper tattoo; it showed the flesh opening outward, exposing wires and rods, cyborg-style. It was oddly realistic-looking, thought Cleaver, as if the skin had been peeled back to show the innards of a machine. Over his shoulder, Cleaver looked at the screen. Someone out there had just finished writing a sentence:

```
My hair spreading out like rays of
the sun as you kneel next to me be-
side the waterfall.
```

The boy typed back.

```
>yes, yes. And then . . .
```

```
and softly you caress my cheek and
then gently, you place your hand
upon my sex.
```

Cleaver recognized the stilted style, the almost Victorian prudery of text sex. The boy shifted in his seat and began pounding the keyboard. Cleaver could not see his reply. The boy hit a button, spun around in the chair, and lifted a beer by hooking his hand upside down around the can. He took a long swallow and smiled, oddly enough, at Cleaver.

The skinhead was still talking with a laborious intensity.

"Now, Moravec, he talks about the postbiological universe. The new cyber life-form will outstrip us. They'll become more and more complex and procreate and leave us behind in the dust. We'll have no choice."

"So we're slaves?"

"Unless we join them."

"And how do we do that?"

"We'll have to download our minds into computers and link up and leave our bodies behind."

"I thought that was Kurzweil," said a girl sitting with her legs crossed. "He says computers are going to be smarter than us in the next twenty years. So it's just a matter of time. If we're going to survive, we have to connect up with them somehow. It's the next big step in evolution."

"No shit," said a young man as thin as a rail. "I can see fucking a machine, but how do you get little baby machines?"

"That's Moravec," said the first boy. "He explains it. You download your human consciousness into a computer. A robot surgeon removes your skull. They use a high-resolution magnetic resonance to make a simulacrum of your brain. They do it bit by bit and layer by layer, throwing away the brain stuff once they're finished with it. Until finally the braincase is empty. Then they just disconnect life support and your body's thrown out."

"Just like Hannibal Lecter," said the thin young man. They giggled.

"Fred, you asshole," said the girl.

Quincy leaned over to the second girl.

"I've got to go into the city," he said. "You can take the car to J and R. But don't wreck it again, for fuck's sake."

She grunted.

On the way out the front door, Quincy unbuttoned

his blue work shirt in the sunlight, looked up and down the deserted street, and turned back to Cleaver. He carried a motorcycle helmet in his right hand.

"Funny shit, huh? All that talk. If they only knew."

It was faster crossing the bridge from the Jersey side. Quincy led the way on his motorcycle, his shirt flapping in the wind, tufts of hair waving demonically below the helmet. Cleaver drove behind in his car, irritated. To begin with, he disliked following anyone. And this . . . following a motorcycle, it made him feel stupid. Quincy could slip in and out of the interstices between cars and shoot way ahead, which he did from time to time. Then he slowed down and looked back with annoyance until Cleaver caught up. The only reason Cleaver had gone to New Jersey in the first place was to be sure that Quincy would show up. Unreliable geek. They were all unreliable, the whole collection of them in that commune, stoned-out computer heads and spaced-out hackers, sitting around getting high on their millennial mysticism and technophile riffs. He despised dealing with them. The only problem was that they were so damned smart. There was no firewall they couldn't breach, no program they couldn't devise. And Quincy was the smartest of them all.

They took the Henry Hudson to the West Side Highway and turned left onto Canal Street, crossing town past all the open-air markets. Quincy thundered past Chinatown, pulled over on the Bowery and shut off the engine. Cleaver parked the car behind him. Clicking the lock shut with the remote, he heard the answering bleeps. The curbside was littered with glass. He always felt nervous leaving his Lexus on the street, especially downtown.

They walked half a block, past two empty storefronts, until they came to a six-floor brownstone. Inside, in a vestibule, was a panel of black buttons. One of them read BRAINTRUST.

Quincy pulled out a key to open the inner door, which was made of thick, reinforced steel. "Come on up.

You might as well see what you're getting for your money."

He held the door open, only a few inches, so that Cleaver had to push it. It was surprisingly heavy.

They walked up three flights, Quincy striding upward quickly and not even using the banister. Cleaver began to feel one of the waves of intense dislike that periodically overtook him whenever he was with Quincy.

"Not so fast," he said.

But Quincy rounded the landing ahead of him and started up the next flight without so much as a pause.

On the fourth floor, by the time he got there, breathing heavily, he found a door ajar and walked inside. Quincy had already thrown open the windows. A racket was coming from one side: a door pounding on its hinges and behind it, a frenzied scratching. Cleaver listened in alarm. A large animal. Quincy had locked him in the adjacent room.

"A mastiff," Quincy said. "Low-cost insurance."

"But who looks after him?"

Quincy shrugged. "Me," he said. "When I'm here. It's good if people know you have one."

He told Cleaver to avoid any sudden movements and opened the door. A huge gaunt gray dog bounded out, running over to Quincy and then sniffing Cleaver's pant leg. He circled the room four or five times and bucked under Quincy's outstretched hand, slobbered a bit, and eventually settled into a heap near the door.

Cleaver shook his head.

Quincy was irritated.

"Look, it's not the Waldorf, all right. It's cheap—you shouldn't complain."

"I'm not. It's just—that dog smells to high heaven."

" *'High heaven!'* Where'd you pick that up?"

Cleaver held himself in check and remained silent. It wouldn't do to get into an argument at this stage.

Quincy walked to the rear of the room.

"Well, what the fuck—do you want to see it or not?"

"Of course. That's why I'm here."

With a slightly theatrical mincing gesture, Quincy unlocked the door and flung it open. Cleaver could see that it had metal backing.

"Ta-*dah*," sang out Quincy. He was being ironic.

Cleaver held his breath and walked in. The instant he crossed the threshold, he got excited at what he saw. All this time . . . Quincy really was building it. He felt a pang of guilt: *And to think that I doubted him.*

The laboratory was large and airy, two floors joined together so that the brick walls were twenty feet high and sunlight streamed in through two rows of windows. Below, there were four long worktables crammed with wires and zip drives and boosters and bowls filled with computer chips. Along one wall were two huge cylindrical vaults that looked like truncated MRI machines, complete with sliding plastic stretchers. Inside them were large helmets with visors, arrayed in cocoons of wires.

Quincy patted one of the machines.

"The first fully operational transcranial stimulator-receiver. It's fucking brilliant."

Despite himself, Cleaver was impressed. He had given Quincy piles of money—it had been easy enough to divert grant funds from Pinegrove—and he had provided him with assistants and time, lots of time. But somehow he had never backed him with the requisite confidence.

"Does it work?" He scarcely dared to ask the question.

Quincy didn't answer right away. Instead, he busied himself throwing switches and checking connections. He acted as if Cleaver weren't there.

Cleaver repeated the question. Quincy scowled.

"Well, we won't know that until we try it, will we? One thing's for sure—it's a lot better than those fucking space goggles you use over at Pinegrove. You still running experiments with those patients? Isn't that against the law or something?"

Cleaver ignored him. "When's it going to be finished?"

Quincy shrugged.

He's playing the role of the temperamental inventor, Cleaver thought. *Try flattery.*

"I have to say—I never thought . . ."

"Yes?"

"Well, that you would come so far. I mean, it certainly looks impressive."

"*Looks* impressive. It *is* impressive."

Quincy walked over to the tube, patted it, and peered inside.

"Look at this," he said. He reached in and unsnapped a helmet, then brought it out and set it on a table. It touched down with a thud. The device had what looked like a face guard in the front, holding in place two concave disks that looked like eggcups.

"Inside here," said Quincy, fingering the side of the helmet, "are five hundred thousand recording electrodes, extremely sensitive. They're arranged in a flat, hexagonal array. They're like the ones you used before in your transcranial magnetic receiver but much finer. Their ability to record electrical synaptic transmissions is five times greater. The signals they pick up are deeper, too, all the way to the brain stem. It paints ninety percent of the brain."

"Ninety percent," repeated Cleaver. "So what's it miss—the rear of the cerebellum?"

"That's right."

"And that's for fine motor coordination. So we don't need it."

"Exactly."

"What's the operating principle?"

"It works like your TMR—only better. I've coated it with a silastic that reduces interference from the skull. The moving electrons in the brain create a magnetic field that's picked up by the electrodes. The brain activity is registered and scanned into a neuro-model on the screen there." He dipped his head toward a computer console nearby. Then he touched the eggcups.

"Now here's the breakthrough. The scanner allows us to read the brain and see what it's doing. But how can we send messages back to it? That's what these little babies are for. Each one fits inside your eyelids and covers the eyeball completely. You can't blink, so we inject saline solution continually through these side vents." He pointed to tiny tubing.

"Why the eyes?"

Quincy threw him a supercilious look. "The visual system is the most efficient pathway into the brain. The optic nerve is our point of entry, and we can ride it like a superhighway—right smack inside." He now seemed expansive, now that he was warming to his subject. He continued.

"What happens when you see something? The retina transforms light into neural signals. The signals are sent to the interneurons, which relay them through the optic nerve to the lateral geniculate nucleus and then to layer four of the primary visual cortex."

"In the occipital lobe."

"Right. So basically all we have to do is to encode signals from the computer to mimic the retinal signals. That fools the optic nerve that carries it into the occipital lobe. We're home free."

"So you can not only listen to the brain—you can talk to it."

"Right," said Quincy. "Decoding and encoding, both. A perfect loop."

"And you think you can actually feed in information? Concepts?"

"Information, yes. We convert it to megabits through the computer and download it. Abstract thoughts, concepts, are more difficult. They involve more than one brain center. We won't know about that until we try it."

"Will the information stay in?"

"No reason for it not to. We're counting on the brain's ability to sort it out and send it to the proper area. We might be able to tap into the vast portion of the cortex that just sits there unused. We could, in theory at least, hook you up and give you a second language. Or implant you with the theory of relativity. Or an encyclopedic knowledge of Renaissance painting."

Cleaver found it hard to suppress his admiration, and

he hesitated before asking the question that was burning inside.

"So, do you think—is it possible that it could work the other way?"

"Meaning . . . ?"

"That the brain itself could travel out?"

Quincy laughed.

"It's possible, but far-out. Who knows? I talked about a highway—a highway runs in both directions. It might be feasible, if the neural transmission runs in the other direction, for the brain to hook itself up to a computer and to rummage around inside it and access all the information there."

Cleaver felt his heart rate quicken, and he willed it to slow down. This was what he was waiting for.

"So you'd create external intelligence, an addition to the brain outside the brain."

"An exo-brain. A form of artificially enhanced intelligence. Imagine if you could hook up Deep Blue to Kasparov. You'd have the sweep of human intelligence combined with the computation speed of the computer."

He snapped the helmet in place and slid the stretcher back inside the tube.

"The only thing is . . . it would have to be a short match."

"And why is that?"

"This draws so much power, the micro-encrypting, that the system can't handle it for long without crashing. We figure it will last seven minutes."

"And what happens to Kasparov?"

"If he's still out there, I'd say he's fucked. That part doesn't come back. And Deep Blue—he starts ordering caviar."

"Very funny."

Cleaver tried to make his words sound sarcastic, but it was hard. He had suddenly gained too much respect for this unkempt young man whose face was blotched with angry red pimples.

"Now let me ask *you* something," said Quincy. "Are

you still obsessed with that whole thing—what do you call it?—the anima?"

Now it was Cleaver's turn to smile.

"Yes and no," he said.

Chapter 9

Scott paced around the waiting room for five hours. He already felt he knew the place inside out, as if he had been coming here for years. The same old coffee table of mud-brown varnish spread with torn magazines, the same dust-covered venetian blinds, and the same faux-English prints on the walls—red-coated riders leaping across the countryside on a fox hunt.

He was not good at waiting. Nor was he good at dealing with large institutions like hospitals. Their size put him off, and their bureaucracies offended his sense of individuality and called up an almost childish rebellion. He tended to think of all of the nurses and doctors and aides in the collective generic, embodied in the single pronoun *they,* as in: *They don't tell you what's going on. It wouldn't kill them to give out some information.* And now, in this particular hospital, he felt totally bereft and dependent upon them, powerless. It wasn't their fault—*they* were nice enough, especially that one surgeon, Kate. It was just that he was a man in crisis, watching helplessly as his life went down the drain, and they were his only lifeline and he didn't trust them.

Time had come to a complete stop—he was no longer conscious of it—and yet everything, even a turn around the room, seemed to take forever. The world was happening in slow motion, except when it fell off its axis and lurched about madly.

They had told him, when they were briefing him the other day—when was it? only a day and a half ago?—that the operation would be lengthy. But this was so lengthy it was interminable. Yesterday morning, when he had phoned to give his consent, Kate had responded sympathetically and had made him feel better, stronger in his certitude, by saying, "I think you made the right decision. You want to give him every chance." And when he had arrived this morning, unable to eat breakfast, fumbling for money to pay the taxi driver, she had sat him down and calmly explained to him the intricacies of what they were going to do. She had made it all sound feasible by using a matter-of-fact tone, but he could sense the huge void of uncertainty at the core of it. Then Saramaggio had waltzed in, stooping reflexively in the doorway the way tall men do. His demeanor was solemn enough, but Scott couldn't avoid the impression that he was barely able to contain his excitement. After all, he was about to embark upon a "procedure" that medical students might be reading about for years to come.

Saramaggio had once again taken him into his office, and Kate had followed. There, the doctor had motioned for the two of them to sit down, side by side, as if they were a couple. He had put his tweed jacket into a closet, donned a white jacket, and seated himself behind his desk to explain some of "the fundamentals," as he put it.

"Good news," he began. "The review board has approved the operation." His eyes met Scott's across the desk. "Contingent—of course—upon your approval. Kate ... Dr. Willet, here ... has told me you agree. That's a sensible decision. The only decision, really."

He seemed to feel that Scott needed bucking up, that he wasn't sufficiently enthusiastic.

"If this had happened five years ago," he said, "you and I wouldn't be sitting here. The field is moving that fast. In another ten years, we probably wouldn't be here, either—because you would already know about it. One day, it'll be routine. Someone has to be first."

He seemed to feel the occasion called for the philosophical long view. Scott didn't feel reassured. He still had questions.

"You said last time that a computer is going to be involved. And Dr. Willet just described it to me. But I don't get it. . . . How can a computer tell a body what to do? How does it work?"

"It won't do any thinking, if that's what you mean. We're a long way from that. All it does—and I don't mean to minimize it, because it's truly extraordinary—but what it does is ensure that the involuntary brain functions continue, that the autonomic nervous system stays in operation. It does this by taking the functions over—or rather the guidance system for the functions. Think of it as replacing a human pilot with an autopilot. Or as a pacemaker—except it's for the brain, not the heart.

"Basically, we're going to make a complete map of your son's brain. We do this from top to bottom by making high-resolution magnetic resonance measurements. The measurements go into the computer one by one, layer by layer, so that by the end of the process, his entire brain is scanned. The computer holds all this information—in effect, it replicates the brain's entire architecture. Then we implant electrodes into the real brain. They record the activity and forward it into the computer, which reads it and stores it. The computer can then imitate the neural transmissions by firing off similar electrical impulses. We feed them directly down the brain's motor pathways of the spinal cord. The lungs, the heart, the glands—they don't care where the signals are coming from as long as they keep coming. And in the meantime, we can, in effect, disconnect the brain and work with it."

"But I thought you said you might not need the computer. I thought it was . . . like a safety net. Backup—that's what you called it."

"I don't think so. I certainly didn't mean to give that impression. No, we will need the computer. You see, to extract the stem cells, we will have to shut down his brain stem. The computer will have to take over."

He paused and looked at Scott to see if he was following him. He was, and he seemed horrified—and angry.

"But what happens then? I mean, at the end, can you reconnect it?"

"Well, yes. If we couldn't do that, the whole procedure would be out the window."

"But have you ever done it?"

Saramaggio hesitated a millisecond.

"It's been done, yes. But as I said before, with animals."

"But not humans."

"Not humans, no. Mice mostly. Once in macaque monkeys. We've done the entire operation. And monkeys are quite predictive of what occurs in humans. It's the same setup, basically."

"And what were the results?"

"Well, they seem to be good. They recover; they function. Impairment seems to be minimal. Of course, it's a little hard to tell with monkeys."

Saramaggio looked down at his desk blotter.

"Look," he said finally. "Your son has undergone extensive brain damage. I don't know if I can bring him back. I don't know if he'll ever be the same. But I do know that this operation, as radical and frightening and unique as it sounds, is his only chance."

Scott tried again not to let his anger show. Blackmail. Hobson's choice. But he didn't want to do anything to jeopardize his son's chances. He let Saramaggio continue.

"Now—you've given your permission. You can withdraw it if you like. But once we get under way, once I walk through those doors of the OR, I don't want—"

"I think he understands," put in Kate abruptly, in a tone that suddenly silenced him. She rose, and Saramaggio, with exaggerated courtliness, sprang up also. Then Scott stood, slowly and warily.

"I'm not going to change my mind," he said. "I just want to know all the details."

Saramaggio explained that there were, in effect, two operations—one to extract the metal object, install the computer, and extract the stem cells, and then some weeks later, once the cells had multiplied to many millions in the lab, another one to plant them.

On the way out and almost as an afterthought, Sara-maggio had touched Scott lightly on the elbow and had said, "By the way, this first part—the MR scanning—it takes a long time."

"How long?"

"Well, with a monkey, almost two, three hours. With a human, it's hard to say, but it's bound to be longer. We can't say for sure."

That certainly hadn't bolstered Scott's confidence.

Operating Room 7, Saramaggio's favorite, was out of the question; it wasn't large enough to fit the operat-ing table with all the new computer equipment, and it was too far from the room containing the magnetic resonance imager. So they had to use OR 9. It was spacious and spanking new, but Saramaggio was not happy with it. Like most neurosurgeons, whose need for exactitude bordered upon superstition, he felt comfortable working only among familiar surround-ings. If your patient suddenly began bleeding uncon-trollably, you didn't want to start looking around for the bipolar electrocautery.

Nor was he happy with the MRI. He had wanted the slightly older version, snug as a cigar tube, because the resolution was fractionally higher, and Cleaver, throw-ing his weight around, had also insisted upon it. But the closer walls of the older model increased the danger of infection, and he had finally decided the risk was not worth taking. As it was, two aides had been swabbing down the machine, every surface and every curve, for two hours.

A team of fourteen had been assembled. The anes-thetist had two residents backing him up; the scrub nurse had two circulating nurses; Saramaggio had Gully Singh and Kate and Thomas Greer, a fifty-nine-year-old neurosurgeon known as a levelheaded thinker, who would be good for a quick opinion on the spot. Then there were the three MRI technicians and a computer

expert to assist Cleaver. Furthermore, all kinds of neu-
rologists and surgeons would be dropping in for a while,
probably even the administrator himself, Calvin Brewster, the old buffoon. They'd stand around in a corner,
kibitzing and straining to get a look, all to be able later
to say that they had been there when the great event
happened—provided, of course, that it turned out all
right. If it didn't, they'd disappear into thin air.

Saramaggio was not entirely sanguine. But he made a
point of exuding an air of supreme confidence all morning—amazing how theatrics enters into our profession,
he used to tell himself. He believed he'd handled the
conference with the boy's father successfully, no matter
what Kate thought. He could tell she faulted him for
lack of what she might call sensitivity, and this bothered
him; if there was one thing he prided himself on, other
than the surgery itself, it was his ability to explain things
in a simple way to concerned relatives. He even liked
doing it. But Kate seemed to have this air of recrimina-
tion. And perhaps he had imagined it, but she had
seemed to end the meeting abruptly. He had to admit it:
She was beginning to get on his nerves. She seemed to
think *she* had all the answers. He hoped he hadn't made
a mistake in choosing her. She *was* intelligent and capable; he had to give her that. And it was good to have a
beautiful woman around—just the scent of her perfume
was enough to call out the bantam swagger in him that
always helped him do his best work. But if she was
going to turn into a judgmental harpy, then the whole
thing wouldn't hang together. Not to mention the fact
that he wouldn't be able to lure her into bed. Ah well.
He sighed. Maybe he *was* getting old for this.

He called the surgical team together and explained
that the operation would proceed in four stages. First
would come the removal of the foreign object. In many
ways, that would be the most dangerous part: extracting
it without ripping out essential brain tissue. Next, provided the damage was not too substantial and the patient survived, would come the total MRI scan. That
alone would take some four or five hours. Then the elec-

trodes would be implanted and the computer switched on. The fourth stage would be the removal of the neural stem cells from the subventricular zone below the fluid-filled lateral ventricles. These would be set aside for cultivation exocranially.

Finally, the skull would be replaced, though not secured, and the patient would be kept in a germ-free environment for weeks. During this time, while the computer aided the lungs and heart to function, the stem cells would multiply in petri dishes, using fetal bovine serum as the medium. If they successfully grew into a colony of healthy, undifferentiated neurons and there were enough of them, then further down the line—who knew how long it might take—there would be a final operation. The skull would be reopened, and the neurons would be reinserted into the damaged region by means of a micropipette attached to a syringe. The hope was that they would integrate through the same genetic program that caused the brain to develop in the first place. At some point, if there was evidence that they had taken hold, the computer would be turned off. He didn't have to say how much of the multiple-tier operation had never before been attempted; the team knew it.

"Any questions?" he asked with a rakish understatement, rather like—or so he thought—a group commander giving orders to a cluster of young, scared, but indomitable RAF pilots about to drop their ordnance over Germany.

He looked from face to face; he could read the strain in their features, and he fancied that he felt a sudden rush of affection for his colleagues.

Something more—some words for history—were called for. But what?

"I know what you're all thinking," he said, though in fact he had no idea whatsoever. He paused, stumbling. "And I'm thinking the same thing. But we can't let that interfere with our work. The first X ray, the first heart transplant, the first use of sterile equipment. Medicine advances this way, in starts and lurches, through us, its practitioners. But we shouldn't feel that today—the weight of history. We should just do what's expected of us, just do our jobs."

He looked around again, finished. Somehow, his speech didn't seem to have had the effect he had hoped. Still, the words were eloquent, in a way.

"So," he added. "Let's get to it."

They took their places in the operating room, moving easily with well-timed movements.

Gully broke the ice with another one of his doctor jokes, but the response was tepid. Usually ORs were perfect settings for tall tales, long narratives, shaggy dog stories—"It's like a campfire without the fire; instead we gather around a prone body," Kate's old professor used to say—but in this particular OR, she noted, there was no levity.

Saramaggio looked to his left, near the Gerhardt table. There was a stainless steel rack, still hot from sterilization, bearing a metal pan of tiny electrodes and a series of small petri dishes. He realized that he hadn't seen them there before, and the realization struck him with renewed force, as he understood that he would soon be filling the dishes with tiny cells taken from the very central cavities of the brain, that what he was about to do had never been done by anyone.

The patient was wheeled in, his head swaddled in sterile cloths, that obscene obstruction still there sticking out like a unicorn's horn. The poor boy—his face looked so inert and haggard. Saramaggio knew, from his earliest years in med school, that it didn't pay to look at the patient this way. Better to think of him as a nonperson, a machine that needed to have its wiring rejiggered—that's all.

The anesthesiologist went to work, and soon the patient was deep under, a tube coming out of his mouth, strapped tightly down. The scrub nurse had everything lined up. Kate was there at his side, and so was Greer, a few strands of silver hair peeking out from below his cap. The machines were ticking and humming.

And before Saramaggio knew it, he heard the whirring of the drill and the rending scream it sent out when the resident leaned forward, touching the bit to bone.

Then Cleaver walked in, more than a touch of arrogance to the way he swung open the door. He carted along his machines and quickly started to fiddle with them. Saramaggio hated to admit it, but he felt a wash of relief as soon as he saw him dressed in scrubs and ready to go. He was such an odd, unpredictable man, but face it: The operation couldn't proceed without him.

The route to the cafeteria was burned into Scott's memory, and he walked it like a zombie. Up the hall past the nurses' station to the elevator bank. Press the button with the arrow tip pointing downward, the one that lit grudgingly. Wait an eternity before stepping into the lumbering boxcar filled with doctors, aides, anxious-looking relatives, the occasional gurney. Then out on the second floor and follow the pale green corridor all the way to the end. From there, it was only a few steps to the stainless steel container that dispensed watered-down coffee with the pull of a tiny black lever.

But so befuddled was his state of mind that he lost his way and wandered along the line of garish-looking Danishes and plastic cups of peach halves and grapefruit slices. He wondered in a moment of sudden clear confusion what he had come there for. He began to understand what it must be like to go insane: So many inchoate thoughts were crowding into his head that he could no longer sort through them to separate the meaningful from the accidental. He was lost like a cork in a stormy sea.

He carried his coffee to his customary corner table and sat down, stirring it absentmindedly. Beside him was a window, and he looked at the traffic down below on York Avenue. It was raining. He scarcely noticed the three men who sat down at a table nearby. Only when their conversation caught his attention did he turn to look at them.

"This trumps everything else," said one. "It leaves everyone else in the dust."

"Like Duke," said another. "Nicolelis, eat your heart out."

"Provided—of course—that it works."

"What are you guys talking about?" asked the third.

Scott studied them. Two were young men wearing white jackets; one had a professorial air, accentuated by a trim beard, the other had longish hair swept back over his ears. Clearly, residents or interns to judge from their overconfident airs. The third was in street clothes, and his manner marked him as an outsider; he was the one who had posed the question.

"Miguel Nicolelis—the neuroscientist at Duke. He led a team that worked with owl monkeys. Amazing stuff. This monkey had electrodes implanted throughout his brain. A computer had recorded signals fired off for various movements, so it could recognize them. When he began to think about moving his arm—just thinking about it—the computer spotted it and send out a similar signal to a robot that then lifted its arm."

"Say that again."

"The monkey could move the robot's arm just by thinking about it."

"Apparently," said the second doctor, "they discovered that cells in the cortex that control movement start firing long before the movement occurs.

"It means your brain is planning out all kinds of voluntary movements beforehand. Those movements can be read and acted upon by machines. Think what it means if robots can read your mind and do your bidding."

"What that could mean for paralytics—or anyone else, for that matter—is unbelievable," put in the other. "You could have a robot do whatever you wanted. You could lie on your back and paint your apartment. Or create a sculpture."

"Or unzip your fly."

"You *would* think that."

"Seriously, it's a first step."

"Yeah, but a first step to what?"

"Connecting human intelligence directly to machines without the middleman—our bodies."

"Get out," said the younger man.

"You have no idea what's going on in neurology these days."

"And this thing could be bigger than that?"

"Sure. In terms of neurology, it means we've crossed over a frontier. We're in a whole new country, pioneers in a land where almost anything is possible."

"This is history in the making," said the man with the beard.

"And *you* are there," said his colleague.

"What's it mean for the hospital?"

"For Saramaggio, you mean. For him, it's fame and fortune. Maybe even a Nobel Prize."

"No," said his colleague. "They give the Nobel for research. This is applied medicine. He won't get it, even if everyone admits he deserves it."

"Don't be so sure."

"It'll go to someone like Gould and Gross."

"Who are they?" asked the outsider.

"Elizabeth Gould and Charles Gross. At Princeton. They discovered neurogenesis."

"What's that?"

"They discovered that the brain continues to make new cells. That opened up a whole new area. Before them, it was believed that the brain simply stopped developing. You got your one hundred billion neurons and that was it; you got older, the cells expired, your brain deteriorated, you turned senile, and you died. Now, we know that new neurons are produced all the time."

The other resident chimed in.

"This corresponds to work done at Rockefeller University on canaries—believe it or not. A guy named Fernando Nottebohm showed that canaries grow new neurons to learn new songs."

"So—Frank Sinatra, he was one smart guy."

The two residents ignored the wisecrack.

"And the other interesting thing, considering what's

happening here today, is that the same general region—the hippocampus—is where the brain's stem cells come from."

"And stem cells are . . . ?"

"The basic cell—the undifferentiated cell from which all other cells develop."

"And they're the ones that this guy here, this doctor, is going to take out and grow and then put back in. Is that it?"

"In a nutshell, yes."

"And the chances of success?"

The two interns exchanged looks.

"Considering that it's never been done before . . ."

"Considering that it's largely theoretical at this point and no one can be sure if the theory is even correct . . ."

"Considering all that, I would say the chances of success are about one in fifty."

"You're being generous. I'd say one in a hundred."

"And we're just talking about survival. Never mind the question of regaining faculties."

"And from what I understand, the patient's a vegetable already."

"So now he'll be a supervegetable. Genetically engineered."

"Christ," said the outsider. "And they allow that?"

"Allow it. They encourage it. They beg for it."

"But why?"

"Prestige. Operations like this equal prestige, and prestige equals money."

"Provided, of course, that they're successful."

"Yes, well, there is that little problem."

Their conversation was drawing to a close. It was just as well, because Scott didn't think he could stand hearing any more.

Chapter 10

Kate tossed the surgeon's gown into the steel laundry hamper, the one for deep washing and sterilization, and undressed, tucking her comfortable operating room sandals away in the bottom of her locker. She picked up a towel, wrapped it around her, and headed for the shower. After a long operation, that's what she needed to relax: the strong stream of water pounding down, blocking out everything else.

Saramaggio. She had once again marveled at the man's skill. *He's a genius,* she told herself as she tested the water on her left elbow (like any surgeon, she was protective of her hands). It was nothing short of a miracle, the way his slender fingers moved with such unhurried sureness. Probing the pathways, moving to stanch heavy bleeding, testing damaged areas with his fingers—not a single wasted movement. But beyond that, he demonstrated that instinct to go directly to the correct spot, even when it was hidden behind a mass of brain tissue, almost as if his fingertips could think on their own. She had to give him credit.

Human brains are alike in their fundamental structure, but when it comes to the not-so-fine points—the size of the ventricles, the mesh of blood vessels, the serpentine turns of the cortex—each one is unique. A brain surgeon picking up a scalpel is about to enter a labyrinth of double deception; from the outside it looks like any other, but inside it is a mystery unto itself. The good ones somehow manage to steer clear of the blind alleys.

The water felt cool against her face. She turned to let

it run against her neck and down her back and legs and then reached out for the faucet to make the water cooler still. She did this in stages until the coldness made her gasp. It was the remnant of a game of endurance she used to play as a child, jumping into the frigid mountain rivers of Washington.

Her admiration was tinged with ambivalence that she didn't want to examine too closely. On the one hand, she was enthralled: This was what medicine was all about; this was what she had spent all those years dreaming about—curing the hopeless, helping people, patching back their lives. On the other, she was filled with self-doubt and even envy. For, watching the man work, she wondered: Would she ever be that good? Did she possess that overweening confidence, the requisite assurance that each and every move was absolutely correct? Here she was at the ripe old age of thirty-four, about to enter the surgeon's prime years when coordination marries experience, and she was light-years behind Saramaggio. Sometimes when she made an incision, she felt a dangerous hesitancy. How would she acquire the arrogance to do it passionlessly? Would she have to turn into an egomaniac to become a great surgeon?

And on top of everything else, she was beginning to fixate on Saramaggio's shortcomings as a person. She could see the lust in his eyes. He was parsimonious with his gift. It was expected that a chief surgeon would pass along his secrets—that was how the whole system was supposed to work—but he was too competitive to share them. Why was it, she wondered, that so many good surgeons were deficient in the old-fashioned virtues of magnanimity, generosity, and compassion?

She stepped out of the shower and toweled herself dry. She swung her wet hair to one side to shake the water off and wrapped the towel around it like a turban.

The operation had gone as well as could be expected, but it was the most complicated and risky one she had ever witnessed. It had lasted ten hours. The first five had been taken up with removing the hideous hunk of metal. Kate noticed at one point that Saramaggio was laboring. He would raise the metal rod a millimeter, clean-cut the bottom to minimize extraction of brain tissue, and work his way around in a complete circle. How could he prevent it from falling back? He had an inspiration: He clamped forceps to the rod and used a brace and wire to jerry-build a small hoist. This way he could gradually extract it while continuing to cut free the newly exposed base, while an assistant slowly revolved it to open up space. He moved by minute degrees and finally got the damned thing out, letting it dangle for a moment in midair, an ugly and complicated contraption with four half-moons of metal and wire attached to a long base of parallel bars. When it was gingerly placed in a sterile container, they all felt like applauding. Instead, they showed their relief by banter. Saramaggio chattered away about a recent vacation in Barbados.

But when Kate looked into the injury, she felt her heart sink. How was it possible that such a deep wound hadn't already killed the boy? She stared closely. She could see all the way down to the hippocampus; the damage was widespread. But the more she looked, the more she realized that, remarkably, it seemed to have somehow spared the vital areas. Was it really possible that new cells could grow and be implanted and repair the connections? She began to feel something stirring: Maybe this *was* going to be a milestone in neurosurgery.

"Make sure you get it all," said Saramaggio to the technician running the video. They stepped back a moment to let the camera take its close-ups.

Then Saramaggio set about searching for the stem cells in their hiding place, in the lining of the fluid-filled central chambers, the ventricles. He reached deep inside the lining and extracted forty-five infinitesimal samples and placed them in the petri dishes. Under the microscope, they would look like featureless blobs of protoplasm, and they had tiny waving hairs, like tentacles only thinner, that propelled them around the liquid surface.

Then came an equally delicate phase of the operation, the implantation of 126 hair-thin electrodes made of titanium so they wouldn't be pulled out by the MRI. The placement concentrated on centers controlling the somatic system. Each electrode picked up a nest of firing neurons and relayed the signal to a computer, which read it, learned to replicate it, and stored it, so that the transmission could be reversed later to keep the vital organs functioning. During this phase, they relied upon Cleaver, whose deep eyes, accentuated by the pale green of the mask and the dome beneath the cap, gleamed with intelligence. He had a way of sending a frisson of dislike up Kate's spine, but she had to admit, as she watched him attaching the tails of the electrodes, running the wires, spinning around to check the monitoring by the electroencephalogram, that he was a thorough professional.

Saramaggio let Gully sink some of the electrodes so that he could rest. But a few minutes later, he was back, looking over Gully's shoulder and then, dissatisfied, gesturing him aside to redo some of his work and taking charge again. The kibitzers stood around quietly in the rear, sometimes whispering among themselves. Then came the MRI mapping, in which numerous segments had to be repeated.

Saramaggio worked relentlessly for another two hours. The rest of the operation was restorative—covering the wound, dressing it, sterilizing everything within yards of it, and securing a specially cut plate to cover the hole in the skull. It was made to be removable, for the connection of the electrodes through which the computer would send its signals would have to be checked and changed from time to time. How often, no one knew. Such a thing had never been done before.

At the end, Saramaggio backed off and looked at his handiwork, a helpless body lying there with the head swathed in bandages, almost as if he were contemplating a work of art. Then he doffed his gown, revealing a simple T-shirt and black hairy arms, and said, "Well, let's keep our fingers crossed." He added an afterthought:

"We better make sure we have a backup power supply for the computer."

"That's my department," said Cleaver, hovering over the computer. "He's in my territory now."

There had been intense emotion in his tone, but whether it was jealousy or triumph, Kate could not say.

After the shower, she dried her hair quickly, dressed, and entered the corridor. As she walked past the waiting room, she looked inside and was shocked to see Scott still there. He was sitting on the edge of a chair, his head in his hands, an exhausted bundle of nerves. Was it possible that Saramaggio hadn't come out yet to give him a report? That would be such a breach of protocol, of normal decency, that she could scarcely believe it. But looking at Scott told her it was true.

He spotted her and rushed over. She spoke before he did, hurrying to supply the vital information in the order she thought he would want it.

She told him that Tyler was alive, that the operation was over, and that it had seemed to go well. Everything that they had wanted to do, they'd done. Tyler was resting comfortably, or at least in no pain. The metal fragment was out, and they believed they had secured brain stem cells. The computer appeared to be monitoring his activity, and at some point in the future it would begin to direct it—it was difficult to say when that would be. That would be the next crossroads. In the meanwhile, they would all just have to hope—to hope and to pray.

She answered a few questions and then said she would look for Dr. Saramaggio, who had been, she repeated several times, nothing short of brilliant.

Saramaggio was in his office, sitting at his desk, still in his white T-shirt, his head resting in his arms. At first, she thought he was asleep. But when he heard her, he sat upright, quickly, as if he were embarrassed, and she saw that there were tears in his eyes. He suddenly looked like a little boy.

"Look at this," he said in a choked voice. He held his right hand up, and she saw that it was trembling slightly.

"I honestly didn't know if I could do it," he said.

"Well, you did."

"Yes, I did, didn't I?"

"And now I think you should come and talk to the father. He needs to know what's going on."

He looked stricken.

"My God, I forgot all about him. How could I do that?" He stood up. "Where is he? Will you come with me?"

"Yes," she said.

And she opened the door wider for him and was even tempted to take him by the elbow to guide him, but the moment he stepped over the threshold, he seemed to revert to his old self.

She wasn't sorry the episode had happened. *I guess he's human after all,* she thought.

❧

Kate was exhausted. As she rode the creaking elevator to her three-room apartment on West Twenty-first Street, she felt like forgoing supper and collapsing in bed, even though she hadn't eaten since breakfast. She realized that something was troubling her, something about the day's events, although she couldn't say what it was. She scarcely had the energy to figure it out.

Luis, the elevator man, smiled sweetly as he swept the door open for her on the fifteenth floor. She thanked him, walked down the aged hallway, unlocked the heavy wooden door, and tossed her pocketbook on the sagging but comfortable couch. Then she went to the window and threw open the curtains.

Twilight was settling in. Spread below for five or six blocks was a valley of low-rise buildings, tar-covered rooftops set apart by low brick walls. They were crowned with wooden water tanks; she loved the look of the tanks and had counted them when she first arrived—seven in all. In the mid distance behind the valley was a wall of higher buildings that rose up like steep cliffs. They were close enough so that she could watch the people taking morning coffee on their balconies or could spy upon scenes of domestic harmony or strife through the occasional curtainless window. Behind the wall, still higher buildings loomed, mountainous skyscrapers that marched off to the north all the way to midtown. Now, at dusk, lights were appearing everywhere. Entire floors of office buildings were blazing, and new lights were flicking on in the faraway residential towers, tiny glowing squares that illuminated as she watched.

The sight set her blood racing. It was the reason she had rented the apartment six weeks ago when she'd arrived from San Francisco with two suitcases and a backpack. It seemed to sum up everything she was feeling about the city, all of its infinite possibilities as well as its gifts of anonymity and privacy and even loneliness. You can remake yourself here into anything you want, it seemed to tell her; it's all the same to me.

Out of nowhere, she thought of her mother. So brave after her husband died in Vietnam, raising her alone in a small mountain town outside of Seattle, teaching her the importance of education. *We're tough women,* she had said, speaking of herself and her own mother, who had come all the way across Canada from Greenland. Generations of tough, single-minded women. *We've ice water in our veins,* her mother used to say.

It was odd, the other day in the cafeteria, how she had told Scott Jessup how her mother had died. She didn't usually open up like that to strangers, but he had seemed to need to hear about someone else's loss. And strangely, she had omitted the most important part of the story, how her mother on the Washington mountaintop had known of her husband's death in Vietnam. Her mother had said that she'd seen him at the moment of his death, that he'd appeared before her in his military uniform. She was not superstitious, but ever afterward she'd insisted that her husband had come to say good-bye. And who's to say it was impossible—the other side of the earth notwithstanding—if the spirit is willing and the love is strong enough? And then, years later, long after her fall, when it came her time to die the long slow death of cancer, she'd seen him again near the end, materializing at the foot of her bed, and she was no longer afraid.

That was a story Kate rarely told, and even today, when she was turning it over in her mind, she didn't know what to make of it. She didn't for one moment deny that her mother *thought* she had seen him. But had she actually? Could the timing of his death have been a coincidence? And if she had seen him, was he inside her mind or was something actually there outside herself? It was a fundamental riddle that challenged her scientific bent, and she'd settled the contradiction by shelving the whole thing. She believed it and disbelieved it at the same time.

And there was something else she hadn't told Scott, or anyone else for that matter. She didn't like to think of it, and when she did, she cringed mentally and tried to turn her mind to something else. When her mother had been dying, in the final days, Kate was at the tail end of medical school exams; if she had left to take care of her full-time, she would have lost her scholarship and a precious year or maybe more. Her mother had understood fully the need to go to a nursing home; it was the only practical thing to do, she had said, and she'd meant it. Kate had visited often, every weekend and sometimes during the week. She had buttered up the staff and brought them presents to make sure that they would take special care of her mother.

But—and this was the thought that cut so deep—she did not drop out of school; she did not take her into her own house and nurse her for a couple of months and tend to her the way an only daughter should. She didn't ply her with treats and sit by the bed for long talks and play music and read to her for hours on end. And, perhaps most of all, she wasn't even with her at the moment of death. She was taking an exam and missed it by two hours. At the funeral when she spoke, a sparrow came out of nowhere and lit on her head. It got caught in her hair and she shooed it away, but it came back and she thought it even pecked at her. Later, she had had the odd thought that the sparrow was an avenging spirit sent by her mother, and though she didn't really believe this, she had had nightmares about it for years afterward.

Why was she thinking of all this now? Something was nagging at her; something from the operation was making her think about all this. What was it?

She went to the tiny kitchen with its stained enamel sink and two-burner stove, brewed a cup of coffee, and sat on the couch in front of the scarred but serviceable coffee table she had found on the sidewalk weeks ago, lugging it home like a trophy.

Ordinarily, she was good at plumbing her own feelings. She was a straightforward woman from the northwest, and she wasn't given to pretense and games.

But there was one game that she had learned to play, and maybe that was part of whatever it was that was tugging at her ankles now. It was the surgeon's game of pretending that the patient wasn't really a person. A game with a deadly serious purpose, as had been drummed into her during med school, because it allowed the surgeon to slip a blade into a chunk of pulsating gray matter and excise it, knowing that it might contain a mathematical formula, a snatch of poetry, or a memory of a lost love.

But this time around it was difficult for her to objectify the patient. Something about this case—about the boy who was so young and the father who loved him so much—was upsetting her and involving her on a new level. And now that she considered it, she knew in part what it was—it was her inability to regard it as a "case" at all. But why?

Try as she might, she couldn't erase the image of Tyler lying so small and helpless on the operating table, or Scott during that split second when she came upon him in the waiting room and their eyes met and she felt his worry and loss. The sight echoed something in her and stirred her. It was the profundity of her feelings, and the fact that they seemed threatening to her equilibrium in some way, that she couldn't have predicted.

⁓

She awoke to the ringing of the phone and grunted into the receiver.

"Dr. Willet?"

The voice on the other end was a man's voice. At first she couldn't identify it—certainly not Harry, her ex-boyfriend out on the Coast, who in any case was too considerate to call in the middle of the night.

"Yes."

"This is Scott. Scott Jessup. Tyler's dad."

She turned on the light and looked over at the clock. Two-thirty in the morning. She expected him to apologize for the hour, but he did not. He was too distraught.

"I need to ask you something, and I hope you will answer me straight out."

"Of course."

She was by now wide-awake, and she added warmly, "Ask me whatever you want."

"That doctor today, Saramaggio . . . he seemed to indicate . . . he said that everything had gone okay and that Tyler would recover."

"Yes. I remember when he said that."

"And then I asked him what . . . what he meant by recover. . . . Do you remember? And at first he wouldn't answer—he was talking all this medical jargon—and finally I cut him off and I said, 'But will he get better?' And he sort of looked at me, surprised, and he wouldn't answer for a long time, and I . . . I asked him again. And he looked at the floor for a while. Do you remember that?"

"Yes, I do."

She wondered if he had been drinking. His words sounded . . . not slurred exactly, but rounded at the edges.

"And then he said, 'Yes, he will get better.' But he said it in a way that suggested he didn't really mean it."

She didn't know what to say. She had had that same impression at the time. So she just said, "Uh-huh."

"Well . . . I was wondering what you thought. You were there; you saw the operation. You know . . . you seem to know what's at stake. You . . . you're someone a person could trust. And so I wanted to ask you . . . I wanted to ask if you thought Tyler has a chance, any chance at all of getting better . . . I mean really better, not just living, surviving in an iron lung or something like that. But becoming himself again . . . recognizable . . . Because otherwise . . . I don't know if it's worth going ahead with the second operation. I mean what's the point. . . ."

He was choking up and couldn't go on.

"I'm not sure what to say," she said. "I hear your question and I know—I think I know—how important it is to get an answer. But I'm not sure at this point that there really is one. So much of what happened in there today is new—so new that we don't know much about it."

"I realize that." His tone was suddenly hard. "And I'm not looking for a hard and fast answer, a percentage or anything like that. But for Christ's sake, you know about the brain; you know how much damage he's had; you know something about this new stem cell business. . . . Do you think it could conceivably work?"

She paused. She knew that under his question was another question—should they continue? Should he as the father stop the whole thing?

"Do you remember our talk in the cafeteria?" she asked.

"Of course. And I've been thinking about it . . . about the idea that he may be gone forever, and the question now is whether this new person, a new Tyler, can live a full life and become as much as he can become. But I have to say, I'm not sure that works. I'm not sure I can accept that."

What he needed was information—hard facts insofar as there were any.

"I'm not sure I could accept it either if I was in your place—or at least not right away. I don't know what to say. Why don't I just go over some of the things again and you can ask me questions if you want to and we can go through it together. Okay?"

"Okay."

"First of all, there was, as you know, a lot of damage. If Tyler were to somehow awaken, if that were even possible, we have no idea what he would be like. The brain is a remarkable organ—it can take a lot, it can compensate, it can even grow. But in my opinion, the damage he sustained was severe. It was amazing that the autonomic nervous system was still functioning so well—that it did so is a good sign, in terms of remaining alive. But I don't believe he would have ever really regained consciousness—full consciousness."

"You mean you think he would have always been like that? In a coma? A vegetable?"

"Yes. Now this operation, as we said—it's never been done before on humans. It's complicated and risky on four counts. *One*: taking out the object, which could cause more damage. That was done. It seemed to go well—Saramaggio is the only surgeon who could have done it—but we won't know for a while if the removal itself caused further damage. *Two*: extracting the stem cells and growing them in a lab until they multiply. The first part of this has been done. How fast and how well they multiply, we can't say yet. *Three*: letting a computer run the autonomic system. That's entirely new. It's worked in animals—specifically in monkeys—and so it's theoretically achievable, but I have to emphasize the word *theoretically*. Finally, number *four*: reimplanting the stem cells and encouraging them to take over from damaged cells. That is the most complicated of all. It's on the outer reaches of experimentation. It's been done seemingly successfully with animals—mice—and they seem to take it pretty well. They've been tested, and to outward appearances they seem pretty normal. But of course we can't talk to them, and humans are much more complicated."

"You say *pretty* normal. What do you mean? How do you judge?"

"Perception tests. Learning tests. We run them through mazes or have them press a bar for food, things like that. Some of them seem to be able to do as well as they did before on these tests, but others have difficulty. It may depend on a lot of things—the extent of the damage, how much debris of the dead cells is removed, how strongly the new cells regenerate and establish neural connections to the surrounding cells. Tyler has one thing in his favor—youth."

"How so?"

"He's thirteen. The brain is still growing and establishing connections—up until the age of sixteen, at least."

"That's hopeful."

"It's all hopeful. Every step of the way. It's just that no one has ever taken this particular path before, and so I'm afraid that uncertainty is unavoidable."

He was silent for a moment, then said, "This is a big help. I have one last question."

"Yes."

"Is he . . . is there any chance that he is in pain?"

"No. That's the one thing we can be sure of. The brain feels pain for everything but itself."

"Then that settles it."

"You're going ahead?"

"Yes. There's nothing to lose. And there's everything to gain, no matter how slim the chances."

"That's the way I'd look at it."

"Thank you. You've been a big help. I'm sorry I called so late."

"That's all right."

"Good night."

"Good night."

After she hung up the phone, she couldn't go back to sleep for some time.

Chapter 11

Cleaver walked along the path from the bridge to Pinegrove. It was dusk, a summer's evening, the salt air churning in the heavy heat. Behind him, he could hear the whir of cars crossing the bridge; on both sides, barges and small craft moved up and down the river; above, a plane flew toward the setting sun.

His thoughts tumbled to a drumbeat of excitement. The operation—so far—had been a success. Saramaggio had been superb in the OR; Cleaver had to give him that. It was groundbreaking stuff, the kind of thing that could make him a legend. But the real breakthrough had come with the computers, which functioned perfectly and were beginning to take over command of the boy's autonomic system. Cleaver had held his breath during the changeover, but it had gone as smoothly as a locomotive switching onto a sidetrack. Now—if only it would continue to work.

No one seemed to recognize the importance of the computers. In the excitement, which was consciously held in check—it was after all a hospital—the credit went to Saramaggio. That rankled. But on second thought, it was all right. It allowed Cleaver to continue his research out of the spotlight. And someday it would all be sorted out. Someday they would learn the significance of what had happened. It was almost funny: Saramaggio was puffed up with pride; he thought *he* was the important one because he was in the driver's seat. He didn't realize that the importance came from the new vehicle he was driving.

Cleaver thought back to the days when he'd started

out, twenty-five years ago. Even then he had heard of
Saramaggio, the whiz-kid surgeon performing split-
brain operations in assembly-line style. He was in it for
the traditional reason: He wanted to ameliorate the
symptoms of epilepsy and relieve suffering. Cleaver
was interested in the operation, too, but for a different
reason: He wanted to split the hemispheres apart because he wanted to see what would happen. He wanted
to set them at war. He was gripped by the concept of
dual consciousness. Imagine: two contending personalities in the same body. Which one would win the struggle
for supremacy? The left brain working through the right
hand would perform a certain action, and the right brain
working through the left hand would do the opposite.
The simplest act turned the person into a battleground
of competing wills. He recalled reading about the young
woman patient in North Dakota who was asked if she
had any sensation in her left hand and replied, "Yes!
Wait! No! Yes! No, no! Wait, yes." She was handed a
piece of paper with the words *yes* and *no* written on it
and asked to point to the correct answer. She stared
helplessly; then her left forefinger stabbed at *yes* and
her right forefinger at *no*.

Cleaver, not a surgeon, had of course not operated on
people. But he had operated on animals. Those early experiments, so long ago—he felt nostalgic for them. How
many hundreds of monkeys and cats had he experi-
mented on? How many had he *sacrificed*?—a medical
term whose brutal simplicity always appealed to him.

He thought of phantom limbs and how they had
pointed the way to his life's work. Doctors used to
scratch their heads in perplexity, confronted by am-
putees who insisted that even though an arm or leg was
missing, they could still *feel* it. Sometimes the limb
merely itched, sometimes it seized up in an excruciating
paralysis. People were dumbfounded. How could this
be? They theorized that the sensations must be caused
by damaged nerve endings in the stump.

Only recently was the mysterious phenomenon explained: a mix-up in the brain. Areas of sensation over-

lap—the part that registers a touch on the face, for example, lies next to that for the arm. With phantom limbs, neural pathways spill over onto adjacent ones, so that a touch on the cheek registers as a touch on the hand—it *feels* like it, even though the hand isn't there. And then came a brilliant move by a brain researcher, V. S. Ramachandran, who devised a method to treat a patient with a paralyzed phantom limb. He rigged up a box with mirrors in such a way that the patient seemed to be looking at his phantom arm but was actually observing his good arm. The patient was told to relax his hand and open it—and, miraculously, the paralyzed feeling disappeared. In effect, the brain tricked itself into believing it. Or, as Cleaver preferred to think of it: The brain did one thing and the mind thought another. For him it was final proof, if any was required, that the two were not synonymous. His own work had paid off, providing him with the inspiration to use computers to work on the brain, to search for the anima. It had led Cleaver toward an irrefutable truth: Consciousness is real and palpable, not some phantasmagoric creature of the imagination. It is rooted in physiology, even though it rises above the mechanics of the brain, and it is therefore something that can be located and mapped, like a continent waiting to be discovered.

Saramaggio is good at what he does, but he is a technician. I am more than that, thought Cleaver, *much more.*

He recalled sitting in a classroom, hearing that there were two types of scientists—the integrators and the inventors. The integrators produced systems; they accumulated data, synthesized things, sifted and winnowed calculations to form a theory. It was like constructing a building—valuable work, in its own way. But the inventors—ah, they were the revolutionaries. They cut through everything with one blow, a leap of deductive thinking. They dynamited the entire building and leveled the landscape and made way for something new.

Saramaggio is an integrator par excellence, thought Cleaver, *but I belong to the tiny band of revolutionaries. I am an inventor.*

A line came to him out of nowhere, a snatch of a poem by Wordsworth: "We murder to dissect."

Cleaver could see Pinegrove looming up ahead, lights already on in the bottom floors, the top floors dark. He spotted a figure moving about in the window of the experimental ward where the old lady was.

It was probably Felicity, he thought, fussing over her and trying to make her comfortable. That was hardly objectionable—it couldn't hurt the experiment and in some ways it would expedite it. Still, it was worrisome. Felicity was eager to help and wanted to learn, but her attitude toward the thrust of his research was shifting in a negative direction—he could detect undercurrents of concern. She was keeping her thoughts to herself. And she was meddlesome. That could be dangerous.

He hurried closer, almost broke into a run. At a bound, he was up the front steps, inside the door, and down the corridor. Felicity was backing out the door, and she didn't see him.

"Hello," he said, in a matter-of-fact voice.

She gave a start, then held one hand to her chest.

"You scared me."

"Sorry. I didn't mean to. How is it going?"

"You mean Myra?"

"Yes."

"Okay," she said. "She's about ready to nod off."

"Let's see," he said, opening the door.

"You want me, too?"

"Sure, why not?"

The old lady was lying motionless in bed, the sheet forming a mummylike mold around her frail body. The transcranial magnetic receiver was in place around her head, and the helmet and goggles led to wires that swirled in a Medusalike headdress. That made it difficult to read her expression. Her eyes were closed.

He checked the monitor. It showed that she was approaching the abyss of slumber, the first of four levels of sleep.

"We're looking for REM sleep," he said. "Rapid eye movement. That indicates dreaming." He glanced at Felicity, who was looking back at him. "Did you know that our muscles become completely paralyzed during REM sleep? That's to prevent us from lashing out when our dreams turn to nightmares. It's amazing, isn't it, how our minds try to take account of everything our bodies might try to do."

"Yes," she said uncertainly. "I guess it is."

"Say, we've got some time yet. You want a cup of coffee?"

Felicity surprised him by nodding yes. She did so with a slightly suspicious air.

They stepped into Cleaver's office, and there was a long awkward silence as he put the electric kettle on and spooned out instant coffee into two mugs. He made a show of waiting on her and asking if she wanted cream or sugar. They sat far apart, self-conscious, like two lonely hearts out on a first date. There was nothing to do but begin, he thought.

"So," he said, clearing his throat, "what do you think of what we're doing here?"

"What do you mean? The experiments?"

He nodded yes and busied himself pouring coffee, as if the conversation weren't all that important.

"You really want to know?"

"Yes."

"Well, since you ask, I think they're interesting, probably really important. But I don't see why we have to treat people like that."

"You mean Myra there?"

"Yes, and Elmore."

"I see."

Cleaver took his time in answering. Myra was Elmore's wife. When he'd died and was placed in a pine coffin purchased by Cleaver himself and buried at a service with inmates doubling as mourners, she had had nowhere else to turn. Cleaver had made her an offer, exchanging room and board at Pinegrove for the right to conduct experiments inside her cranium. She had accepted with her customary old-biddy bluster and now was as complacent as an African subject giving herself over to the unfathomable exigencies of a Western anthropologist.

"We took them in, you know. They were both homeless and had no place to go. We fed them and clothed them and gave them a place to sleep. You're aware of that—right?"

Felicity nodded yes, but her words came tumbling out, as if she had been bottling them up.

"But why did you have to do all that to him when he was dying, all those wires and machines? Why not make him comfortable instead—and why not let them be together and let Myra care for him?"

"I suppose we could have done that. But that was the deal. We made him as comfortable as we could under the circumstances. And you know, they were together—that was the whole point. She *felt* she was with him, and he probably felt the same thing. You saw it with your own eyes."

"They may have felt it, but they weren't actually together."

"But if they felt it, they were—don't you see? That's what this is all about. It's about the human mind, how it works, how it experiences the world."

She was quiet.

"You see," he continued, speaking slowly now and trying not to sound as if he were talking to a child, "all of my work is really concerned with a single human faculty, and that is human consciousness. I call it anima. Do you understand?"

"Yes."

"Think of it as a spirit of consciousness, a spark inside that makes you you."

He could tell she was hanging on his every word.

"What are you? A complicated bundle of trillions of cells that is convinced it is separate from the rest of the world. You believe that everything that is you is contained within you, and that your mind is in control of it—but that belief could be wrong.

"Take memory. We think of our memories as replicas of events that happened to us. Almost as if we made little films of our daily lives and stored those films away in brain cells somewhere, canisters that can be opened at will. But now we know it doesn't work like that. Memories are not recaptured—they are made new each time. Our brain tries to construct them out of fundamental elements that are there because they touch us on some deep emotional level. And each time we construct it, the memory is different in some way or other, but we are not aware of the difference. So, strictly speaking, the memory is not of some past event, something over and done with that we are recollecting afterward. It's a current event, a new experience happening in real time. The part of you that creates the illusion that you are *recreating* it—the projectionist for the film that isn't there— is your consciousness. You follow?"

She did.

"Consciousness exists outside of time. The events you believe are over aren't really over. And that's what philosophers mean when they say that every action that ever happened is still happening out there somewhere, and that every person who ever lived still lives on. They are in our consciousness, and our consciousness is not limited to our physical bodies. We use our anima to tap into this larger domain."

Felicity took a sip of coffee. Cleaver felt her resistance crumbling. He wondered if she realized that hungry biographers might someday beg her to reproduce this conversation. He hoped she was listening carefully.

"So what's the experiment all about?" she asked.

"I'm getting to it," he replied archly. "If consciousness rises above mere mechanics, then there's no reason to assume that it's confined to the physical vessel of the human skull, is there? Why shouldn't it be able to roam?"

She nodded.

"In fact, if you're honest with yourself, you'll probably admit you already know this. How many unexplained mental phenomena can you think of? How about ESP—doesn't it stand to reason that some perceptions can happen outside the five senses and that some of us are more adept at gathering them in? Dreams that are incomprehensible and fill us with incredible dread or incredible well-being? Blind sight— the phenomenon of seeing something without being aware you are perceiving it?

"How about all those stories of dying people who are able to appear before loved ones at the precise moment of death? Or people who have died for a second and describe the out-of-body experience of rising up to the ceiling and seeing themselves stretched out below? The white light at the end of a tunnel. Is it so unreasonable to think that your consciousness—at the final moment, the moment of death—can summon up all its energy and will in order to perform some dramatic act, some final farewell?"

Cleaver's voice dropped a notch, a hint of intimacy.

"In point of fact, Felicity, you have seen this. You've seen the objective measurement of anima. You saw it with Elmore, who appeared before our friend there in the other room."

"What I saw was that Elmore appeared before her just as he was dying. She saw him. And why not? They loved each other deeply."

"Exactly, Felicity! What she saw was his anima. And I am the first person to prove it exists. And not only prove it, but document it, measure it, locate its site in the brain. I know where it resides—in a subcortical spot no bigger than your little finger, the amygdala. The amygdala and the hippocampus, the centers of emotion and memory. And that's what the anima is, what makes each of us different and special—our emotions and our memories all wrapped up together, being newly created all the time.

"This is pioneer work. Because . . . well, think about it: How can a scientist grapple with consciousness? Consciousness is elusive. As the ultimate examiner of everything else, how can it examine itself? Have you ever tried to write down your thoughts exactly as they occur without leaving any of them out? It's impossible, like trying to catch lightning in a bottle. So one must find traces of consciousness. One must leave powder on the floor to catch the footprints of the ghost. Construct mirrors. And that's what I've been doing: devising experiments to capture the reflection, to see where the ghost has been and what it can do."

"And that's what you're doing in the next room there? With Myra?"

"That's all. I'm just monitoring her dreams, trying to catch her consciousness as it roams. It doesn't hurt her. We're not causing her to have dreams any more than we caused Elmore to die. We're just going along for the ride."

He stood and motioned for her to follow him into the room next door. Myra was still lying motionless. Cleaver walked over to the monitors.

"She's dreaming right now," he said.

"How do you know?"

"For one thing, her EEG is active. Only in dreaming is a person's EEG the same as when she's awake. Now, take a look at this."

He tapped some keys on the computer and turned several dials, and a cross section of her brain appeared on a recessed screen. The view was from above, so that it looked like the meat of a walnut cut in two.

"See that?" He pointed to an area where dark spots were exploding like shell bursts. He turned another knob and they turned into colors, brilliant blue and green and yellow. That was from a tracer element that flowed through her IV.

"What is it?"

"It's a particular pattern of brain activity that I have come to recognize. It cuts through a number of deep brain centers. The pattern varies a bit from person to person, but for any one individual it's always the same. You can see it involves a large number of neurons. They always fire in the same sequence."

"When she dreams?"

"Yes."

"And that means her—what did you call it?—her anima is outside her body?"

"No, not entirely outside. It's still rooted in her brain. But it's able to extend itself far beyond the waking mind and experience things outside the body. It's like a dog that roams on a leash—until death. Then the leash drops away."

Felicity stared at the screen, fascinated.

"Freud thought dreams were the product of the unconscious mind. The metaphor was something bubbling up to the surface from the lower depths. But it's much more than that. It's like stepping into a large lake and being aware of everything else that's in the lake. Some of those things are wonderful and enthralling, and some are monstrous and dangerous.

"Now I'll show you something else."

So saying, he pushed a button, and out came a black-and-white negative of the picture on the screen. He slipped it on a luminous board next to another picture of a brain scan. They looked remarkably similar.

"The one on the left is Myra when she saw Elmore at the moment of his death. That's what people who deal with death every day, people in hospices, call a visitation. The other one is Myra dreaming. In both, her consciousness is in a state of high arousal. You see how similar they are?"

"Yes. It *is* interesting."

"And *important*."

"Yes, I see that."

"So now you see what we're doing. And you have to understand what we're doing with these people—Myra, Elmore, and the others. They're not being treated as guinea pigs. They're living their lives out as they would, only they're doing it—I hope this doesn't sound too corny."

He hesitated.

"What?" she asked. "What are they doing?"

"They're doing it on *the altar of science*."

Felicity brushed a wisp of hair away from her broad forehead, a characteristic gesture that he suddenly found fetching. Her face seemed slightly flushed. She seemed to feel it was time to leave. At the door, holding one hand on it, she turned back and looked at him, square in the eyes.

"Thank you," she said.

"Don't mention it. I should say *thank you*."

She closed the door behind her.

Cleaver finished his coffee and checked the monitor. Then he went to a supply cabinet, filled a syringe, stepped over to the old woman's bedside, and raised her thin wrist, exposing the upper arm. He jabbed the needle in. He slipped behind the bed and fiddled with a valve, cutting off her oxygen. After a moment, she gave a little heave in bed, twitching slightly and raising her chin. Then her head dropped to her chest, and she remained still of all movement. Cleaver watched her closely. After a short period, he turned again to the valve, opened it, and gradually she came to life again.

He returned to the computer and pushed a button. The negative that came out this time looked different. The explosions were larger and had shifted to an opposite corner of the lower brain. He put the negative on the viewing light board, opened a drawer, and extracted yet another brain scan, which he placed next to the new one. It looked very much like it.

He compared them avidly, the one from the drawer that he'd taken from Elmore at the moment of death and the other one from Myra just a minute ago. Very similar, very similar indeed. Two different brains and they registered the same activity in the same regions.

Another breakthrough.

He wondered what Felicity would have made of that. If she had been there to ask him one of her questions—"So what does it show?"—he could have replied, "That's what the brain looks like when it gives up the ghost."

And if she had persisted, asking, "And what did you do to Myra?" he could have replied, with an untroubled conscience, "Nothing much. You can see she is breathing normally now. She simply went for a plunge—in a very large lake."

Chapter 12

The following day, Cleaver met Quincy again. Quincy had persuaded Cleaver to accompany him on the chance that he might meet Cybedon, whom he had described as his "virtual Virgil." And so there Cleaver was, on the outskirts of an abandoned, packed warehouse in Williamsburg, Brooklyn, fighting to get inside, where the pounding, monotonous techno-music had ratcheted up the dancers into a frenzy. There were bouncers outside the entrance, which was through a loading dock, and spaced-out druggies worked the crowd, wearing the initials of their chemical wares on signs taped across their foreheads.

Quincy reached back to help Cleaver up onto the dock.

"Just follow me," he said.

"Who are all these people?" Cleaver shouted back. He was surprised that so many of them were so young.

Quincy shrugged.

"Cybergypsies, booters, starpunks, you name it. Technopagans, cocooners, mystic mercenaries, silicon hippies, crystallites—hackers and bounty hunters of all kinds."

"All here for the convention?"

He had seen two men in suits, which prompted the question.

"More like an *anti*convention," said Quincy. "These are people who wouldn't be caught dead at the Javits Center. The computer companies try to crash because this is where the next is."

"Next what?"

"The next next."

Quincy ducked under the arm of a bouncer into the cavernous room. Cleaver followed, and the heat and smoke and music struck him like a wall. He could feel the drumbeats against his cheek. About forty people bounced on the dance floor, jumping up and down like Masai warriors, and Cleaver spotted small mechanical robots on the floor, bouncing in rhythm.

"That's X-Mundo," shouted Quincy, pointing toward the DJ, who was stripped to the waist and sweating like a pig. He had not a single hair anywhere—even his eyelashes had been plucked—and Cleaver spotted a shunt sticking into his shoulder. Quincy followed his gaze.

"Goes straight in," he said. "Hits him sixty miles an hour."

Quincy threaded his way through the crowd toward the back of the warehouse, where there were booths and bridge tables with computers and displays. It looked like a conventional sales conference, except that the material on sale—virtual reality setups, bootleg computers with megahertz drives—were anything but conventional. In one booth, an artist was drilling cyber tattoos. Across another, a curtain was drawn, and looking through a tear, Cleaver saw a young woman lying on a cot, naked except for a Turkish towel across the midriff and a steel mask upon her face and electrodes attached to her breasts and thighs and lower abdomen, quivering slightly.

They went down a broad staircase and into the basement, where it was quieter. Quincy opened a door, and inside sat about sixty people on folding chairs, facing a fat man standing at a lectern. He was old enough to have a face crisscrossed by wrinkles and had yellow-white hair tied into a ponytail.

Quincy took a seat and motioned to Cleaver to sit next to him.

"Cybedon," he whispered.

A woman in the back finished speaking and sat down. She had apparently asked a question.

"Okay. What is my concept of the postbiological

change, and how does that differ from escape velocity?" the man repeated, looking out over the audience. He took a breath.

"Escape velocity, as used by Mark Dery, is a metaphor. It occurs when speed and distance reach the critical point at which a moving object—a planet, a spaceship, anything—breaks out of the gravitational pull. It achieves hyperacceleration and moves into another dimension.

"This idea—of a striving and a sudden break with the past that will lead us into a new world—is not new in Western thinking. It's found in the myths of Prometheus and Icarus. It's in Janus, the god of the doorway, and in the Garden of Eden and *Paradise Lost* and Shangri-La. It's in Socrates and Plato and Marx and Adam Smith and modern thinkers like Marshall McLuhan and Teilhard de Chardin.

"What I and others have done is recognize this theme for what it is—deliverance from human mortality—as applied to the scientific principles of Darwinian evolution."

The woman stood up again. She looked frustrated.

"But how does that apply to machines?" she asked.

"Machines are evolving rapidly. The first modern computer was Colossus, built by the British in 1943 to decode the Germans' Enigma machine. It was powered by two thousand vacuum tubes. When ENIAC went into operation in 1946, it was the size of a room. Then came transistors in the fifties, integrated circuits in the sixties, and microchips in the seventies.

"As the machines got smaller, they got smarter. And now they're getting smarter quicker. The first computer to play chess was designed in 1958. It took thirty-nine years for Deep Blue to arrive and beat Gary Kasparov. But it was inevitable: Deep Blue's thirty-two separate microprocessors can examine two hundred million chess moves per second. It can look thirty-five moves ahead. Kasparov can see four, maybe five, moves. In contrast to the computer, neural connections in the human brain move at a snail's pace.

"Ray Kurzweil says that computers will exceed human intelligence by 2020. He foresees that man and machine will link up and evolve together. This is inevitable once machines replicate themselves. And so the only answer for humankind is to figure out a way to enter into that system of evolution. If we don't, we'll be left behind. Evolution teaches that there is room for only one entity in any particular niche, and the niche we're talking about is the one reserved for the planet's supreme intellect.

"So how is this evolutionary conjunction going to take place? It's a little difficult to imagine people mating with machines. That's where my theory comes in. My contribution is to posit the medium for the connection to occur. There is only one area where it can happen, and that is through defused and incorporeal artificial intelligence."

The questioner, the woman with a whiny voice, was still on her feet.

"Explain, please," she said.

"Artificial intelligence has grown exponentially since the 1970s, and it has organized itself into a quasi-life-form encircling the globe. I speak of the Web. Its pattern of growth mirrors that of a multicellular organism. It fulfills the two criteria for life: It expands through a process of regeneration, and it can communicate with its furthest parts. It even has natural enemies, in the form of viruses.

"If we conceive of the Web as the ultimate expression of machine intelligence, and the bundle of neural connections we call the brain as the expression of human intelligence, then it is at the point where they converge that a linkup will occur. Both operate on electrical impulses, so they speak a common language. As a consequence, I believe that at some point soon, human intelligence will merge with computers in cyberspace.

"Next question."

"I can see why we would want to merge with machines. They have superior calculating abilities. But why would they want to merge with us? What do we bring to the table?"

"Consciousness. The spark of creative intellect that can drive the calculations and make sense of them by directing them to a higher purpose."

"But exactly how will it happen?"

The old man shook his ponytail. "I'm not a prophet. I'm not a futurist. I don't do *how*. I also don't do *when*. I am talking about the larger forces of history here. It's for others to work out the details."

"And will that be the end of us?"

"The end? Far from it. It will be the beginning. It will be the quantum leap that science and religion promise. The moment of deliverance. Our minds will no longer be bound to our bodies. Perhaps if we can truly shake off our physical vessels, we will achieve an immortality of sorts. The *mysterium tremendum*. Physicists call it escape velocity. Pentacostalists call it the Rapture."

At that, the woman sat down.

Cybedon took a quick look around at the audience, ignored several hands in the air, and stepped away from the lectern. There was no applause, but many of his listeners appeared rapt in thought. Some rushed up to speak to him; he all but disappeared in a tight knot of admirers, save for his ponytail, which bobbed up and down above the group like the mane of a skittish horse.

"What do you think?" asked Quincy.

Cleaver shook his head in amazement. He didn't respond.

"That's what Leo Marx calls 'the rhetoric of the technological sublime.' Want to meet him?"

"Not if it means fighting through that bunch."

Quincy walked over, and as soon as Cybedon caught sight of him, he broke free from the throng and came over with both hands outstretched.

"My boy, my boy," he said several times, grinning. He held Quincy by both shoulders and pulled him into a violent hug, enfolding him into his flab.

Cleaver was surprised. He hadn't expected the man to be so genial.

"Beer?" asked Cybedon.

Cleaver heard the thumping of the dancers above.

"Sure," said Quincy.

He introduced the two. Cleaver felt the dark heat from Cybedon's stare.

"I . . . I liked what you said. How you said it," he said, feeling foolish as soon as the words were out of his mouth.

"You can join us," replied Cybedon.

They went upstairs, Cybedon moving with surprising agility for such a fat man. They negotiated across the dance floor—a path seemed to open up before their Moses—and then walked outside behind the warehouse, where a crowd had gathered. Three young men seated at a card table gave up their chairs. Quincy went off for three beers and was back in a flash. People dispersed in front of the table so that they could see. They were at the edge of a parking lot. Hanging from a lamppost was a gigantic human effigy, the head outsized and misshapen.

"What's that?" asked Cleaver.

"That's the Melting Man," said Quincy. "The raison d'être for the whole festival. It started twelve years ago, when this man here"—he gestured across to Cybedon—"was fired from Microsoft."

"What for?"

"Insubordination," cut in Cybedon. "That, and free thinking."

"And morals," added Quincy.

Halfway through the beers, a murmur of excitement ran through the crowd. A man appeared, holding a small candle, and a humming began that seemed to come from everywhere. Cleaver knew the tune, but it took him a while to identify it from the soundtrack to *Chariots of Fire*: "Jerusalem," the English hymn from the Blake poem that never failed to moisten Albion eyes.

The man with the candle approached the effigy, and the humming grew louder. Cleaver sipped his beer and looked around at the ravers and sci-fi fanatics and technopagans and hackers. How odd they looked, with all kinds of dress, from hippies to bikers to nerds to suits, and all kinds of hairstyles, from dreadlocks to skinheads. The only common denominator was youth. He and Cybedon were practically the only ones over thirty. The realization made him feel like an intruder. Who knew such a tribe existed?

The flame from the candle licked at the left foot of the effigy. It sparked and traveled upward—a fuse. Suddenly, a crack rent the air and a shower of fireworks burst out of the belly, pinwheels and fountains and Roman candles pouring out streams of color amid the *rat-a-tat-tat* of exploding firecrackers. In no time, all that was left was the huge paper head, still grinning as it slowly burned.

The crowd cheered and lifted their glasses.

"I give up," Cleaver whispered to Quincy. "What's the point?"

"The point?" Quincy was engaged in the spectacle and barely paying attention to him. "No point," he said absentmindedly. "Not everything has to have a point."

Cleaver peered around at the New Age revelers and downed his beer. Across from him sat Cybedon, his eyes half-closed, his bulk settled onto the chair like a gelatinous mass, a big sleepy toad.

Strange that the proposition of the mind casting off the body should come from such an unprepossessing person, Cleaver thought. Or maybe, come to think of it, not at all strange.

He felt suddenly emboldened.

"Let me ask you something," he said. "Do you think in everyday life the mind—our consciousness—is inextricably bound up with the body? Or can it lead a separate existence?"

The toad opened both eyes slowly. "And what do you think?" he asked.

"That consciousness can roam, but we just don't know what to call it. Visions, religious ceremonies, dreams, near-death experiences, visitations from the deceased—they're all examples of the same thing: consciousness spilling out of the physical vessel."

"Congratulations," he said, "you've discovered the multiverse."

"The multiverse?"

"Because we spend most of our waking lives in the narrow dimensions of our singular universe, we don't acknowledge all these clues that there are many universes out there, all of them existing side by side. Who knows what they contain? Memories, dreams, every action that was ever taken, every word ever uttered, every person who ever existed, anything and everything that our consciousness has ever experienced, all parallel to each other like hundreds of circuit boards in a computer." He closed his eyes again, then muttered softly, "Many rooms are there in my father's mansion."

A strange biblical metaphor, thought Cleaver. But he was feeling a thrill he could barely suppress, a warm flood of self-satisfaction. Never before had he encountered someone who could put into words everything that he had been thinking, everything that he had been working on, his theories that had now finally reached the ultimate scientific stage of experimentation.

He felt drawn to Cybedon, understood his power. He glanced over at the fat man sipping beer. If Cybedon only knew what he was up to. If he only knew . . .

Cleaver savored the secret thought that someday Cybedon would have reason to look back and remember this meeting, reason to remember meeting *him*.

As Kate was leading Scott toward the special ward, they were called back to the nurses' station and told that he had to sign in.

"But he's the boy's father," she protested.

The nurse, a battle-scarred veteran of hospital wars, stood her ground. Everyone had to sign in—those were the orders, she said, though she had the grace to show a blush of embarrassment.

Kate was furious. It was the bureaucratic mind-set that she had been fighting ever since she went into medicine. But Scott didn't object and signed the log. He still had the look of someone lost in the daze of mourning.

He hadn't expected to find such an elaborate setup. They came to a locked set of glass doors that could be opened only by a coded ID card. Kate kept hers on a chain around her neck, and as she held it over a scanner mounted on the side of the wall, the door clicked. She pulled it open and held it for Scott to go through first.

Then they came to a dead end before an observation window that was thick and ran up a good eight feet, stopping three feet short of the ceiling. Behind it was a hospital bed pitched at a forty-five-degree angle, on which lay a small immobile figure. With a shock, he realized it was Tyler. His son's head was swaddled in so many cloth bandages that his face seemed scrunched into a tiny window in a tower of white. Tubes ran out of his mouth and nose, and his eyes were shut and swollen round with bruises. He scarcely looked human.

"I know how hard it is to see him like this," said Kate softly. "I wish we could get closer, but we can't. He's being kept in a totally sterile environment. That's necessary because the wounds to the skull are still open. That's to gain further access if necessary. The computer is activated, and if an electrode slips we have to quickly reinstall it."

Only then did Scott see a sheath of thin wires, neatly bundled by a plastic tie, rising up from the back of the bandage and fastened to the bedsheet above. It looped around to the wall and then ran to the corner and through the plastic into the back of a desktop computer. With a shudder, he realized that the wires began in his son's brain.

"They carry the computer's signals," Kate continued. "The electrodes may have to be moved from time to time. And Dr. Saramaggio will need to reimplant the stem cells at the final stage. So it makes no sense to subject Tyler to the trauma of a whole new operation."

"But this way, it's like . . . the operation never ends."

"I know it seems that way. But now, for example, he's

resting quietly. He's tranquil. He's in no pain. It's a kind of suspended state. So he's recovering."

"And how do you care for him if you can't touch him?"

"We can."

And just then, as if to prove the point, the door behind them clicked and a nurse joined them. She was carrying a metal container. She unlocked another door, this one to the right and marked MEDICAL PERSONNEL ONLY and entered the small antechamber where the computer was. She reached into a wall cabinet, pulled out a sterilized envelope containing rubber gloves and a mask and put them on. Then she pulled out a syringe, lowered the sheet to Tyler's waist, raised a sleeve of his gown, and quickly jabbed him in the shoulder.

With the sheet down, Scott saw that Tyler was belted to the bed.

"We have to do that, I'm afraid. We can't take the chance that he might move and rip out the electrodes. But he's not aware of it, I'm sure. And we will change his position often so that he won't get bedsores."

"How the hell do you know what he's aware of and what he's not?" retorted Scott. The anger in his voice surprised even him.

By way of answer, Kate rested her hand upon his elbow. The touch was startling to him.

"Of course we don't know, really," she said. "But we have some idea by looking over there."

She pointed to a bank of machines near the bed, and Scott looked at the loathsome battery of monitors with their irrepressible green lines moving across the screens—oxygen level, blood pressure, and the rest. He felt he knew them all by now, knew what the needles and fever lines measured and where they should be if all were normal. They never were.

"I don't know if you noticed," she said, "but that one there"—she pointed at a round window with the jagged lines of pulse racing across it—"sped up when we came in. I think that means that he can hear us. On some level, he's registering our presence."

Scott took hope from her words.

"Tell me which one registers his brain waves," he said. "And what it's supposed to look like."

"This one here," she said, pointing toward a small round screen with a bouncing movement that went across it.

"The spikes should be larger. About twice as large as they are now and more pronounced, sharper. But they will be—someday. I'm convinced of it."

She sounded as if she meant it, and that made him feel a little better. He saw another machine he didn't recognize.

"What does that one indicate?" he asked.

"Brain swelling. That one's important—well, they're all important. But the swelling has to come down if he is to be . . . to have a chance."

"And where should the needle be?"

"About halfway where it is now."

He stared at it. One thin little piece of black metal, hardly larger than a toothpick. He could almost imagine it moving downward if he stared hard enough.

"Look over there," said Kate. "Next to the computer. There's a second bank of monitors. That measures the computer's activity. We've converted the outgoing impulses into signals of body functions. You can compare the two banks of monitors and see that they're in harmony."

The nurse put the syringe back inside the metal container, then opened the side door and gave them a small smile. She stood next to them looking through the window at Tyler.

"We're doing a little better," she said.

We. Scott looked at her with horror. *We.*

Then he felt Kate's hand on his arm again, and he looked away and tried to collect himself. But it was hard. No one knew what he was going through, really. No one could understand, even if they tried, like Kate. And the funny thing was that the more he allowed himself to believe that there was a possibility that Tyler could someday heal, the worse he felt. Because that thought was

followed by the thought that it was only wishful thinking. *Who are you trying to kid?*

He didn't know what to wish for, really. It was all so
incalculable. These doctors knew how to say things,
hopeful things, but what did they know, really? He
couldn't calculate how much hope to let into his heart.
He felt he had already died. Why die a second time?

Chapter 13

Scott knew by heart the inside of his darkroom, tucked away at the rear of the loft, so much so that he literally could have worked there in the dark, without the eerie red glow from the single bulb in the ceiling. He knew where the large plastic bottles of chemicals were and, by their weight, how much of each was left. He knew the exact location of the developing trays, the enlarger, the taps for the faucets and every piece of equipment. He had spent so many hours there, day after day, year after year, that he used to take comfort from the boxlike room, like a phantom prisoner not altogether unhappy with his confinement, laboring away in solitary.

But no longer.

Now, three weeks after the operation, comfort was out of the question. Still, the lab was a sort of refuge. He could lose himself there and, for whole minutes almost, not think much of anything. That deadweight of emptiness was still in his gut, and he lugged it around like a piece of shrapnel, but he could keep it more or less under control, keep it from rising up and exploding in his brain, through the mindless routine of makework.

His stretch in the darkroom had begun two days after the operation, when he had stayed up late drinking scotch at home, wandering aimlessly around the loft, going into Tyler's room and picking up his things—his shirts, his old video games, his soccer trophies, the signed photograph of Sean Connery, the koala bear—then wandering back to the kitchen and pouring another drink. He had fallen asleep in his clothes and awakened in a cold sweat, his heart racing, at dawn.

Then he had remembered something: the undeveloped negatives. He'd leapt out of bed. They were in a series of coffee cans, rolls of film that he had taken as a matter of course on outings around the city or just hanging around, back in the days when he was never without his camera. He had known instinctively when a roll was worth developing; the others he tossed aside the way an artist will discard preliminary sketches. Except that now they were priceless. He hurried to the lab and began developing them. Some were so old they were barely discernible, but still, by highlighting the film, he could make the figures out, ghosts on a membrane. He lived for that moment when the naked white paper floated gently in the bath of developer, and magically dots would form and gradually assemble themselves so that gray shapes would materialize. Then sometimes, the rare pearl in the oyster—the shapes would darken, become recognizable, and then out of nowhere Tyler would gradually appear, coming to life.

Sometimes, Scott remembered instantly where the photo had been taken, in front of the Museum of Natural History on that sunny day in October or on a bench in Central Park that time they'd talked about death for three hours. Other times, he had no recollection at all and he stared at them and lined them up on the kitchen table and thought about them for a long time. Among them was a real prize: three rolls of Tyler taken as studio portraits, full 4-by-5 negatives. He remembered the shoot well; he'd used backlighting and had worn white to reflect in his son's eyes. He had focused the camera perfectly, using Tyler's eyelashes, those long fetching eyelashes. Why had he not developed them? Too busy, no doubt. But now they were a godsend. He enlarged the close-ups to the size of a broadsheet newspaper and tacked them to the walls. How handsome the boy was— *is,* damn it. After two days, he noticed he was running through the rolls too rapidly and he began rationing them, one every other day.

He was not rationing his drinks. He began drinking earlier in the day, and sometimes when he was up until four or five in the morning and dozed for a couple of hours, he took a shot or two to get started. He was smoking so much that his lungs ached. He was doing almost no work. He began turning down jobs; he didn't say why—he couldn't bear to talk about the accident, and the one or two times he did, he hated the saccharine sound of sympathy that crept into people's voices. Soon enough the phone stopped ringing. Kind of remarkable, he thought, how soon that happened. Only a few of his old clients kept calling, three or four photo editors at magazines who themselves had been photographers. He missed deadlines for the first time in his life.

Something else was happening. He was having horrible nightmares. Some of them were constructed around deep-seated fears, as if the entire dream had been choreographed to produce a moment of pure horror. In one he was pursued by hounds across a marsh and fell into a pit that turned into an open grave, where he lay pinned and helpless while dirt and rocks rained down upon him. He awoke on the floor, half under the bed. In another, he felt himself go insane and watched himself as he walked through a house, turning off lights one by one, mounting the stairs to his son's room and seeing him asleep and smothering him with a pillow. In another, his body began to decay, and the blood vessels on his wrist turned into long bloodsucking worms. And there were others—which he tried to repress immediately—about his mother, from the time when she was drinking.

It became hard to separate the nightmares from the drinking. The images of horror were so vivid and stayed with him so long afterward that he wondered if he was having DTs. He noticed sometimes, reaching for a carton of orange juice in the morning or trying to shave, that his hand was shaking, and that scared him greatly. He knew the signs of alcoholism, and he kept discounting them in himself. And then he remembered that that—the denial—was the surest sign of all.

Even Comet, lying in a large ball sleeping most of the day, seemed depressed.

In spite of the drinking and the loneliness and the fears, he never missed a day at the hospital. The nurse would swipe a card to unlock the door to the observation area, and he stayed there for hours on end, pulling up a chair and observing his son. Every so often, rarely but enough to keep him vigilant, he could see Tyler's eyes twitch; during those times he thought his son must be dreaming, and that brought him a sort of solace; if he was dreaming, he might wake up. No? The chest moved slowly but steadily up and down, and the machines never varied. The needle that indicated brain swelling, he thought, had moved down perhaps a little.

He thought he noticed by scrutinizing the monitor of Tyler's heartbeat that it sped up a little when he appeared and when he spoke. So maybe Kate was right—maybe on some level Tyler was still partially conscious. The pulse rate that came out of the computer did not change, however. Its rhythm was invariably, inhumanly, always the same, a perfect pattern of jagged lines marching across the screen.

Then Scott noticed something that puzzled him greatly. Sometimes when Kate would appear, Tyler's heartbeat would accelerate even more. The thumps from the monitor came in rapid-fire staccato. Even more mystifying, this did not happen every time Kate was there, but only sometimes. He pointed it out to her and she, too, was stumped for an explanation.

Partly to humor Scott, a hospital resident set up a speaker system so that he could talk to Tyler, and this he did incessantly. Then he brought a book—*The Adventures of Huckleberry Finn,* of course—and read to him. He was convinced that his son could hear him; even if he couldn't follow the words, he would perhaps recognize his speech patterns, and on the off chance that his son was lonely and having horrible nightmares, too, locked away somewhere at the bottom of a grave, he wanted him at least to hear a familiar, comforting voice.

Sometimes the bed was rotated so that Tyler was suspended upside down, facing the floor and held in place by thick bands that ran across his chin and chest and abdomen and legs. This was to avoid bedsores. But it was even worse seeing him like that—he appeared lost and small in all the paraphernalia surrounding him, a doll-like figure in a machine that looked like a giant gyroscope.

A daily routine was established: the hospital, a coffee shop for half a hamburger or a tuna fish sandwich, then home to walk Comet and spend more time in the darkroom, and finally drinking almost to oblivion late into the night.

One day as he was leaving, he ran into Kate, and she seemed to be looking at him closely. That evening, he examined himself in the bathroom mirror and saw that he looked a mess; his chin was covered with stubble, his eyes were red, and his skin looked flaccid and pale. He shaved, but it did not help.

The next morning, she called. When he heard her voice, he feared that she was calling with bad news about Tyler, but she quickly calmed his fears.

"It's my day off," she said. "If it's not too much to ask, if you're not busy, do you think you could do me a big favor?"

"What?"

"There's an exhibit of photos at the International Center of Photography, and I'd like to see them. But I want to see them with somebody who knows about photography. Would you go with me?"

He paused a long time, long enough to be rude. He didn't want to go. But he couldn't think of how to say that, and so, finally, he said yes. As soon as he hung up, he regretted it. He thought of phoning her back to call it off, but that was too difficult. He put on his jeans and a T-shirt and left.

He found her on Sixth Avenue, waiting for him on the sidewalk, leaning up against a building. He hadn't expected to come upon her just like that, and so he found himself looking at her for the first time. It was odd to see her without her doctor's coat. She was wearing a silk blouse, with a single strand of pearls, and her arms were crossed, casually. She smiled pleasantly when she saw him. The photographer in him noticed that at that moment she would have made a strong subject.

"I was beginning to worry you wouldn't come," she said.

He looked at his watch, confused.

"I'm sorry," he said. "Did it take so long? I left right away, more or less, I think."

"No, no, it's all right. I got here too early. I called you from near here."

He mumbled another apology, but she was already off, turning the corner to the entrance. He noticed that she pulled two tickets from her pants pocket. She stepped aside to let him go in first.

"I've been wanting to see this exhibit. I read about it in the *Times*. Mostly news photos. Three or four of them won a Pulitzer."

The exhibition was called *Up Close*. The first section, titled "The Urban Landscape," was replete with the usual bleak photos of inner-city ghettos, kids playing against a stream of water from a hydrant, and world-weary old folks staring out from the stoops. But every now and then Scott spotted a shot that went against the grain and captured something surprising. He knew many of the photographers, and he could identify most of their work at a glance.

Kate was standing in front of one that showed a group of black teenagers hanging out in front of a candy store, a subway entrance in the background. She seemed absorbed by it.

"I like this one a lot," she said. "Though I'm not even sure why."

He stood next to her.

"The kids, they're smiling, probably at something this one's done." He pointed to a young man who was making a long face. "They're flirting. Just at that age, twelve or thirteen. A rough age. Sex on the brain. There's anxiety in the air despite the smiles. Three guys and two girls—a dangerous combination. The guys are probably figuring one of them's going to be left out."

She nodded and added her own interpretation.

"And each of the girls is worrying that the other one is more attractive," she said. "That one smiles halfheartedly, like she's trying to hide braces."

"And if you look through the store window, you can just make out an old white guy looking at them. He looks amused."

She smiled.

"Now I see why I like it."

"There's a lot going on there, and the camera catches it all," he said. "Looking at it makes you want to make a story up about it."

They moved on, through a section called "Catastrophe" that depicted fires, explosions, floods, and earthquakes. Humans of all sizes, shapes, and colors reached out, peered out, were carried out of flattened houses, mounds of rubble, charred timbers. After a while, so much suffering was numbing.

"This is a lot to take all at once," Kate said. "I guess you photographers get to see the seamy side of life."

"Some do. News photographers, mostly."

He started thinking of the photojournalists he had known, the seedy-looking ones who listened to the police band radio and raced out after the big calls, the high-flying international types who worked for Magnum and Sygma and jumped on airplanes to get to places that other people were desperately fleeing from. Most were burnt out. Some had been killed. None of those who survived seemed like whole human beings.

"They're not what you would call a happy lot."

As if by design, they came to the next section, titled "The Scourge of War," a mix of shots from Afghanistan and Kosovo and Chechnya and the Congo and West Africa. One after another, the corpses piled up. Kate was horrified in particular by three photographs from Sierra Leone, young boys who had been captured by rebels and had had their hands severed by machetes, lying back on dirty hospital linen and holding stumps into the air. She shuddered and shook her head slowly to herself and then fell silent. Scott tried to hurry her through, but she lingered and forced herself to look at every picture.

"It's enough to make you despair for the human race," was all she said.

They came with relief to the next section, "People and Portraits," a hodgepodge of shots of Americans at work and play. Boys skateboarding, construction workers on lunch break, models on the catwalk, families picnicking and river rafting—it was all there.

Then she gave a short gasp. She was standing in front of an arresting photo. It showed four men with their sleeves rolled up, tilting back in wooden chairs that rested against a brick wall. Above them, sticking out of the wall, were large lightbulbs in different colors, blue and green and red, and nearby a man with his jacket hanging over his shoulder by one finger was talking to two policemen. It was eveningtime and hot. The men on the chairs were sweating and looking bored, but ready to jump into action. The picture had a strange mystery to it.

Scott almost did not recognize it at first.

"That's yours," she said in amazement. She had been reading the wall label. "It's called 'The Police Shack.' What's that?"

And so he explained. He told her about the old building on Mulberry Street where years ago reporters from the major papers all had grubby offices, each with only one piece of furniture, an old desk. Police radios were constantly blaring, and in the hallway an old bell would clang in code from time to time, signaling the call box for a fire. On hot nights, the reporters would sit outside and shoot the breeze with the cops. When the home office rang, a colored lightbulb outside would tell them which paper was calling.

"It always struck me like a hospital emergency room, long stretches of boredom and intermittent times of

panic. I liked that weird sense about the place—of utter
lassitude that could break out into frenzy at any moment. That's what I was going for."

"Well," she said. "You got it."

He could see the respect in her eyes when she looked
at him.

In the next room was a photo that he wished was not
there. As soon as they walked in, it seemed to reach across
the room and grab him. He tried to avoid it, but he was
drawn to it. It showed a man and a boy sitting on a dock
in summertime, their legs dangling into the water and
sending out ripples. The man was speaking—he looked as
if he was explaining something, maybe communicating
some important fact about the world or maybe just telling
a story—and the boy was taking it in. His face was rapt in
seriousness. This was clearly an important talk. And the
father—for it was clear that the man was the boy's father—was just as clearly investing himself in the talk. He
seemed deeply serious and somehow deeply contented.

Scott walked over to the picture and stood before it,
transfixed. He was there quite a while, and he lost track
of time until he felt a gentle pressure on his elbow. Without words, she guided him away.

They went outside and walked for a few minutes
without saying anything. Then they came to a coffee
shop and went in and sat down at a booth. They signaled
to the waitress, who brought them two cups.

"You know, I'm not good at talking about my feelings," he said. "And sometimes, a lot of the time, I don't
even know what I'm feeling. It's so intense it doesn't
have a name."

She nodded.

"I'd like to say what I'm feeling about what's happened. Anything I can say—that my whole world is
shattered, that there's this great void, that life isn't
worth living—it all sounds trite. It's a cliché. And yet it's
true. I feel all of it and even more. Things I can't come
close to expressing."

Now she leaned across the table and rested her hand
on his wrist.

"The only thing I know is that I have to be with him. And whatever happens, if there is even a little shred of him left, I want it to live. I want him to live. But if he's gone—if he's truly gone—then maybe he should go. I don't know. He was so wonderful, so alive . . . so—this sounds ridiculous, to pick up on this one thing, but—he was so *funny*. He was such a *presence,* even as a little kid. He used to sing around the house, all the time, different voices, corny little songs, making believe he's a rock star or a blues singer. He was always one for games, for fun, all kinds of projects. He threw himself into them. I don't even know where the ideas came from. Like once he made a video tour of our loft, acting like he was one of those stupid announcers with a deep voice. It was wonderful, so funny.

"People loved him on the spot. He had all these contacts, these relationships—I couldn't keep up with them. I'd go into the deli and it turned out he and the counterman had been pitching nickels. The counter guy joked that Tyler owed him a lot of money, so one day he came in with a suitcase with a whole bunch of fake money in it. He put it on the counter and flipped it open dramatically. The whole place just cracked up. We'd walk down our block and people would wave to him.

"He was one of those truly special ones—you know it when you meet them. People would just see him, his smile—it spread across his whole face—and they would just fall for him. People would meet him once and ask about him every time afterward. He was like that. So smart, so friendly, so open. So . . . so much his own person, really different . . . really special. I just don't know . . ."

She held his hand now and squeezed it, and he began to cry. The tears felt good, so he just let them come, not even wiping them off his cheeks.

He realized that, for the first time, he was talking about Tyler in the past tense. Did he think about him in the past tense?

The waitress approached with a pot of coffee, then looked at them and retreated.

Kate smiled at her, and Scott was grateful for it. He took a deep breath, and she softly moved her hand away.

"I want to say it's good for you to get it out," she said. "But, I feel foolish saying that—I mean, speaking of trite—"

"No, it *is* good. Except that it doesn't really get out. But for the moment—right this second—it's good."

He finished his coffee, and now the waitress refilled their cups.

"And you know, when I was looking at that picture—yes, of course, it was painful. But somewhere, on some level, it felt at least like I was connected to something outside myself. Fatherhood or something . . . universal. It wasn't all a bad feeling."

"No, you *are* still connected."

He paused and looked at her, then said, "I've got to stop drinking. I've got to pull myself together."

Saying this, out of nowhere, surprised him. He felt suddenly embarrassed.

But she said only one word.

"Yes."

"You know, I'm not always this self-absorbed. I mean before all this happened, I didn't use to just talk about myself."

"I'm sure," she said—and she was.

A few minutes later, as they were leaving the coffee shop, he held the door for her and she brushed past him. He suddenly got a whiff of something so strong, so unlooked-for, so deeply familiar, that he felt dizzy.

"Your perfume," he said suddenly. "I recognize it."

"It's *Je m'en souviens* by Lanvin."

He halted, uncertain.

"My wife used to wear it. The very same one."

She smiled. He looked pained. Then abruptly, she cried out.

"My God," she said. "Do you think—is it possible?"

"What?"

"Do you think that could be why Tyler has such a strong reaction when I come into his room?"

He stood there openmouthed.

She didn't say the rest of the thought out loud, because she knew it would upset him. The rest of the thought was this: It would be logical for smells to register with Tyler, because the sense of smell was the only one that is hardwired into the lower part of the brain, the only part still functioning on its own.

Chapter 14

All morning, Cleaver had busied himself with make-work at Pinegrove, filling out grant forms, checking pharmaceutical supplies, and making rounds of the patients—though this latter duty consisted of little more than strolling through the ward where pairs of darting eyes regarded him with suspicion and fear. Leaving the ward behind, he walked down the main corridor, his steps echoing with buoyancy. Once again he experienced a surge of boyish excitement. He relished the sensation even more by suppressing it. It was delicious—like a spy's secret.

He had phoned Quincy so often that he had rattled the young man, who'd turned off his cell phone.

"For Christ's sake," Quincy had screamed during their last call, "it'll get there when it gets there. Now piss off." Then he had hung up.

Cleaver decided he couldn't get angry at him—not under the circumstances.

That afternoon—finally—Quincy was to deliver the TSR.

At three o'clock, the movers came. Cleaver, running down the back stairs to the loading dock, suppressed a pang of annoyance at seeing a large U-Haul truck and a ratty old Chevrolet. Four young Hispanic men got out, the driver hitching up his belt, and one of the olive-skinned passengers tugging down his T-shirt at the waist to emphasize the bulge of his muscles. To Cleaver, they had the look of illegal aliens. A third lit a cigarette and exhaled smoke in a thin slow stream.

This was not what he'd expected—hardly the harbingers of the grand occasion he had been anticipating.

But one glance at Quincy, who stepped down from the U-Haul cab with a six-pack under his arm, told him to tread lightly. Quincy was smoldering. And he looked a little unsteady on his feet. Had he been drinking already?

"I figured you didn't want anyone to see us unloading it," he said pugnaciously.

"No problem. It doesn't matter. This is all aboveboard."

"Like hell it is." He walked to the back of the truck. "You mean to tell me you account for all this shit?"

"To the letter," Cleaver lied.

Quincy climbed up to the loading dock and lay down, leaving Cleaver to direct the workers in his fractional Spanish that made them laugh. He fussed about like a mother hen, pointing the way, probing the padding under the crates, making sure that the machine wasn't bruised in the freight elevators that carried it to the special room in the basement. At one point, exiting from the elevator, they crashed into the wall, smashing a hole and setting off a mini-avalanche of plaster. But the machine itself was unhurt.

The room had been worked on for weeks, and now it was ready, soundproofed, well lit, painted, fed by high-gauge electrical cables, and cleaned spotless. Once inside, the workers attacked the crates with claw hammers. Cleaver had them take away the wood and the padding. Then he directed them in placing the machine where he wanted it along one wall, standing back for the full effect, indicating an inch or two to one side or the other with an extended forefinger.

He couldn't wait for the movers to leave, and when they finally did and he was alone, he walked around the room surveying the machine from every angle. He ran his fingers along the sleek outer cylinder. He moved the sliding stretcher back and forth and held the tight-fitting helmet with its two eye receptacles that looked like eggcups. The idea of fitting them underneath the

eyelids to send messages directly into the brain gave
him a tiny shudder of anxiety.

Quincy appeared in the doorway, sauntered over to a
chair, and sat there, swigging from a beer bottle, turning
it upside down and pouring it down his gullet with a
kind of fury. His acne was erupting in half a dozen tiny
white-tipped volcanoes.

"This is gonna cost you a pretty fucking penny," he re-
marked, wiping his chin. "You're going to subsidize my
whole fucking commune for a long time to come."

Cleaver was bothered by him, everything about him.
And imagine talking about money at a time like this.

"Don't you worry your pretty little head. I'll pay what
we agreed upon. And maybe more if I decide to give
you a service contract."

Quincy scoffed at the idea and tossed the empty bottle toward a wastebasket. He missed.

Cleaver retrieved the bottle and delicately placed it
inside, standing up. He rose and looked again at the
transcranial stimulator-receiver. Quincy had built two,
which was good. A scientist demands backup. Important
things always came in twos. Fat Man and Little Boy.

"Let me ask you something," he blurted out suddenly.
"Why did you leave the other one in your lab? What are
you planning to do with it?"

Quincy grinned unpleasantly.

"A spare. I need it to make improvements. And especially if I'm going to be on a service contract."

Cleaver couldn't tell if he was being sarcastic or not.

"Let's get started. Show me how to run this thing."

"You're going to need an assistant."

"I have one. A young man. Felix. Not the brightest
bulb in the place, but he'll do."

He buzzed for Felix on the intercom.

"You'll need something else," Quincy observed, detached now, almost philosophical.

"What?"

"Someone to put inside it. And . . . how can I put this?
Someone who might not be missed if things go wrong.
Someone *expendable*."

Cleaver permitted himself a false hearty laugh. "No problem there," he said. "I've got a whole ward full of candidates."

"And are they ready to sacrifice themselves for the great god Science? Have you asked them that?"

"They've all signed waivers, if that's what you mean."

"Hmmm. Informed consent, was it? From nutcases."

At that moment, Felix appeared in the door and, standing next to him, under his outstretched arm, was another man, a patient, to judge from the faded seersucker bathrobe that hung from his shoulders. Quincy looked at him—a mousy-looking man in his fifties with eyes that seemed to bounce around the room, taking everything in. He had red marks around his eyes as if he had been wearing goggles.

"Ah, and here's one now. How convenient."

"Come in," said Cleaver, sounding like a genial dinner party host.

Felix gave the man a little push, and he stepped forward uncertainly.

"Meet Quincy. Quincy, this is Herbert Mann. He's been with us for some time now—what is it? Must be fifteen years or so. Herbert's a little disoriented. He feels people are out to get him. But we're not—are we?"

Quincy stood up, but not to shake hands. Instead, he walked out of the room.

"Don't be afraid," said Cleaver. "Nothing's going to happen. I just want you to become familiar with this room. Today, it's simply orientation. Like the first day of school."

He led Herbert over to one of the machines.

"Now, why don't you try this? Just lie down. Right here. I want you to get used to this machine. It's going to help you. See how this stretcher slides back and forth? And it moves right into that big metal thing. See? Nothing to be frightened of. It'll make you much better."

He was tempted to try the machine on the spot, but he resisted. Things weren't ready, and the experimental protocols weren't in place. He told Felix to take the patient back to the ward.

Quincy returned with another beer and provided rudimentary instructions to run the TSR, but his heart wasn't in it. Besides, the machine was so simple and revolutionary that it was actually easy to operate.

"There's really only one thing to remember," Quincy said. "That's the time limit. Seven minutes and not a second more. After that the whole system crashes."

"And then?"

"Who the fuck knows."

As he left, he glanced at Cleaver over his shoulder.

"Don't forget—Deep Blue starts ordering caviar," he added.

That night, Cleaver slept at Pinegrove, in a little bedroom attached to his office. He often stayed over if his work—his experiments—kept him past midnight, when the tramway cars to Roosevelt Island ran few and far between.

But he had trouble sleeping soundly. He fell off quickly enough, but it didn't last, and when he awoke two hours later, his heart was racing and he was sweating heavily. He listened to the wind outside, rattling the panes. Two trees rubbed their trunks, an unearthly creaking sound. He knew what was upsetting him—he was having a dream, a nightmare. Ever since his research on anima, on consciousness roaming outside the body during REM sleep, he was apprehensive about his own dreams. They no longer seemed harmless, and their incoherence no longer seemed insignificant. To the contrary, they seemed dangerous and freighted with dead-on meaning.

And this dream was more dangerous than most because it was about someone from his past, the dark shadow so close to him. Cleaver's father had been a respected Methodist minister in their tiny New Hampshire town. He loved his only child, or so he sometimes said, but his calling kept his preoccupations heavenward. He was a stern disciplinarian; whenever anger seized his features, turning the blood vessels in his temples crimson, the boy knew what to expect—the belt whipping through the loops of his father's baggy black pants, soon to land across his back. Cleaver's mother—God rest her soul—was a quiet woman with long, graying hair who wore simple print smocks and was reluctant to step into the fray. She never opposed her husband, never raised her voice.

At the raucous public school, Cleaver was shy and always without playmates. He stayed indoors at recess and played with miniature cars and trucks, humming in harmony with their movements as he propelled them along tabletops and molding. He began stealing items at the hardware store: switches, circuit breakers, timers, magnetic coils, anything that looked mechanical. He kept them in a box under his bed and carried them one by one in his pockets to school. He played with them for hours on end, arranging them in artful patterns. He took apart clocks and wired the alarms to his door to keep intruders out, although his father and mother had not set foot inside for years. By the fifth grade, his teachers called the parents in to tell them that their son was brilliant, that he scored unimaginable grades on any test put before him. The father was proud, as was his mother, but by then the relationship between man and boy had taken a bad turn. Chess games that had been fun were transformed into subtle battlegrounds, and now Cleaver always won. When he beat his father and looked into his eyes, he knew that the victory was costly.

He was caught shoplifting, and his father beat him and locked him in a closet and threw away all of his machines. They sent him away to school, his mother weeping when he left. There, a chilly little New England religious school, the other boys picked on him while the math and physics teachers doted on him. He developed skin rashes and then boils and eczema, and it became so serious that he was sent home. He knew from the look his father gave him and the silence across the dinner table that first evening that he had failed, that he was an excrescence, a soul lost beyond redemption. He began rocking, thumped his head upon the pillow at night to sleep, and finally found salvation through computers.

He spent endless hours at the keyboard, took the computers apart, built his own. His submission to the high school science fair on algorithmic complexity was turned away; no one could understand it. He graduated from high school two years early and went to MIT, staying in a small six-bedroom house on a leafy street that was set aside for brilliant but maladjusted students. Not once did he date a girl, though he began fantasizing about a thin young woman with stringy hair in his computer linguistics class. She worked in the experimental psych lab, and so he spent time there and developed an interest in the subject.

In a stab to become well-rounded, he took courses in philosophy and one in the Romantic poets: Keats, Shelley, Byron—he liked Wordsworth the most, for his improbable, old-fashioned sensibility. One day, he had an epiphany: The center of the universe lay in the human brain. He would learn its architecture. He began on rats, then cats, and finally monkeys. *"We murder in order to dissect."*

When his father died, when he got that late-night phone call in winter from his mother, sounding strangely calm as she relayed the news, he looked out the window at the ice on the tree branches. He walked out into the falling snow and promptly blacked out. He left college then, with eight months to go in his senior year. But it didn't really matter—the graduate schools were all after him and willing to overlook the truancy.

Cleaver's palms were still sweaty. He couldn't believe how heavily his heart was pounding. Had he really seen his father in his dream only a few minutes ago, the long, slender fingers undoing the belt? He wished he could pan the vision off as a mechanistic neural phenomenon, some random sequence of firing synapses, but he no longer believed in that. He saw his father because somewhere, on some level, his father *still existed*.

All of his work, his research, his formulations, his instinct, conspired to convince him of that.

Cleaver put on an old terry-cloth dressing gown and slippers and decided to go to the half-refrigerator in his office and have a glass of milk. The cold liquid spread across the back of his throat—it tasted good. He wished, for the first time in years, that he could have some chocolate chip cookies with it.

He felt oddly frightened at the prospect of returning to his tiny bedroom, so he walked the dimly lit corridor, past the attendant's station. He looked in and saw the night duty man asleep, his shoulders in a heap and his face pressed out of shape like a rubber mask on the surface of a desk. It was quiet. The ward was dark.

On an impulse, he went into Room 35 and there was Benchloss, strapped down, awake as he knew he would be. He was looking up at the ceiling, and his eyes were wide open—two wide whirlpools of panic surrounded by dark circles. Poor Benchloss, suffering from the most bizarre syndrome of all, Cotard's syndrome.

Cleaver decided to talk to him. He walked in.

"Benchloss, my poor friend. Still awake, I see."

Benchloss could not, of course, respond, because in the deepest recesses of his mind he believed himself to be dead. And dead people could hardly talk, now, could they?

Cleaver stared at him. His skin was covered with jagged red rivulets of scars where he had gouged himself picking off the larvae and worms visible only to his own cracked mind. He looked closely at the eyes. Were they moistening up a little? Was it emotion—fear or dread, forever entombed in there? Or did he in fact feel absolutely nothing? Had he achieved a nirvana of affectless tranquility? Cleaver felt his heart soften, uncharacteristically.

"I wish I could do something for you," he suddenly blurted out.

He reached over to touch Benchloss, something he had never done before, his fingers coming to rest lightly upon the man's forearm. The skin in fact felt cold. The patient gave no perceptible reaction. How could a dead man possibly react?

Then Cleaver once again felt the odd feeling of eyes staring at him from behind. Could it be? *My father!* He turned around—not too quickly, in case his fears would prove out, but calmly and slowly as he had trained himself to do. No one there, just the dim light shining from overhead, a chair, a wastebasket on the floor. Or was that a flicker of movement through the window on the door?

He quickly went outside. Nothing in the corridor; it was empty, though it was possible that there was a sound from the stairwell, a door closing just ever so much or maybe hurried footfalls on the stairs. He went to investigate, down a flight, all the way to the basement. Was that his own shadow moving against the wall down there or the rippling back of a preacher's black coat?

The special lab was straight ahead. He hesitated before the door, certain somehow that the specter he was chasing had taken up station on the other side. He felt the doorknob, turned it slowly to one side, pushed gently. His hand glided inside along the wall, found the light switch, and flicked it downward. Instantly, the room exploded in a whiteness that seared his eyes. He blinked them furiously, trying to accustom them to the light.

He looked around—quickly.

Everywhere, up and down, back and forth. The computer, the machine, the cylinder. Then the shape caught his eye, the anomaly of it, the black figure within the pristine sterile alabaster whiteness of the transcranial stimulator-receiver. Cleaver's body registered the sight first, an alarm deep within the amygdala that spread outward through the limbic system like cracks in glass. The smell of fear in the air.

Then, just as abruptly, his brain processed it all, put it together, and the fear disappeared like a puff of smoke. Nothing to be afraid of. Not a specter, not his father. He saw who it was. Herbert Mann. The patient, the paranoid.

He was lying down on the stretcher, ready to slide into the cigar tube headfirst, a funny look on his face, a smile playing upon his lips, trying to please.

Cleaver almost burst out laughing.

Chapter 15

As Kate dressed in her apartment—she was becoming a New Yorker and no longer lowered the window shades in modesty—she found herself thinking of Scott. He popped into her mind at the oddest times, a snapshot of him here, a snatch of his voice there. It was hard for her to say why this should be—she certainly wasn't infatuated with him, though she could see how, in other circumstances, he could be attractive. The reason for it, she was convinced, was pity, and pity, she had been told, was not a good foundation for a relationship. But still, it was hard to say where her natural empathy for his horrible situation ended and other feelings began. The whole story was so dreadful. Who wouldn't be thinking about it a lot?

And lately she had begun to worry about Tyler's prognosis. It had been almost three weeks now since the operation, and he hadn't moved so much as a finger. She knew in her rational mind not to expect change—and an unchanged status was in fact what was to be hoped for while his stem cells were being cultivated in the lab. But she had seen patients in deep comas more reactive than him, and the more time passed, the more radical Saramaggio's treatment appeared. Scott's words still resonated in her memory: It *was* beginning to seem like a single *endless* operation.

Her doubts about medicine had been growing on a number of issues lately. All those contradictions born of so-called modern-medical miracles. Yes, a premature baby barely twenty-four weeks old could be saved by all that fancy incubation equipment, but would he live a healthy life? Yes, an old man on the threshold of death could be kept alive on a ventilator, but was that living? Maybe things had been in some ways better in the not-so-distant days when the cycles of life played out like the natural rhythms of the seasons and we bowed down in our communal helplessness before the Grim Reaper. At least they were more human—whatever that meant. Black and white: You knew when to give merciful thanks on bended knee and when to beat your breast in grief.

She attached her bra in front, shifted it around, put her arms through the straps, and pulled a light knit sweater over her head. She knew her thinking was heresy. Doctors, never mind surgeons, were not supposed to ruminate this way. But her mother had always encouraged a bit of heresy—*going against the grain,* she had put it with a widow's pride. Without it, we'd all still belong to England, she used to say.

That was another thing. Kate was thinking more and more about her mother these days. Why is it, she wondered, that when you are deeply touched in one area, your emotions fan out to other areas; they're like ripples across a pond when a stone is dropped in—nothing on the shoreline remains untouched. Maybe it was because she felt she had never completed mourning; the wasting away from cancer had been so prolonged and the image of her mother as helpless and emaciated had blocked out all the happy memories. There had even been a certain relief when she was finally gone, which had pulled Kate away from the natural inclination to weep a daughter's tears. And then Kate had kept her grief inside because her mother's dictum against self-pity resounded in her ears: We Willet women don't feel sorry for ourselves; we get on with life.

But there was more to the story than that, and Kate knew that sooner or later she would have to deal with it. The guilt that crept in around the edges because she felt she had abandoned her mother in her hour of need was becoming too strong to ignore.

She went to the kitchen and poured herself another

cup of coffee and read the newspaper and then sat at
the dressing table (thirty dollars from the Salvation
Army) brushing her long honey-blond hair. She looked
in the mirror, and her sky-blue eyes stared back. She examined her skin, still pure, without blemish. Must be
those tough genes forged back in Greenland, the generations raised among the sharp rocks and sea spray.
Those were her good features. Then she looked at her
nose, held it in profile, tilted it upward. Not so good.
Crooked to one side, a bit too long. She cocked her head
again. The ears seemed too large—at least she could
cover them with hair. Some wrinkles developing around
the eyes, across the forehead. Thirty-four years old.
How many years were left to her to remain single? Was
she becoming too much of a careerist to think of marriage and family? She had always thought she would be
a good mother. She had wanted to have children, lots of
them—the dream of an only child raised by a single
parent.

She shook her head, a rebuke. Time to end idle daydreaming.

She stood up, straightened her skirt, and made the
bed, and as she placed the coverlet over the pillow she
noticed that the double mattress had developed a life-
sized indentation on the left side where she habitually
slept. She made a mental note to try to switch to the
right.

Kate had never been to Rockefeller University, tucked
away on the eastern edge of Manhattan along the bus-
tle of York Avenue. She entered the gate and followed
the path beside the main drive. Cool green lawns under
a canopy of oaks, and ivy climbing brick walls. Ahead,
up an incline, was a massive building set on a hill, a temple to the gods of science.

Inside, at the receptionist's desk, she gave the guard
the name of the man she had come to see—Ira Rosenfield. He was a legend in neurology and neurosurgery,

forty-five years in the operating room, now retired. He was close to her mentor, A. B. Reinhardt, the professor of abnormal psychology who had set her on her path and from time to time guided her career by remote control, largely through his extensive network of professional buddies.

Rosenfield received her graciously in his third-floor office, a cramped room whose walls were covered with teeming bookcases from floor to ceiling. On his desk, stacks of reprints and articles were crowding a leather desk set on which he had been writing a letter, she noted, in fountain pen ink.

He fussed over her and offered her chamomile tea and brewed the water in an electric pot. His smallish pink eyes crinkled in delight. The two exchanged pleasantries, mostly about Reinhardt, whose puckish sense of humor tended to come out in practical jokes that were famous on both coasts. He cackled at the recollection.

"And what brings you to see me?" he asked finally. "You mentioned something about St. Catherine's and Saramaggio."

She thought she caught a tone of disapproval in the very mention of the name, but maybe she was imagining it.

She told him the story of Tyler and Scott from beginning to end, congratulating herself for the detached tone in which she delivered it.

"And so . . ." he said finally.

She stammered and blushed slightly.

"I just wondered what you thought of it—of the whole thing, the operation, the chances of success."

"Ah, that, well—it's hard to say. I don't know the facts of the case . . . the state of the research."

Rosenfield blew on his tea, took a noisy sip, and settled back in his chair with his hands behind his head, looking up at the ceiling. It was not a flattering posture—folds of skin hung from under his chin like turkey wattles.

He was quiet a long time, thinking it through. Then he looked her square in the eyes. She realized he was taking her measure, wondering whether he should be totally honest. He came to a decision.

"Let me declare at the outset—I put great stake in medical progress. Who among us does not? But I more than most. I'm a believer in the pioneer spirit. I was present at one of the very first liver transplants. And it was wonderful to witness, not for the patient—in fact, the patient was miserable; it was a long and painful recovery, and it was never complete. It was wonderful for the operation itself, the sheer marvel of the doing of it. Because it was one of the first. You knew that it was the precursor of many such operations to come. You knew that with time they would be refined, that surgeons would improve the technique, that new drugs would come along to fight rejection and make things more bearable for the patient. You felt history breathing over your shoulder. You knew that an advance was being made, right then and there, the way an army fighting on its belly for territory inch by inch knows it's moving ahead when it sees the flag planted forward. It was an advance because it was the right time for an advance."

He leaned forward, took a sip of tea, replaced the cup on an envelope used for a coaster.

"Like everyone I know, every doctor, I'm a proponent of gene therapy. We will use it to eliminate diseases, hereditary diseases of all kinds. We will wipe them off the face of the earth. I believe in stem cell research. I think stem cells hold incredible potential for repairing and replacing damaged organs and body tissue. In three to five years, we'll be in clinical trials for all kinds of diseases, strokes, spinal cord injuries, Parkinson's, heart disease—you name it. Everything but cancer. And someday we'll get there, too.

"But the advances have to come at the right time. Move too soon and you threaten the whole endeavor. Every general knows that—keep your battalion grouped and don't move too far ahead of your supply lines. Or you risk defeat.

"All this publicity about stem cells has raised a lot of expectations. They're running way ahead of us. The potential is light-years ahead of the research. We can dream about these things, but we can't do them yet. Christopher Reeve will not walk again anytime soon. And people will still be getting Alzheimer's and slowly losing their minds."

He stopped and stared at his teacup, then continued.

"You know, I do a fair number of lecture tours, and I talk a lot about stem cells. And you know what question I'm asked a lot?"

She shook her head.

"Afterward, a man will come up to the lectern, sometimes more than one, and he'll hem and haw a bit and then come out with it—he'll ask me if I can use stem cells to build him a bigger penis. And sometimes it's a woman—she wants one." A small sigh. "That's what the public is thinking about all our great advances. That, and are we killing babies to get the cadaveric fetal tissue."

"So you think it's too soon? You don't think Saramaggio has much chance of success?"

"I didn't say that. I'm loath to criticize a fellow surgeon, especially one as renowned as he is. But rebuilding a brain! The arrogance of it! We can't build a new liver or a kidney or a heart yet—much less a brain. I mean do you know how many neurons we're talking about?" He looked at her and halted, flustered. "I'm sorry, of course you do." He stood up to cover his embarrassment, began pacing around. He was smaller than she expected.

"Well, as I tell my patients, if you're talking about the entire nervous system of a single human being, you're in the neighborhood of four trillion neurons. Do you realize that that's approximately the same number of stars in the sky?"

She looked at him, skeptical.

"Well, maybe not exactly. No one knows how many stars there are. But it makes my point, and my patients get the idea. A human being is as complicated as the entire universe. Every neuron is connected to approximately one hundred other neurons. Those long pathways, all the way down the spinal cord, they're formed in the embryo. If a neuron doesn't connect with the right neuron, it dies away, and they keep dying until finally the proper connection is made and two of them survive. They're a micromillimeter apart, then they grow—they elongate with brain expansion. As the infant grows, they grow, too. How can you achieve that with a thirteen-year-old boy? He's almost full-grown. His brain is all laid out. As you well know, it's the pattern of connectivity that counts. All those connections zapping around the cortex, they give us memories, make our personalities, make us fall in love—they're *learned*. They're pathways formed over time, by habit. Why does one neuron connect with a second neuron and not the ninety-nine others? Habit, that's all. It happened last time, so it's likely to happen again. The same synapse fired before, so it'll probably fire again. It's a pathway in the literal sense, worn through use, just like a dirt path across your lawn. So what happens? You get ten thousand of those neurons firing as they did last time and you can lift your spoon. You get hundreds of millions of them, billions of them, following some kind of crazy pattern, and you get a complete human being. It's as simple as that—and as complicated.

"So tell me, even if Saramaggio is somehow able to replant all those baby neurons, how in God's name is he going to replicate the connections?"

"A computer. He's got a lot of the brain activity simulated by a computer."

"And how about the part of the brain that was damaged? How can the computer simulate that? Do you think that if a real person emerges at the end of all this, there is the remotest chance that he will resemble the boy he was—in any way?"

Kate looked down. Rosenfield saw this out of the corner of his eye, but continued to press home the point.

"And what if something goes wrong? Have you thought about that? Tell me, do you have that much confidence in computers? Would you want to trust your life to one?"

She shifted her position uncomfortably, but he didn't let up.

"You know what your Saramaggio is trying to do?"

She was tempted to say that Saramaggio was not *hers*, but held herself back.

"Nothing short of trying to reconstruct the entire universe. He's trying to string the stars in the heavens."

Rosenfield went back to his desk and sat down. He picked up his tea, and the envelope stuck to the bottom of the cup and traveled up to his chest. But he didn't notice, so intent was he upon Kate. He put it down again without drinking.

"Now I didn't mean to harangue you," he said. "As you can tell, I feel rather strongly about this whole thing. We have real guinea pigs, you know; we don't need to use humans. I knew Christiaan Barnard. I knew them all. The first one who operated inside the heart by touch—he lost his first four patients. The first to use a heart-lung machine—he had one success, then lost the next four and never did another heart operation. For heart transplants, the early mortality was incredible. Of the first two hundred or so, one hundred twenty died within months. About twenty lived for one year. Out of two hundred! And that was the heart! A muscle with four chambers and a bunch of valves. The kind of thing Saramaggio is attempting—how many will it take until there's a halfway decent chance of success? A thousand, maybe more."

Kate sat up, nodded.

"Well," she said. "I'm glad I came. I wanted to hear what you think, and you certainly told me."

He chuckled, now suddenly avuncular.

"I do get carried away," he said softly. "The prerogative of old age. I'm sorry—lecture over." He gestured down at his pen and inkwell. "I'm very old-fashioned. I don't even use a computer to write a letter."

He bounded up again.

"Come—let me show you around."

He escorted her through a rabbit's warren of offices and laboratories and libraries. In an adjacent building, they passed a large room with swinging doors that had small diamond-shaped windows. She glanced through one and saw a large oval-shaped table surrounded by a dozen or so wooden chairs, all occupied. On a podium up front, a man stood before a blackboard.

"Stuart Kauffman," said Rosenfield. "Complexity theory. Theoretical biology. Good stuff. You should hear him sometime."

"What's he speaking on now?"

"Today? I think it's what he calls the concept of the adjacent possible."

"What's that?"

"Let's see: How does he state it? Ah, yes. For any set of objects or states, the adjacent possible is the set of all objects or states that do not yet exist, but are just one simple combination away from coming into existence. In other words: Watch out—you never know what's likely to happen."

"Like our neurons. One hundred of them lying next to the one that wants to fire."

"Sort of," he replied politely. "It's easier to think of chemical reactions—how one chemical compound can abruptly catalyze into another. Or the cup of tea I just made—how the water got hotter and hotter until suddenly it changed altogether and began to boil. If you didn't know anything about water, would you have predicted that? Large bubbles suddenly jumping all over the place."

They came to the ground floor.

"But Kauffman applies the theory to any complex system—economies, societies, and of course organisms. It's intuitively obvious, but he's looking to formalize it so that it will shed light on the history and dynamics of evolution."

"Evolution?"

"Yes. On ancient earth there were simple molecules—ammonia, methane, and so on—and now 4.5 billion years later, we've got ten to one hundred trillion kinds of organic molecules, ranging from simple enzymes to gigantic complex proteins and DNA chains. How did this incredible diversity happen? Life creates it, steadily expanding into the adjacent possible. And every time it ratchets up its complexity a little, the range of opportunity for further expansion increases. Imagine a Rube Goldberg tower rising up, getting more complicated the higher it goes."

He pushed through the front door, still talking, and they found themselves on the front stoop of the building she had entered forty minutes earlier.

"Basically, Kauffman speculates that life is persistently drawn, as though by some inexorable force, into the next stage—into its adjacent possible."

"And no one can predict the next stage?"

"No, no one. Not even a computer. Unless maybe the computer's the next stage, and in that case it'll probably keep it a secret," he said with a chuckle.

They shook hands in the sunlight, and he cupped hers with both of his and held on to it for some time.

"I think," he said slowly, "you're troubled by this whole business with Saramaggio. I think you came to me because you wanted to hear the answer I gave you, and now that I've given it to you and put it into words, you will have to decide what you are going to do."

She nodded, partly to return his earlier politeness, partly because what he said had struck a chord.

He's right, she thought, as she descended the stairs, too preoccupied to turn and wave. *I am troubled.*

Her pace picked up as she walked down the incline of the pavement.

Expansion into the adjacent possible.

She couldn't say why, but she didn't like the sound of that.

Kate came in to work early the following Monday because St. Cat's had organized a private symposium on Saramaggio's operation for a select group of neuro-anatomists, neurobiologists, and neurosurgeons. She had received notice of it only the Friday afternoon before. Word of the remarkable operation was already beginning to make the rounds, a memo explained, and so it was best to confront the talk head-on and explain just what had been done and how well the patient was doing so far. All of it, of course, off the record—until such time as the *New England Journal of Medicine* would carry Saramaggio's own account.

As she joined the others in the small auditorium on the fifteenth floor, a cozy wood-paneled room with a glass wall that gave a spectacular view of the river, she spotted some big names among the surgeons. Sitting in the second row was Alex Berenstein of Beth Israel, and there two rows behind her was Nick Barbaro of Moffitt. Could he have flown all the way from San Francisco for this? She noticed audiovisual equipment at the ready—another sign that this was not a session hastily thrown together at the last moment.

Calvin Brewster, the administrator, took the floor first, speaking from a lectern that had a control panel with an impressive array of switches and gadgets. He fumbled a bit with the microphone, feigning modest embarrassment when the feedback squawked. He welcomed the group, noted that there were coffee and Danishes in the rear, joked that it would hardly be necessary to ask such an eminent gathering to observe a pledge of secrecy, and then did just that. The twenty or so people there quickly agreed. His introduction to Saramaggio was downright fawning.

The lanky surgeon uncoiled himself from a seat in the middle and sauntered languidly to the front. Applause would have been unseemly, but Kate thought she detected the discreet acknowledgment of heads bowing ever so slightly. Like reeds in a gentle breeze, she thought.

As the only woman there—a position she often found herself in—she felt conspicuous.

Saramaggio began with a recitation of the early research. He acknowledged the work of Dr. Cleaver in "the realm of computer-driven artificially enhanced intelligence," and as he did so, his eyes cast to the back of the room. Kate turned. Cleaver was sitting by himself in the last row. He was slumped down in his seat. Did he make it a habit to slip unnoticed in and out of rooms, or did it just seem that way?

Then Saramaggio recounted the accident that befell Tyler, whom he called a twelve-year-old. She wondered: How could a doctor so meticulous in the operating room get the age wrong? The question crystallized her growing uneasiness. Then she felt a pang—maybe she was being too critical. Maybe her little talk with Rosenfield was pushing her around a corner.

"So you see what we were confronted with," said Saramaggio. "We were at a crossroads. We have a patient in a desperate state facing death or lifelong severe mental incapacitation. And we have promising but incomplete research in advanced medical techniques that could conceivably alleviate his condition. It was, perhaps, a fortunate conjunction."

A dramatic pause. She thought she had rarely seen anyone more pleased with himself. A sudden image of the helicopter landing on the roof flashed through her mind, Scott holding on to his son's hand as the team rushed across the tarmac.

Saramaggio pushed several buttons on the control panel. A blackout curtain drew across the window, the lights dimmed, and a silver-flecked screen lowered behind him. A minute later, it was alive with images, movement, light. It took her a few seconds to recognize the operating room. There were the green cloths draped above Tyler. A close-up of him with the metal object protruding out of his skull—she thought she could hear a doctor nearby give a shallow gasp—and then she began to recognize individuals. The anesthesiologist, Gully, herself. In the center, the prima donna himself, Saramaggio, moving with fluid self-assurance. Odd how she hadn't been aware of the camera at the time, though it had been visible behind a tinted wall panel.

In a laconic voice, Saramaggio narrated both operations. As he painstakingly removed the hideous hunk of metal, he stepped aside from time to time. Was he doing that intentionally to give the camera a clear shot? Kate chastised herself for letting the thought flicker even briefly.

With the device out, there was a close-up of the injured brain. Saramaggio froze the frame on the screen and used a pointer to describe the wound. Kate was shocked as the camera zoomed in for a close-up. The gash seemed wide as a ravine. The damage was even more substantial than she had realized at the time. Then the video resumed, showing the extraction of the stem cells—enlargements of them in the petri dishes—and the implantation of the electrodes. Slow, painstaking, boring to watch. Cleaver appeared on the screen, working his infernal machines. Soon the video was over and the lights came back on.

Saramaggio took a few questions, mostly narrow and technical. He seemed eager to move on, and sure enough, he cut an answer short and made an announcement: "Now, we've arranged a special demonstration for you."

Lights off again. There was Tyler lying immobile in his bed, slightly blurry and indistinct behind the two sheets of glass. A closer view. You could see his chest moving up and down barely; he was breathing. His face twitched, ever so slightly.

"This is our patient today, right now. You see all the signs of a coma. We want above all simply to keep him stable."

The screen went dark for a second; then another image came up—a petri dish with hundreds, thousands of tiny spheroids, dark around the edges. They looked like shadowy raindrops on a pane of glass.

"These pictures were taken yesterday. As you can see, the colony of stem cells continues to grow. So far, they are multiplying even faster than we had predicted. At the current rate, in two, three, maybe four weeks, we will have enough to begin reimplantation."

A hand shot up. A question.

"Are you using any catalytic agents?"

"Fetal bovine serum with two proteins: fibroblast growth factor and leukemia inhibiting factor."

"Do you see any variants among later generations?"

"No, the newest appear to be exact duplicates of the oldest."

The screen went dark again, then back to Tyler. The camera was moving now—it was mobile, someone was handling it. It turned toward the bank of machines next to Tyler.

"This footage is live. Right now. These monitors show the patient's vital signs. Look closely at the EEG." The screen showed four portholes, each with an impulse tracing a path from left to right. "We have installed four submonitors to record brain function in four different locations, three of them in the limbic region. Now watch closely."

The screen split into two. The four monitors were on the left half. On the right, Kate recognized the bank of machines from the computer in the room adjacent to Tyler's bubble.

"This represents the impulses coming from the computer. Here, too, we have four submonitors." The right screen zoomed in for a close-up and also showed four separate monitors. There were now eight altogether.

"The four on the left are directly from the patient's brain. The four on the right are from the computer. You see how perfectly synchronized they are. It is impossible to tell if the patient is originating the activity or if the computer is doing it and sending it to the brain, which then registers it as its own. But we do have a way of finding out which of the two is calling the shots.

"Shift to master monitor," Saramaggio said. Only then did Kate realize that the microphone he was using was hooked into an audio headset for whoever was handling the video camera. The screen now showed a single green monitor window with a black needle. To the left side was a large zero and to the right a large number one. Kate realized that she had seen the machine before, but had never bothered to inquire about its function.

"This is undoubtedly the single most important measurement we have. Every sixty seconds, we institute a minute time delay in the impulses from the computer. If the computer's monitors lag behind the patient's, then we know the patient's brain is sending the signals all by itself. If the patient's monitors don't register anything until the computer kicks in, then it is the computer that is doing the work. This indispensable device tells us which one is paramount.

"You see the needle pointing to zero. That indicates that the patient is still brain active. If the needle sweeps to one, then the computer has taken over."

They all peered. The needle was indeed solidly pointing to zero.

"A very simple but effective indicator. We are indebted to Dr. Cleaver's ingenuity for it."

Some turned around to look at Cleaver, who acknowledged them with a thin smile.

"Now watch this."

By the time they turned back to face Saramaggio, the split screen showed Tyler on the left side and a bank of monitors on the right. A figure, a nurse, could be seen approaching his bed. Abruptly, the nurse clapped—loudly.

Just as abruptly, a line on the monitor jumped suddenly, sending forth a little peak that gradually trailed down to a normal progression of slender spikes. The nurse clapped again, and the line jumped up again.

"As you can see," Saramaggio said, a hint of swagger in his voice, "the patient, though in a coma, can register sound. Nothing unusual in that. But there's a catch here. The monitor you are looking at is *not* the monitor hooked up to the patient. It is the computer's monitor.

"In other words"—and here he drew out the sentence for emphasis—"the sound is entering the boy's ears, but he is not the one reacting to it. That is being done by the computer."

The nurse clapped a third time, and this time all eyes were upon the monitor. They stared in silence at its little peak, as if it had suddenly acquired the aura of magic.

Chapter 16

W hen he called, she could tell by the background noises that he was in a bar. The TV on high, a ball game. The murmur of voices, indistinct, a burst of false laughter. She imagined it darkly lighted, old wood stained with glass rings, a brass footrail and jukebox. The kind of place Frank Sinatra would go to forget a woman.

It wasn't that late. She could join him. Except—he hadn't invited her.

Scott wasn't drunk, or at least he wasn't slurring his words, but he was in a state, hyperemotional, excitable, angry. He had learned about Saramaggio's demonstration.

"Were you in on it?" he demanded. "Did you just sit there? Didn't you say anything?"

Finally, she got from him the name of the place. McHale's, Eighth Avenue and Forty-sixth. He wouldn't have given it to her if he hadn't meant for her to come.

"Stay there," she said. "I'll be right there."

His response was drowned out by another burst of laughter.

She jumped in a cab, and fifteen minutes later walked through the door.

The TV shone down from a mounted perch on up-lifted faces, all men. The announcer was excited, fans cheering, runners rounding the bases, a close-up of the white ball bouncing in the outfield on a sea of bright green grass.

He was at the end of the bar, sitting on a stool, leaning his cheeks against his fists, looking down. The stool next to him was empty, and she lifted one leg high to swing onto it. It was higher than it looked, and for a moment she felt she would topple over backward. She gripped the bar with both hands. Some entrance.

He looked over at her and smiled. She hadn't expected that. Where was the anger? In the cab, she had been rehearsing her lines: It wasn't the way you imagine it; this kind of thing is done fairly often in medicine; it's a means of sharing important advances. It's not as impersonal as it sounds; it's not intended to objectify—*is that really a word?*—the patient.

"Want a drink?"

She nodded. "Absolut, with ice."

He ordered for her and motioned for the bartender to refill his glass. Scotch. She wondered how many he had had. He looked all right—for a man in hell. He took a long last drag on a cigarette and crushed it out in a black plastic ashtray that was half-filled with butts.

"Look," he said. "I'm sorry for those things I said on the phone. Some of them, anyway. I don't want you to think I'm getting paranoid." He paused and added, "Just because everybody's against me." He gave a rueful grin.

"Of course. I understand."

"It's just that, when I heard about all those doctors gathered around, talking about him. Analyzing him. The video feed, *live*—for Christ's sake. And him just lying there, helpless."

He stopped, raised his glass, and took a sip to hide the crack in his voice.

She wondered for a moment who had told him—another doctor, probably, or maybe a nurse, some of whom felt sorry for him. It wouldn't do to ask—that would make it seem as if she was ferreting out an informer, as if a conspiracy indeed existed.

"They don't really care about him, you know," he continued. "Especially Saramaggio. He's out for prestige, fame, money. Who knows? They're all the same. For them, this is the big one."

He halted for a second, then motioned toward the TV and lit another cigarette. "Bases loaded. Two out, behind by two. Look at the batter; look at his jaw. He lives for this moment. They all do. Same thing. Moment of truth. The big one.

"I thought at first, that's okay. To hell with them. I can handle it. I can exploit it. What we have here is a marriage of convenience. They want to get famous. I want them to fix up my son. Motives are irrelevant. It's the end result that counts. I'd kiss the butcher, the devil himself, if it would help."

She was still struck by his dispassionate tone. Whatever it was that had overcome him, that emotional storm that had caused him to phone her, it had passed.

"To hell with all of them, I thought."

She noticed that he said *them,* not *you.* He seemed to have the same thought.

"Except for you. You were different. You understood and you cared. You were what held me together, and I'm grateful for that. I guess that's why I was upset when I learned you were at that session. But I know that's not being rational. It's just that the whole thing, putting on a demonstration, turning my son into some kind of specimen . . . I mean, I don't care if they think that way, but they shouldn't act that way."

She felt she had to say something. But what?

"I know it's hard," she said, wincing at the banality of her words. "Maybe some of what you say is true—about motives and all that. Maybe all of it's true. Except for one thing. They are doctors. And they do care."

"They treat him like a piece of meat." He raised his glass again, gave a slight shudder. He stepped back from anger into irony. "Piece of meat. Amazing how clichés come to you at a time like this. I guess it's because they're true after all."

She felt the need to defend her profession.

"They've been trained. They've learned some of that hardness. You'd be surprised at some of the things that go on in the OR, jokes, discussions about golf, stocks— all kinds of stupid, immaterial, irrelevant things. But I've seen those same surgeons, the ones who act like they couldn't give less of a damn, the ones who act as if they're sitting in on a hand of cards, I've seen them, when they lose a patient, sink into a depression you wouldn't believe. One of them, a guy in San Francisco, he used to just walk right out of the hospital, and people coming in would say he looked like he was crying. He'd come in the next morning as if nothing had happened. It's a macho thing."

Scott was silent for a moment, taking it in.

"Okay," he said finally. "I'll buy it. Maybe they are human after all. But that doesn't change my decision."

Her stomach knotted.

"What decision?"

"I'm going to take him off life support. I'm going to end the whole thing. The whole goddamned, pioneering, brain-stem-celling, son-of-a-bitching thing. The whole experiment. I've already called the chairman of that group—what's it called?"

She knew right away what he was talking about. The IRB—the Institutional Review Board, which passes upon experimental operations. Once the IRB approves the protocol, as it did in Tyler's case, the patient's parent is given the chairman's phone number. Precisely for this kind of situation.

"The IRB," she replied. "That would be Kellman. And what did he say?"

"They'll meet. Tomorrow at nine o'clock. And guess what?"

"What?"

"I want you to help me."

A whoop went up from the other end of the bar. The batter walked away from home plate, dragging the bat in the dust. He had struck out.

"Missed his big moment," said Scott, draining his glass and taking another long pull on his cigarette.

———

Before strapping Herbert Mann into the TSR, Cleaver and Felix gave him a double dose of Valium. Cleaver hadn't wanted to do that to his *subjects*—it was impossible to call them *patients* under the circumstances. He had wanted them to retain clear mental faculties, and he feared the medication would introduce a contaminating variable into the experiment. But the principle quickly dissipated once they were in the basement.

Out of nowhere, Mann had rebelled at the prospect of entering the room. He braced himself with both arms straight against the doorjamb, refusing to take one more step, and there was a moment of awkward uncertainty when they tried to jackknife his elbows and force him inside. He was strong for a little man, and at one point held on to the jamb with both hands, like a sailor clinging to the mast in a storm. His fit would have been comic if it weren't so damned inconvenient. It was an odd display, given that he had seemed ready, even eager, to try out the machine not so long before. Cleaver thought back to the night when Mann had lain down in the TSR all by himself, smiling like a babe. That's the trouble with paranoids, he had thought, you never know what mood you're going to catch them in.

Cleaver led him back upstairs by the elbow, murmuring sweet blandishments in his ear, and gave him a cup of tea, spiked with two ten-milligram tablets that he'd crushed hurriedly in his office, using a saucer and spoon as a mortar and pestle. He waited half an hour, watching Mann's eyes take on a glazed sheen, and led him, now docile, back downstairs. Even primed with the medication, Mann's face puckered with a moment's alarm when they crossed the threshold. As directed, Felix had a straitjacket waiting on a stool, but Mann abruptly relaxed once inside the room, and Cleaver could tell they wouldn't need it.

"That's right, Herbert. Come along. There's nothing to it. That-a-boy."

Cleaver's high-pitched wheedling sounded insincere, even to himself.

They lowered him onto the movable stretcher at the mouth of the machine as delicately as a bag of apples. Standing over him, Cleaver got hit full in the face with a stench that almost made him gag. He could tell by the expression on Felix's face that he was smelling it, too.

"Looks like our boy soiled himself," Cleaver said with distaste.

"Should we change him? It won't take a minute."

Cleaver thought it over. What if the Valium should wear off? Wasn't worth the risk.

"No. Let's just get going."

With that, Cleaver threaded the thick strap into the buckle and pulled it so tightly across Mann's upper body that his shoulders hugged his chest. Felix strapped his feet in place across the ankles. There were two smaller straps for his wrists, which lay palms upward. Standing up and looking down at him all trussed up and lying in a bed of gleaming metal, Cleaver thought he looked somehow shrunken, a corpse. He had the momentary sensation that he was dispatching his subject off to cremation and the nonexistent afterlife—pull the lever and the casket would slide away into an oven. And an odd thought came out of the blue: *How fleeting and peculiar and pathetic it is, this whole messy business called life.*

But Mann was hardly lifeless: His face was twitching and his eyes were darting back and forth like windshield wipers.

"It'll be all right. Don't worry. It's like taking a little snooze." This time, Cleaver thought his words struck just the right tone. He felt it, too—he badly wanted Mann to calm down. Mann's face relaxed a bit, and Cleaver was touched. He looked over at Felix and gave a quiet nod: Time to proceed.

Moving slowly, so as not to alarm him, Cleaver pulled down the helmet with its tangled array of wires.

"Now this won't hurt at all. We're going to fit this around your head, and it will keep you nice and snug."

The helmet slipped on, surprisingly easily. Then Cleaver lowered the eggcups so that they barely touched Mann's eyes. He turned a knob on the side, and the metallic cups retracted into curved horizontal strips. Mounting them in place was difficult: He and Felix had to lift his lids one at a time, first the upper, then the lower, pulling them up by the lashes and using a blunt scalpel to pry open a sliver of space. Mann lay perfectly still—he seemed to have resigned himself to whatever fate might bring. Once the metallic lip of the strip fit under the edge of the eyelid, Cleaver turned the knob again to expand it to its full convex oval shape. An automatic switch turned on the wash of saline solution; Cleaver watched it slowly ascending through the translucent tubing.

It was a bit of a relief, he confessed to himself, not to have to look into Mann's panicky eyes.

Mann was the third subject to be hooked up to the machine. The first had been a young man with a severe affective disorder who played solitaire for hours on end and mumbled to himself. The second had been a borderline personality who'd dug holes so deeply into her heels that she'd reached the bone and could no longer walk.

Cleaver couldn't say precisely what effect the experience had had upon them, and this bothered him no end. Where were they going, and what did it feel like? He used injections of 2-deoxyglucose to read the brain activity, and that part of the experiment worked perfectly. The tens of thousands of minute electrodes inside the helmet picked up the electrical impulses and fed them into the computer, which displayed them in real time. He could literally watch the brain think—and he could listen to it, too. Quincy had rigged up an analog sound system. It reminded Cleaver of bursts of static. The first time he used the audio, he turned out the lights. Standing there in the semidarkness watching the screen and listening to the speakers, he felt he was in outer space, observing the explosions of sunspots and hearing them tear at the fabric of the universe.

But the experiment was intended to be much more than observational. The idea, after all, was to link the brain to the computer. The first step was to try to feed information from the computer directly into the cortex—and it was here that the uncertainty lay. For the young man, Cleaver downloaded a variety of new data, all kinds of information transmogrified into on-off electrical pulses—even, ever so quickly, a version of an Italian card game called *sette mezzo*. Whether it took or not was impossible to tell. Cleaver ran various tests on him for days—including, of course, providing him with the requisite deck of cards—but they never turned up any sign that the information had been processed or was in an area of the cortex that could be accessed by the conscious mind. The same was true of the woman. In her case, Cleaver fed in snatches of Polish, answers to riddles, even a piercing sound that preceded a tiny electric shock, repeated ten times. Again, once the woman was taken out of the machine and allowed to rest, she showed no indication that she had taken any of this on board, except for a response to the sound, which caused a spike of anxiety. But that, theorized Cleaver, was a simple case of Pavlovian conditioning and had nothing to do with the computer.

He was feeling doubly frustrated. One problem was clearly the time limit for each session. Quincy had warned him that the system would crash after seven minutes, and to give a margin of safety he had triggered it to turn off automatically after five minutes. There was an override button that would keep it going, but Cleaver sensibly declined to use it. Who knew what might happen to the apparatus if it kicked into overtime? And contrary to Quincy's predictions, he discovered that the programs for encoding information were cumbersome—not very much information could be packed into five minutes.

And then there was the problem of the subjects. Lunatics were not fit for the job. They were unable to articulate anything that happened to them, and they could hardly be grilled about newly acquired knowledge. Sooner or later, Cleaver thought, he would have to enlist a mature, rational human. But who? It would take a mighty persuasive tongue to convince anyone halfway normal to lie down inside that cylinder.

Did the experience cause no change whatsoever in

the subjects? Cleaver was not prepared to conclude one way or the other, though he had noticed one unusual occurrence. He'd happened to patrol the ward on the night each of the two had undergone the session and he'd seen that each of them was tormented by nightmares. He had tried to make out what they were saying, but could not. A coincidence maybe, but he made a mental note to drop by Mann's bed this night.

He swabbed the soft skin under the forearm with alcohol, gave him the injection, and waited a few minutes for the tracing compound to work its way through the system. Finally, he looked up at Felix.

"All set then?" he asked, a peevish tone setting in. He still disliked his assistant and thought him incompetent. But he had gone this far with him, and besides, if he fired him, who knew what Felix might do? Those dull eyes were in part a masquerade—he was certainly capable of scheming.

"Yep. All systems go." Felix was standing at the computer controls, which apparently made him feel he was about to launch a rocket.

Cleaver rolled the stretcher on its tracks and watched as Mann disappeared headfirst into the tight cylinder until only his feet were protruding. He gave a little shudder of empathetic claustrophobia, straightened up, stretched his back, and walked over to take the controls from Felix.

The first thing he did was to start the large clock set in the console, its big black hand marking off the seconds in melodramatic lunges.

He flicked a few switches, and the screen leapt to life: an image of the helmet with its recording electrodes, arrayed in limitless hexagons, lit up like Christmas tree bulbs. By pressing the edges of a directional button, he could rotate it 360 degrees in any angle.

He turned more switches, and Mann's brain image popped onto the screen. He turned wheels that rotated the brain and allowed him to enter and pull back at any point, like a cinematographer on a boom camera. He sat for a full thirty seconds, just watching the brain work and listening to the sound of its infinite machinations. Sunspots exploding.

He caught himself; they had work to do. The large hand on the clock was marching forward inexorably.

They had decided to feed Mann algebra. They knew from his dossier that he had not advanced beyond simple mathematics in high school, hampered by personality quirks that were precursors to his illness. Painstakingly, Cleaver, helped by an assistant at St. Cat's who had no idea what purpose the work was serving, had loaded algebraic formulas and theories into the computer. Testing whether they had taken—provided they could get Mann to concentrate—should be possible.

He downloaded the material and looked again at the clock. Three minutes had gone by. Still two minutes left.

On impulse, Cleaver decided to perform an experiment within the experiment. He stopped transmitting electrical impulses from the computer and flipped all the switches open. That might, in theory, unobstruct the optic nerve. It would let the impulses flow in whatever direction they wanted, like water seeking its own level. It was, he thought, tantamount to lifting the gates on a series of locks connecting oceans at different heights. Which way would the water flow?

He gave it a full minute. The sixty seconds ticked by, slowly, silently, tensely. Outwardly, nothing was happening. It was a suspended moment, like holding your breath.

Cleaver started the process of shutting down the connections. Felix didn't seem to have a clue about what had happened.

When they extracted Mann from the machine, pulling down the stretcher on its rollers, removing the headgear carefully and then undoing the straps, he seemed a bit dazed and befuddled, but otherwise unchanged. It could have been the Valium that disoriented him; once again, Cleaver, holding his nose against the smell, cursed the fates that had forced him to use it.

Mann stood up unsteadily, like an astronaut back on earth, but soon regained his equilibrium. They helped him out of the room, which he left in grateful haste. Upstairs, they cleaned him up, put him down for a rest, then awakened him gently, gave him a light lunch of soup and a cheese sandwich, and set him down for tests in the old smoking veranda. Sunlight was streaming in through the grime-covered windows, reflecting off a swirl of dust motes.

With forced casualness, Cleaver handed him a yellow pad and sat beside him. He wrote on top of it:

$$4y = 12$$
$$y = ?$$

"Now take your time," he said. "See if you can figure it out."

But one look at Mann was enough to realize that he hadn't the slightest idea what the figures meant. The experiment was a failure, like the two others before it.

Cleaver tried two other formulas, but by the end didn't even bother to slide the pad in front of Mann. He had to curb a rising sense of anger: Couldn't the poor slob try a little harder? How in God's name did he manage to get so dumb? And to think this little mouse murdered his entire family.

"I give up," Cleaver said. He stood up wearily. It had been a long day. He looked down at Mann, sitting there in his striped seersucker bathrobe, rocking slightly, the picture of contrition.

"I'm leaving," Cleaver said summarily.

"Cześć. Do zobaczenia."

Cleaver barely paid attention. But then suddenly he whipped around.

"What did you say?" he demanded.

"Mówię po polsku," said Mann. "I'm speaking Polish."

"When did you learn to speak Polish?"

"I don't know. I just did it. The words just came out."

Cleaver's thoughts came fast and furious. They seemed to echo around his head as he walked down the corridor.

So it did work after all. But in the wrong direction. His brain went out and went into the computer and rummaged through it and came up with the file intended for the other subject. My God! Who would have thought it possible?

Walking down Second Avenue, Kate was having second thoughts. She didn't know what had possessed her—maybe it was the Absolut. Maybe it was Scott's resolution and the new strength it had given him. But in any case she had clearly gotten carried away and made a pledge she might come to regret. She had told him that she would back his decision. The odd thing was that he had barely registered a reaction; it was almost as if he had expected nothing less of her.

She stopped into a deli and absentmindedly picked up a wire basket and began filling it with the small foragings of a person living alone—one quart of skim milk, a barbecued chicken, a head of lettuce, Pepperidge Farm Orange Milano cookies.

But it could lead to trouble for her, no question about that. Saramaggio would not take it lightly if she crossed him. Already he didn't like her. He was the sort of man who would take a certain pleasure in ruining careers.

The thought of placing her ambition ahead of her instinct to do the right thing shamed her. And she was even more ashamed by the thoughts that followed: She was tempted to go back on her word to Scott, but one thing stopping her was the question of how she would tell him. She didn't think she could face the opprobrium. And he wasn't a gentleman who would let her off the hook easily. She wondered why his opinion of her had come to matter so much.

Leaving the store and hugging a bag with one arm, she thought she recognized a figure up ahead, the jet black hair. *Gully!* That's just what she needed, someone to talk it over with. They could go for a cup of coffee.

She hurried ahead, half trotting, awkwardly. The figure stopped at a light, and she caught up and was about to speak when he turned around to face her.

It was someone else, not Gully at all. The man's eyes registered momentary alarm at the intensity of her look.

Walking back to her apartment, she felt twice as bad and twice as alone. She set the groceries down in her kitchen and decided to go up to the roof, walking up the flights of stairs, unhooking a thick metal door, and stepping out onto an expanse of buckling tar paper. It was warm, and the sky overhead was spectacular, with a shimmering aura from the skyline around her. Directly overhead, in the blackness, the stars were gleaming.

She thought—out of nowhere, it seemed—of her father. She had been only two when he'd been killed in Vietnam, bombed by an American plane in the Mekong Delta—"friendly fire," as that arrogantly lying oxymoron put it. She didn't remember him at all, though her mother had described his departure so often she almost felt she could. A large man with a barrel chest and a mustache (this from a photo on her mother's dresser), he'd picked her up and hugged her and said, "I'll be gone a long, long time, but I'll be back. Don't forget that—I'll be back." Then he'd turned and walked out the door and she'd run to the window to watch him walk away down the flagstones outside. The scene was so strong in her mind that she was sometimes sure the memory was her own.

When she was young, reciting the Lord's Prayer— "Our *father* who art in Heaven"—she often pictured her own father up there, looking down on her, watching out for her, arranging things. It was comforting. And now she felt, looking up at the bright stars, a little foolishly, that she would like to feel that way again.

That evening, for the first time in a long while, she thought of calling Harry in San Francisco, just to talk to an old boyfriend, to hear his voice and maybe feel less alone. She picked up the phone to dial, but then placed the receiver back on the hook. It wouldn't be fair to him, she thought, to lead him on, especially when she'd hardly thought of him in weeks.

Chapter 17

$\mathbf{K}$ate walked into the hearing room with trepidation, which she tried to mask by making herself conspicuous. Her heels resonated loudly against the wood floor as she stepped inside. Her hair was pulled back in a bun, and for the occasion she had chosen her dark blue pin-striped suit with angular no-nonsense lapels; it was cut snugly but conservatively around her bosom and hips, and she thought of it as her "power suit"—much as she detested the word, in fact the whole concept. Still, she needed something to bolster her in this male bullring. An exoskeleton might do the trick, she thought.

She noticed right away that the fifteenth-floor room had somehow transformed itself. It was the same place where Saramaggio had held his little demonstration three days earlier, but it looked entirely different. Gone were the movie screen and refreshments and the lectern. The atmosphere was stolid, businesslike. She glanced over at the window. Even the view of the river seemed to have changed—it was a drizzly morning, with wisps of mist circling the bridge towers, and boats moving sluggishly upstream into the fog. Of course, it wouldn't be sunny, not on a day like this. An interloping thought broke into her stream of consciousness: What was that called, back in college days, when the outside world mirrored your inner emotions? *It rains in the town as it rains in my heart.* Ah-hah—the *pathetic fallacy*. She was pleased she had reclaimed that half-fragment from a long-ago life. Cleaver—she suddenly thought of him. Gully had once told her that

Cleaver had quoted a stanza of Wordsworth. Imagine that—the computer maven frolicking through hills of daffodils. Her heart sank—he would undoubtedly be here for this.

A podium had been arranged, a panel almost the width of the room in front of ten empty chairs. The chairs would be for the Institutional Review Board members. Black vinyl with high backs, the kind that swing. Modern-day thrones, she thought. And look how the podium is raised a full foot off the ground. It's revealing how some authorities feel the need to demonstrate status through physical elevation.

The first question, of course, was where to sit. She would sit next to Scott—she had resolved as much already—but where would *he* want to sit? And if she got there first, should she actually save a seat for him? She felt small, not for the first time, for worrying over such inconsequential details, which reflected her own self-absorption, especially when this hearing was a matter of life and death to him.

Problem solved—there he was. First row center.

She took the seat to his right. He turned and gave her a little half-smile, forced.

"How are you?" she asked.

He didn't bother to answer, instead asking a question of his own.

"Have you ever sat through one of these things before?" He tossed his head vaguely at the room. She detected the ember of anger burning beneath his words and already knew him well enough to know where it came from. She would try to calm him.

"Once or twice. In San Francisco. Every hospital has an IRB—at least every one that gets Medicare funds. They're not really as formal as they look, despite all the trappings. I mean, it's not like it's a court of law."

She was rattling on, but it eased her nervousness.

"What's it like?"

"Well, the officers are from different places—senior physicians, some of them retired, chiefs of departments, the chairman of the ethics committee, one or two community representatives. Don't worry—they don't wear horsehair wigs, and nobody bangs a gavel."

He didn't smile.

"First they usually hear from the records division. They get all the background on the case. Then they hear from the doctor. He says why the operation is necessary or whatever it is that's under dispute. They usually interrupt him with questions. Sometimes they take cases passed up by the ethics committee—say, if a baby requires blood but the parents are Jehovah's Witnesses and refuse to allow it. If it's about a patient who's been badly diagnosed or threatened or something's gone wrong under some mysterious circumstances—well, then the questions can get pretty tough. And by the way, it's all private. No press, no outsiders come in—except of course interested parties. Like you."

"Yeah. I'm an interested party all right."

"You will probably be asked to speak, as I told you the other night. They'll ask you why you want to take Tyler off life support. And the more straightforward your answers, the better. These are doctors and scientists, for the most part. Sentiment doesn't get to them, common sense does."

"What you're saying is I shouldn't say what I feel."

"No, not at all. Just be a little careful how you say it. Don't throw everything at them all at once. Don't get their backs to the wall."

"I'm the one with my back to the wall."

"Well, they're not criminals. They're not trying to hurt Tyler. Don't forget—this all began with them trying to save him. And at first you were in favor of it. What's happened is you have changed your mind, and they haven't."

"Because they want to try out their new toys. Not because they're really thinking of him."

"Maybe that's part of it. But so what? What does it matter if there's some professional pride coming into play, even arrogance? It doesn't matter as long as they end up doing good."

"That's what I thought, too, at first. But that's changed now."

His voice was rising, and she worried that he was attracting attention from the somber men beginning to file in and take seats. This was not what she wanted to do—she wanted to calm him down, not wind him up.

More people came in, doctors, some in handsome, hand-tailored suits, others in flashy casual wear, linen jackets with tight Italian shoes. She saw the scrub nurse and the circulating nurse. They sat side by side in the rear, whispering to each other and looking over at her. She wondered what they were saying, then decided she didn't much care.

"One other thing," she said, cupping her hand around her mouth, because the seats around them were filling up. "This may sound strange, but technically, their decision isn't binding. What I mean is—even if they decide against Saramaggio, he could continue the operation. It just means that he'd be on his own and running a risk."

"And what's that supposed to mean?"

"Well, for one thing, he wouldn't have much of a leg to stand on if you decided to take it further ... to go outside."

"You mean—if I take it to the courts."

"Yes."

The ten chairs on the podium were almost all filled now. Robert Kellman, the chairman, sat in the center. He looked the part—senatorial, with wisps of white hair gently capping his ears. A urologist, whispered Kate. The others were mostly middle-aged men, equally somber-looking, almost interchangeable—dried peas in a pod, thought Scott. There was one woman, pale and unsmiling, thin as an ax blade, whom Kate explained was the chief nurse. One seat was empty. Finally, a ruddy-faced priest came in to claim it by placing a briefcase next to it, then moved down the line, working it like a politician, giving a hearty handshake here and a backslap there.

Scott didn't like that: A gregarious establishment priest likely to uphold the sanctity of human life could hurt his case.

"By the way," he said, "how do they decide? Do they vote—or what?"

"Yes. They vote."

He felt her stiffen beside him. And when he turned, he saw why: Saramaggio had taken a seat directly across the aisle, next to Brewster, the administrator. The neurosurgeon was looking at Kate, shooting darts at her.

For the first time, it dawned on Scott that by associating herself with his cause, Kate might be putting her career in jeopardy. He felt a sudden rush of gratitude—along with a touch of remorse. He had been so self-centered, so obsessive, that he hadn't even considered the repercussions for her. Were these doctors accustomed to the dissent that comes with contentious debate? Or would her defection be viewed as treason?

The proceedings began with a lengthy description of Tyler's condition at the time he was brought to St. Catherine's, replete with arcane medical terminology that sanitized his injuries and made the recitation easier to listen to. Still, some terms he couldn't pretend to ignore—phrases like "massive destruction of the lateral left cortex" and "traumatic invasion of the limbic system." Sitting through this would be even worse than he had envisioned.

Scott was shocked to learn that the method Kingston Hospital had used to medevac Tyler to New York, wrapping the head in ice to cut down on brain swelling, was no longer the recommended procedure for containing brain injuries. *Don't they notify people about changes like that?* he wondered to himself.

Then Saramaggio was called upon to present his views. He seemed to treat the occasion as an opportunity to bask in the esteem of fellow practitioners. He actually moved his seat to be closer to the panel and began a long recitation of the operations: how much preliminary research had been done, how well things had gone with animals, how Tyler's case fit the protocol for the first ever Computer-Assisted Neural Stem Cell Extraction, Cultivation, and Reimplantation. He was the soul of sweet reason and sympathy.

One of the doctors leaned forward to ask a question: "And could you tell us about your consultation with the patient's father and whether you fully explained the procedure to him?"

Saramaggio gave an account of their two meetings and somehow made the sessions sound more thorough and methodical than Scott remembered. He told how he had precisely described the penetration of "the blunt instrument," the chances that it had already caused irreparable damage, the new research into stem cells, and the effectiveness with which they had been reimplanted in animals. He told of how he had simply placed the alternatives before Scott and made it sound as if he himself had been as disinterested as a waiter who offered a choice between dishes.

"Excuse me, Dr. Saramaggio," asked one panel member. "How long would you say these sessions lasted?"

It was a softball question, but Saramaggio seemed put out nonetheless.

"How long?"

"Yes."

"Well, the first occurred right after the preliminary investigation of the patient, and I would say it was an hour or so. It's hard to—"

"Doctor," the priest interrupted. "You first met the father, eh, Mr. Jessup here"—he glanced over at Scott paternally—"*after* the first operation? Not *before*?"

"That's right."

"Is that customary? I would think that you might want—"

"It *is* customary when the patient is *in extremis*. You understand that in such a situation, every second counts. I myself rushed back to treat him—on my day off, I might add. Massive hemorrhaging, blood loss, shock to the system. Anything could happen to bring on instant death." His voice was rising, indignant. "And what is the point of meeting with the father, might I add, when there is absolutely nothing you can tell him because you know nothing about the status of the son."

It was a statement, not a question, and the priest quickly replied, holding up his hand, meek as a lamb.

"Of course. Of course. I did not mean to imply that you *should* have met with the father first. I was merely asking a question to find out about procedures."

"Well, since you've asked, the *procedure,* as you call it, is to tend to the patient first, to do what needs to be done and to get him out of danger if at all practicable and as soon as possible. If you care to suggest another way to conduct business around here, we're all ears."

The priest reddened and looked down.

"Of course not," he said. "Our purpose here is not to second-guess you. But not all of us are as familiar as you are with the customary practices."

Saramaggio was puffed up with indignation. *Like a rooster preening his tail feathers,* thought Scott. *Maybe the priest isn't so bad after all, but I would have liked him better if he had held his ground.*

"Dr. Saramaggio," said Kellman, speaking in a basso voice and weighing each word as if he were an Olympian arbiter of reason, "could you please tell us what the chances are—in your view—that the patient will survive the operation?"

Saramaggio had clearly been expecting the question, but he paused before answering, as if reflecting deeply and searching for the precise words to express a fine balance of ambiguity.

"I would say, all things considered, that they are good. We're sailing on new waters here, and so predictions are fraught with imponderables. But will he live? Will he survive the procedure itself? Of that I have little doubt."

"And how about survival postoperatively?"

"Difficult to say. All I can do is provide a progress report. For the moment, the stem cells are reproducing normally and rapidly under good laboratory conditions. They belong to him, and so they will prove compatible when they are reimplanted. His bodily functions are stable. The computer is now matching his brain activity, and it stands by ready to assist if need be. In other words, everything is running smoothly so far and I have no expectation that they would do otherwise postoperatively, though of course we cannot say for certain what might happen."

"And his quality of life?" It was the priest asking the question. He seemed to have regained his composure.

"Ah, there we cannot predict with certainty. I see no reason that his stem cells shouldn't function normally. The neural connections already made, however—rather those that had been made—some of them will perhaps not persist into the postoperative state. We cannot say with one hundred percent assurance that he will retain all of his preoperative characteristics."

"Do you mean his personality may be different?"

"His personality? As men of science, we can't talk knowledgeably about such an abstraction. He will have many new tasks to learn, some of which he may once have known and may have to relearn."

Scott was sitting bolt upright in his chair, glaring.

"Will he—for example—know his father?"

Saramaggio hesitated, looked at Scott, then away.

"That could well be problematic. If he does not know him right away, however, I would say he would be perfectly capable of learning to know him again."

"*Learning* to know him?" Now the priest was almost truculent.

Saramaggio jumped back into the fray.

"Yes, he will have a lot of learning to do. The main thing is he will be around to do it. I'm sure that if his father is like any other loving father, he wouldn't want his son to cease to exist simply because the filial bond might have to be reestablished." He looked back at Scott. "You can ask him."

"That we will do," said Chairman Kellman. "In the meantime, we thank you for your cooperation. Is there anything more you would care to say?"

Saramaggio paused a beat, then added, "I would like to repeat what I said earlier. The waters we are navigating are new and uncharted. Where they lead is not known. Our young man will be the first to cross them, the first to set foot upon a new land. When he returns, we cannot say for certain what he will be like. But he will be a pioneer, and generations to come will know his name and be thankful to him."

Scott could no longer keep quiet.

"*Your* name is more like it."

The chairman turned toward him. "I beg your pardon."

"I think Christopher Columbus here is thinking about his own name, not my son's."

The room was shocked into silence.

"And I resent—deeply resent—the implication that my only concern is that my son won't recognize me if and when he wakes up. I'm worried that I won't recognize *him*—that I won't recognize him because he won't *be* him. I'm worried that he'll have half a brain or be impaired in some horrible way or be so emotionally damaged that his whole life will be a nightmare. Or that he won't wake up, ever, that he'll continue in a coma. Who knows what it's like being locked in there—maybe it's agony, the worst torment imaginable. Maybe he's already in a nightmare, begging for release. Or maybe he will wake up and he'll be so unable to function that after I'm dead, he'll end up in an institution where no one will care for him, no one will tend to him. . . ."

His voice trailed off.

The chairman cleared his throat, then spoke. "Yet you gave your consent for this operation to take place. And now you've changed your mind?"

"I have."

"Can you tell us why?"

"At first I had hope. Who wouldn't take up such an offer? *We can save your son's life, we can make him whole. It's hard to say for certain, it's risky, but we think we can do it. We can do wonderful things these days— you have no idea.* Who wouldn't say yes? Even if it's grasping at straws, it's better than the alternative. It's better than just letting him slip away into nothingness. Anything's got to be better than that—one day he's there, he's off for a weekend with a friend and hugs you good-bye and runs out the door, and then suddenly he's just gone. Anything's better—even a never-ending round of operations where he's sliced and cut and put on machines and breathing through tubes—at least it seems so at the time.

"But now weeks have gone by, and I have no hope at all. He's still breathing through tubes, and now a computer is doing it for him. I don't think it will work. The enormity of it all has sunk in. I've been reading up on this stuff. People talk about brain death—there is no such thing as brain death. That central piece—the limbic system—it keeps going long after the rest is gone. And you can probably keep it going forever if you feed it the right amount of oxygen and glucose or whatever. But there's no one there, no person inside. No human by any definable term. That's not living. That's a jellyfish sloshing around in a tidal pool. A piece of meat connected to a machine.

"I saw a documentary once on television, one of these magazine programs. It showed a woman whose daughter was in an accident and in a coma. The doctors wanted to pull the plug, but the mother wouldn't let them. She took her daughter home and she kept insisting she was going to be all right. The camera filmed her as she put her daughter in a bikini and floated her in their swimming pool, holding her head out of the water. And the thing is, when I saw that, I thought, Who could ever do that to their child? Who could be so crazy? And now, I understand it. That's me. That's what I've been doing to Tyler."

He looked directly at Saramaggio.

"You're not saving Tyler. You may think you are, but you're not. You're killing him off, bit by bit. You're sacrificing him in pieces. And when you're all done and there's nothing left of him, you'll end up dissecting what's not there. And writing it all up. *Pioneer*—my ass!

"So, yes, I've changed my mind, but it's not because I'm fickle. It's because I've wised up and now I see that I was duped. I know what the right thing to do is. I demand that you take my son off life support. As his father, I demand it."

When he finished, there was a rustling among the audience. The chairman declared a fifteen-minute recess.

Scott collected himself and rose to go to the men's room.

There he opened a window a crack, stood next to it, leaning against the wall, and lit a cigarette, inhaling deeply.

A man came in, an Indian or Pakistani, with jet-black hair and a pleasing face. Scott held his cigarette up apologetically and said, "Sorry—but I really need this."

"That's all right," said the man, offering his hand. "My name's Gully. I heard you in there. You were very . . . persuasive."

Scott nodded.

Gully frowned as if he were on the verge of saying something more, then spoke.

"I'm afraid this one is going to go all the way."

"What do you mean?" asked Scott. "What're you saying?"

"Did you happen to see that gentleman in the back? The one taking notes . . ."

"No."

"He's a lawyer. Curtis and Reinfield. That's the firm the hospital uses for court cases. They're already preparing the way, you see."

Scott did.

When the session resumed, the chairman invited various others to speak. Several doctors took the floor. Then Brewster spoke, full of platitudes. The hospital wanted only to do what was right. It was trying to balance the needs of the patient as articulated by the father—most eloquently, he might add—with those of research, for the hospital was both a place of healing and a center of learning, so that those in future generations might also be served. It sounded to Scott as if he were speaking for the court record, and he noticed for the first time that positional mikes were recording. They had been there all along.

Cleaver was asked to speak about the functioning of the computer, but he declined by shaking his head from side to side, almost vehemently, much to Saramaggio's annoyance. Scott, who had not seen him before, studied him, watching his abrupt movements, his eyes scanning the room. He worried that such a person was on the team caring for his son.

Finally, the chairman looked at Kate.

"And do you have something to add?" he asked kindly.

She froze, looking uncharacteristically frightened. Then she moved up to sit in the same seat Saramaggio had occupied an hour before.

"I wasn't going to," she began. "I did not come here prepared to speak. And I doubt that I can add much to the medical nature of the testimony."

"Please, please," interrupted the chairman. "Not *testimony*. This is not a court of law. I hope I haven't given that impression."

Kate's cheeks flushed slightly.

"No, I know that. Forgive me. What I meant to say was simply that I can add little to what has been said already, as far as the operation itself goes. It's new to me—it is new to everyone in this room. And so it follows that much of what we say, virtually everything we say—no matter how deep the conviction that underlies it—is going to be conjecture. None of us can say for sure what will happen, because none of us can possibly know. We can only guess what the outcome of this operation will be. There are no precedents to guide us, no statistics, nothing in the literature. As Dr. Saramaggio pointed out, we have set foot on a new, unknown terrain."

She paused, thinking, and when she resumed, she spoke with more assurance.

"Because it's new, the few meager instruments we have to guide us are abstract principles. They are our map and compass—the time-honored traditions of our profession. Foremost among these, we all agree, is the Hippocratic oath that says, 'First, do no harm.'

"We cannot say today with complete certainty whether we have observed this ancient directive or violated it. But because the situation was so dire, we were in a situation of force majeure. Did we cause more harm than good? We may have to face the possibility that the answer to that question is ultimately unknowable. But that doubt does not mean that we were in the wrong. Faced with a patient in such a desperate, life-threatening condition, with a grieving father and the prospect of so much further suffering, who here would not have made the same decision? Especially since the tools to treat the boy were at hand, even if they'd not been tried before. So I think we can all agree that the initial decision to proceed with the operation was the right thing to do."

Scott looked around. Saramaggio was beaming, Brewster's face was clothed in self-satisfaction. Kate took a deep breath.

"But now," she continued, "the situation has changed. It's changed because the father, who is legally charged with making decisions on behalf of his son, wants the procedure to stop. How can we ignore his wishes? How can we pretend that he doesn't know what is best for his own son?"

Saramaggio's face was beginning to sag now.

"It was said earlier that he has changed his mind. I don't think he has really *changed* it. When he gave his consent—and I was there—I think he had not fully formed his thoughts. He was looking to us for guidance, and like the rest of us, he was just going along hoping for the best, because there was little else to do. And you always want to do *something*. But now, clearly, he *has* made up his mind. He's thought and learned and watched us, and he has come to a decision. And he is the only one who knows the patient, who loves him, who will have to care for him if things do not turn out right. Who else can be said to be thinking only of the patient? Not of medical science, not of other patients to come, not of research or the hospital's reputation—but only the patient, and nothing else."

She spoke the final words like a defense attorney winding down a summation.

"He has spoken, finally. His is the one voice we

should listen to above all others. I believe we would be immoral and someday face judgment if we did not."

She stopped and heard her last words echo back to her. The room fell deadly quiet. She rose and walked back to her seat, this time with a self-consciousness she could not disguise.

Saramaggio and Brewster exchanged looks, then Brewster and Kellman. Kellman waited a full thirty seconds, and in the silence, an air of drama grew. Then he cleared his throat, as if he were about to make a significant pronouncement, and fixed Kate with a hard stare. He asked a question instead.

"Dr. Willet, can you please tell us—and I advise you to think carefully before answering—have you established a close personal relationship with the father of the patient?"

Chapter 18

Cleaver sent Felix with a gurney into Room 35 to collect the patient with Cotard's disease and waited anxiously in the basement near the TSR. Truth was, he was becoming a little spooked by the patient with the bizarre malady that turned him into one of the living dead. Benchloss. Only twenty, and yet his full head of hair had gone all white. Even his past was sketchy—his file was the thinnest of all. A young man from Detroit. He had had a cousin who worked on an automobile assembly line who'd looked after him and then gotten fed up as he drifted off into the netherworld of psychosis. What could have happened to him, Cleaver wondered, that metamorphosed him into such a psychological freak? What deep-seated part of the brain had gone haywire? Did it happen by itself, some kind of monstrous gene that exploded like a time bomb? Or was there an external agent, some outside event so unspeakable that it took away his tongue, his sight, his touch? No matter. He was ripe for experimentation. And being dead, he certainly wouldn't complain.

Not for two nights, since the time he had put Mann into the machine and discovered that somehow Mann's brain had connected with the computer, actually entered into the memory of the damn thing and pillaged it to come up with some snatches of Polish, had Cleaver been able to sleep well. He had worked frantically, loading one diseased subject after another into the TSR, turning all switches into the OPEN position, and waiting nervously for the five minutes to roll by, pulling out the stretcher expectantly—the image of a chef lowering the lid of an oven to examine a soufflé passing fleetingly through his mind—as he removed the subjects and then sat them down to watch for telltale signs that they had been transformed by their mysterious journey in the tube.

He was not always disappointed. Some of the subjects showed advances, along with a new kind of weirdness. They did indeed seem in possession of some new information—data that they didn't have before. But the information wasn't fully integrated—it came out in fits and starts and didn't seem to do them all that much good. Transmission of a complete, coherent body of knowledge seemed beyond reach.

But of course it was hard to tell—they were, after all, out of their minds to begin with.

Bruce, the young man who thought his parents were "imposters," had been a major disappointment. Cleaver had been anticipating his turn in the machine; he was smart, reasonably well educated, articulate—you could have a normal conversation with him as long as you avoided the subject of family relationships. Surely he would be able to demonstrate the effects of a psychotelegraphic experience. But it hadn't worked out in quite the way that Cleaver had hoped. To begin with, Bruce had balked at going into the TSR; in particular he was fearful for his eyes and resisted having the eggcups inserted under his eyelids. When finally this was done, he gripped the sides of the stretcher as it was being loaded into the tube, so that the little fingers of both hands were mauled. They pulled him out and dressed the wounds. Then they used the straps, which upset him further, so that he actually began to scream once inside, the sound oddly muffled as if it were coming from inside the folds of a giant cocoon. Cleaver waited a full two minutes for him to calm down a bit, and this threw the calculations off. Since the machine had been partly started, Cleaver wasn't sure whether or not to subtract the two minutes from the allotted time, then decided it was safer to do so. Observing the safety margin, that

meant that Bruce had only three minutes or so with the
throttle fully open. Nonetheless, he came out dazed.

Cleaver took him to the smoking veranda and had
Felicity bring him the obligatory cup of tea. Bruce refused it, saying he hated tea. That was odd, seeing as
how he customarily drank three cups every morning.
Cleaver set up a chessboard, having loaded the computer with advanced proficiency at the game and knowing that Bruce had never played it. Bruce's first move
was educated: He moved his queen's pawn two spaces.
Cleaver's heart leapt up and he leaned across the board
eagerly—his young opponent had learned the rules. But
after four or five moves that were nominally correct,
Bruce's game fell apart. He seemed totally unable to devise any kind of strategy or even to relate one piece to
another. More worrisome, he suddenly developed an
odd tic, a tug at the left corner of his mouth that gave
him an odd-looking grimace, which in a certain half-
light made him look sinister. And soon his eyes began
darting around. Cleaver knew where he had seen that
before—the telltale sign of Mann's paranoia.

"What's this here for?" Bruce said abruptly, looking
down at the board. Then he shouted, "Roaches, roaches,
everywhere!" He slapped the edge of the board hard so
that the chess pieces flew up in the air. Cleaver was
struck on his dome by an errant knight on the way
down. It smarted. He looked over anxiously at Bruce,
who was in the throes of a psychotic break. "Get out of
here! Get off me!" he yelled, slapping his forearms, then
falling on the floor in a convulsive heap. Felix came running and pinned his arms to the floor. Then Bruce gradually calmed down—he calmed down too much,
abruptly turning mute and descending into a psychotic
stasis that at first blush resembled catatonia.

Cleaver, who witnessed the scene with a clinical detachment, was deeply perturbed. The guy seemed to
have gone literally bugsy. Yet many of his new physical
manifestations were familiar: They were the manner-
isms and defense mechanisms of other patients who had
preceded him in the TSR. Was it possible? Did the pa-

tients, or rather *subjects,* somehow leave something behind in the computer, an imprint, bits and strips of themselves, their anima? Did others somehow pick this up when they traveled on their own solitary trips into the unknown? He would have to study the question, make detailed notes, maybe compile videotapes.

In the meantime, he was preparing for Benchloss. In the past, Benchloss had managed to call some pity up from him. But in fact his fountainhead of pity was not bottomless, and he had begun to view the unfortunate man exactly as Benchloss himself did—as a creature beyond humanity's pale. Benchloss believed himself to be dead, and so in Cleaver's eyes he was at death's door already. No great matter if something untoward befell him.

Felix wheeled him in. Felicity had helped him slide Benchloss onto the gurney—never an easy job, as he was a literal deadweight—and now she was lingering at the doorway, too curious to leave. Cleaver ignored her. In any case, they hadn't done a good job of it. Cleaver saw that Benchloss's arm was partially pinned under his back. A few more minutes like that and he would lose circulation there. A couple of hours, and the damn thing would turn blue and then black and then probably begin to rot. Not that Benchloss would even notice. What the hell—he'd probably take it as confirmation that he was already decomposing in the grave.

Cleaver lifted him, moved the arm, and lowered him, a silent rebuke to Felix, who seemed not to get it. Cleaver stared closely into Benchloss's face. Did he detect a flicker of fear there? Something rustling behind those eyes, usually as lifeless as a shark's? No question about it—the guy was creepy. Cleaver felt a shudder overtake him. He might as well admit it—he was frightened, deeply frightened, by this most unnatural patient. Benchloss's mouth was open, a hole into a fathomless black well. Cleaver leaned down and put his cheek to it; he could feel nothing, no breathing. He put his ear to it; there, in the far distance way down, a dim rattle. The lungs working themselves, some elemental reflex pumping them on. Or was it? Maybe he was imagining it? He shuddered again. Why did that black hole conjure up his father, the fear, the belt buckle opening to deliver punishment and humiliation? He began sweating. In the old days whenever he felt like this, he could divert himself—the cyborg slave fantasy or sometimes just numerology, systems and systems of numbers multiplying, square-rooting, dividing, and subdividing. A system, pure science, pure religion.

"So—are we going to put him inside?"

Felix's question startled him. It was sudden and rude, and he wondered how to express his disapproval. At the door, Felicity was still hanging around, so Cleaver walked over and shut it in her face, none too softly.

"Of course," he spluttered. He meant it to be a command, but it came out like an uncertain whine.

They lifted the man onto the stretcher, Felix taking his shoulders from behind like a wrestler and Cleaver hugging the legs—less strenuous but undignified. Again, he was surprised at how heavy Benchloss was. Was it possible for the mind actually to leaden the body like that, bloat it, flooding the cells with water in preparation for the final decay? Or was it just Cleaver's own imagination?

They straightened him on the mobile stretcher. Cleaver felt faint and let his assistant do most of the work.

Felix pulled down the helmet, with its helter-skelter bird's-nest of wires, and fitted it onto Benchloss's head. He picked up the eggcups and retracted them into bands.

"At least this one should be easy," he said.

But it wasn't. The deadweight of Benchloss's eyelids made it difficult to fit the band underneath; the upper eyelid, held open while working on the lower one, would spring loose and half close. For a moment, Cleaver suspected Benchloss of faking it, trying to sabotage the experiment. But there was still absolutely no sign of life. Felix kept at it. Finally, between the two of them, they fitted the eggcups in place and turned the dials to extend them, watching the characteristic oval bulge under the thin skin across the eyeball.

He was all ready to go. But Cleaver held off. He needed to collect himself. Mumbling an excuse, he left the room, walked up the stairs, and went outside. He sat on the stoop and looked at the water sparkling brightly in the sun. At that moment, a strange thought invaded his consciousness. It seemed to come of its own volition, out of nowhere, an arrow sailing from the long-gone battlefields of the past. A memory, long repressed and dangerous. It was of his father. He thought again of how he had learned of his death while a student at MIT. And he suddenly realized with a certainty that he had never before had the courage to admit that he had known of his father's death the moment it happened, before the phone call. He was absolutely sure. It all came back. Looking at the snow outside, he had seen his father, a dim shadow against the white, staring up at his window, a funny look upon his face, as if he had just been laughing—laughing at what? At the joke of seeing his son again in the final second of departure, at this visitation to a patch of snow near the Charles?

More than anything in the world, Cleaver feared being dead. Not the pain of it, not the last lingering moments of life, but the state of deadness itself.

Never before had the thought collected itself in such a crystalline way and presented itself to him as a hard, immutable truth. He shook it off, turned away from the water, feeling his eyes burning from the brilliant reflection of the sun on waves, and went back downstairs.

Felix was there, looking at him curiously.

"Let's get started," Cleaver said.

He heard the rattle of metal against metal as the stretcher slid upward, and he watched Benchloss slide off into the tunnel, the wires barely missing the sides. He could see scrape marks where other subjects had moved back and forth.

Felix was in place at the controls.

"I think I'll take this one," said Cleaver, motioning

him aside. Felix stepped away, a slight sulk to his shoulders.

"What are you doing?" he asked.

Cleaver was fiddling with the timer. He had turned off the automatic override so that the machine could go beyond its safe allotment of five minutes and even into the danger limit of seven minutes.

"I see no reason why we can't try something new," he said.

"But you said Quincy told you never to do that," Felix complained. "You don't know what's going to happen. The whole thing could overload. It's not safe."

"Not safe for the subject or not safe for the machine?"

The question stumped the thick-browed assistant, who thought for a full five seconds.

"I'm not sure. Either one, I guess."

"Well, if you have to guess, I'd say you don't know."

Felix lapsed into silence.

They heard the hum of the machine starting up. Cleaver turned two knobs, and Benchloss's brain sprang to life on the screen, the familiar large clenched fist. Another knob and it rotated slowly, showing itself from constantly changing viewpoints—the lava-hill ridges, the deep cleavage between the hemispheres, the wrinkled lines separating the lobes. It was disembodied like a hologram.

"A little accompaniment?" said Cleaver, covering over his fear with forced lightheartedness. He switched on the audio, and out of two speakers came once again the rush of static, neurons firing their electrical charges. This time the crackling sounded like rifle fire from a distant battle.

He checked the timer: two minutes. The electrodes had all found their targets; the coverage was complete.

By now Cleaver had seen enough subjects to interpret the firing of the impulses. He could stand back with enough distance and objectivity to see the forest, not just the trees. He was able to read the overall pattern of neural activity—an increase concentrating in the midbrain, building up rapidly to a crescendo, and then tapering off to almost nothing. Felix had noticed the pattern, too. "Like popcorn in a microwave," he'd said last time. "It starts slowly and then the popping comes all at once and finally it peters out." Cleaver had deemed the metaphor infelicitous, but he knew the pattern was significant. It's the way the brain would sound if its waves were moving outward—*into the computer*. And then, when the time was running out and he began reducing the power to the computer, the waves rushed back—back *into the brain*. Like pouring water from one glass into another, he thought, though he knew it was hardly that simple.

He manipulated the hydraulic dials to bring up a cross section and then honed in on one side of the lower brain. He spotted the major structures: the layers of the cingulate gyrus and the fornix, the septum and mammillary body, the hard nugget of the thalamus, the curving hippocampus opening outward like a horn of plenty, and the central pineal gland—the innermost organ that secretes melatonin to regulate biorhythms so that primitive man hidden away in his cave could keep track of daylight. Poor Descartes, looking for "the seat of the soul," had found it here; maybe on second thought he wasn't so far off—every computer starts with a clock. Finally, the dials led him to the ultimate treasure, the twin organs, slightly darkened and perfectly almond-shaped—the amygdala.

Odd, how his heart was racing. *Why am I so afraid? What am I afraid of?*

He looked at the clock. Four minutes had gone by. That was approaching the safety zone. What happens if they reach seven minutes?

He looked at the amygdala. It was small; if he had it in his hand, he could crush it between his thumb and forefinger. *What kind of thing is that to think?* It looked odd, somehow . . . what? *Empty, bleak.*

When he was younger, Cleaver had used numerology to combat anxiety. He could go on for hours, working formulas, reciting square roots, enumerating pi: three . . . point . . . one . . . four . . . one . . . five . . . *What comes next?*

"Dr. Cleaver," said Felix, "I think it's time to turn back."

Nine, I think. Or eight . . . no, nine . . . then two . . .

"We have to turn back; we really have to."

And after two . . . what? His father had looked so strange there, standing in the snow, looking up at him. But Cleaver had had no doubt—it *was* his father. And his hand *was* on his belt buckle.

Five minutes gone. Then six.

He was vaguely aware of Felix on his left, brushing up against him. But he held his ground. The room seemed to be spinning. Pi . . . the mystery of a never-ending number.

Gradually, he began exiting from his reverie.

It was strange how the colors and the tracing of the neurons firing on the screen looked just as they had during the death of the old man while his anima departed and he appeared before his wife one last time.

Sounds inside the tube, more neurons firing, or was it a thumping?

Seven minutes now. A sputtering and the screen went black. Not all at once, but as if it were burning out, first dark around the periphery and then all across the middle, leaving only a diamond of light in the center. The diamond lost its luster, turned dull, and shrank away, extinguishing itself.

Felix was quiet, aghast. Cleaver shook himself, shook off the fear, feeling a little better, as if a nausea had lifted. His head was clearer. The computer was silent, the screen vacant. Should they pull him out? Why not—his time was up.

Felix took one side of the stretcher, and Cleaver took the other. It didn't require two people, but both of them were curious, drawn to it the way one is drawn to a car accident, driving past the shoulder slowly, staring at the underbrush, senses all atingle.

Down the stretcher came, and it wasn't really a surprise at all. There he was, Benchloss, lying immobile, all animation drained from his slumped body. It was hard to say what the difference was; he had been almost lifeless going in and now was totally lifeless coming out. But there *was* a difference. No one could have mistaken this heap of cold flesh for a diseased man playing at being dead.

He *was* dead.

And there was something else. His face was contorted, frozen in a grimace, as if he had died of something horrible. As if he had died afraid.

Cleaver wondered about that. He felt bad about it, sort of. But what struck him, and what bothered him, was that he didn't feel nearly as bad as he thought he should. He felt mostly a kind of lightness and only a modicum of shame. He hoped he hadn't gone so far down the road that he was no longer capable of regarding these patients as human beings.

What struck him, and what he couldn't escape, was the final arrow of irony in fate's quiver: The patient with a disease whose main symptom is believing himself to be dead suddenly comes alive and then at the end does die.

Poor Benchloss. And now that he was finally, truly, irretrievably dead, Cleaver found it strange that he was at last able to think of him as a *patient*. Not a *subject*.

❧

Scott was working again, a four-day shoot of nightspots in SoHo for *Brio,* a new hip magazine. Ordinarily, he would never accept an assignment like this. He didn't respect the magazine or its editors, and the photos themselves—crazed dancers strung out on Ecstasy, young women dressed to kill waiting in a sleazy alley to be admitted—posed no special challenge. But he had to do something. Kate had convinced him that it was necessary for his own sanity. This job paid a lot. And it had the added advantage of night work, which left the days free to stay with Tyler at the hospital. In between, somehow, he grabbed a few hours sleep. The last time he had looked, his eyes were puffy and hung by bags the color of dark ash.

He dragged his camera bag into the loft and collapsed in bed. Comet bounded around and jumped on the covers, licking his face. Scott groaned; he would have to take her for a walk.

Last night had been long and exhausting because his heart wasn't in it. He had hit three clubs, two of them in the newly fashionable meatpacking district. As often happened, especially when he had his old Nikon strapped around his neck, women came on to him. The camera emboldened them. In one spot, Mickey's Roadhouse, a woman in a blue dress had followed him into the men's room, perched upon a sink, and opened her legs. When he'd walked out, he could hear her cursing. He had come back home, developed twenty rolls, and took the prints to the magazine. All day, until evening, the editors had dithered over the choice. He found he didn't care.

He thought of Tyler all the time and wondered if the day would ever come when he would stop. It had been four days since the hearing, and he had yet to know the decision. Why was it taking so long? It wasn't as if the board needed more information. Perhaps they had already come to a decision; perhaps they were waiting for a decent interval to lend the appearance of a spirited deliberation, like a jury that reaches its verdict in the first hour and then sits out the clock playing cards.

He had bothered Kate with calls at all hours. Had she not heard anything at all? She tried to sound encouraging, but he could tell she was doubtful that the decision would come their way. She was trying to give him reality in small doses.

He was worried for her, around the edges. She had been brave to speak on his behalf; he had seen the look on Saramaggio's face as they filed out of the hearing room. He knew that one day she might be made to pay for her principled stand. Just one more thing that he owed her. But all of that—everything she had done for him, even the fleeting thought that she cared for him, beyond the obvious sympathy—all that was relegated to the periphery of his consciousness. He wished it could be otherwise. He wished, as he had told her weeks ago, that he could be less self-involved. But he couldn't help it right now. After Tyler, there was not room left over for much else.

He took Comet out for a walk all the way to the river. He took off her leash and watched her zipping through the waterfront park, dashing this way and that, turning from time to time to make sure he was still there. Such simple joy. It did him good, for a minute or two, to watch it. Darkness fell quickly.

When he returned to the loft, he heard the phone ringing, but by the time he opened the door it had stopped. Then it started up again—not a good sign, that would mean an important call. His heart rose up in his throat, pounded his ribs. A premonition of bad news.

He lifted the receiver and said not a word. He heard her voice: "Hello . . . hello . . ."

"I'm here," was all he said.

"Scott, oh, I'm glad I reached you." There was a pause, which his heart made longer.

"I don't know what to say. I heard, informally, that the board reached a decision." Another pause, which told him the answer. "It's . . . it's not the one you want." Then she spoke more quickly, gathering strength. "They've decided to go ahead with it. They say they think Tyler has a reasonable chance to survive and that's why they want to do it, not because it's some kind of experiment that they want to see how it ends. I know it's not what you wanted or what I wanted, but maybe it's not so bad, at least if they see some hope. You see? And if you still disagree, there's always the possibility of filing an appeal to the courts. So it's not really over. You see?"

But by this time, Scott had stopped listening. He mumbled "Thanks" and replaced the phone slowly, one hand mindlessly rubbing the ruff on the back of Comet's neck.

The bastards, he thought. *The heartless bastards.*

Chapter 19

Kate entered the freight elevator wet from the rain and pressed the button for the fourth floor without a second's hesitation. She glanced down at the business card she held in her hand. Scott's address was printed in neat block letters, with the tiny icon of an old-fashioned viewfinder Brownie in the lower left-hand corner. She had no idea what she would say to him once she got there or what she would do.

She knocked softly on the door. No answer. She grasped the knob and found that it turned with no resistance—this was not surprising to her; she was beginning to feel an odd sensation that inexorable, unnamable forces were guiding her. She simply had to give in to it—and that, she had realized, made everything less complicated. She didn't have to think so much.

The door swung open. A large dog greeted her happily, its tail thumping on the wooden floor. No one home. She patted the dog and put her raincoat over the back of a chair and looked around the huge loft. Tall crowded bookcases, two bicycles, intriguing abstracts on the brick walls, a plethora of mounted photos. She took a moment to reflect: She had guessed that his place would look like this; she was pleased to be right.

On a coffee table were stacks of black-and-white photos. She felt a stab to the chest—they were all of Tyler. She realized that she had never seen him without the injury; he was a handsome youth. The eyes, the cheekbones, the set of the jaw were all like his father's.

She crossed the floor and stepped inside a smaller

room. It took a microsecond for her eyes to adjust to the dark. She gave a start.

There he was!

Lying on the bed, next to a small object propped up on the pillow beside him, an animal of some sort. A stuffed koala bear.

He looked horrible, closed in on himself.

Scott did not move, but his eyes shifted to her. He was not surprised to see her; he barely seemed to register her presence. She tried to think of something to say.

"I thought . . . I thought I should come here."

No reply.

She saw a bottle of scotch on the floor, half-empty. She walked over and sat on the foot of the bed, and she could smell the alcohol on his breath. But he didn't appear to be drunk. He sat up.

"Thank you," he said in a distant monotone. "I'm glad you came."

He swung his legs around to sit on the edge. Side by side, they were almost touching thighs. He bent over to lean his elbows on his knees and cradle his head in his hands. When he spoke, his voice had changed, was more emotional.

"I didn't expect it, somehow," he said. "Though now, thinking back, I can see how deluded I was. There was no chance. All along, there was no chance. They wanted to continue it, and nothing was going to change their minds."

She put one hand on his back.

"Maybe you're right. But it's not over. There're things we can do, more steps."

"The courts. And how long is that going to take? Meanwhile, he's lying there more dead than alive."

He stood bolt upright.

"I just don't get it. Who are they to make the decision? I'm his father, for God's sake." He began pacing around the room.

For the first time, Kate realized the room was Tyler's. How could she have missed that? The movie posters, the Rollerblades, the pile of shirts, the adolescent mess. She surmised that everything was probably just as Tyler had left it. That's the way it always was in literature; and now, here they were, in life. On the bed, the koala bear fell to one side, its shoulder fur worn to bare patches—from Tyler's hugs, she guessed. The boy was becoming more real to her by the minute.

Scott was working himself up.

"You know what angers me more than anything? I didn't tell you this at the time. What really pissed me off was when that guy, the head of the hospital—what's his name?"

"Brewster."

"Brewster. When he started in questioning me and he asked if I understood that Tyler was suffering no pain. No pain! Here he is hooked up to those goddamned machines, sunk in some kind of coma and going through who knows what. Maybe there *is* no pain. But maybe there is. Maybe every time he flicks an eyelid, he's passing through some hideous nightmare. Maybe he's in perpetual agony. Or maybe he feels lost or alone or abandoned. Who's to say? They don't know. Nobody knows. Not even me, and I feel so close to him, sometimes I used to think I could read his mind."

He paced around some more. His voice softened.

"You know, when he was little and I put him to sleep, I would tell him a story. It always began the same way—about a house with a thousand rooms. I would lie next to him—right there—and I would put my head on the pillow next to his, and I swear, I would look deep into his beautiful eyes, and I could *think* what he was thinking, I could *feel* what he was feeling."

She nodded, speechless.

"And even if he's not in pain, he should still . . . they should still let him go. He's not Tyler anymore. I can see that. They don't want to see it."

He stopped and looked directly at her.

"Let me ask you something. When you called just now, did they tell you to tell me?"

"No. I heard about it. They're planning to tell you formally tomorrow."

Scott nodded. He seemed to be working up to something, but he shook the thought away for a moment. Instead, he asked her a polite question.

"Would you like a drink?"

To her own surprise, she heard herself answer yes. And then, "Very much."

He picked up the bottle by the neck and left Tyler's bedroom, walking across the loft into the small, cluttered kitchen. He picked two dirty glasses out of the sink and rinsed them out. She sat on the couch in the large room and watched him as he poured them both a half glass and walked over to the couch and, standing above her, handed one to her. He leaned down and touched glasses, a reflex done distractedly.

She took a deep swallow. She felt it burn her throat, then her chest, and spread out to her arms and legs. The warmth felt good.

He took a sip and put the glass down on the coffee table and sat next to her and looked directly at her.

"I wonder if I could ask you something, if you could do me a favor. I wonder . . ."

"Yes?"

"Do you think you could take me there so I could see him?"

"When? . . . Not now?"

"Yes. Now."

She looked out the window. It was dark. She could see by the lights across the street that it had begun to rain even harder.

"This very moment?"

He nodded.

She paused to think it over, but that was a bit of play-acting—she had known from the moment he asked that she would do it.

"I guess so. But you know—I think they've taken away my authorization to enter that ward. Officially, I'm off the case."

He seemed stunned. *For the first time,* she thought, *he's thinking of what this means for me.*

"I didn't know. I'm sorry."

"Oh, it's no big deal," she lied.

He left his glass where it was, but she finished hers in one large gulp. Then they went outside in the rain to flag a cab.

⌐——⌐

The hospital was quiet, and they were able to walk past the nurses' station without being spotted. But halfway down the corridor, a voice boomed behind them.

"Excuse me—where are you going?"

It was the nurse on duty, and her battle-ax tone suggested trouble. They turned and walked back toward the counter with its computers, clipboards, and paraphernalia. They were no longer dripping water, but their shoes were still soggy.

As soon as she saw Kate, the nurse's demeanor changed.

"Oh, Dr. Willet. I'm sorry. I didn't recognize you."

Kate relaxed outwardly. But her mind was racing: What if the pass code had been changed and her ID swipe card no longer worked on the outer door to Tyler's ward? In that case, they couldn't reach the observation room to observe him through the glass wall, never mind the second lock that closed off the inner chamber with the computers and his medical equipment. If not, how could she come back here and talk her way through the locked door? Scott didn't look as if he would stand being denied the chance to see his son.

"That's okay. We're just . . . making a visit." Kate smiled. "After hours," she added unnecessarily.

"I see." The nurse's expression suggested that she did not. She hesitated for a full five seconds. "Well—he has to sign in, boy's father or not."

Scott went to the log with barely suppressed anger and scrawled his signature. The nurse insisted that he add the time. Kate didn't want Scott to get into an altercation with her. That would surely end everything. He looked the worse for wear. He had insisted on hitting a bar a block away, a dive with a linoleum floor and

men in T-shirts who looked as if they lived there. The
bartender knew him. Another round of quick drinks. It
was not a casual stopover; he had insisted, and there had
been a hardness, almost a desperation, behind his insistence. She wondered: Was he trying to fortify himself to
see Tyler?

And as for Kate, she hadn't felt this unsteady for
some time. She noticed, leaving the bar, that the lines of
linoleum seemed to waver. And when they stepped into
the elevator, she had hesitated before the bank of buttons, blanking momentarily as she tried to remember
the floor.

Now, the nurse was looking at her with opprobrium
dancing in her eyes.

They turned around, and Kate felt the stare follow
her like an icicle dripping down her back. The hairs on
the nape of her neck rose up. Their footsteps were so
loud they echoed, and as they traversed the corridor, it
seemed endless and the green pastel walls with white
wainscoting seemed to be narrowing, closing in on both
sides. It took a long time to reach the end. She didn't
dare look back.

Kate opened her purse and pulled out her ID card.
Her hair was wet, but it felt hot and clammy as it clung
to her forehead and temples. Her blouse was wet
around the shoulders and she shivered, but from cold or
heat, she couldn't tell. Her stomach tightened—she was
suddenly nauseous. She wondered for a fleeting instant
if she could just turn to Scott and tell him that she didn't
think this was such a good idea after all, and couldn't
they just go back to the bar and have another drink and
talk? She shot him a sideways look. He was standing
there, leaning forward expectantly, waiting calmly. He
would not be denied.

Her hand shook slightly as she aligned the card over
the slot and swiped it, holding her breath.

Click. The lock sprung.

She breathed, felt relief wash over her, and leaned
over to grab the door handle. But Scott was already
there, anticipating her, tugging the heavy door open

fiercely. He was inside before she knew it, and she had to hurry before the door clicked closed again.

Scott was at the glass, both hands up over his head, leaning into it, staring through it. His body was tense, as if an electric current were running down his spine.

Tyler was inside, behind the glass, suspended upside down in the frame of the bed, held in place by straps and surrounded by tubes and wires. She looked at his face, which appeared wooden, fixed as he hung in space, as sculpted as a ship's figurehead.

Something nagged at her. Something was wrong.

Was it the sounds of the machines, slightly different, quieter? Or something in the lights crossing the round window of the monitor, a low undulating line where there should be jagged bouncing peaks and valleys? Or something in Tyler himself, a gray cast to his features, an immobility?

"My God," said Scott softly.

He had noticed it too. He began banging against the glass.

Kate let out a gasp.

"Look," she said. "Look at the machines."

Scott turned, looking around frantically, then back at her. She pointed to the computer in the room next door. There, the signs of life were everywhere, lines pulsating across the screens with vigor and intent, lights blinking, rhythmic purposeful beeps.

They didn't understand. The monitors on the left, connected directly to Tyler's body, were barely operating. The lines screening his heart, his brain, his breathing, his body temperature—all were barely moving. The EEG was flat. The ones in the room to the right, coming from the computer, were newly active.

"What's going on?" demanded Scott. "What's happened? Something's wrong. Look at him."

"And over there," she said, her voice high and nervous. She pointed, and Scott spun around to see what she was looking at.

The master monitor, the device that revealed which of the two, patient or computer, was in command of the signals that told the body to function, had its needle pointing squarely to one. Not to zero, but to one.

"That means the computer's registering activity before he is," she said.

"So the computer's taken over."

Scott froze a moment, then spoke rapidly.

"And when *you* came in, he registered nothing. The machines didn't jump. Tell me—are you wearing that same perfume?"

"Yes. Yes, I am."

She rummaged quickly through her purse and pulled out the bottle and removed its top. She sprinkled some on her arm. The aroma filled their nostrils. They watched the monitors.

No response. The needle didn't fluctuate at all.

Kate pulled out a handkerchief, poured out the contents of the bottle, held it upside down until it all splashed out on the white cloth. She dropped the empty bottle in her purse and held the handkerchief up by two corners. The smell was overpowering.

They peered through the glass.

Still nothing, no response.

Je m'en souviens.

So Tyler could remember nothing. Not even his primordial self, his primitive second brain, just above the stem where the olfactory sensation was supposed to shoot like a bullet.

"He's gone. He's totally gone," said Scott, his voice cracking.

Kate wondered whether she should speak. Because it was worse than that. Some words came back to haunt her: *expansion into the adjacent possible.*

She decided she had to tell Scott. She owed him the truth, now more than ever.

"No, not entirely gone," she said finally. "His own brain is not operative. But whatever was there—that part of his mind that regulated his bodily functions—has gone over there." She pointed to the machines in the room to the right. "It has flowed into the computer."

Scott struck the glass with his forehead and remained there for a while, not moving, staring at Tyler. His son wasn't totally ashen; he was receiving blood. But there was a lifelessness to him that was very apparent now that he knew to look for it. There were no flickers of the eyelashes, no little tics that he had come to know over the past weeks and seize upon as harbingers of hope. Instead, Tyler's face was a kind of waxen mask.

He found it hard to put the thoughts into words.

So this is what it amounted to. His son's body was an empty shell, kept functioning by wires and tubes. His mind had fled. Whatever had been in him that had made him unique, that made him the special loving living human being called Tyler, had traveled down the wires and taken up captive residence inside the computer.

The computer was more his son than the inert shell before him. The computer had kidnapped him.

They had finally done it. They had finally done something worse than kill him.

He felt like screaming.

And so he did scream.

Security guard Juan Montoya received the alarm shortly after midnight. Even before the nurse called down, almost hysterical, he could see trouble on the video monitor. A man up on the third floor moving around, his figure discernible in oddly rapid movements through the snow on the black-and-white screen. And when Montoya turned on the sound, he could hear shouting—a man's voice, low and angry, and somewhere in the background a woman screaming, "No, no, don't!"

Then came the call. Nurse Beadham, her voice tinged with uncharacteristic fear.

"Come quick! It's the father of that boy in the isolation ward. He's gone berserk."

Montoya allowed himself a moment of confusion.

"Isolation ward?"

"Saramaggio's patient. The one who's a vegetable. Anyway, it doesn't matter—just get up here right away, damn it."

She paused, horror-stricken. "My God, he's coming my way. No, he's not. He's going into a room. What's he doing?"

Montoya was standing, staring at the monitor. The man had walked out of the camera's line of sight. He looked at another screen and saw nothing.

A few seconds later and Nurse Beadham answered her own question. "He's coming out again. He's got a chair. What's he doing with that?"

On the monitor, Montoya could see what he was doing with it. The guard watched in a kind of frozen fascination as the figure hoisted the metal chair over his head and then, summoning his strength, pitched it against the glass in the observation room. In the background, a woman's voice, begging him not to do it. There was a dull crashing sound. The glass shook a little, but it held. Montoya saw the man pick up the chair again. He indeed looked like a madman.

"I'll be right there," he said into the phone.

"You better," yelled back Nurse Beadham. Unvoiced but powerful threats lurked in her words.

Just as soon as reinforcements arrive, Montoya thought to himself. He was no fool: He had hit the emergency alarm button, plugged directly into the station house one block away, even before her call. The phone rang again. This time it was the police, and he told them to come as quickly as possible. While he waited, he went to his locker and searched for his nightstick and found it in the bottom, under a stack of newspapers. He hadn't used it once in his four years on the job. He picked it up and thwacked it into his left hand. *Ouch.* It was heavier than it looked, weighted in the upper end. *That could cause some real damage,* he thought.

Hardly five minutes later, two police officers, a man and a woman, rushed in through the emergency room.

"What's going on?" asked the male cop. Montoya

told them the little he knew and pointed to the monitor, where the figure was still banging against the glass. The cops stared at the screen, almost transfixed, then the woman said, "Let's go." The three ran down the corridor to the elevators. Montoya pressed the button, and they waited in nervous silence for what seemed like a long, long time, until the car finally arrived.

It didn't take long for them to subdue the man. Perhaps he had already tired himself out by tossing around the chair, which lay upended to one side. The thick plate glass was unbroken. Behind it, an apparition that unsettled Montoya: A boy swathed in bandages was suspended upside down, held in place by straps.

The door that was normally opened with an ID card had been propped open by a shoe. That was so the man could go down the hall, fetch the chair, and get back in, figured Montoya. He must have had some damn strong reason to want to smash that glass.

"Take it easy, take it easy there, bud," said the male cop, holding Scott down by planting a knee, not too gently, into the crook of his shoulder.

"Officer," interjected Kate. "Please, don't hurt him. He's the child's father."

The male cop looked at the female cop, and she gestured toward the glass. Slowly, comprehension dawned on the cop's face—he glanced again at that horrible view of the boy suspended upside down—and he lightened the pressure on his knee.

"You gonna behave yourself now?" he asked, almost rhetorically. It seemed like the right thing to say under the circumstances. He didn't really expect an answer, and he got none.

"Why's the boy like that, anyway? Upside down?"

Kate moved into his view, standing just above Scott. "It's to prevent bedsores."

"What's wrong with him?"

"He's had an accident," she replied, not wanting to go into it any deeper.

"And he's the father?" the cop said, none too quick a study.

"Yes."

"So what was he doing up here late at night? And how did that chair get there?"

"He was trying to smash the glass," said Nurse Beadham, who had waddled over to join them, sounding even more officious than usual. "God only knows what he would have done if he had succeeded." She seemed to feel that the cop's sympathies were shifting over to Scott.

"And who are you?" said the female cop, addressing Kate.

"I'm a doctor. Dr. Willet. I've been handling this case."

"Aha. Well, what do you think? You witnessed the whole thing, I take it."

"Witnessed it. She helped him get in," put in Nurse Beadham.

"Please. I'm not talking to you. I'm talking to Doc Willet here."

Kate thought quickly. What would defuse the situation?

"His father—Scott's his name—had just gotten some bad news about his son's prognosis. He was upset, understandably. And he wanted to come and ... see him, maybe for the last time, I guess. And the situation sort of got out of hand—"

"And you aided him—is that right?" said the female cop. "I take it you need a swipe card to get in there. Is that how you and he got in? With your card?" She motioned to the card resting on Kate's chest.

At that moment, Scott began to struggle and bellowed out, "Let me up, goddamn it."

"Hey, take it easy there, fella," said the male cop.

"Watch out," yelled the woman.

For Scott had raised one leg and, arching his back, hooked his ankle around the man's shoulder. With one swift jerk, the policeman went flying on the ground. He leapt up, red-faced and furious, while his female companion jumped on Scott and pinned him to the floor by holding her nightstick against his windpipe.

"*You* take it easy," said Kate, rushing over. "You're hurting him."

"Hey, shit," said the woman, leaning down into Scott's face and inhaling deeply. "This guy reeks of alcohol. He's drunker than a skunk."

The other cop pushed aside her nightstick, grabbed Scott by the collar, and hoisted him to his feet. He took his own nightstick and jabbed him in the ribs.

"Lemme see you walk. Lemme see you walk a straight line."

Scott refused. He looked at the cop and shook his head.

"Looks like we got an uncooperative guy here," said the male cop.

"Wait a minute," said Kate, interposing herself between them. "Let's all calm down a moment."

"You calm him down. He struck me. That's an offense. I'm going to run his ass right down to the precinct."

"But surely there's some way to work this out. He's distraught. He's worried about the life of his boy. Have some sympathy."

"Lady, he just struck an officer of the law. As far as I'm concerned, that just stopped all my sympathy right there."

The man swung Scott around, gathered his arms behind his back, and clamped a pair of handcuffs on him.

"What's he going to be charged with?" asked Nurse Beadham, not without a trace of excitement.

"Could be a lot of things. Drunk and disorderly. Assaulting an officer. We'll see when we get there."

"I'm going with you," said Kate.

"Like hell you are."

"Well . . . where's the precinct?"

"Lady, look it up."

They marched off, Scott between them looking down, each with a hand on his shoulder.

"Come with me, Doctor," said Montoya softly. "I have the address downstairs."

Kate left, after turning to take one last look at Tyler, behind the sheet of glass. He hadn't stirred one iota, lost in another world and snug in his medical cocoon, wrapped up like a fly in a spiderweb.

Chapter 20

As Kate was about to leave the security guard's office, a shadow loomed in front of her, cutting off her exit. Instinctively, she stepped back. It was Saramaggio.

He was glaring at her, his face red and puffed.

"You will come to my office," he commanded. "Right now."

"I can't. I've got to go to the police."

"Police? What for?"

"Scott Jessup's been arrested."

"I saw them dragging him off. Serves him right."

"No, he didn't do anything wrong. They shouldn't have arrested him."

"That's not the way I hear it."

Saramaggio turned to the guard.

"You there, what's your name?"

"Montoya, sir."

"All right, Montoya. You will kindly escort Dr. Willet to my office."

With that, Saramaggio spun on his heels and walked out. Montoya cast a beseeching look at Kate, and she nodded at him. He checked the directory for the office number and led the way, but once they got to the floor, he stopped, unsure. She showed him where it was, and he opened it with a master key. The room was empty. Montoya gestured toward a chair, and Kate sat in it, uncertain whether the security man was being a gentleman or holding her hostage. They waited a good ten minutes for Saramaggio to arrive—apparently, he had been inside Tyler's ward, casing it for damage. Kate fig-

ured he'd been thorough and had taken his sweet time
about it.

He walked in and dismissed Montoya with a wave of
his hand and sat behind his desk, heaving a world-weary
sigh. He was dressed in a green knit sweater, khaki
pants, and Timberland Top-siders. It struck Kate that
she had never seen him in casual dress. A five o'clock
shadow darkened his jaw, his hair was mussed, and even
his salt-and-pepper beard was unkempt. The effect was
unsettling; he looked like a businessman at a convention who had just returned from a night on the town.
Evidently, he had been staying somewhere in the city
and had been roused from bed, probably by Nurse
Beadham.

He cleared his throat portentously and looked down
his nose at her, much the way a teacher confronts a truant.

The thought crossed her mind: *He's enjoying this. He's
luxuriating in his power.* She resolved not to show a
flicker of discomfort. Another thought popped up, but
she ignored it—for the moment.

"I suppose you know . . . ," he began slowly, measuring his words like tablespoons of castor oil, "at least I
expect you know—I can't imagine otherwise—that
what you have done here tonight is most serious, grave,
unheard-of. It is—in one word—simply scandalous."

That's two words, she thought. She looked up at him,
waiting, and put on an expectant expression, as if she
were merely curious about what he would say next. He
didn't care for that at all. She played again with her private thought.

"Proceeding against all instructions, under the cover
of darkness, invading the hospital at an ungodly
hour . . ."

He's making me sound like a World War II saboteur,
she thought.

". . . bringing with you an unauthorized party . . ."

*Unauthorized party, he's the boy's father, for Heaven's
sake.*

". . . and who only knows what you had in mind, what
your objective was . . ."

Objective. . . . There's that war jargon again—

Saramaggio stopped cold, folded his hands upon the desk, and focused his eyes on a spot above her head.

"I might as well ask you outright—and I advise you to think carefully before answering. Were you or were you not, together with the patient's father, planning to remove the patient from life support?"

Kate leapt forward in her chair. "What! Not at all. That's the craziest thing I ever heard."

"Well—that's what it looks like from here. The father wanted to pull the plug. You, having thrown away all pretense of professionalism, took what you construed to be his side and decided to assist him in his campaign. You know, you've fought us every step of the way. You testified against us at the board. And when you lost fair and square, when the decision went against you, you decided to ignore it. You decided unilaterally to disregard the findings of your peers, your superiors, and so you resolved to achieve your goal through underhanded means. That goal, purely and simply, was to thwart our important research work and our attempts to return this poor young man to a state of health and normal functioning. Dr. Willet—do you realize how serious this is?"

He sat back in his chair, his hands linked behind his head, a prosecutor satisfied with his summation.

But clearly, he had one more iron in the fire, one final ace up his sleeve. He was winding up to deliver the coup de grace. He was preparing—and his mouth was already forming the words—to fire her.

He never got to it.

At that precise moment, Kate decided to unleash the thought that had settled in her mind. She took command. She fixed him with her toughest stare and said, "Dr. Saramaggio, I'm glad you're sitting down. Because there's something you should know. I'm surprised you don't already know it from your visit to the isolation ward."

In truth, she was more than surprised. She was aghast. How very typical of him, she thought, that he would check the damage to the glass, the chair, and everything else before checking on the status of his patient.

Saramaggio looked miffed, a trifle confused. His hands unlocked and returned to their resting spot on the desk.

"What in hell's bells are you talking about?"

"I'm talking about the fact that the operation has gone all wrong. The boy, Tyler, is no longer in a coma; he's sunk to an even lower state than that. He shows no signs of life whatsoever. He's not functioning on his own; he's not doing anything. The computer is doing it all for him."

"What! That's impossible!"

"No, it's not. It's happened. The computer has seized total control of his brain. There's nothing left of him but an inert body. That's why his father got so upset."

"I don't believe you."

"Go see for yourself."

"That's exactly what I'm going to do."

"And if you find I'm right, there's only one possible course of action."

But Saramaggio, without another word, had already bounded out of his chair and was halfway out the door, leaving Kate sitting across from an empty desk.

Well, she thought to herself, *no reason to stick around here.* She left Saramaggio's office. No security guard in sight. She decided to leave her raincoat where it was, on the third floor, lest she run into Nurse Battle-ax or his Malevolent Majesty, and she took an elevator down to the lobby and stepped out into the rain.

There were no cabs on the streets, and so she had to walk the eight blocks to the police station.

Saramaggio's hand was shaking as he dialed the number. He heard the phone ringing—two, three, four times. He thought he could hear his own heart pounding over the line, a tintinnabulation in his ears. The storm of his own thoughts, maybe.

But how—how is it possible?

The whole grand experiment had gone haywire. The patient was lying there just as she had said; the boy was in something worse than a vegetative state. He had no EEG at all, no brain activity. He wasn't alive; he wasn't dead. The computer had taken over everything, all of his autonomic functions. Saramaggio had never seen anything like it.

Goddamn it—why doesn't he pick up?

Finally, on the ninth ring, there was the sound of the receiver being picked up, some rustling and grunting in the background, and then Cleaver's sluggish voice thick with sleep.

"Hullo."

Saramaggio didn't waste time with any niceties.

"Come right away. I need you. Please. Something's gone wrong."

A momentary pause while Cleaver pieced together who it was, what he wanted. He quickly became alert. It hadn't escaped him that Saramaggio had used the word *please*. That was most unlike him.

"Where are you? What's gone wrong?"

"I don't know. If I knew, I wouldn't be calling you, would I?"

The words were meant as sarcasm, but they couldn't camouflage a trill of weakness, which Cleaver detected immediately. Something big was up—and the more Cleaver thought about it, the more excited he got.

"So . . . tell me."

"I'm at the hospital. Something's gone wrong with the boy. He's totally nonresponsive. The monitors show no signs of activity at all."

"So is he dead?"

"No, not really. It's hard to tell."

"But is he breathing? Is his heart pumping? Are his lungs working?"

"In a manner of speaking, but he's not doing it."

"What do you mean? Explain yourself."

"The master monitor is at one. The computer is doing everything. It's almost as if . . . well, I don't know any other way to put it."

"Go ahead."

"It's almost as if his mind . . ."

"As if his mind what?" Silently, Cleaver began to curse Saramaggio.

"As if his mind were gone, as if it had just disappeared."

"Disappeared?"

"As if it had been sucked down the wires and into the machines."

"I'll be right there."

Saramaggio had no way of knowing it, but his particular way of putting it plucked a deep, unforeseen chord in Cleaver, who jumped out of bed and put his clothes on over his pajamas. He had never moved so fast in his life. That's what happens when you hear something that might just mean that your life's dream is on the road to being realized.

~~~~

Cleaver got there in half an hour flat, despite the rain. He traversed the nearly deserted hospital lobby, nodding to the receptionist, who was half asleep, and tried to walk calmly, as if nothing had happened. He took the elevator to the third floor, where he found Saramaggio pacing back and forth, a pained expression upon his face.

From the moment Cleaver saw him, and saw his sagging shoulders, the worry lines creasing his forehead, his stupid salt-and-pepper beard, he knew that Saramaggio was scared.

Well, well, the great Saramaggio. It's times like this that test our mettle. And I'm beginning to wonder if you've got what it takes.

The surgeon rushed over, a half-relieved, half-anxious look upon his face that he tried to disguise.

"I'm glad you're here. What took you so long? I haven't touched anything. I haven't told the nurses that something's wrong, but I think that one over there, the big one—don't turn around, she's looking our way—I think she suspects something."

He led Cleaver down the hall, talking. He told how Tyler's father had come to the ward along with Dr. Willet and found that the machines—

"That woman! What was she doing here? I thought she was denied authorization."

"Well, she was. But she didn't actually enter the ward. I mean, not the inner room. She just went to the observation room."

"I don't care. She shouldn't have been here."

"I know—the lock was supposed to be changed. I guess it wasn't."

"You know what this means. She's got to be suspended—or better yet, terminated."

Saramaggio told him about the incident with the chair.

"Well, there you are!" exclaimed Cleaver. "They must have disturbed something, wrecked the equipment, altered it in some way. That would explain the patient's deterioration."

"I don't think so," said Saramaggio. "She said that they saw the problem before then. That it was when they saw it that the father went . . . got so upset and threw the chair against the glass."

"But she would say that, wouldn't she? It's a perfect way to try to cover her tracks and throw blame elsewhere."

"I don't know. . . ."

They reached the ward. Cleaver took out his ID card and swiped it through the slot on the wall; the door clicked, and they entered. Cleaver's eyes moved quickly from machine to Tyler and back to machine; he took in everything—the master monitor, the bank near the computer, the nearly flat lines on the screens. The boy was suspended upside down in the air with his white gown and his arms strapped to his sides. He looked like an angel frozen in midflight.

Cleaver felt his heart pounding in his chest, his nerves tingling with excitement. It was obvious that his condition had changed drastically.

Saramaggio broke the silence.

"Well, what do you think?" he asked.

Cleaver ignored him for some minutes, walking slowly behind the observation glass. Then he used his pass to open the inner door and switched on the button to turn the bed ever so slowly. The outer frame rotated like a huge gyroscope until the bed faced upward and Tyler was resting on his back. No longer was he straining against the straps, and the sheets and bedclothes fell back upon him lightly. One wrist was bent backward, caught in an odd position that emphasized his complete helplessness. The effect was of someone struck down and gone—like a corpse found upon a battlefield. And yet upon closer inspection, a subtle difference emerged. Cleaver was able to spot it right away—the body was flaccid, not rigid. The skin tone was waxen but still had tiny splotches of red. Supine upon the bed, the boy might be in a profound sleep. From a quick observation, there was no reason to doubt it: This was a person whose mind had fled from his body but who was not technically dead. An empty vessel that was still strong on the outside and able to be filled once again—if only one could locate the precious elixir of life.

Cleaver washed his hands, dried them, and touched Tyler's forehead. The boy did not move. He poked Tyler's arm, and his finger left a white circle that faded quickly—another sign of normality. He stroked his cheeks, opened one eye and looked at the pupil and the white rim, and felt the slow, steady, throbbing pulse in his neck. He opened his mouth and examined his tongue. His temperature was a perfect 98.6.

A grim play upon an old joke tickled him: The operation was a success, except that the patient *didn't* die.

He withdrew his hands, washed them again out of habit, and turned to Saramaggio, who was waiting in the observation antechamber.

"Let's go somewhere where we can talk," he said. "This is obviously extremely serious. I wish you had called me sooner."

"But I just got here," Saramaggio protested. "I only found out about it just now."

"Proper security might have avoided the whole problem."

Cleaver didn't really believe that—he was just amusing himself by being cruel.

———

The spacious room on the fifteenth floor was dark, and they kept it that way at Cleaver's insistence. He hadn't wanted to confer in Saramaggio's office because it was cramped and windowless, not right for the grand proposition he was mulling over. At the same time, he felt a strange need for darkness, not because he feared that his emotions could be read upon his face, but because it suited his mood.

My, how the lights on the river are grand, he thought. *Just like diamonds scattered on a velvet blanket. Nothing like a little excitement to unleash our poetic natures.*

"What do you think you should do?" he asked Saramaggio. He emphasized the *you.*

The question was disingenuous. Cleaver was enjoying the moment. He wanted to feel his rival sweat. He wanted him to hang twisting in the wind, as that marvelous Watergate metaphor had put it.

Saramaggio hesitated.

"Well," he said finally, his voice none too confident. "We've got to take action. We've got to pull the plug and end the whole thing. I was just wondering how to do it, what to say."

"You mean what to tell the board?"

"Yes."

"Well, I can see how that's a problem for you. Especially since you were so cocksure that the boy would remain in good shape until the implantation procedure began."

Saramaggio remained quiet.

"Especially since you denied the father's demand that the boy be taken off life support."

"I didn't deny it. The board denied it."

"Yes, well, you spoke out against it—rather eloquently, I thought."

"I didn't notice you saying anything at all."

"No, you're right there. This horse was yours to ride. I didn't want to get in the way."

"I wish you had."

"Me, too," replied Cleaver. "That way I could have shouldered some of the blame now."

Saramaggio squirmed in his seat. Cleaver couldn't see it, but he felt it.

"And then there's the problem of the woman," Cleaver continued—he never called Kate by her proper name, not to mention her title. "What do you think will happen when she tells the board what she's discovered?"

Saramaggio shrugged.

"Where is she, by the way?"

Saramaggio looked up into the dim light.

"I don't know. I left her in my office. I doubt . . . I don't think she's still there."

"I'm sure she isn't. I wouldn't be surprised if she's gone off looking for the boy's father. You say he was taken away by the police?"

"Yes."

"That's probably where she is. We may be able to use that."

"What do you mean?"

"Never mind. I'll handle everything. I might even be able to come up with a plan that will get you off the hook."

"A plan?"

"Yes, but you have to do exactly what I say. And I don't want you asking a whole lot of questions. I'm tired of your questions."

"Well, I don't want to do anything illegal. You're not contemplating something like that—are you?"

"Saramaggio."

"Yes?"

"That's a question."

Cleaver rose, walked over to the doorway, and flicked on the lights. The room seemed flooded with brightness that made Saramaggio feel even more vulnerable. And

Cleaver was being quiet again, which unnerved him even more.

"I just never thought this would happen," he said. "I don't understand it."

Cleaver ignored him. He was pacing around the room, then stopped, looked at Saramaggio, and said, "For openers, you've got to deal with that nurse. I need to get her off the floor for a good two hours."

"Two hours. What're you going to do?"

Cleaver stopped and looked at him.

"Saramaggio—I told you to stop that."

"What?"

"Another question. In fact, two of them. I guess you don't follow instructions very well. I hope you're up to this."

Saramaggio decided to bite his tongue. He had already come this far; he might as well see what kind of plan Cleaver could come up with. The man was smart—maybe he *did* have something up his sleeve. There was always the option of going to the board and admitting that the experimental procedure had failed. How he hated that word: *failure*. The board would insist that it be ended right away. Maybe they could do that on their own, which is probably what Cleaver had in mind. That way there would be no complicated explanations, no backtracking, no apologies.

He sighed.

He looked out at the river, a ribbon of blackness snaking its way alongside the concrete banks of the island of Manhattan, and he felt his heart plunge into utter despair.

How had it come to this?

Nurse Beadham was not in a good mood—far from it. First, it had been a trying night, what with that man coming into the hospital and raising such a ruckus— she had known there was something fishy about the way that Dr. Willet had tried to slip by without signing in—and then the security guard being called and the police arriving and everything else. Most upsetting. And then Dr. Saramaggio coming in at this godforsaken hour, and him pacing around so nervouslike, and finally that Dr. Cleaver arriving—he gave her the creeps, the way he never looked you in the eye. Always seemed like he was scheming.

She checked the clock. Another two hours till quitting time. She wished it were here already.

At that precise moment, the elevator opened and who should step out? Cleaver himself. She gave a start and almost felt as if she had conjured him up from some dark sulfurous place.

He walked over, and she saw him glance at the nameplate pinned onto her breast pocket, a white rectangle with the sunken letters a deep blue.

"Ah, Nurse Beadham," he said unctuously. "Has anyone informed you about the tragic situation here?"

She shook her head no.

"Our young patient, sad to say, has taken a turn for the worse and is now beyond our assistance. He has no hope of recovery. Dr. Saramaggio tells me that this occurred while the father and Dr. Willet were here. Apparently, they created some kind of disturbance, which triggered an attack and precipitated the boy's sudden collapse. I take it you witnessed this?"

He glanced over at the sign-in sheet while she nodded yes.

"Good. I'll need a full statement from you. You can go up to Dr. Saramaggio's office to compose it—he's waiting for you there. But first, I need you to go to the boy's isolation ward and mark down all of the indicators. This is extremely important. Take your time, write down all the numbers, and sign the sheet. Then go upstairs."

She hesitated.

"But who will take care of the floor? I can't leave my station until two a.m."

"Don't be silly," he replied. "I'm here. If there are problems from any of the patients, I know where to reach you."

"And what will you be doing?"

"If you must know, I will be withdrawing life support. It's all quite legitimate. Dr. Saramaggio is phoning Dr. Brewster and other members of the board right now."

She dawdled, uncertain.

"Get along now," he said, as if speaking to a child.

And she did what she was told.

Cleaver couldn't believe his luck. Alone at last, he made the necessary calls over his cell phone—he didn't want any hospital record of them. Then he checked the floor to make sure all was quiet, walking down the corridor to the south wing and back and ending up at the isolation ward. He used his card to gain entrance, the click of the lock sounding unreasonably loud.

He felt calm. He knew what he was doing. Now if only Felix came through. He wished he had more confidence in that young man.

He leaned up against the glass and found a nick about shoulder high. It was probably there that Jessup had struck with the chair. Cleaver allowed himself a moment of compassion for him—poor guy, he really had been put through the wringer. Well, soon enough all that would end.

He looked through the glass at the boy. Even with the bandage around his head, he looked handsome. And at peace. That was important—that he be at peace, the outer shell from which life had been extracted, the empty vessel still standing.

It was a historic moment. He almost wished someone were here to witness it and to record it, a Boswell to his Johnson. The consummate man of science, the innovator about to take the great leap into the uncharted world, to "shift the paradigm" of received human wisdom, as that philosopher Thomas Kuhn would put it.

What would Cybedon say if he were here?

But come—he was delaying.

Cleaver entered the inner room with a self-assured swipe of his card. He opened a drawer under the computer and found what he needed, not much really, just a simple connecting cord. He searched along the base-boards for an outlet and couldn't find one.

Christ, wouldn't that be perfect? For want of a nail, the battle was lost.

He pried a machine two inches from the wall and peered behind it. Aha! There it was! He shoved and pulled the machine, swiveling it from side to side until it was six inches from the wall. He reached behind and attached the cord to the phone outlet. Then he slipped the other end into the computer and sat down in a chair to reflect.

It was hard to say what would happen. But he knew that the time had come to take the big step, that the world required an anima—the quintessence of human intelligence—to enter into that ether and glide through all those megamillion bytes and make sense of it all and reconnect back. Humans and machines, united at last.

He looked back at the boy. He appeared even more handsome in the glow of the hospital light. Maybe he was looking at him and knowing, the knowledge that he was going to be the first. . . .

Cleaver stood and turned to the computer. He hit the keyboard quickly and typed in all the right codes without a moment's hesitation. He stepped back. The machine was waiting, blinking obediently. Was it crazy to think that it knew what was about to happen, that it too desperately wanted it to happen?

Maybe someday we can ask it, he thought; *maybe someday its feelings will be known.*

And that was the final thought Cleaver had before he made his climactic move, before he leaned down and hit the *send* button and sent Tyler's anima—his mind, if you will—careering down the wires and out into the infinity of cyberspace.

III

The Recovery

Chapter 21

Scott paced around his cell for five hours, following a path that he repeated over and over, as any caged animal will do. His was a circle that brought him by the bars, then past a bunk, then back to the bars. The routine of it allowed him to think, though the thoughts were as repetitious as his movements. His pacing got on the nerves of his two cellmates: a black Dominican with dreadlocks who had picked a fight in a bar and gotten the worst of it, and a lanky young white man whose glazed eyes told a tale of heroin use and who now slept stretched out on the floor.

"Hey, man, give it a rest," the Dominican shouted at one point.

Scott looked over at him without a word and then sat on the floor leaning back against the bars. But a few minutes later, he was up on his feet again, pacing. He couldn't help it. The Dominican had no more protest in him, and soon he lay down on a steel cot hanging from the wall, resting his head upon one arm like an innocent child.

"Man, you all fucked up," he said, shortly before falling asleep. He snored, but Scott scarcely heard him.

Fucked up. That just about says it all.

Scott replayed the night in his mind. When he came to the scene on the hospital floor and called up the image of Tyler lying there, attached to the machines but without life, his chest moving like a bellows, his heart pumping like a metronome, nothing happening of its own volition, he closed his eyes and tried to shake it away. But it kept coming back, and the only way to rid himself of it was to force himself to consider what might happen next. Surely now, if they had any decency at all, they would take Tyler off the machines and let him die. If not, he himself would sue them and compel them to do it—he would get the best lawyer in town, a killer lawyer, whatever the cost. It was too late for any kind of death with dignity, but Scott had given up on that long ago. What he wanted now was simply to put Tyler to rest inside the ground, once and for all. That was it. Nothing else mattered.

The drink had left his system, forced away by adrenaline and anger. His mouth had a taste of bile and his gullet burned, and he had bruises on his wrists where the handcuffs had been, but he was thinking clearly. He felt oddly calm. He was looking forward to taking them on—Saramaggio, Brewster, the review board, the whole lot of them. He was eager to do battle and the sooner, the better. But he had to get out of this place first, and he would do whatever it took to accomplish that, even if it meant swallowing his rage and hanging his head before a judge. Revenge would come soon enough.

He began pacing more slowly, thinking. He should conserve his strength. He looked around. The jail stank. He wondered if the heroin addict had crapped in his pants. There was a toilet bowl without a seat in one corner. The cell had bars on three sides and one brick wall peeling white paint. Light came from two bare bulbs hidden behind a metal mesh.

He should try to get some rest. He walked over to the steel cot that was unoccupied and sat down, dangling his legs over the side. They felt cramped, tense.

The only other time he had been behind bars was on a weeklong trip to Somalia when had he photographed an old woman in a marketplace and nearly created a riot. It had been one of his rare times outside the country without Tyler—he'd left him at his mother-in-law's—and he'd worried the whole time that the incarceration would delay his return. Luckily, he had gotten out quickly, polished off the assignment in another two days, and made it home on schedule.

His mother-in-law—it had been almost a year since they had seen her. Scott and she had never gotten along, and, oddly enough, after Lydia's death, she had seemed to lose interest in her grandchild. She moved into a condo in Florida, sent dutiful checks decorated with marlins for Tyler's birthday, dropped by during infrequent trips to New York to catch some theater, and that was it. When Scott telephoned her about the accident, she was horrified but she didn't come up.

"Hey, you. It's your lucky day."

It was a cop, meandering down the corridor and stopping in front of their cell. He had a cup of coffee in one hand and lifted it to his lips, blowing and slurping. He looked at Scott.

"Get up. Come get your stuff. You can go."

He balanced his coffee cup on a crossbar and opened the cell door. Scott rushed over and walked through. The Dominican leapt up.

"Whoa. What's this? What's goin' on? Why he gettin' out? He got privileges or somethin'? He got con*nec*tions?"

The cop stared him down.

"That's right. He's got 'em and you don't, which means you'll be on the next bus to Rikers."

"Aw, man. White cops is always lookin' after they own. Whole system's fucked-up rotten."

"Maybe, but it can still catch scum like you."

"Man . . ." The Dominican slumped back on the cot and closed his eyes. "Leastways lemme get some fuckin' sleep."

"Nighty-night." The cop made it sound like a threat.

Scott followed him, the cop's backside and belt with its massive array of equipment—handcuffs and flashlight and radio and ticket book—swinging slowly side to side. Only the gun was missing from the holster.

At the front desk was another cop with a large beer belly, who handed over a manila folder with Scott's name on it. Inside were his belt, wallet, and keys. He could see through a window that early-morning light was breaking.

"So, am I being released on my own recognizance? Do I put up bail?"

"Naw, nothing like that. You can go. No charges. You just needed a night to cool off. But don't go creating any more disturbances."

Scott shook his head. He would say anything to get out of there and return to the hospital.

"And you might want to thank her."

At that moment, Scott felt a hand on his right arm, and he turned to face Kate.

"She explained everything," the desk cop said. "Sounds rough."

He looked away, as if Scott had a disease.

Kate smiled and with her hand coaxed him to turn and move toward the door. Her hair was tousled and her white silk blouse wrinkled.

"Have you been here all night?" he asked.

"No, in and out. They kept saying they couldn't make a decision until the sergeant came back. There was some kind of trouble in East Harlem, so he was away until just now. A nice guy, named Paganelli. He was the one who said it was okay to release you."

"Thanks to you."

"When they heard the story, they were sympathetic. They just needed a pretext—a doctor telling them it would be all right, that you weren't some kind of nutcase."

"I'm not too sure about that."

Outside, the sun was bright and shining down upon them. It hurt his eyes.

"You don't look so hot," she said.

"Let's go to the hospital."

"I think you should go home first, change your clothes, shave, get a cup of coffee."

She gestured toward him with one hand, and he looked down. His shirt was torn, and on the front was a trickle of blood, dried to a deep brown.

"We've got a long day ahead of us, a lot of meetings, demands, fights, who knows what. And frankly, you'll argue your case better if you look a little more presentable."

"You sound more like a lawyer than a doctor."

She smiled and felt like saying something supportive. "Right now I'm neither. I'm just a friend."

They reached the corner of Lexington. He raised his hand for a cab, and when it stopped and he opened the door, he was surprised that she slipped right in.

An hour later, they pulled up in front of the hospital. As soon as they entered the lobby and saw the face on the receptionist, they knew that something new had happened. She looked nervous and reached for a phone.

"Dr. Willet. Please—just a moment. Dr. Saramaggio has given instructions for you to wait right here. I'll call him."

Scott was already moving toward the elevators.

"You do that," said Kate over her shoulder. "Tell him I'll be up on the third floor."

She hurried after him and stepped in just as the doors were closing. There were three other people inside, staring straight ahead. She looked at Scott—it was easy to see that he was overwrought. He was facing forward, his eyes narrow, his shoulders raised and his hands balled into fists.

The elevator stopped on two, the doors opening with maddening slowness, and a doctor in a white jacket entered and pressed a button and the doors closed, again languidly. Scott pressed the third-floor button three times, hard. No one spoke.

At three, Scott was out before the doors fully opened, and Kate was right behind. They hurried to the nurses' station—again an odd look from the nurse there, half shock, half worry—as they turned right, down the corridor toward the special isolation ward. As soon as they came within fifty feet, they saw that everything was different.

It was gone. The ward was no longer there.

The normally locked doors were wide open, and they could see clear through to where, only a few hours ago, there had been the glass partition of the observation room.

Scott ran the rest of the way down the corridor. Then he stopped and walked slowly through the doors, as if in a dream, staring at the blank walls around him, the empty outlets, the newly scrubbed floor. It smelled of Lysol.

Scott turned, and Kate saw his face drawn in bewilderment and confusion. He knew what had happened, and he looked as if he didn't know what to feel—he both feared and desired it.

They heard footsteps behind them, Saramaggio hurrying up, his coat flapping behind him. He appeared anxious and uncertain.

"I wanted to catch you first to tell you," he said, slightly out of breath. "I'm sorry that you found out this way. You see, we had no alternative. After what happened . . . after what you saw earlier today . . . last night, we decided . . ." He paused, took a breath, and plunged ahead. "We had to take your son off life support. There was no reason to continue. . . ."

He looked at Scott, appealing. Scott took a step forward, and for a moment Kate thought he was going to flatten Saramaggio. Instead, he stared at him, his body shaking with fury.

"You goddamned, stupid, selfish . . ."

He stopped. It looked as though he had gathered control of himself, but no, he had not. He walked over to a wall and leaned against it with his left hand and then heaved a deep sob and smashed his right fist into it. In the small room, the noise was loud. He did it again and again until the wall was dented and a thin rain of plaster fell out and formed a tiny white volcanic mound on the floor.

Saramaggio stood frozen, and his head was bowed. Kate saw that tears were silently streaming down his cheeks.

So he was human, after all.

"I'm sorry," he said finally, in a thin voice. "I wish there were something I could do. I wish . . . I wish we had never done this. I didn't mean for it to end badly. I wanted to . . . I wanted to save the life of your son."

"You wanted to run your experiment on him. You didn't give a good goddamn for him!"

Scott turned, still resting his left hand upon the wall, and glared at the doctor.

Saramaggio took a deep breath and looked back. Slowly, he nodded.

"I guess there is some truth in that," he said. "Maybe you're right. I did want to do the operation. I wanted it very much. I'd been preparing so long, thinking about it, what it could mean . . ."

He trailed off, waved his hand vaguely in the air, then covered his eyes.

Kate was surprised to see what happened next: His shoulders began twitching and then heaving so violently that she thought he was having some kind of attack. He was sobbing uncontrollably, from somewhere deep inside, so that his upper body was actually flopping. When he took his hands away, his eyes were blinking madly as the tears streamed out and his face was contorted and squeezed into a pathetic red ball.

What followed was even more remarkable. Saramaggio walked toward Scott and actually put his hands together as if he were praying.

"Please, I'm sorry," he blurted out. "Please, please forgive me."

And he continued to approach him until he was standing right in front of him. He opened his arms as if to hug Scott, and he put his arms on his shoulders and moved his hands around his back. But Scott stood there erect, unmoving, his hands tight at his sides.

Saramaggio took a step backward and looked beseechingly at Scott, then at the wall.

Kate felt a sudden rush of pity for this man who had let his dream carry him off too far on a path he never should have taken. For a moment, she thought of giving him comfort, telling him what he needed to hear—that he had transgressed but could be forgiven, that his soul was not yet lost.

But she, too, just stood there, not moving. Things had gone too far. Things had happened that never should have happened. Too much pain and misery had been caused, and all so needlessly.

Scott had won his point. Saramaggio had been transformed by a night of epiphany, and now he stood before them, a forlorn and abject figure. But neither she nor Scott felt good about that.

Later that day there were meetings of the Board of Ethics, the Institutional Review Board, and the hospital's governing board, forms to fill out, the beginnings of inquiries—all the meaningless paperwork and formalities of officialdom that a large institution turns to in time of trauma.

Scott refused to be interviewed, and this was noted by an investigating medical expert, who wrote in a box on the appropriate form that the "nearest relative" was "uncooperative." All of those present during the operations, including Kate, were debriefed for a comprehensive report that would be issued in due course. New guidelines were to be drawn up to cover similar situations; from the tone of the questions posed, Kate was certain that they would end up being toothless. Brewster made a point of expressing full support for his staff, including Saramaggio, whose contrition surprised them all, and who requested and was granted two weeks' leave. It seemed to be generally agreed that the areas of stem cell cultivation and implantation and computer-assisted surgery were fruitful to pursue, despite what everyone called "the recent tragedy."

Almost nothing was said about Scott and Kate's late-night visit to the ward or about Kate's role in the whole business. Clearly, there would be no overt reprisals against her, and the thought occurred to her that by not pressing charges they might be buying her silence. She couldn't imagine assisting Saramaggio in an operation again. *They* might be willing to forget, but she wasn't.

Kate found Gully alone, sipping coffee in the surgeon's lounge, a small room of easy chairs and mismatching tables and lamps on the fourth floor. They talked and she soon found that she was unburdening herself. Her doubts about Tyler's death did not find a sympathetic ear.

"What's so strange about it?" he said. "It was an experimental operation to begin with. Everyone knew the risk of using computers to assist the boy."

"*Assist!* Spare me from that kind of assistance. *Finish off* is more like it."

"Now, don't be harsh."

"Why wasn't there a rigorous investigation of what actually happened? Who knows why the damn thing failed? It looked like the computers actually caused him to die."

"How can you say that? He would have died long before if they hadn't kept him alive. Please don't get yourself all in a snit about this. Please don't get into any more trouble. You were doing so well here and we all like you so much."

Gully drank delicately from his cup.

Kate was hardly assuaged.

"I don't know—the whole thing seems wrong. I think the computers malfunctioned in some way. They're responsible for his death—don't you see?"

But Gully just shrugged and turned away. His face looked pained, but his gesture bespoke a rudeness that he wouldn't have displayed two weeks before, she thought.

———

The funeral was held in the afternoon at a parlor on Amsterdam Avenue, an assembly-line kind of place with three separate service rooms, so that to enter the correct one, mourners had to read the replaceable white letters on a black velvet bulletin board.

A surprisingly large crowd turned out, including most of Tyler's class at Horace Mann. The service was short. Tyler's coffin was closed because of the damage done to his head and face or, as the mortician had put it in talking to Kate earlier, "restoration difficulties." The casket was simple wood. Scott left the choice to Kate—in fact, he left almost all the decisions to others. He was in an odd state, not dazed but removed, as if his emotions had finally shut down.

Kate sat next to him during the service and couldn't help thinking of the last occasion when she had sat next to him—the board meeting that would determine Tyler's fate. So much had happened since then. It seemed so long ago.

He had placed a wrapped package on the pew next to him. She watched the others file in and noticed a large contingent of people her own age who had an artistic look about them—Scott's fellow photographers, she surmised. They looked at him with concern, and three or four of them came over to whisper to him or put a hand on his shoulder. One leaned down to hug him. There was a family of three, with a boy about Tyler's age, sitting across the row from Scott. All three of them looked stricken, especially the boy, dressed in a heavy black suit, who stared ahead blankly, his cheeks flushed.

A handful of people came from the hospital. There were some nurses who had attended to Tyler, seated all together, and Gully and another surgeon. Brewster, looking solemn and official, chose a place halfway back, close enough to be noticed but not so close as to intrude. Saramaggio, who had appeared to be waiting for Scott in the entryway and then had watched him pass by without uttering a word, sat in the back row, clearly distraught. Cleaver was nowhere to be seen—no surprise there, thought Kate.

One thing Scott did was choose the music. The first selection was the Rolling Stones' "You Can't Always Get What You Want," then Bob Dylan's "Like a Rolling Stone," and finally Tom Petty's "Free Fallin' "—all songs that had been meaningful to Tyler. He had heard them for years, Scott told Kate, listening mindlessly to them along with his father and then abruptly making them his own in that voracious way of adolescents.

There were only a few speakers. One was a teacher who talked of Tyler as a student, the intelligence that crackled in his eyes, the humor and curiosity and love of Latin and science and Greek mythology and biology and learning for the sake of learning. "He loved life," the teacher said. "He opened himself to it and wanted to drink deeply from its cup." Another was a Cub Scout leader who said Tyler had tried everything—canoeing, archery, photography, painting—hanging back until he was ready and then jumping in and embracing them to the fullest. In baseball, he had played left field, singing scraps of arias during the dull moments and so acquiring the nickname "Figaro." At night, sitting around the campfire, he had mesmerized the other children with scary stories that seemed to spring from a bottomless, fecund imagination.

Then Scott stood up to speak. His voice was shaky at first, but as he went on, it gathered strength. He told stories of Tyler as a young boy and as a man-child and then as an almost adult, story after story, and by the end everyone there who knew him felt that he had been fully rendered, and the few who did not know him believed they had missed an extraordinary person. Finally, Scott spoke briefly about the accident, and then he seemed to address the doctors and others who had cared for him.

"I've been thinking a lot in recent days about the operations he went through, those that were necessary in an attempt to save his life and those that he was subjected to for additional reasons, as well. The difference, if there was one, was sometimes difficult to distinguish. The ordeal was hard—perhaps hard for him and definitely hard for those of us who loved him. I've had some tough words for doctors recently, and I'm not going to take them back. But I would like them to know, everyone who cared for Tyler, that I appreciate what they did and that I understand it. It is not a bad thing to want to come up with a new operation to lessen human suffering over the long run, even if in the short run, it brings hardship and heartache to the individuals who first undergo it. Please do not think that I do not recognize this fact, even in the midst of my rage over the days he spent in the hospital and over the final outcome."

He paused a moment, collected himself, and went on. "If Tyler's death has contributed, even in some small way, to medical science, to an understanding of how the brain works and how it can be helped to recover from a deadly accident, then what happened to Tyler will not have been as meaningless as it now appears. So whatever you do, please do not stop your effort to advance the cause, despite what you may hear from me and from others like me. And now that I have said this, what's on my mind, I don't want to talk about it or think about it anymore."

He sat down, and music played once again, this time the final chorus from Haydn's *The Creation*. Then he filed out, with Kate close behind, onto the steps, where he absentmindedly accepted more hugs and handshakes of commiseration. Kate noticed that the family of three hung back a little before coming over. When they did, Scott put his arm around the boy and said, "Johnny, I hope you know that this was not at all your fault. You were smart and brave, and because of you, Tyler was able to stay alive a little longer."

The boy looked grateful.

"Here," Scott said, "this is for you." He handed him the package.

The burial was held in Westport. Kate sat with Scott in the first car of the cortege.

"What was in that package you gave that boy?" she asked.

"A koala bear. Tyler's. That was his best friend, Johnny."

She put her hand on his and they rode in silence for an hour and a half. The graveside ceremony was mercifully brief. Tyler's grave was next to Lydia's. Scott looked away as the coffin was lowered and then threw down a small handful of dirt upon it, gently and reluctantly.

On the way back, as their car entered the city, the driver asked, "Where would you like to go?"

Scott was still silent. He shook his head as if ridding it of a loathsome thought, and looked at her.

"What do you feel like?" she asked. "Where do you want to go?"

"I don't know. I just feel tired. I want to—you know what I want? I just want to go someplace and sleep."

"I know just the place," she said, and she gave the driver the address.

When they arrived at her place, it was already early evening but still light outside. The sidewalks were filled with people coming home from work, men and women in light business wear, toting briefcases, walking quickly with self-assurance. The late-summer air was electric, had that sense that anything could happen.

She paid the cab. The elevator operator seemed to pick up the mood, didn't say a word as they ascended to her floor. She unlocked the door and tried to hold it open for him to walk through first, shifting her foot against it, a moment of awkwardness.

He looked around but without really seeing, at her furniture, the prints on the walls, the view out the window.

"Want a drink?" she asked.

He shook his head no.

"Want to sleep?"

He nodded his head yes.

She led the way to her bedroom, embarrassed at the mess—the tapes stacked precariously next to the TV set, the open sewing box, the magazines scattered about, a towel over a lamp neck, a pair of panties resting on the back of a chair.

But he didn't seem to see any of it. He headed straight for the bed. She left the room and closed the door behind her.

Then she read for hours, without really concentrating, and ordered in Japanese food—enough for two, just in case. But he slept on.

Later, when it came time for her to sleep, she crept into the bedroom and saw that he had left his jacket and shirt hanging on the back of a chair and neatly folded his pants and put them on the seat. In the bathroom, she changed into a cotton nightgown, brushed her teeth quietly, and turned out the bathroom light before she opened the door back to the bedroom.

Ever so carefully, she crossed to the other side of the bed and lifted the sheet and slipped underneath, hovering on the edge of the mattress. She could hear him next to her, breathing deeply, lost to sleep for the first time in weeks. She lay awake for a while, listening to him, to the regularity of his breathing, and she wished him peace from the bottom of her heart.

Chapter 22

Walking down Gansevoort Street, Scott faced the breeze blowing in from the Hudson and felt a bite in the early September air. He lifted his head up to it. The first stirrings of autumn—once his favorite season, a time of sweet endings and crisp beginnings.

Not now. Now he was barely coping, trying to crawl out of the black hole. September already. How quickly it had sneaked up on him. Time does that—it's so cruel the way it continues in the rest of the world when grief grinds our own clock to a halt. He felt that he had aged years over the past summer.

His lips were dry. He wanted a drink, wanted it badly, but he would resist, force himself to, as he had for almost two weeks now. He had had his last one—forever, he vowed, because he had hit bottom. The binge that had started a week after the funeral had been one for the books, days upon days of steady drinking—double scotches, triple scotches, going from bar to bar, finding the ones along the waterfront that stayed open until dawn. Then staggering home, collapsing into bed, and spiraling down into a deep sleep and waking up in the afternoon and eating something—an egg, a sandwich—and starting off again with a couple of beers. One morning, he awoke lying in the doorway of his building. Later, when he poured orange juice his hand trembled so much he spilled it.

Kate had tried to help, but even she had given up, powerless before his inner demons and outer fury. But now he would whip them.

He hadn't seen her for—how long?—not since he

went on the wagon. He barely remembered their last talk.

He turned into the art gallery, tucked away in the meatpacking district, a chic address for those who liked to shop avant-garde among loading docks where quartered carcasses and hacked joints were carried by men in bloodstained white smocks.

Vickie was there, reading a magazine, and she smiled up at him, dark red cropped hair cupping her face like slender fingers.

"You're early," she said.

"Got a lot to do."

"You've still got two days. The opening's not till six o'clock, so three really."

"I know. But I'm behind."

"It looks finished."

"But it's not."

Scott entered the wide room to the rear.

He *was* behind. Over the past two weeks, he had gone through hundreds of photos, sorting them, choosing them, cropping them, enlarging some, discarding others. They had to be just right. They were sent out for mounting and he still wasn't satisfied and chose others to substitute. Then he had to hang them, leaving just enough space against the white walls. And of course they had to be arranged in the proper order—they had to tell a story. He was getting there, but still he wasn't quite satisfied.

The exhibition had been Vickie's idea. A sometime girlfriend, their romance had lapsed years ago by mutual consent and they had remained close. She had made it big in the art market of the nineties and kept up her downtown contacts. She'd wept at the funeral and, five days later she'd dropped by his loft in the afternoon, waking him up. Leafing through the photos of Tyler, she'd been struck by a thunderbolt—or so she said at the time. (Later, Scott was to wonder, Had she planned the whole thing?) "You know what?" she proclaimed. "You've got such good stuff here, you've got enough for an exhibition. How about it? Why don't you show these photos of Tyler? I'll loan my gallery. It'll be a tribute to him—think of it that way." Her enthusiasm had been infectious, but Scott had been in no shape to catch it. He'd grunted something noncommittal and said he would think about it. Nonetheless, the idea had worked on him in his alcoholic stupor. He had kept returning to it in moments of clarity, began conjuring it up, putting the photos on the walls in his mind's eye, rearranging them, fixing the narrative. So eventually he came to the decision without ever making it—even now he couldn't pinpoint the exact second he'd realized he wanted it more than anything in the world.

He would call the exhibit "A Boy's Life." It would begin with pictures of Tyler as a baby and then follow him through all the years of growing up, the arc of his brief existence. Assembling it had been a painful backward journey for Scott, but he remained convinced that the enterprise would be redeeming. There were so many outstanding photos—maybe he could capture him, explain him to people who would never know him, people like Kate and others, strangers. But at other times he was discouraged. He thought of those millions of spontaneous moments that went unrecorded by the camera, times when Tyler's face would open in delight at some discovery or turn morose at some hidden thought. Those unlooked-for moments of joy, contemplation, fear, boredom, anger, petulance, love—those were the significant ones. That's when the thing called life poked through so that others could see it and experience it. And even those moments were little more than signifiers on the surface. Because real life happened inside. Could he even pretend to come close to documenting it? Make any sense out of it at all?

How presumptuous he was, he thought.

Scott sat at a large table stacked with prints. They were sorted in manila folders by year, by camera, by theme, by season, by mood.

In his pocket was a roll of undeveloped film, the last roll he had taken. They were pictures of Tyler in the hospital ward, shot through the observation window on an afternoon when Scott had felt a sudden need to record it—for what reason, he could not say. Should he throw it out? Or should he develop it? Include it in the show, an accusatory coda? It cut too deep—too personal, too intrusive. But what was the point of a piece of work if it sidestepped ugly truth out of some high-minded sense of dignity? And there was no dignity here, only the long lonely misery of death.

He lit a cigarette. What would Tyler have wanted? Hard to say. He remembered a discussion they'd once had when Tyler had read an article by a writer whose daughter had contracted a dread disease. How could someone do that? he had asked, looking up from the magazine at his father. How could someone turn a horrible private experience into something public—and for profit? Wasn't that obscene? And yet scarcely a year later, he'd become a stickler for unflinching truth when he'd begun nibbling at the edges of literature and admired writers like Philip Roth and Frederick Exley who had the courage to turn their own lives inside out and strip them bare for art.

Scott put the roll of film away in a drawer.

He began looking through the manila folders, going over the prints one by one. They were from years ago, back when they lived in the old house in Connecticut. There was Tyler as a toddler, squatting in knee-deep water in Long Island Sound, the rocks hurting his feet, his face contorted in crying. Never had any child looked so miserable. Scott smiled as he remembered how, years later, Tyler would upbraid him for taking that photo—"Why didn't you just come and rescue me?" he would ask, joking. "What kind of parent were you?" Another shot of Tyler standing on a porch—one which was long ago forgotten—and here he was older, maybe four or five, naked as the day he was born and oblivious to it, his penis falling naturally to one side, his right fist held across his chest like a Roman emperor.

It was then that he came across a bunch of pictures in a folder that was not labeled. They were puzzling, instantly familiar, though he couldn't at first place where they had been taken—a dozen or so shots without anyone in them. Yet they must have been important; why else would he have shot them and gone to the trouble of developing them and saving them all these years? He held one up, looked closely at it. There was a wall, familiar wallpaper, a door jamb. It struck a distant chord—he knew the pictures were for some reason important. Then the memory hit him with a jolt. Of course. He had taken them inside Tyler's room, not long after Lydia had died. The camera was angled up from Tyler's bed, at his instruction, to frame the door. It was after that strange episode.

Scott thought back, the memories coming together. Tyler had received the news of his mother's death quietly, seemingly with the forced stoicism of childhood. And then, days later, he had made a confession of something that bothered him and he'd talked about it for weeks afterward—he'd insisted that he had seen her standing in his doorway at the moment her plane crashed. He was scared of going to sleep, and so his father had tried to convince him that nothing was there, that photos would pick up any disturbance, even things not seen by the human eye. For four or five nights, they'd taken the pictures together, and of course, they showed nothing. They did not, however, do the trick. Tyler was still anxious every night at bedtime. And so his father would stay and tell him stories—about Jingo and the house with the thousand rooms, and behind each and every door lay a new adventure, sometimes funny, sometimes scary.

Scott had to stop. Enough for now. His stomach was churning, and he felt the hole inside growing bigger. A ghost of desire passed through him, but he shook it off. He had to be strong—he was not going to try to fill that hole with alcohol. Not now, not ever.

He took Vickie out for a cup of coffee, wanting company. She talked, as she always did, nonstop. Then she looked across the table at him and said, "You haven't heard a word I've said, have you?"

He smiled. The truth was, he hadn't. He had been thinking of someone else.

~——~

He spotted Kate at once coming out of the hospital—a gray suit, honey-colored hair spilling onto her shoulders, pointed chin, a vigorous stride. He realized, with a start, that she was good-looking—very good-looking. He had known that before, but hadn't paid much attention to it.

"Hi," she said, as soon as she saw him, her face spreading in a warm smile. No recriminations.

"Thought I'd meet you after work. Doing anything?"

"Not right now."

He fell in beside her.

"I'm glad to see you," she said. "How're you doing?" She stepped back, a bit theatrically, and looked him over top to bottom. "You look better than the last time I saw you."

"I *am* better." He searched for the words. "I thought the time had come to clean up my act."

"Good."

They walked by the East River along a promenade, cars whizzing by below, the river choppy with tiny whitecaps.

She turned toward him and looked him in the eye.

"You know drinking will get you. Sooner or later, it'll kill you—in your case, probably sooner. I'm your friend, but now I'm speaking as a doctor."

"I know that. I've stopped—for good."

"Are you in a program?"

"You mean AA?"

She nodded. "I've seen it work—for lots of people," she said. "Some of them so far gone you'd think they're beyond help."

"I tried it a couple of times before. I have a problem with the 'higher being' part. But I've assimilated some of the concepts. One day at a time, and all that."

"Still, the other people help. They support you. You need that."

"You're probably right."

"You should go again. Do it. Promise me you will."

He promised, and meant it—much to his own amazement.

They sat on a bench. Scott told her about the exhibition. She was excited, seemed genuinely happy for him, and promised that she would be there for the opening.

"I can't wait," she said.

Scott described the experience of sorting through all the pictures of Tyler. He soon found that he was telling her about the photos of the bedroom doorway, Tyler's insistence that his mother had appeared before him at the moment of death, standing there and making a gesture with one arm, a waving sort of motion that he couldn't interpret and couldn't describe.

"I know it sounds strange," Scott said, "but I believe him—I mean he was so certain that he saw her. And why would he make it up?"

"Maybe it was his mind playing tricks on him. Maybe it was somehow his way of dealing with the loss—convincing himself that she loved him so much that she had to come back and say good-bye."

"But if that's the case why wouldn't she do something loving, hug him or something, instead of making some vague gesture that filled him with fear whenever he talked about it?"

"I don't know," she replied.

"I tend to be a skeptic about supernatural things but this one . . . I'm not sure—I think it happened. And another strange thing—when I had to go in the next morning and tell him that his mother died, he seemed to know it already. He didn't say that, but I could tell by the way he was acting."

Kate nodded vigorously.

"You know—this is going to sound crazy," she said. "But my mother claimed to have had a similar experience, the exact same kind of thing."

"What do you mean? Like what?"

"When her husband . . . my father . . . died in Vietnam. We lived on this mountain in Washington—I think I told you that. It was way out in the wilds. On the day he died, there was a wedding at our house. Our house was a big old beautiful ramshackle kind of place, with a barn and everything. It was poor, but we had land, about twenty acres, even a small apple orchard. Down the road was a young couple, and they would come up and do odd jobs for us every once in a while, help out with hauling hay for the animals or baby-sitting me. I don't remember them all that well. Anyway, it turned out they were just living together, they had never gotten married, and one day they decided to, so my mom offered our place.

"In our backyard we had a large sycamore tree transplanted from the East, a beautiful thing, and they were married under that. A local justice of the peace performed the ceremony. After the ceremony, after the dinner when most of the people had left, as my mom was cleaning up, she was washing a wineglass at the sink and suddenly she felt strange. It came out of nowhere and it was a strong sensation, really powerful. Later, she said it felt like she was dizzy. And she knew instantly that something was wrong and that it was about him—my dad. She stepped outside to catch her breath and went under that same tree and went to sit down and just sank to the bottom of the trunk, and she knew right then that he had been hurt. Just like that. She spoke to him over and over—'Darling, what's wrong? What's wrong?'—but he didn't respond, not at first. And then he appeared before her, no more than twenty feet away, and he just looked at her, a long look—she said it must have lasted a minute at least—and he didn't say anything but just looked. Then he disappeared as quickly as he had come. And another thing—he was wearing his uniform, and she had never even seen him in his uniform before.

"And two days later, a car came up to our mountaintop and a retired colonel delivered the news, not looking her in the eye but looking down at the dirt. I was hanging on her skirt behind her—I don't remember that; she told me it later. The colonel said he wanted to talk to her alone, so I was shooed indoors. Then he said that my dad had died. He said at least he went quickly, no suffering. And she asked the question: When did it happen? And he told her. After a few more words, the colonel went away, and that night she took me in her arms and rocked me and rocked me until I fell asleep. Then she carried me into the bedroom and put me in bed and went to the kitchen table and pulled out an atlas and did the calculations—the exact spot in the Mekong Delta, the time difference, no daylight savings—and sure enough, it all matched up perfectly."

Kate's gaze moved from the river to Scott. She saw that he was hanging on her words.

"My mom wasn't superstitious. She was the last person to believe in that kind of spiritual stuff—'mumbo jumbo,' she called it. But ever after, she said that her husband had come to say good-bye just as he was dying. And who's to say it's impossible? *'There are more things in heaven and earth, Horatio.'* So what if he was on the other side of the earth—if there is such a thing as a spirit, then who's to say what it can do and what it can't do, if it's willing, if the love is strong enough? And there's a final chapter. Years later, when it came *her* time to die—a long slow death from cancer—she saw him again near the very end. He materialized at the foot of her bed and spoke to her, and she wasn't afraid any longer."

Kate's words trailed off. She was feeling a little drained. She had never told anyone that entire story before—it had been too close to her heart—and when she looked down, she was surprised to see that she was gripping Scott's hand. She couldn't say whether he had reached over to take hers or she had reached over to take his.

She removed her hand to wipe her eyes, laughing a little at her silliness for crying. She hadn't told the whole story, the part about her mother dying alone in the nursing home without her daughter there or the sparrow who'd lit on her head at the funeral.

Through the cigarette smoke, the chatter, and the bobbing heads of the crowd, Vickie saw Scott and gave him
a thumbs-up: The opening was going well.

Inwardly, Scott blanched.

She was always one for a big party, he thought.

He knew he was being uncharitable, but couldn't help
it. It was nice that so many people had turned up. The
gallery was packed with more than half of the city's
photographer community—though that was hardly the
proper word to describe such a disparate, querulous,
and reflexively antisocial group of people. Not that
many invitations had been mailed out, but word had
gotten around.

Scott could have taken the turnout as a tribute to
himself, a token of the respect with which he was regarded. But he chose not to. Why put such a positive
spin on things when negativity is there to guide you?

Vickie worked her way over to him. She was holding
her wineglass unsteadily and spilled some on the floor,
then pulled his head down as if to whisper confidences
in his ear.

"It's a smash," she said, so loudly that he recoiled.

He forced himself to smile.

She continued, speaking in a higher, squeaky register
to get through. "A lot of people have come up to me and
asked if they can buy some. Why not?"

"Because they're not for sale."

"But why not?" she pressed on, giddy from the wine.

"Because I don't want to sell them—that's why."

"Oh, Scott. You're so down. Here—have a glass of
wine."

He found a hole in the crowd and darted through it.
He was sweating profusely and felt stifled. There was
nothing in the world he wanted more right now than a
glass of wine. But, thank God, so far at least he had been
able to quash that desire. He worked his way to the end
of the room, where four people were grouped around
the final picture—a shot of Tyler in the hospital ward.
At the last minute, he had decided to include it and had
given it pride of place. The instant he'd put it up, he was

sorry, but then again he'd felt that it belonged there and couldn't bring himself to remove it. Vickie had encouraged him to keep it in the exhibition—but, of course, she would. It made for a powerful climax.

He dreaded to hear what the group was saying, but couldn't resist and so he moved closer. Two young men and two women—none of them known to him.

"Just horrible," said one of the women. "Really horrible. I heard it was some kind of mountain-climbing accident."

The other woman chimed in: "How old was he? Fourteen or fifteen? Isn't that young to be mountain climbing?"

"This picture gives me the creeps," said one of the men.

Scott made a break for it, pushing around the edges of the crowd to reach the glass front door. He put his hand in the small of a man's back and nudged him out of the way, none too gently. Finally, he came to the door, lunged for the handle, and pushed it hard.

"Ow," came a sound from the other side.

He looked—there stood Kate, rubbing her nose.

He stepped outside.

"Don't go in there," he said.

"Why not?"

"Just don't."

"Don't be silly—I've come all this way to see it." She was still rubbing her nose. "You might say *I'm sorry*."

"For what?"

"Never mind, I'll recover. But let go of my arm."

She shook him off.

"I mean it—don't go in."

"You'll have to give me a good reason."

"Because I don't want you to see it. It doesn't work. The whole idea—it's wrong. I never should have tried it."

"There's a big crowd—they look like they're enjoying it."

"*Enjoying* it. They're not supposed to *enjoy* it."

"Okay. So I used the wrong word. What I meant to say was your pictures seem to be affecting those who view them. There—is that better?"

"Not much."

"What's the matter with you? You look strange."

"This whole thing was a mistake."

"How can you say that?"

"Because it's true. And if Tyler were alive and saw this, he'd be . . . he'd be mortified."

"I don't think so. I mean, it's a way of presenting his life, who he was."

"Who he *was*. What do you know about it? You never met him."

"What's wrong with you? Why do you say that?"

"It's true. You came in at the end when he was no longer himself."

"Still, I feel I know him in some way, I've heard so much—"

"You didn't know him."

"No, but I almost feel I did."

His mind was on the bar inside, the hip-looking bartenders handing out glasses of white and red wine to anyone. It would be so easy. . . . And it was an opening; that's tough on anyone.

"I never should have included that last picture, the one in the hospital."

"You can take it down."

"It's too late. I should have just put up a shot of all the doctors, a group picture, standing there, maybe in their surgical gowns—"

"Scott—c'mon."

"—smiling for the camera."

"Scott . . . don't say that."

"Why not?"

He stormed off down the street in the direction of the river. Halfway down the block, he turned and looked back. She was standing there, indecisive, one hand on the door. She didn't see him looking. He hurried on.

Then the door swung open. A couple came out and headed for a waiting limousine, the woman's laughter carrying across the street in the late-afternoon silence. With the open door beckoning, Kate looked down the street at his retreating back and stepped inside.

Chapter 23

It was close to midnight when Scott let himself into the gallery with the small brass key Vickie had given him. The detritus from the crowd was everywhere. Empty and half-filled plastic cups covered the tables and windowsills, some containing waterlogged cigarette butts that opened like rancid flowers. The smell of stale smoke hung in the air. A small black purse had been left behind in one corner.

The fancier the crowd, the more piggish the litter, he thought.

He kept the lights low, and the photos all around him took on a ghostly appearance in the half-light. He walked over to the last display wall and gently lifted off the picture of Tyler in the hospital bed and carried it under his arm into the workroom to the rear. He flipped the light switch and was momentarily blinded by the glare of the overhead lamps. He placed the photograph on the worktable and sat before it, staring at it. It filled him with dread and anger, as it always did, only more so this time, alone at night in a stifling room.

He felt unaccountably strange. He looked around, surveying the place, checking out the shadows in the corners, over there behind the filing cabinet, the dark reflection of his angular profile in the lone window on the back wall.

A wave of anxiety swept over him. He had the feeling—absurd, he knew—that someone else was there, watching him.

He tried to push the feeling away, to get on with the task at hand. He turned the photograph facedown and gently pried open the stays at the back, removing the cardboard backing, then the white beveled frame. He lifted out the picture and turned it over to look at it. He felt a shiver seize his back and move up into his shoulders.

There it was, the last photograph of his son—the white sheets, the antiseptic bed, the small figure encased in white, wrapped up like a mummy. Tyler's face—the face that Scott knew so well—was scrunched down by the bandages into a grimace so that he was almost unrecognizable. He scrutinized it, tried to look through the shadings and shadows. Were those lines on his face lines of pain? Were the cheeks swollen by the accident or the operation? Was his look so waxen because his body was trying desperately to pump its life's blood up to the damaged brain? The longer he looked, the more questions leapt up to plague him. Now, he could almost hear in the background the cursed machines droning on and on. He could hear them, the steady beat of electronic pulses that mimicked life's rhythms.

What had ever possessed him to put this photograph up for thousands to view? It made a mockery of the whole concept behind the exhibition—it was not life, not a boy's life, but the exact opposite, the absence of life, artificial life. His own brain was trying to purge this very same image from his memory, and here he had plastered it on the wall as the conclusion to his son's recorded life.

Again, free-floating anxiety gripped him. He was sweating madly. Maybe he was being punished, was punishing himself, for bad faith. The lyrics to a song popped into his head:

'Cause I'm free . . .
Free fallin' . . .

Where had he just heard it? My God, it was at Tyler's funeral—of course.

He picked up the photograph and held it with two hands and then very carefully pulled it in two and ripped it down the center. He put the pieces together and ripped them again and then made smaller piles, ripping each one.

He imagined that he was listening for a scream, but of course he heard none. So who was this other person here? A guilty conscience?

He tossed the pieces into a wastebasket, and as soon as they touched bottom, he felt a strong urge to flee this suffocating place.

But first—one more thing to do.

The exhibition was on the gallery's Web site. He would have to go there through the gallery's computer if he wanted to fully expunge that single hateful image. He sat before the computer and switched it on and waited for the screen to fill, and as he did, he stopped sweating and began to feel strangely cold. What was going on? *Have I fallen sick? Why am I shivering like this?*

The screen was ready. A desktop of swirling leaves, icons, a click to go on-line. The machine demanded a password and he prepared to enter Vickie's. His fingers were posed over the keyboard. And then, before he touched a single key, there it was. *His own password appeared all by itself.*

It read, letter by letter:

    JINGO

But how was that possible? *I don't recall entering it into the computer.*

Besides, passwords were not supposed to be displayed like that. And why had it come up letter by letter, almost as if there was someone on the other end, someone laboriously typing it in? On the other end of . . . what?

There must be a virus, he thought. Either that or the computer had somehow lifted it from the last time he used it. He didn't like that at all—these things are supposed to be inviolate. Maybe somehow some hacker had gotten hold of it. Who knows what damage he could do? Scott started thinking back over his files, what kinds of information were kept there—financial information, e-mails, the usual sort of thing. Nothing really personal, nothing that would mortify him if it got out. His life was not interesting enough to have deep dark secrets, he thought sardonically.

But then his ruminations came to a dead stop. Because the screen came alive. His hands were nowhere near the keyboard—yet *the words were appearing on their own.*

Again slowly, letter by letter, as if someone—somewhere—were pecking at the keyboard. *Is it going to be gibberish?*

THE

He waited breathlessly as the words kept coming, the sentence took shape.

THE LITTL

And when it did, when the sentence was complete, he nearly jumped out of his skin. Because it was far from meaningless.

THE LITTLE BOY FELT BORED.

No one else knows that—no one but Tyler and me. He must have told someone. Someone has hacked into the computer. And they know our secret ... our secret way of talking. The story I told him every night.

It didn't stop there. The computer kept going, all on its own, picking up a little speed now, until it had finished its message.

SO HE REACHED UNDER HIS BED AND THERE HE FOUND HIS MAGIC PEBBLE. HE RUBBED IT AND SOMETHING VERY STRANGE HAPPENED.

Damn right it's strange, Scott thought. Strange and sick. *But I'm going to get to the bottom of it. And whoever is responsible is going to pay.*

He switched off the computer without even clearing the screen. Then he turned out the lights and stormed outside, so angry that he walked all the way home. He took Comet outside and passed by a bar twice, congratulating himself that he didn't go in, but worried because the pull he felt was so strong.

—————

Johnny's father was surprised to hear from Scott—surprised and a little nervous because he hadn't expected a call and because they hadn't talked since the funeral, a month ago.

The family was trying in its own way to pull itself together and patch over the past. Johnny wouldn't talk about the accident. His mother and his father had each tried to draw him out, to tell him that it wasn't his fault, that he had done everything that could have been expected. But their words just fell away like drops on a windowpane—nothing could reach the boy. He'd constructed a shell around himself. After two weeks, they'd taken him to a therapist, but the results were not much better. Johnny had cried once, full out, the therapist reported, in describing how Tyler had fallen and how he himself had tried to hurry down the cliff to reach him but couldn't find him at first. Then he had fallen silent and resolutely refused to talk about it anymore.

"Why is it," the father asked the therapist after the last session, "that children take so much guilt upon themselves? Why do they think that bad things are their fault?"

The therapist had shrugged and had looked the father square in the eye and replied, "And not just children."

And now here was Scott, calling and asking to speak to Johnny.

"Of course, I'll get him," said the father. But he lingered on the line. "Tell me, how are you—how are you doing?" He felt foolish using such ordinary words, the way you might talk to someone who had been out with a toothache.

"Okay," replied Scott. "How's Johnny? I worry about him. He didn't look very good the last time I saw him."

"No, he's not."

"Does he talk about it?"

"No, he doesn't. That's one of the problems. The bear you gave him was a kind thought, though. It means a lot—he sleeps with it every night." Still, he lingered. "Scott, can I ask—what do you want Johnny for?"

"I want to ask him something."

"What? If I may ask."

Scott paused, thinking, then said, "Well, a strange thing happened. When I went to use a computer last night, my password jumped on the screen without my doing anything, and then . . . other things appeared. Words were written all by themselves, and some of them—look, this is hard to explain. I know it sounds crazy."

"Go on."

"Well, one of the things that appeared was something that only Tyler and I knew about, as far as I know, and so I want to know if maybe Tyler told Johnny about it."

"What would that prove?"

"I don't know. But I need to know how this thing happened. Whether there's a hacker or what."

"Do you think Johnny would be mixed up in something like that?"

"No, I don't. Not at all. I know he wouldn't be. But like I say, I need to know what's happening, and I thought maybe he would have some idea where to look."

"Ah . . . listen. Wait a minute."

Johnny's father covered the receiver with one hand. His wife was at his side, having heard his end of the conversation, her eyebrows raised in concern. He filled her in. Scott heard more muffled sounds, then the father's voice, exasperated, speaking to her: "I know, I know."

He came back on the line.

"Well, we've talked it over, Sarah and me, and here's what we think. We think we will definitely try to get an answer to your question. But maybe it's better if we talk to him. I mean, I know it's nothing compared to what you're going through, but this whole business has been rough on him, too."

Scott said he understood and that he worried about Johnny. But he wanted an answer; he had to have one. And the boy might tell his parents more easily than he would tell him.

"Okay," he said. "Well, what you have to ask him about is a made-up character . . . called Jingo. That's a boy that I used to tell Tyler about for a good-night story, and every time the story began the same way. What you have to ask is how the story began."

Johnny's father felt a rush of sympathy. "How it began?"

"Yes, that's all. And call me back—soon. I need to know this."

"Sure thing."

"And I hope Johnny's okay."

"Thanks."

They hung up.

Later that day, when Johnny's mother fixed him a lunch of tomato soup and a bologna sandwich—his favorite—and put it before him, she gently broached the subject. Had he by any chance heard of a made-up character by the name of Jingo? A sort of nursery-room fairy-tale character? He was dumbfounded—no, not at all. Why was she asking, he demanded, and she replied, "Oh, no reason, really. Just curious," as if it were the most natural question in the world.

Johnny's father called Scott back and told him. As he hung up the phone, he turned to Sarah and shook his head sadly and said, "Lord, he's in a bad way. Hearing things, seeing things. I wish there were something we could do for him."

"But he's got to ask for help," she said. "He's got to reach out."

"Johnny didn't."

"That's different," she said, putting away a dish. "He's our son."

Scott went back to the art gallery that evening. Vickie was talking on the phone when he entered. Cradling the receiver against her neck, she pointed a well-manicured forefinger at him and rubbed the other one against it, a cutesy-pie you've-been-a-naughty-boy gesture. She prattled on while he waited and then hung up, gave a loud sigh, and proceeded to upbraid him, halfheartedly, for walking out on his opening.

"One of the biggest shows of the year and you pick that moment to turn into a sensitive artiste—you of all people. Christ, you used to shoot slums, famine, wars. Now look at you—a few big spenders from the Upper East Side and you turn tail."

He remained silent.

"If I could have sold your pictures, you'd be looking at a rich woman right now. 'Course, you can always change your mind."

He shook his head.

"And I see you took down the last photo. Not smart. Leaves the whole thing hanging. I just wish we could have talked about it first."

Then she noticed he was preoccupied. "And now—you're not listening to me. Am I right or am I right?"

"I need to use your computer," was all he said.

She turned one wrist toward the back room, a diva's motion.

"Help yourself, Mr. Artiste."

The rear office looked exactly as it had the night before. The papers were stacked in the same piles on the filing cabinet, and the ashtray was overflowing with butts ringed in lipstick. The wastebasket still held the shreds of the photo he had destroyed. And in the middle of the desk, its keyboard extended, its screen dark and tilted upward as if in eager expectation, sat the computer.

He circled around it once, sat down before it, and stood up again. He approached the door and shouted out, "How much longer you going to be here, anyway?"

"Not long," she said. She came to the door and leaned against the frame. "Why? You planning on visiting some porno sites? Careful—that can be traced, you know. I don't wanna be closed down."

He turned his head away.

"Art's one thing," she continued. "Porn's another."

He turned his back.

"Oh, well, I know when I'm not wanted. I was leaving anyway. Just take a minute to gather my things."

Her high heels clacked against the wooden floor.

"Don't forget to lock up," she yelled.

He waited until the front door closed. Then he sat down again and braced himself and stared at the blank, gray-brown screen. There was depth to it, which he had not realized before—he could see his reflection. His face staring back looked lean and haggard. His eyes were wells of sorrow. He looked down and ran his fingers over the keys like a man sitting down for the first time at a piano. He waited a while. Then he leaned down and switched the computer on and sat back in the chair, far away from it. He heard the humming sound of the machine booting up. He squinted at the screen and waited some more while lights flashed and incomprehensible numbers and letters marched across and then the familiar desktop appeared, swirling leaves. It made him giddy to look at them.

He felt an artery throbbing in his neck—he could hear it, too, beat-beating inside his ears. The hairs on the back of his neck bristled. He was beginning to sweat, just like last night, and thought he was beginning to shiver, too, unless—unless he was imagining it.

He watched the screen carefully. He clicked the icon to go on-line. It asked for his password. The cursor blinked.

Nothing happened.

Absolutely nothing.

He waited. Still blinking. How long should he wait?

Then it dawned on him, the thought that he hadn't wanted to entertain, and he put it in the form of a question to himself so he could almost hear himself speaking: *What if it doesn't come again?*

And he didn't know the answer. Another question posed itself: *How would I feel?* Deep, deep relief, like the passing of a nightmare, or disappointment? Why disappointment if he was fully convinced, as he had told himself he was, that last night's occurrence had been nothing more than a malicious prank? What else could it possibly be? He knew it was, but still he was intrigued: Who out there could possibly have known about their secret ritual?

Should he go on-line?

He did. A quick punch of his password—

    JINGO

—and he was there.

Now what? He didn't know.

He waited some more and not knowing what else to do went to a browser and then a search engine and began typing idly, or not so idly:

    ONCE THERE WAS A LITTLE BOY WHO
    FELT BORED.

He hit *enter*.
Nothing.
He continued:

    SO ONE DAY HE FELT UNDER HIS BED.

Enter.
Still nothing.

    AND THERE HE FOUND A MAGIC PEBBLE.

Enter.
He waited for a long, long time. Until he felt foolish and confused and, none the wiser, shut off the machine and the lights, locked the door, and walked home.

Scott heard Comet barking even before the elevator came to a halt. He felt guilty—he was leaving her alone far too long these days. On top of that, he was sure the dog missed Tyler, who used to take her for long walks through Chelsea Park and let her sleep on his bed.

Sure enough, he spotted a puddle as soon as he opened the door. She just couldn't wait. Comet herself was in a state of high excitement. She jumped up to greet him, placing her forepaws squarely on his rib cage, and then backed off and leapt around the loft. He had never seen a display like this—she was whining for joy—and it only made him feel even guiltier.

"Okay, old girl, okay. Take it easy. I'll walk you in a minute," he said as he ruffled the fur on the back of her neck, then rolled her over and scratched the creamy pink flesh of her belly, causing her back leg to dance in the air. She certainly was excited.

"There's just the two of us now," he added, out of nowhere.

He used paper towels to clean up the mess, which he put in a plastic garbage bag. Rummaging under the sink for a replacement bag, he knocked into some bottles—a sound he knew well. He rose up out of the squat and leaned back against the sink for a while, thinking.

What the hell, he decided. *Let's do it.* And so he reached back down and pulled out a bottle of J&B, then another, and a third that was half-full. One after another, he poured the contents down the drain. The familiar sour grainy smell went straight to his brain. He hoped he was doing the right thing. He had been meaning to dispose of the stuff for a while now, but something had always stopped him: the comforting knowledge that the liquor was there if he really needed it. At the same time its presence endowed him with a false sense of willpower—for being able to refuse it when it was so close at hand. Either way, he figured, he was still a slave to it. Better to be rid of it once and for all.

No regrets, he thought as the last of the brown liquid swirled out of sight. He caught a view of his face in the small shaving mirror over the sink—he looked okay, maybe a little ashen, a few more wrinkles, but still himself, despite what he had been through. And he thought he better say it out loud, so he did, looking right into his own eyes. "No regrets."

Then he picked up the garbage bag and took Comet's green leather leash off the hook by the door. Usually just the sight of it was enough to send her spinning in circles, but this time she appeared confused and continued to whine, her tail low.

"C'mon, old girl."

She sat in the elevator. His love for the dog was more intense now that Tyler was gone. He didn't care to analyze it, but he knew that the reason was that the dog was one of the few living connections to his son.

Together they went out into the night air, now unseasonably cold. Scott tossed the garbage bag and the empty bottles into a trash can and walked east on Twenty-eighth Street, passing the LIEBERMAN BROTHERS sign on the old storefront. The sidewalks were empty except for a man and woman strolling arm in arm across the street. He was glad it was not a man and a young boy. Whenever he passed such a couple, the pain became so palpable he could hardly bear it. Only that afternoon, he had walked by a father and a boy holding hands, the boy babbling along and asking questions quick from the hip—"Dad, how come things look different if I open one eye and close the other real quick?" and "Why is that man begging for money? Why isn't he at work?" Scott had felt like grabbing the father by the arm, issuing dire warnings, frothing at the mouth like the ancient mariner, saying, "By God, enjoy your blessing; every second you spend is a treasure beyond belief."

Taxis slowed on Eighth Avenue—not for him, for a man across the street. A person walking a dog rarely hailed a cab. He took the corner, then back west on Twenty-seventh, facing the wind from the river, and then up a block and east again to his own doorway. Again, in the elevator, Comet seemed agitated. Once inside, she began whining again, so he fed her. But she did not eat.

Scott's computer on the desk was still on from a letter he had been writing earlier. For no particular reason, he sat before it and touched a key, causing the screen saver to drop away and the white screen to spring to life.

And then it began spelling words, all on its own, in that slow, laborious fashion. And the words it spelled were:

```
AT FIRST HE FELT HOT, AND THEN HE
FELT COLD
```

A long pause. Longer still. Scott put his fingers on the keyboard, his breath knocked out of him. He typed:

```
And then he felt warm and then he
felt cool.
```

He waited, confused, scared, not angry this time. The computer barely skipped a beat in answering, the letters coming quicker now:

```
AND FINALLY HE FELT JUST RIGHT.
```

Scott panicked. He wasn't sure he knew the rest of the words. Maybe he had to get them just right; maybe the spell would be broken. How was this happening? How could any computer do this? He typed rapidly:

```
There was a big white mansion, and
so Jingo went up the front steps
and opened the front door and
stretching before him was a long
corridor as far as he could
see . . .
```

He stopped and waited, breathless. Nothing happened. *Maybe I got it wrong. What happens if the words are wrong? Maybe I went on too long.*

He felt he had broken an incantation, a summoning. And the longer he waited without a response, the more he became convinced that he had done something wrong and the more panicky he became. Should he type in a question? Ask who was doing this—how it was happening?

But then—to his relief and to his horror—more words did begin to form themselves, coming slowly, as if from a deep place, and when he read them, he felt his heart being ripped from his chest.

     DAD. HELP ME. HELP ME DAD

Scott leapt at the keyboard. He pounded the keys furiously.

     Tyler, Son. Is that you???

There was no answer. He waited a long time, trying to silence the pounding in his ears, trying to think. Should he try again—would that disrupt the answer from— from wherever it was coming? He did try again.

     Tyler, where are you???

And this time the answer came back even more slowly than before, each letter taking five, ten seconds, so that before the word was finished, he knew what it was going to say. And he knew that it would be with him forever and that his life would never be the same.

The answer was a single word:

     E-V-E-R-Y-W-H-E-R-E

Chapter 24

Saramaggio walked into the cafeteria at St. Cat's carrying his tray and searched for someone friendly to sit with. He saw some people looking at him and he half imagined that they were talking about him, or would be as soon as he turned his back. He scanned the room almost desperately.

After taking so much time off, he was a bit nervous about being back, and he was doubly nervous at the prospect of operating. He had once heard a story about the men who walk across steel girders at construction sites as the building grows—that they're fearless when they rise from the ground to dizzying heights floor by floor, but let them be out for three weeks and return to a building that's gone five or six floors higher and they get the heebie-jeebies. He felt a bit like that now.

Following the harrowing night that Tyler had died, he needed the leave. He had been heartened by what Tyler's father had said at the funeral—his words about medical progress and the need to lessen human suffering over the long run showed a spirit of magnanimity and forgiveness that almost brought tears to his eyes. He felt that they were intended for him, and he took them personally.

But he couldn't convince himself that he deserved them. Nor did they lift a burden of guilt. For he was honest enough to admit that he had plenty to feel guilty about. He had ignored the implications of Scott's pain and pressed ahead with Tyler's operation, partly because he wanted to advance the frontiers of medicine but also because he wanted to further his own ambition.

And he'd stepped across the line and across the boundary of the Hippocratic oath when he'd put so much trust in Cleaver's machines; a voice deep inside had told him that relying upon a computer to direct the functioning of the autonomic nervous system was so problematic that the odds against it succeeding were daunting. He had always prided himself on the surgeon's second sight, and this time he had disregarded it.

And there was more. He had shown bad judgment that night; he had folded under pressure and done something whose implications he was only now beginning to discern. One result was that he felt under Cleaver's thumb, which was insupportable. He had always disliked him—everyone did—but before, he had been able to accommodate the feeling by looking down on him. Now, after their secret collusion, he had the impression that power was slipping away into the other man's hands. Their relationship was like a seesaw; and suddenly Cleaver was the one with both feet planted on the ground, while Saramaggio's swung helplessly in the air.

After a week moping around his house in Greenwich, occasionally meandering along the paths of the Audubon Center while the first leaves of autumn toppled down around him, he'd decided to seek professional help. He'd chosen a psychiatrist named Bill Swenson, whom he knew socially but not too well. They belonged to the Round Hill Country Club and nodded to each other on the golf course with a distant respect, members at opposite ends of the medical fraternity.

Swenson agreed to see Saramaggio instantly—almost gleefully, Saramaggio thought—and initially without fee, the not-quite-spelled-out understanding (contained in the words "you'd do the same for me") being that sometime in the future *he* might require surgery. The arrangement broke down when it was clear that more sessions were required, and Saramaggio extended his leave by adding on vacation time.

At the first session, the surgeon was guarded and silent much of the time. Swenson told him that he was being hostile, and Saramaggio replied, with only half a smile, that he was just acting normal. In subsequent sessions, he was able for the most part to keep up the air of defensive aloofness, though once or twice, in discussing Tyler, he felt himself on the verge of tears.

One time, he fixed his eyes upon Swenson and asked, "Tell me, is it true this notion of patient confidentiality?"

"What do you mean?" Swenson asked.

"If I told you that I had done something ... unethical ... maybe even illegal, certainly enough to possibly lose the right to practice ... would you be honor-bound to keep it to yourself?"

"Of course. Provided that no one's life was at stake. Why do you ask?"

"I just wondered."

"Come, come. Something is troubling you."

And Saramaggio said that indeed something was, but he threw up a smoke screen, saying that he was concerned that he could never operate again. Dramatically, he held up his right hand to arm's length and rotated it so that his slender fingers turned orbs in the air. When he voiced the fear, there was enough hidden truth to it that Swenson bought it and followed a red herring.

But in other ways Swenson was good—not for nothing could he afford a home in Greenwich—and after several more weeks of intensive sessions, and with the aid of little white pills, he pretty much had Saramaggio back on his feet, though to the discerning eye the surgeon's old confidence wasn't what it had been. And on the morning that Saramaggio returned to St. Cat's, he actually nodded to doctors and even interns when he passed them in the hallways.

Kate saw him enter the cafeteria and looked down at her tray, but to her dismay, when she looked up, he was standing before her.

"Mind if I join you?"

She didn't see how she could say no, but she couldn't bring herself to say yes, so she gave a half-nod, which he took as assent. At first they didn't say anything, and then they engaged in awkward small talk. But finally Kate, who had begun to soften toward him despite herself, found that she was burning with curiosity. She fixed him with her piercing eyes and said, "I don't mean to intrude—and please tell me if I am—but I feel I should ask you something."

"Please, by all means," he said, not meeting her gaze.

"Are you . . . are you all right? You seem different since you've been back."

"Different? How? I mean, in what way?"

"You seem—well, you seem less cocksure." She had deliberately chosen a word that he might find insulting.

"I do," he replied quietly. It was a statement, not a question.

And that was all it took to get him going. Perhaps it was the reaction of someone who had undergone a crash course in analysis, but he actually talked about himself and his emotions. He said that it had been hard for him to get over Tyler's death and that he even felt a certain amount of guilt about it. He talked about the specter of depression—what Churchill called "the black dog"—and how he, too, had his own black dog that was tailing him. He even came close to admitting that he felt a little worried about walking into the OR and picking up a scalpel.

Amazing, she thought—truly amazing. One brick is pulled out and the whole wall comes tumbling down. And she felt she wanted to rebuild it, though not as high or as impenetrable as before.

"You know," she said, "I think you made a mistake, a horrible mistake. But what makes a difference is when someone can profit from the mistake, when he can recognize it and learn from it, and that you're clearly trying to do."

He looked at her directly.

"Well, that's true. Maybe a bit trite, but true."

And she went on to tell him that she thought his skill as a surgeon was as good as anyone's she had seen, that he had a gift and owed it to himself and others to put it back to work. There was one area, one major area, where she thought him deficient, she said, and that was in empathy. She quoted her mentor, A. B. Reinhardt, as saying, " 'A surgeon who cannot imagine what it is like to undergo the horrors that he is perpetrating upon another human being is neither a good surgeon nor a good human being.' "

He nodded quietly.

"I don't mean to sound like a fortune cookie," she continued. "But I believe it's true—empathy and compassion begin with our own suffering. Only by knowing pain ourselves do we understand pain and learn how to avoid giving it to others."

He took it in.

"Let me ask you something," he said. "The father, Tyler's father . . . what's his name?"

"His name is Scott—and incidentally, you might begin your new leaf by learning the names of your patient's relatives."

"I suppose you're right. Anyway, I was just wondering—how is he doing?"

She hadn't expected the question, and it threw her.

"I . . . I can't say for sure. I haven't seen him lately."

"Oh." He paused. "I thought—I thought the two of you were kind of, you know, tight."

She blushed—and was ashamed of herself for it.

"Well, we are. I don't know. I just haven't seen him recently."

"Ah, I'm sorry."

She cast back to Scott's exhibition, to his strange behavior and how deeply angry he had been, for no apparent reason. It had only been two nights ago and she had tried to reach him the following morning, but he hadn't called back. She had held off trying again. That was why she was dancing around Saramaggio's question. She felt small and resolved to call Scott again—right away.

They started talking about operating again, and she had the feeling that Saramaggio was about to ask her to assist him. She wasn't sure, frankly, whether she could

bring herself to say yes, because she hadn't forgiven him
for the way he had treated her. In the new confessional
atmosphere, she was tempted to let him know. But at
that moment, she caught him frowning. He was peering
over her shoulder toward the entrance of the cafeteria.
Turning around, she saw that Cleaver had come in and
joined the line, pushing his tray along the rails in a
jaunty manner. Somehow, his display of bravado struck
her as even creepier than when he used to skulk around.

It was the oddest thing, she thought: Why was everyone acting so out of character?

She was walking toward her office—a plain windowless
room that she'd inherited as the newest surgeon—when
her beeper rang. It displayed an extension she didn't
recognize. She dialed it from a wall phone.

"Dr. Willet, this is the receptionist—down in the
lobby. Could you please come here?" The woman's
voice dropped to a confidential level. "There's a man
here asking for you. He knows you—or says he does."

"What's his name?" she asked. But she knew—or she
hoped she did.

"Mr. Jessup. He says his son was a patient here. He's
acting a bit . . . I don't know—agitated."

"I'll be right there."

As she hurried to the elevator, she felt a frisson overtake her. It was surprising, and so she indulged in a
bout of self-examination: She was willing to admit to a
welter of feelings—gladness, relief, and worry all together. Even a little excitement. She had tried hard not
to think about Scott over the past forty-eight hours, and
as always in such cases, the effort was its own worst
enemy. Now that he had come to see her, now that he
was the one to make the first move, she could admit it.
She was even prepared to be magnanimous. No hard
feelings. But what did the receptionist mean—*agitated*?
Was he drinking again?

As soon as she saw him, that particular worry

dropped away. But another replaced it. Scott was pacing in the ground floor atrium. He looked high-strung and keyed-up, as if his system was addled by amphetamines.

When he saw her, he didn't smile.

"You've got to come with me," he said. "I'm going crazy—I don't know what to do."

She knew from his tone that he wasn't talking about how much he had missed her.

He put a hand under her arm and was trundling her toward the door.

"Wait a minute—I can't just walk out like this. I'm at work."

He stopped in his tracks, perplexed. He hadn't considered that.

She continued. "What if I have to operate?"

"Do you?"

"No."

"What if I have to see patients?"

"Do you?"

"No."

"Then let's go."

She relented. She really didn't have anything more to do at work. "Okay. But let me get my coat."

"You don't need it. It's warm out."

"Okay."

"I've got a cab waiting."

He escorted her in double time and disappeared ahead of her, out the revolving door.

"But you'll have to tell me where we're going," she shouted after him. She meant to make it sound like an ultimatum, but it struck even her as a modest demand. "I'm glad to see you, too, thank you very much," she muttered, stepping into the spinning chamber.

The cabdriver was querulous, none too happy to have spent time idling at curbside when he could have been out cruising for a new fare. Scott held the door for her, got in quickly, and yelled his address through the plastic partition.

"So that's where we're going," she said playfully, trying to lighten the mood. "You're full of surprises."

He didn't want to play.

"Sorry," he said, staring out the window. "I should have told you."

He looked so preoccupied that she felt bad for teasing him.

"Scott. What's wrong? You seem really upset."

"I don't want to talk here," he said, tilting his chin at the driver, who had cocked his head to the left in order to chatter nonstop into a cell phone.

Great, she thought. *He's turned paranoid.*

"Really?" she said. "I don't think he's listening."

"Still . . . no, it's not that. It's that it sounds so incredible and so strange that I'm afraid you won't believe me. I want to sit you down and explain the whole thing and—maybe, hopefully—show you."

"*Show me?* What do you want to show me?"

But he didn't answer, instead turning away to look outside once more. She settled back for the ride and also to save her spine—the cab had begun hitting potholes as if its life depended on it.

She poked Scott on the thigh.

"Not even an inkling?" she ventured.

He glanced again at the driver, still jabbering in some conspiratorial language.

"I think there's a chance, a good chance—I don't know how to explain it really—but I think that maybe Tyler is still alive. At first I thought it was some asshole playing a stupid joke, like maybe somebody from the hospital board or something. But I don't think so anymore—or at least I'm not sure."

She looked away and bit her lip and groaned inside. *Oh, the poor, poor man,* she thought. *He wants it so much to be true that his mind is playing tricks on him.*

⁙

Despite his promise to sit her down and calmly tell her everything at length, Scott was so energized that he began spilling out his story halfway up in the noisy elevator. He told her about the computer in the gallery and how it had sent the signal of his own password to him and then mysteriously answered him with responses that were secret, that only Tyler knew. And then how his own computer had done the same thing the next day and finally Tyler himself had sent a message—at least he said he was Tyler—and had asked for help and was clearly in trouble.

She asked him for the exact words of the message, and he told her—he had memorized the exchange perfectly.

Once inside the apartment, she requested coffee, playing for time while she considered what to say. Before he got the coffeemaker ready, he rushed over to his computer, stepping back from the desk to look at the screen with an expectant air, the kind a pilgrim might make gazing upon a venerated icon.

Then he went to grind the beans at the kitchen counter. She turned her face to him, inviting him to continue.

"I don't know how to explain it," he said. "I've gone over it and over it, as you might expect, and I can't even arrive at a theory. It doesn't make sense—no matter how you look at it. The only explanation I can come up with is that somehow, somewhere, Tyler is still alive—not only that, but he's conscious and able to communicate with me, and he needs my help."

"Maybe, as you said, it's just some horrible stupid prank, somebody who is incredibly malevolent or vindictive—"

"Of course, that makes sense. But I've racked my brains. Nobody I know would do that. That would be pure evil. And besides, nobody—and I mean absolutely nobody—knows about Jingo and the stories I told Tyler."

"Surely there is some kid, maybe somebody who slept over and heard the stories."

"No, I never told them when he had a sleepover. It was our private little ritual."

"Someone he could have told about it."

"No, I checked the only person he might have told.

And anyway, Tyler wouldn't have done that. Like I said, it was just something between the two of us. That's what made it special and magical."

She marveled again, for the hundredth time, at what a good father he had been, raising his son alone. Someday she would like someone like that to be the father of her children.

He brought her the coffee. She sipped it, blew on it, and put the cup down. Time to take a different tack.

"Scott, you know, if you step back from the situation, it's hard to believe that Tyler could still be alive," she said gently. "We went to the hospital that night, you and me together. Remember? We saw that his vital signs had stopped. That's what angered you so—that he was . . . virtually dead."

"We saw that *he* wasn't doing the breathing and *he* wasn't making his heart pump. The machines were doing it. But it was getting done. Technically, you'd have to say he was still alive. *Virtually* dead isn't the same as being dead."

"But they took him off life support. And we know he couldn't survive that."

"They *say* they did. How do we know they really did?"

"Scott—there are all kinds of things you have to do in that situation, a whole procedure. You fill out forms, you get another doctor's verification. It's not something you can do just like that."

"And who was the second doctor? Answer me that."

"I don't know, but I know there was one."

"Can you find out who it was?"

"I guess so, but, Scott, that won't prove anything."

"I don't trust that place or anyone in it." He looked at her and quickly added: "Except you, of course—I trust you."

"I would hope so," she said, not even ruffled. But inside, her mind was racing. "But we went to the funeral—you and me. We sat there together."

"Yes, but it was a closed coffin. The funeral home said the damage to the head was so bad it couldn't be open.

So I never actually saw him there—I was too upset. I just took their word for it. I regret that now."

"So who would be buried there, if not him?"

"I have no idea. Like I say, I can't explain this."

His voice was beginning to get testy, but she felt that it was important to press ahead with the tough questions.

"That means someone in the funeral home saw him, too, probably worked on the body. Scott—this is too crazy. If there's some kind of wild plot—I don't know, some kind of conspiracy—then they'd have to be in on it, too. This is getting out of hand."

"I've thought of that. I've thought of everything you've said. But believe me, if you saw what I saw, the message coming from that machine"—he pointed to the computer—"then you wouldn't sound so sure of yourself."

He was making it personal, drawing a line between them. She finished the coffee and put the cup down with a definitive thump.

"All right, show me," she said.

He sat down before the computer, his face reflecting a ghostly glow from the screen, and pecked at a few keys. He typed:

```
JINGO
```

He waited—and waited. Then he typed:

```
Once there was a boy who felt
bored.
```

Minutes went by, five, then ten. He hit the keys again:

```
Tyler
```

Nothing. Then he typed:

```
Tyler Tyler Are you there? Speak
to me . . .
```

During this time Kate had been walking around, looking out the windows and reading whatever she came across—cover lines of old magazines, messages left over on a bulletin board, cereal boxes.

"Why don't you stop that—all that pacing," Scott said. "It makes me nervous."

She just looked at him.

"Sorry," he said. "You know, it doesn't always work like this—not right away."

"How many times has it . . . worked?"

"Twice."

She looked at him again.

"I know what you're thinking," he said. "Twice is not a lot. But each time there's, you know, back and forth— a real exchange."

"I see."

She decided to change the subject and came upon a photo in a propped-up silver frame on the kitchen table. It was of Scott, his wife, and Tyler, taken many years ago, Scott wearing long hair that almost touched his shoulders, Tyler flashing a toothy smile, a sweet boy looking serenely content to be next to his parents, each with a hand resting on his shoulder. They were standing in the doorway of a cottage by the sea somewhere—the photo had a blue, washed-out quality—and the door frame was white bordering upon weathered gray shingles. At their feet was a smooth paving stone surrounded by sand, and above the door, now that she looked more closely, was the carved figure of a whale.

But of course she was looking most closely at the woman. Her eyes were so stunning—a deep rich brown like the center of the earth—and they shone with intelligence and seemed to pull at your gaze so that it was hard to look away. Her hair was dazzling, falling all over the place; her nose was strong and forthright; and her mouth had a quizzical, sad turn to it. She was the center, the maternal center, of the trio, and she was certainly one of the most beautiful women Kate had ever seen.

All in all, there was something about the photo that was gripping and moving to Kate, something in the glaze of the light, the threesome standing and looking directly at the camera, a bravery in their posture, the casualness of their love for one another—the knowledge that this family was soon to be split by a lightning bolt. It almost took her breath away. She clasped it and looked at it for a long time.

"Taken in Nantucket," Scott said.

Kate was still staring at it.

"Her name was Lydia," he said. "There, she was about twenty-seven. We'd been married seven years. Tyler would be . . . let's see, about five. We rented this little cottage—Tyler's room was no bigger than a closet. The beds were lumpy; the walls were thin; sand everywhere. But it was right smack on the ocean. You got up and walked across a sandy beach and fell into the waves. We loved it."

"I think . . . there's something wonderful about this picture," she said. She remembered it from the exhibition. She didn't tell him the half of it; she didn't say that the photo filled her with a longing that was almost bottomless.

"I like it, too," Scott said. "I carry one around."

He lifted a wallet out of his back pocket, slipped out a small photo, and handed it to her. The picture lost some of its power in its reduced version, but only some—she could still see Lydia's burning gaze, Tyler's serenity, Scott's paterfamilias pride.

"Let's go out for a bit," she said abruptly. "I need some air." She looked over at the computer, and added, "You know what they say: 'A watched pot never boils.' "

They walked east to Broadway and then uptown to Times Square. The sidewalks were crammed with humanity: travelers, deadbeats, hucksters, businessmen, delivery boys, Africans selling women's purses laid out on sheets spread upon the pavement, teenagers screaming up at the MTV windows, middle-aged men looking for porno shops, tourists gawking at the news zipper around the old *Times* building and the flashing lights of the Nasdaq and Reuters signs.

Scott felt good in the midst of it, renewed as it all washed over him. So many different people, running around in so many directions with so many different destinations and destinies. He thought of a Humphrey Bogart line from *Casablanca,* about the world being at war and the troubles of two people not amounting to a hill of beans.

They walked and walked, all the way up Broadway to Lincoln Center, where they sat on the rim of the fountain and talked. Then they crossed the street to a sidewalk café and had cappuccino, and after that strolled through Central Park.

It was almost dusk by the time they returned to West Twenty-eighth Street. In the elevator up, they were quiet, both thinking about the computer. But thinking different thoughts—Scott wondering if there would be a message, wondering what it might say, and Kate worrying about Scott, worrying about how to comfort him and help him over the disappointment when he saw that there was none.

Once inside, they didn't have long to wait. For there it was, staring out at them in black and white, the letters gleaming against the ghostly background:

    IT'S ME. TYLER. HELP ME

Chapter 25

Scott paced back and forth in front of the Nineteenth Precinct on East Sixty-seventh Street, trying to figure out what to say. He was also attempting to screw up his courage *and* to calm down. He knew that his demeanor in presenting the problem would count for a lot, because the problem was out of the ordinary, to say the least. He had to be straightforward and rational, a civic-minded parent bringing a complaint over a possible crime—a serious crime, his son's disappearance. In other words, he told himself, don't come across as a raving lunatic.

As he reached the corner of Lexington, he found that he was doing more than mouthing the words, he was speaking them out loud. He realized this when a woman pushing a stroller shot him a frightened look and gave him a wide berth. Not a good start for someone trying to play down the lunatic angle. He gathered his thoughts again, turned, climbed the steps into the old red-stone-and-concrete station house, and went up to the desk officer.

"Sergeant Paganelli here?" he asked. Somehow, in the blur of confusion and anger on the night he'd been arrested—not arrested, *detained*—he'd remembered the name of the sympathetic officer with the beer belly.

This desk cop had a beer belly, too, but there the resemblance ended. He looked at Scott with a weary, jaded eye.

"Naw. Comes in the late shift."

Scott's question dropped the verb, and the cop's answer dropped the pronoun. Not an auspicious beginning, he thought.

"So . . . what time does he come in?"

"He starts at six p.m."

"Okay, thanks."

He turned to go. The cop called after him.

"Can it wait?"

"Oh, yes."

Scott was at the door now.

"And who do you want to say called for him?"

"Nobody. I'll come back later and look for him."

"Suit yourself."

The law office of Klinger, Klinger, and Beaner occupied the second floor of a squat modern building in depressed downtown Bridgeport. The members and their longtime clients parked in a basement garage, pressed the levered bar on a metal door, and took the cement staircase up the two flights—not a particularly alluring entryway and certainly not befitting one of the best law firms in Connecticut.

Steve Klinger was one of Scott's oldest friends, though their professional lives were on such divergent paths they did not see one another all that often. They had met twelve years ago, when Scott had been assigned to do a magazine shoot on hotshot lawyers. He'd followed Steve around for two days, and they'd gotten on. Steve was an amateur photographer, and Scott gave him tips. Steve's father was a hefty man with a cherubic halo of white wispy curls who smoked huge cigars, gave big bear hugs, drove a Cadillac El Dorado, and was one of the wiliest criminal defense attorneys in New England. He'd taken a special liking to Scott and Lydia, and when Lydia died, the Klinger family had adopted Scott and Tyler. They'd plied them with lox and bagels on Sundays, propped Scott up with solace and single-malt scotch in the proper proportions, and attended Tyler's school plays so he would have a large rooting section. An ersatz extended family.

"Mind if I smoke?" Scott asked, sitting next to Steve on a couch in his office. The walls were covered with plaques, degrees, and pictures. Over Steve's shoulder, Scott saw a photo of Steve's father standing shoulder to shoulder with Huey Newton, from the New Haven Black Panther trials of the early seventies.

Steve, lean and intense, grimaced. Smoking wasn't allowed, and they forced their secretaries to step outside, even in winter.

"For you—okay," he said, getting up to open a window. When he sat down at his desk, he was facing a pile of papers.

"After we talked on the phone, I did some research on exhumation. I've only requested one exhumation in my life, and someone else in the firm actually handled it. So I'm no expert. I checked the law—it's section 19a-413 of the Connecticut general statutes, by the way."

Scott looked at him blankly. Steve added, "That's should you need it for future reference."

"This is the only one I'm planning on," said Scott.

Steve went on.

"The statute empowers the chief medical examiner to exhume a body under certain circumstances. Let's see ..." Here he consulted a thick book that lay open on his blotter. He hummed and muttered and read aloud in an undercurrent so that only a few phrases could be deciphered: "... if death occurs under circumstances warranting ... a body is buried without proper certification ... the chief medical examiner notifies the state's attorney ... presents facts to the judge of superior court ... and so on et cetera et cetera."

He closed the book with a thud, a movement he must have performed in front of hundreds of clients. It made Scott feel that there was a whole new side to his friend that he didn't know at all.

"Scott—let me ask you this: I'm assuming that because of the nature of the case ..." His words had an impersonal ring, and he had the grace to pause and back up. "Sorry. I don't mean to go all technical on you. I know how hard this is. What I mean is, Tyler was in the hospital for a long time, and the procedure they put him through was highly experimental—right?"

"Highly experimental. It had never been done before. On humans. And it wasn't a *procedure*. It was an *operation*."

"Right. But what I'm getting at is we have to assume that they were following normal protocol, and that would mean that in such circumstances, since the operation was experimental, once a patient dies they would do an autopsy. Do you know for sure if they did?"

"Yes, they did."

"Hmmm."

"Hmmm what?"

"Nothing really. It's just that autopsies used to be fairly common in Connecticut, and now they're rare."

"So?"

"So that makes it a bit more difficult for our side. When a judge sees an autopsy has been performed, he tends to stand up and take notice. It's more suggestive that things are on the up and up."

"The up and up?"

"Yeah. In the sense that the body's been properly examined, and all that rigmarole. The fact that it's already been examined makes it harder to get an exhumation, assuming of course that the autopsy's in good order. I guess you have no . . . no reason to think it's not?"

"No."

Steve paused and rested his elbows on the desk and put the tips of his fingers together. "See, the statute sets out five or six conditions under which an exhumation can be ordered—a sudden or violent death, suspicious circumstances, a death related to disease or while employed or related to public health, that kind of thing."

"*Suspicious circumstances.* We've got that here—in spades."

"Ah, you mean that computer business you told me about? The messages?"

"Exactly."

"Well, it's not as straightforward as that. The *suspicious circumstances,* as I read it, refers to the mode of death, not, you know—things that happen afterward."

"How about the fact that maybe he's not dead at all—wouldn't you call that suspicious?"

"Well, sure, but we're dealing with a court here—or at least a judge, and he's got to be able to see it right in front of him. We've got to get him to agree that it's suspicious, if you know what I mean."

"Damn it, Steve, whose side are you on here?"

"Yours, of course. Hold on, now. I'm just saying it's not so easy. I'm not saying it's impossible—it's just not, you know, a pro forma thing. To get an exhumation ordered by the court, you need one of these conditions cited here—say, suspicious circumstances—*and* the absence of an autopsy. And you have an autopsy, which makes it harder."

"Can you do it or not?"

Steve looked out the window again, then picked up a pen and started writing on a long yellow legal pad.

"I think so. I can certainly try. What we have to go for here is the possibility of mistaken identity."

"Mistaken identity?"

"Yes. We have to assert that someone else was buried in Tyler's place, or at least that we have reason to believe that the identification of Tyler was faulty in some respect . . . that it was incorrect or maybe not sufficiently certain."

He made a list on the pad and handed it to Scott.

"I'll need this information, as best as you can get it. Oh, and what's the name of that woman who worked at the hospital, the one who sat near you during the funeral?"

"Kate Willet. She's a neurosurgeon there."

"Right." He wrote it down, then stood, seeming a little awkward now that the business was out of the way.

"Well, I guess that does it," he said.

"Steve, do you think we'll be able to do this?"

"Yes. Eventually. I don't think a superior court judge is going to deny an order for exhumation from the single living relative. But the problem is, because of these things I was saying before, it's not going to leap ahead on the judicial calendar."

"So how long are we talking about?"

"I'll be honest. I don't think anything will happen before two, three months."

"*Months.* I don't have that long. Christ, Steve, this is urgent. Something really strange is going on. Tyler's out there somewhere and I've got to find him. I don't know where else to start."

"I know, okay. I'll do whatever I can to speed it up."

"You've got to."

"We'll move as fast as we can on this."

Scott said good-bye and left quickly.

Steve looked after him as the door closed. Then he picked up the phone and tried to reach Kate. He didn't know what he was going to say exactly, other than to introduce himself as Scott's friend and tell her that he thought Scott needed help of some kind, perhaps even a really good therapist. He knew that she was a new acquaintance, but given her position at the hospital he figured she might be able to recommend someone.

She didn't answer. Rather than leave a message, he thought he'd call back later.

Kate waited until late afternoon, the slow period when few people were about. She walked into the records division as if her visit were only one of a series of chores.

The attendant was standing at a counter, filing microfilm. She looked up and raised one eyebrow.

"I've got a bunch of stuff to get. Mind if I just go back there myself?" Kate asked in a matter-of-fact tone.

The attendant frowned and went back to what she was doing, dismissing her. For once, Kate was glad to receive a New York brush-off.

The files were meticulous up until 1985, when computerization had begun. After that they were more scattershot. The rows extended back like library stacks, fifty feet deep on either side of narrow aisles, the top ones reachable only by small stepladders on wheels. Kate was relieved to see that the most recent files—where she would be searching—were not the ones closest to the counter.

She found the section with the *J* drawers and pulled out *JAS–KAM*. It wasn't hard to find "Jessup, Tyler"— the folder was newer than those on either side. Stapled to it was a message typed on pink paper that read: "Do not give out. Notify Dr. Saramaggio of requests."

That was odd. She flipped through some of the other files to see if any had similar notes attached. None did. She looked up and down the aisle—no one was around. She pulled the file out and read through it quickly. Much of it she was familiar with—the write-up of the operation, the charts, the day-to-day records, minutes of the meetings of the Executive Board and the Ethics Board. She was startled to find a paper in her own writing, then remembered it—the form she had filled out that very first day when Scott arrived on the helicopter with Tyler.

At the back she found what she was looking for. There was the Certificate of Death, a simple straightforward piece of paper, innocuous given the weight of its official character. The cause of death was listed as "heart and respiratory failure" after "lengthy postoperative decline." The time of death was listed as "approximately" midnight—interesting. That would put it at the time that Scott and she were in the ward. Why say it happened around midnight when he had probably been dead sometime earlier? She looked at the signature and saw the wavy hand of "Saramaggio." He'd signed in three separate places as the presiding physician. Nothing out of the ordinary about that. Next to the certificate was the autopsy report, which she read through quickly. Again, there was nothing untoward; it seemed to be just another inventory of another body's inability to carry on—specimens taken and examined, body fluids analyzed, organs weighed. But there was one tidbit of information that she hadn't expected. The second attending physician—since two are required in unusual cases—was none other than Cleaver. *Cleaver.* Of all people. What in the world was he doing there at that hour? Why not simply ask the resident on duty to come by and sign the report?

Kate heard footsteps, and so she quickly folded the file, slipped it back, and closed the door. As she did so, the attendant stepped into the row and stopped, looking at her quizzically. Kate looked back at her. Best to stare her down, she thought. They held each other's gaze for a full five seconds.

Finally, the attendant gave way.

"I thought you might require assistance," she said mildly.

"Not at all," replied Kate, keeping the advantage. "I'm perfectly capable of doing it myself." She smiled. "But thank you."

It was Saramaggio's day off, and Kate's as well. She thought she'd take advantage of the coincidence and catch him off guard by meeting him on his native ground. It was unseasonably warm—even hot.

Scott insisted on driving her to Greenwich. They took the Merritt Parkway and drove for half an hour through the lush four-acre-minimum estates of the "back country" north of the parkway before finding his house, a handsome old white clapboard Colonial with green shutters. A maid answered and told her that he was to be found at his yacht club, Belle Haven.

It took them another forty minutes to find the place, a sailor's paradise on the town's Gold Coast. It occupied the tip of a peninsula, set around a snug little harbor. On the opposite side, huge stone and Tudor mansions occupied high ground; their manicured lawns sloped gently for several hundred feet and ended at the water's edge in stone walls, and in whitewashed wooden piers that rose and fell with the tide. In front of the club were red-clay tennis courts on which thin, rich-looking women in tight white tennis shorts darted back and forth. The thwacks of the balls were just about the only sounds—that and the deep baritone of fat happy bumblebees plunging into the lilac blossoms. In the back, a clipped green lawn led to an open deck from which bobbing sailboats at anchor could be seen, and beyond them two small islands and then the choppy gray waters of Long Island Sound.

Fifty feet from the clubhouse was a small beach and a fenced-off swimming pool. In front of it, in a handsome line of a dozen or so parked cars, was Saramaggio's black Ferrari.

"I'll wait for you here," said Scott, pulling over in the shade of a small maple.

"Okay," she replied. "I hope I do better than you did with that policeman."

Scott had to smile. He had told her about the conversation he'd finally had with Sergeant Paganelli at the Nineteenth Precinct. The cop's eyes had grown wider and wider as Scott tried to explain that his officially dead son was actually trapped or kidnapped somewhere and was sending SOS messages by means of a computer. He was not entirely unsympathetic, and he heard Scott out, but Scott could tell that other thoughts were flickering behind his secretive cop mask. The final tip-off came when he put an arm around Scott as he walked him to the door and recommended that he calm down and maybe take some time off from work and go someplace nice.

Kate walked through the open gate of the white fence, past a brick bathhouse on the left. The place was not crowded. On the right was a children's wading pool, where a boy and a girl, both wearing plastic water wings, splashed each other and ran screaming to the safety of their Latina nannies. Half a dozen teenagers cavorted in the main pool under the bored eyes of a lifeguard, a high school girl in a one-piece orange bathing suit and sunblock, who sat high on a wooden perch.

Kate spotted Saramaggio off by himself under a beach umbrella, lying on a reclining chair that was facing the Sound. He had a bathing suit on. A book lay upon his lap, but he seemed lost in thought, staring out to sea. She felt strange, approaching him out of nowhere. But maybe the element of surprise would favor her mission.

"Dr. Saramaggio, hello."

He took off his sunglasses and looked up at her, momentarily confused. He couldn't place her for a half minute or so.

"Ehh, Dr. Willet? Kate Willet? What are you doing here?"

He blinked, large owl blinks, then looked around. He was trying to figure it out. "Do you know someone . . ."

"No, no. I don't know anyone here. Just you. I came to talk to you."

"I see." He sat up, balancing himself uncertainly on one extended arm. He had a belt of rolling flesh around his midriff, and she thought how deft a dashing green surgeon's gown was at camouflaging flab. As he stared at her, searching her face for some kind of answer, his manner began to change. The change was something she felt rather than observed. No longer surprised, he now seemed oddly reconciled. He didn't ask how she had come or how she had managed to find him. It was as if these questions dropped away before something more profound now that they were together on the edge of the ocean.

They moved over to one side and sat at a metal table in the shade of an umbrella. The sun was hot for September, and Kate began to feel it. The armpits of her white blouse were damp.

"Would you like . . . ?" He gestured vaguely in the direction of the bathing house where, she now saw, there was a snack bar. The smell of frying oil carried even this far.

She wagged her head no.

"Dr. Saramaggio—"

"Leo. Please, call me Leo."

That was odd. He had never said that before. Why had he chosen such a moment for informality? The more she looked at him, the more she became convinced that it was not a polite concession. It was a gesture of appeasement.

My God, she thought, *he's nervous.*

"Well," she said. "I've come to ask you some questions about Tyler's death."

He gave a slight sucking sound, an almost imperceptible intake of breath. And then he nodded slowly.

"I don't see how I can help you." A half-second pause, then he added, "What is it you wish to know?"

She noticed that he didn't challenge her, a subordinate, over the right to pose questions. *Best to start with the easy ones,* she thought.

"A number of things, if I may. One is, just how did you determine that he was dead, and how did you fix the time of death?"

"You were there. You saw it. In fact, if I'm not mistaken"—a hint of sarcasm here—"you were the one who alerted me to it. Were you not?"

"Yes."

"So you saw that he was gone, that all of his vital signs had stopped and that he was beyond resuscitation."

"Yes, but the computer was still carrying on. So how does one define death in such a situation?"

"It *is* an unusual situation, I'll grant that. But I chose to determine that it had occurred when all of the patient's vital signs had stopped—those coming *from* the patient—so that he would clearly not be able to survive a single moment once the computer was no longer helping him."

"I contacted you after midnight. Why did you put down midnight as the time of death?"

He stiffened. He looked out to sea, and she thought for a moment that he would revert to the old Saramaggio, that he would stand up and demand to know where she got off interrogating him and bellow for her to be thrown out on her ear. But nothing of the sort occurred.

"It was a rough approximation. I put down midnight by extrapolation—I thought that was about the time you were there and saw him and that therefore that was the earliest known time he had ceased to exist."

He's good, she thought. *In a court of law, he would make an unflappable witness.*

The lifeguard blew a whistle. It let out a screech that seemed to violate the genteel surroundings.

"Parents' time," she yelled.

One of the teenagers groaned. Slowly and sullenly, they emerged from the pool, hoisting their lean, tanned bodies up over the side. Their place was taken by demure women in bathing caps, who stepped into the pool gracefully and then swam the breaststroke, their heads moving like stately vessels through the water.

For a minute or two, Saramaggio and Kate were silent. He was the first to speak.

"So I take it you've seen the death certificate?"

"Yes."

Again, he looked away, out to sea—almost longingly, she decided.

"And the autopsy report," she added. "I noticed that Dr. Cleaver signed the second signature. May I ask— why him? Why not just the duty resident? What was he doing there at that hour?"

"I called him."

"You called him?"

"Yes. I thought he should come in, since half of this whole procedure was his. He was the one who set up the computers, and he was the one who should be there if anything went wrong."

"Went *wrong*?"

"Well, Dr. Willet, I assume you'll agree with me if I say that when a patient dies, something can be presumed to have gone wrong."

Good, she thought. *He's flying along in that old superior way now. It's a good time to ask him the question I came here for.*

"Dr. Saramaggio—sorry, Leo—did you actually perform the autopsy? Or did someone else?"

He looked away quickly, but not quickly enough—for his eyes told the story. He had been ambushed, and they'd replied for him before he had a chance to censor them. No, they said, I didn't.

"Of course I did." Then he worked up a show of

anger, halfheartedly. "Do you mean to suggest that I would falsify a death certificate? Do you know what the penalty for that would be?"

"I do. So I wanted to ask you more about it, how you did it, including the abnormalities you found."

"Abnormalities?"

Now he looked worried.

"Yes."

He paused, finally replied, "I don't recall any abnormalities."

"Do you happen to recall the name of the aide who took the body away?"

"No."

"The attendant who was on duty in the morgue?"

"No."

"The time?"

"No. After midnight, that's all. You know, I was very upset by this whole thing."

The admission was more than an admission of weakness, she thought. It was an admission of guilt.

"On second thought," she said. "I think I would like a cup of coffee. Would you mind getting me one?"

When he came back, a tall figure carrying the cup in a hunched-over way that made him appear even older, she pretended that he had convinced her and changed the subject. He was grateful for the pretense. He wasn't one hundred percent certain that he had succeeded in quelling her doubts, but with time he knew he could persuade himself.

The lifeguard blew the whistle again. She shouted, "Parents' time over," and the transfer that unfolded— adults stepping out of the pool, boys and girls jumping in—struck Kate as some odd suburban ritual.

Meanwhile, she asked him a few idle questions about Cleaver, where he worked when he wasn't at St. Cat's or Pinegrove, who he worked with—in particular, his assistants in the mental asylum and the people who helped him build the computers.

Saramaggio, relieved to be talking about something else, spoke freely.

Half an hour later, when she stepped outside and motioned to Scott to pick her up, he thought he could tell by the tilt of her head that she was pleased with herself.

"Any luck?" he asked.

"Yes."

Chapter 26

Scott turned onto the George Washington Bridge and stole a glimpse at the distant skyscrapers on the horizon to his left, shrouded in a haze. From the bridge he used to spot the World Trade Center towers, and their absence never ceased to stun him.

He turned toward Kate, who was looking ahead. The angular light from the late-afternoon sun bathed her hair and made it gleam.

The rush hour slowed them. He moved into the right lane to take the turnoff to the Palisades.

"Thank God that guy has such an unusual name," he said. "What is it again?"

"I've told you three times already. Quincy. Quincy Penderglass."

"Sounds like something out of Dickens, a bookstore clerk—not a computer genius."

"Just be glad we got it at all."

Once they'd obtained the first name from Saramaggio, Kate had looked him up in the hospital's database and found him under a subsection of the affiliate's billing file for Pinegrove. Cleaver had been paying him a monthly retainer of over three thousand dollars for unspecified computer work. Kate guessed that the charge was padded. But in any case the file contained his full name and home address.

They got lost in Englewood. Even when they found the right street, they circled through the development twice because the ranch houses looked so similar, distinguished mostly by the elaborateness of outdoor play sets or the size of their raised garish blue swimming pools.

"That's got to be it," said Scott, pointing to a brick house with a sagging gutter. "Jesus. What a mess."

"I think we can safely say they don't care too much about outward appearances."

Scott parked across the street.

"We'll have to play this by ear," he said. "We've no idea if this guy knows anything."

Halfway up the path of broken flagstones, they heard the throbbing beat of techno-music from within. Scott knocked, but no one heard him. The door was ajar, so he pushed it and it swung inward. The music was blasting now, and they saw a young man, stripped to the waist, seated before a speaker on a card table.

He looked up disinterestedly and pointed toward a hallway. They followed it. At the far right was a closed door, and when they opened it and their eyes adjusted to the dim light, they saw an extraordinary sight—a man so fat that his body formed a perfect pyramid of blubber. He was seated cross-legged on an imposing bed with raised sides and a wooden canopy, all of it elaborately carved and lacquered in black and red. Scott recognized it as a Chinese opium bed.

The man opened his eyes slowly—he appeared to have been meditating—and gestured for them to sit down on wooden chairs that lined one wall. He, too, did not seem surprised to see them. His face was wrinkled, and his long hair was drawn back in a neatly tied yellowish gray ponytail.

"Yes?" was all he said.

"We're looking for Quincy," said Scott.

"And who might you be?"

Scott and Kate introduced themselves, and then rose to shake his hand, which was surprisingly strong inside all that flab.

"I am Cybedon. But of course I imagine you knew that."

"Not really," said Scott. "And who are you exactly?"

"The question is," he replied in a lugubrious basso, "who are *you*?—*exactly*?"

"We came looking for Quincy," Scott said, "because we hoped he could help us."

"Please do sit," Cybedon said. "I hate to be a negligent host. Would you like some beverage? They treat me well here, but the service is not all that it might be."

"No, thank you," said Kate. "We're really here for some information."

"Please tell me in what way you had hoped Quincy might help you," he said, smiling patronizingly.

Just like the caterpillar with the hookah on the mushroom, thought Kate. *And he probably makes about as much sense, too.* She wondered how much information Scott would give and was surprised when he settled back and told him almost the whole story of Tyler, from his accident to the operation and his death and finally the computer messages. She was even more surprised that Cybedon didn't seem taken aback by the story.

"I see," he said, rocking his head slightly, which had the effect of sending ripples down his body as if to spread it out even farther. "I believe all of what you told me has an explanation."

She felt Scott stiffen.

Cybedon looked at Kate. "And you are . . . ?"

"A friend. And I'm a doctor, a neurosurgeon. I was part of the team that did the operation."

"Ah." His eyebrows rose.

Scott was about to say something, but Kate placed a hand on his arm to stop him.

"Please explain what you mean by an explanation," she said.

"Certainly. It would be my pleasure. But your occupation may make it more difficult for you to understand what I'm about to say. You are bound to have your own view of the human brain, and I hope it is not a narrow one. I hope you do not agree with Francis Crick when he summed up that view by saying, 'You're nothing but a pack of neurons.' "

"I'm acquainted with his work, of course, but not with that particular quotation."

"But do you agree?"

"I need more information before I disagree. But surely we're not here to—"

"Oh, our blessed scientists. Always so congenial and sentimental when it comes to the theories of their colleagues. Always so loath to take on the giants of our age, no matter how misguided they may be."

"Please," said Scott testily. "Get to the point."

"The point, Mr. Jessup, is that Mr. Crick and others like him adopt a mechanistic view of the brain, which retards progress. We are on the verge of some very important discoveries here, discoveries that fall into that complicated area known as the mind-body problem, and from what you tell me I would say that your son has become, willingly or not, a pioneer."

"A *pioneer*?"

"Precisely."

"Goddamn it, explain what you mean," Scott said.

"Scott, please." Kate turned to Cybedon. "Tell me, does what you're saying have something to do with computers?"

"Ah, the surgeon's knife hits the mark."

"Somehow the computers did something to Tyler."

"They didn't *do* anything to him. They provided him with an opportunity. You see, all the computers did was to open a door—he was the one who walked through it."

"So where is he?"

"He is in an entirely different realm than the one we inhabit."

"Where is it?"

"All around us, I believe. It is everywhere. Is it better or worse than our own?—Who's to say?"

"Shit," said Scott.

"Wait," cautioned Kate. She turned back to Cybedon. "Can we see him?"

"See him? I doubt it. The question is, Can he see you? I tend to doubt that also, though I admit I am less certain. You may, however, talk to him."

"*Talk to him?*" said Kate.

"Yes. Through the computer. As you tell me you already have."

"You mean he's in some halfway world and he can

send us messages from there and get our messages?"
said Scott.

"Yes—in so many words."

"Let's back up a minute," said Scott. "Can you explain to us what's going on—the whole thing, from the very beginning?"

Cybedon sighed, so deeply that his immense belly shook. "Where to start?"

"How about at the beginning?"

"But what is the beginning? This is but one more chapter in an ancient and continuing narrative." He paused, then resumed. "What we are witnessing is something that has long been a striving of mankind. Forgive me, my dear," he said, turning to Kate. "I've never been able to adopt that awkward expression—what is it? *Humankind.* It sounds so odd to the ear."
Kate nodded, hurrying him along.

"Philosophers and other such thinkers, epistemologists in particular, have long wondered about the human mind, its capacity to know things that would seem to lie outside of its daily existence, even things beyond its physical capability. A whole raft of experience comes to us without explanation—dreams, intuition, the famous 'sixth sense,' our spiritual beliefs. Have you ever known something, known it to be true even though it did not appear to you through one of your five senses?"

Kate thought immediately of her mother and the vision she'd seen of her husband. She said nothing, made no sign of assent.

"This knowledge might seem to be less certain by virtue of the fact that its origin is obscure, but actually the opposite is true. We believe in it *more,* and we do so *because* the source is not in the realm of our everyday senses. It is liable to become a deeply held belief—like faith. Faith in the existence of a higher being threads itself through much of recorded history, from the Crusades, the Inquisition, the expulsion of the Huguenots, and so on—a distressingly sad litany of events that are epic in their violence. It continues down to today—Iran, Afghanistan, the Middle East. I'm tempted to add

Northern Ireland, but being part Irish myself, I tend to think of *the troubles,* as they are so euphemistically called, as sui generis."

He smiled. Kate sensed Scott's impatience and didn't smile back.

"So the question arises, How do we know these things? Since they are known by the mind, it is natural to assume that it is the mind that does the knowing—notice that I employ the word *mind* here, not the word *brain*—in other words, at certain times the mind has a capacity to range beyond the physical vessel that seemingly contains it. Especially, I should add, at critical times, such as illness, states of extreme emotion, and—it goes without saying—the most critical time of all, death.

"Some people are specialists in this netherworld. They are born with the gift of higher insight, and we consequently look upon them as guides—Socrates at the moment of drinking the hemlock, Christ on the cross, Muhammad meditating in the caves outside of Mecca.

"Others, lesser mortals, attempt to train themselves to accomplish the feat of leaving the body. This is done either through the repetition of some physical act, as by the whirling dervishes or shamans or our modern equivalent, techno dancers, or through some meditative state—witness Buddhist monks who can achieve a trancelike state for weeks on end. A third avenue, of course—and again, it is a symptom of our age—is artificial stimulants. Not for nothing are they referred to as mind-expansion drugs.

"But these methods are unsatisfactory; the experiences are brief and passing. No one—at least no one until now"—and here he looked meaningfully at Scott—"has actually been able to enter this realm, to enter and make his presence known. How could this be done? Only by the mind itself, the pure mind, as it sheds that awkward troublesome vessel, the body.

"In Latin America, you know, there is this saying that at the precise moment of death, the body loses twenty-one grams. Twenty-one grams—that, they say, is what life weighs. I myself do not believe this saying to be literally true, but as a myth I find it psychologically compelling and surprisingly revealing. For something *is* given up at death. The question is, What? The ancients had a word for it—*psyche*. Today we call it *the soul*. Some call it the *anima*."

"Please, please," said Scott. "Get to the point."

"I am, Mr. Jessup, I am getting to the point. I would like to take you there with me, which is why I am favoring you with this lengthy exposition. Shall I proceed?"

"Yes."

Cybedon looked at Kate.

"You know, of course, of the work done by the Danish research team that studied three hundred and forty-four heart-attack survivors? It was published in *Lancet*. More than one in ten experienced visions and lucid thoughts *after* they were declared clinically dead. That makes sense when you consider that your brain dies from the outside in. It shuts down layer by layer, like an egg turning cold. Deep in your interior brain, your primitive brain, is where your anima is located. Why wouldn't it be the last to depart?"

"Sort of like a rat deserting a sinking ship," said Scott.

Cybedon ignored him.

"Imagine now if at the moment of death this quintessential quality—whatever you want to call it—could find another route. If it could find something to ease its passage into the ethereal realm, so to speak. Imagine that there is in place a system of wires and connections capable of carrying electrical impulses deeply implanted in that part of the brain where the anima exists, where the mind actually resides. In short, imagine someone such as your son hooked up to computers who—"

"Are you telling me that the computer took the life out of him and put it—wherever you call it, in another *realm*?"

"In effect, yes, though I find your wording less than felicitous. The computer is a portal."

"And where is this so-called realm? What is it? Cyberspace? Are you telling me that my son is in cyber-space?"

"No, Mr. Jessup. It is not cyberspace. Cyberspace is merely a term to describe a man-made series of connections between systems of computers, first through wires and then through space. This is altogether different. It is clearly not man-made. It is eternal and it has always been with us, like the space between molecules that we cannot see."

Cybedon looked directly at Scott, who returned his stare.

"Think of cyberspace as a medium of communication. That's all. It's like an antenna that can pick up signals in the air and feed them to your television set. Or sonar blips that travel across the ocean and record the sounding of whales hundreds of miles away. It enables you to reach him—and, more importantly, it enables him to reach you. It is that two-way contact that represents the significant breakthrough.

"The wonder is not that Tyler"—the use of his son's first name struck Scott like an electric shock—"has gone or that his consciousness has entered into a world we cannot experience. The wonder is that he has reached this world and succeeded in communicating back. That, one might say, is computer feedback of the highest level."

"So what is this realm like?"

"Who knows? If you stand on the shore and merely look, you do not know the ocean. It might consist of everyone who has ever lived, every deed that has ever been done, every word that has ever been spoken. It might be the same for all of us. Or it might be individualistic—it might represent your own consciousness freed of the body, your pure imagination, the very essence of what you are."

"Let me get this straight. You say he's *gone*. So what you're saying is he's definitely dead—right?"

"No, I would never put it in those terms. I would say he has achieved the mind-body split permanently. And that the situation is actually quite the reverse: He—

meaning his consciousness—has the opportunity to achieve eternal life." Cybedon opened his hands, palms outward. "Though, granted, we do not know what kind of life it is."

"And his body?"

"Well, that, regrettably for you, will deteriorate."

"So there's no return."

"No. At least not in our lifetimes."

"And after?"

"After, I expect that humans will devise a machine that can recapture it. And then we will have achieved a quantum leap in evolution. It will be like the first meeting of the sperm and the egg, and it will lead us into a brave new world."

Cybedon folded his hands and blinked, almost as if he was sleepy. It was clear that the interview—or, from his point of view, the audience—was over.

"Good luck," he said finally. "And do not be disheartened—on the contrary."

They left the room. Scott went into every room in the house. He turned up only three people, including the young man who had greeted them with such taciturn indifference, and none of them seemed to know anything important. The elusive Quincy was not to be found.

They got in the car and began the trip back in silence, but soon Kate turned to Scott and said, "What do you make of it all?"

"I can't say I buy it. Freed consciousness. Anima. The other realm. It's all a bit too fantastic for my taste. But, I don't know—there was one moment there when he was talking and what he said seemed to make sense. What do you think?"

"I feel the same," she said. "I'm skeptical, but only halfway."

For the fact of the matter was that, for all the hard-headed science that had been drilled into her, Kate was open to the belief that the world was a complicated place that hid away its more profound truths. *"There are more things in heaven and earth, Horatio. . . ."*

And Scott, too, was feeling unsure. He was beginning

to think he was like Cybedon's landlubber looking out over the ocean. Our ignorance is so abysmally limitless, he said to himself, that we can't even begin to imagine its depth.

As they crossed the river, the bridge towers were set afire by the setting sun. The sky above was ribbed by clouds that seemed illuminated from within, dramatic explosions of purples and pinks and oranges. It was an unearthly sight, like the end of the world.

Cleaver was feeling frustrated—and rightfully so. After all, he had been the one to dispatch the anima out there into the ether, and now the damn thing was ignoring him. He simply couldn't make any contact with it at all.

He sat at the keyboard in Quincy's lab at Braintrust four floors above the Bowery, alone, pounding the computer keys, hoping to blunder upon something that might call up a response. He was desperate now, even hitting *tab* and *backspace* and *delete*. He had already tried every conceivable variation of JINGO, the password that Quincy had hijacked from Scott Jessup's computer.

Nothing worked. *The perverse little brat.*

The windows were open, and he could hear the street sounds—a car honking, a dog barking, if he listened closely, even heels clacking on the concrete. A perfect, crisp autumn day outside, the kind that used to fill him with bottomless melancholy at his New England prep school and later at MIT. It used to make him feel that while he, the ever-faithful drone, was working at his desk, others must be off having fun—riding around in cars, heading out to Cape Cod for a final clambake on the beach, piling up at a drive-in hamburger stand where the waitresses floated over to the cars on roller skates—whatever it was that young people did.

Quincy's dog was gone, on a walk at least—thank God for small favors.

He looked again at the screen. There had been only

those tentative messages, back and forth early on, enough for him to realize that the great experiment had worked. But nothing since. And now Cybedon, who hadn't had anything to do with it at all, who was lucky to have even heard about it—*that* was all Quincy's fault—was taking it on as if it were his own, talking about it, expostulating about it, theorizing about it, almost as if he were the creator.

Cleaver took his hands off the keyboard and sat back. He thought about cyberspace, tried to conjure up what it must be like. Whenever he did, he imagined it as some sort of vast organic network spreading around the world like some science fiction creature or one of those underground fungi you read about that spreads for miles under the earth, the world's largest living creature. Sometimes he thought of it as a brain, a sprawling global brain oozing gray matter like billowing banks of fog and with sparks jumping across synapses like forest fires across rivers and pulsating centers like underwater earthquakes.

He stopped short and wondered: If cyberspace is a brain or analogous to a brain, does it organize itself according to a principle? Does it sort itself out by organic function so that over time it breaks down into different parts? Is it outlandish to think that all the reams of pure data circulating out there might organize into some retrievable memory storehouse or that all the viruses might congregate into some center of malevolence, a center of aggression? Or that the antivirus systems that try to keep the pathways open evolve into the command stations for benevolent circulatory systems?

Is Tyler's consciousness zipping around through a funhouse hall of mirrors now, or is it locked inside a chamber of horrors too gruesome to be described?

Why does it refuse to communicate? Has it become diffuse, like a drop of perfume in a barrel of water? Or can it summon up will and decide, like a stubborn child, to hold its breath and not open its mouth?

Cleaver sighed. He wanted so much to know—not just in the abstract, but to know from experience. He looked over at the TSR, the backup model, sitting on a desk where Quincy had been working on it. It looked exactly like the model he had delivered to the basement of Pinegrove, the one Cleaver had been using on the patients.

The idea of trying it himself was—he had to admit it—tempting. Just thinking about it set his heart racing so that he could hear his pulse pounding in his ears. How easy it would be. Just set the dials and slip onto the movable stretcher and disappear inside the cigar tube. In just a few moments' time, he would understand what it's like to be out there, to experience the departure from the body, the flight through space, the mind soaring across the heavens.

But—and there's the rub—how about the return? And how to ensure that the trip is accomplished within the mandatory seven minutes without a lab assistant to pull him out? Overstaying his welcome would clearly be catastrophic—he had seen what it had done to Benchloss. The memory of the man's contorted features when he had been pulled out of the chamber was vivid. He shuddered. No one who had looked upon such a sight would willingly undertake the risk of duplicating the voyage. It wasn't so much the end, but the passage to it that loomed as terrifying.

He couldn't say, though, that Benchloss's death had been totally inconvenient. It had, in fact, been nothing short of fortuitous.

He heard Quincy's steps come up the stairs, then pause in front of the door. The dog scratched at the base, and the door rattled. A jangling of keys, a turn in the lock, and the mastiff bounded inside, shaking the floorboards. Quincy followed him, staring none too happily at Cleaver.

"Christ. You still here? I thought you'd left ages ago."

Cleaver ignored him and turned back to the keyboard.

"Still battering away at that machine, huh? Why don't you give it a break—the damn thing's not going to answer you anymore anyway. You know, I think it's pissed off at you. I think you're the last person it's going to want to speak to."

The huge dog came over and smelled Cleaver's pant leg. It lifted its head next to his shoulder, holdings its ears down and its tail low—not a friendly posture.

"Hey, will you call him off?"

"Take it easy. He can smell your fear. So can I, for that matter."

Cleaver tried to listen to see if he could hear a low growl without putting his head too close.

"Don't move," commanded Quincy.

Cleaver froze.

"C'mon," he said. "This isn't funny. Get him out of here."

"No—I don't mean that. I mean don't hit the keys. For Christ's sake, look up at the screen."

Cleaver did. And there in the center, he saw the following words being formed, slowly but surely:

```
P-I-S-S  O-F-F
```

Chapter 27

Kate took the elevator to the hospital basement and walked briskly toward the morgue along a corridor painted institutional green. She detested the morgue. Everything about it grated on her—the church-like silence, the glare of the lights refracting off burnished metal, the long body drawers that looked as innocuous as filing cabinets. Even the sterility was bothersome, rigidly enforced for the benefit of the living—as if it mattered as far as the corpses were concerned. As a doctor, and particularly one whose operations took patients to the very edge of life, she should be on friendlier terms with the place, she knew. But she couldn't find it in her to try. To her, it represented consummate failure, the apotheosis of death.

A young man was on duty. His hair was parted down the middle so that forelocks hung down on either side, framing his forehead. He sat behind a metal desk reading a book—she couldn't make out the title, but saw that it was by Nabokov. He immediately lowered it and looked at her with the air of bemusement and a hint of obstinacy that she recognized as a prelude to flirtation.

"May I help you?" He gave a droll lilt to the question, like a customs inspector hinting that he might be open to a bribe.

She gave her name, title, and department, which pushed him back a bit. Then she said she wanted to check some information—the exact time that a body had entered the morgue and the time it had left for the funeral home.

"I don't know," he said uncertainly. "Was it one of yours?"

"As a matter of fact, it was."

"Oh. Sorry. What's the name and date and approximate time of death, if you have it?"

She told him, and he punched the name into a computer. He frowned. Nothing was coming up. Then he checked the general register, scrolling down. He stopped and touched the screen.

"I have him," he said. "He was admitted upstairs—whoa, nine weeks ago. Is that right?" She nodded. "But I don't have him coming down here. That's odd—I see a date of death here." He hit some more keys, checked more files. "I've got nothing at all for him here. I'd have to say, it looks like he never passed through here. That's strange. Maybe the family insisted that he be taken somewhere else—that's the only way he'd bypass this place."

She thanked him, prepared to go, but he seemed to want her to linger.

"Who signed the death certificate?" he asked.

"Dr. Saramaggio."

He smiled. "Oh, well, that could explain it—maybe he resurrected him."

"Tell me something." And now she gave a friendly smile in return. "If a body is taken out, like to go to the funeral parlor, who is the last one here to actually see it off?"

"That's easy. That time of night, it would be the night porter. The one who works the rear exit. There's a way to check that, but you have to go to the porters' office. It's at the other end of the basement."

Suddenly he had turned helpful.

"One more question, if I may."

"Certainly. You can have more than one."

"If there's an autopsy, it would be done down here, right? You wouldn't do it anywhere else in the hospital."

"Unlikely. We've got all the equipment here, fluids and everything. Hey, you're really investigating this. What's up? Suspect foul play?" His use of the crime-novel expression was ironic. "Need any help? I used to read Dick Tracy."

"No, thanks," she said. "This is more Mickey Spillane."

It wouldn't do to have this guy muddying the waters.

She left, feeling his eyes trail her from behind as she walked away. Just for the hell of it, she gave an extra sway to her hips.

The porters' office in the bowels of the building wasn't easy to find. It was at the end of a rabbit's warren of passageways with peeling paint that led past furnaces and boilers and old storage rooms covered in dust. At last she came to it, just before a flight of steps that led to the rear exit. To one side of the doorway was an array of rusted racks and an old time clock for punch cards. To the other, a coffee machine that looked like it hadn't been cleaned in months. She stared at the machine—a cup of coffee suddenly seemed appealing.

"Only if you're desperate," came a voice behind her. "That machine's temperamental. Never know what's going to come out. It's liable to bite you."

She turned and saw an elderly black man wearing neatly pressed trousers and a sports jacket with an open-necked shirt. His dark neck was wrinkled and his temples were gray, but he looked strong and spry.

"Oh, I'm looking for the porters' office."

"I'd say you've come to the right place. What can we do you for?"

"I'd like to know, if it's no trouble, if you can tell me who was on duty on a certain night last month."

"Come on in." He motioned her to follow and turned and walked into the office. It was a snug windowless box with a battered wooden desk lit by a gooseneck lamp. On the wall was a calendar from an insurance company showing a white-steepled church among rolling verdant Vermont hills, and a shelf of well-thumbed paperbacks. He offered her the only seat in the room, but she refused, so they both remained standing.

"Last month, you say. If it wasn't a weekend, I don't even have to check. That'd be me."

"Good, you're sure."

"Yeah. I've worked nights for years now. I like it better. Less hassles, fewer people to bother you."

Having delivered his considered opinion, he waited, expectantly. So she nodded. She understood.

"This is the night I was wondering about," she said, handing him a piece of paper with Tyler's name and the date of his death written upon it.

"Let's see," he said. He sat down at the desk, put on a pair of glasses, and from the desk drawer pulled out a notebook with a black-and-white speckled cardboard cover. "It's old-fashioned," he said, thumbing through the book and peering at her over the rim of the glasses. "But I trust it more than those computers. Never hear of one of these crashing."

He moved slowly. Waiting for him to find the answer, and trying to will his thin bony fingers to fly through the pages, she realized how overwrought she was. She was seized by anxiety—she could feel it, like a hand tightening around her body, forcing her breathing into short bursts, sending her blood racing, feeding alertness with a surge of adrenaline. They were all textbook symptoms that she had studied to boredom and back in med school.

Her meeting with the morgue attendant had unsettled her. If Tyler's autopsy had not been performed according to proper procedures, it was a serious violation of regulations—and at first blush, that seemed to be the least of it. Outright falsification was a possibility, which was even worse and could lead to dismissal and revocation of the hospital's accreditation. The strangest part was that she couldn't say for certain exactly what she wanted to happen. She didn't want to see the hospital get into trouble, or Saramaggio either, for that matter, nor did she want to be a party to questionable procedures, especially where Scott and Tyler were concerned. She didn't really believe Tyler was alive, but she'd feel better if she could prove categorically that he was not and that the hospital had behaved correctly. But that would mean dashing Scott's hopes; no matter what he said, she knew that deep down he was clinging to the idea that his son had somehow survived.

"Let's see," the old man repeated, needlessly because he had already found the page and had read it through once. He was going back for a second read.

"No," he said. "I see nothing here about a funeral van. But there is a notation here about a patient being removed, and now that I see it, I remember it well. It was raining to beat all tarnation."

"A *patient*?"

"Yep. It was that little boy that everyone was talking about, the one who had that accident to his skull. He was being transferred to another hospital—that's what they told me."

"Who?"

"The ones who took him. The driver and the assistant."

"Did they say which hospital?"

"No, come to think of it."

"What were they driving—a hearse?"

"No, an ambulance. Not from here, a private one."

"Do you know the company?"

"No."

"Could you describe it?"

"I guess. It was just an ordinary ambulance. White and red. I expect it had the name on the side, but I'm afraid I didn't get a good look. If I did, I don't remember. Like I said, it was raining something fierce."

"Was a doctor from the hospital there?"

"Not that I recall."

"So who authorized the transfer?"

"Now that you ask, I'm not so sure. Somebody called down. I think it was a doctor, but now that I think back, I can't rightly say."

"Don't you keep records?"

"No, not on something like that."

She held her breath.

"Could it have been Dr. Saramaggio?"

"Hmm. No, I think I would have remembered that."

"Then who?"

"I just can't say."

"When you say you can't say, you mean you don't remember, right?"

"Right."

One name occurred to her, of course, but she wasn't sure she should mention it. Cleaver hadn't been in to work for three days. She didn't want to run any risk that he could be alerted, even inadvertently.

"Tell me more about the ambulance and the guys who took him away."

"Not much to tell. The ambulance was just a regular ambulance. The guys were—well, I can't say they looked like CPR types. One had long hair—I mean, really long. And the other was kind of scruffy-looking."

"Race?"

"White—both of them."

"Anything else?"

"Not that I can think of right now. I'm trying to cast my mind back."

"Okay. If you come up with anything, will you be sure to let me know?"

"Sure will."

She pulled out a card and also wrote her home number on it.

"Can I ask you something?" he said.

"Sure. Go ahead."

"How come you're asking all these questions?"

She decided to play it straight with him. He had been straight with her, as far as she could tell.

"Well, keep it between us, please, but that little boy— there was a funeral service for him the morning after you saw him."

"No kidding." He shook his head and whistled. "Too bad. So young, too."

"Yep."

"Uh-huh. I guess he must've died somewhere else then."

"Why do you say that?"

" 'Cause he was alive when he left here."

"And how can you be sure?"

" 'Cause of the stanchion."

"The stanchion?"

"Yes. The one that held the IV drip. Plus, there were a lot of machines—you know, life-sustaining equipment—attached to him. They were real careful with it loading him in. Now he wouldn't be needing any IV drip if he wasn't still alive—would he?"

She tried to keep her face blank.

"No, you're right about that."

"So that's why I say I guess he must've died somewhere else."

"I guess you're right about that, too."

"Uh-huh."

She worked her way back through the basement of the building, her mind racing. She was so excited, she realized she had lost all track of time. She checked her watch—my God, she had an operation to perform in half an hour. She hurried upstairs and sat at her desk to collect herself. She knew from experience that she performed best in the OR when she was able to vacate her mind. That allowed her to achieve a thin shield of mental detachment so that she could concentrate on the minute tasks at hand, cutting the dura or slicing with a scalpel, and at the same time visualize the whole operation so that she could take the next step without even thinking about it. This was impossible to do if her mind was somewhere else.

After a few minutes, she felt under control and went to change and wash up. Her last thought before donning scrubs was that she shouldn't tell Scott yet what she had discovered. She needed some more information first. It wouldn't do to give him half the story.

———

Scott tossed in bed that night, victim of his worst nightmare. He had had trouble falling asleep in the first place. It was unseasonably warm, so he'd kept the windows to the loft open and had tried to read. He couldn't concentrate, and at midnight turned out the light. Just as he was about to drift off, a fight broke out on the street below. Two drivers got out of their cars and circled each other like angry curs, letting loose full-throated threats and curses. A neighbor on the third floor across the street made everything worse by screaming at them and finally throwing down a pot full of water, which caused the two to curse him and yell even louder. They banged on the neighbor's front door. Eventually, they jumped into the cars and pulled away, peeling rubber. By then, Scott was wide-awake. He had tried reading some more and had finally fallen off, to sleep fitfully, and after a short while he tumbled into the nightmare.

It was one that he had had before, several times. And even though he was semiconscious, on some level he seemed to know that it was familiar, and this knowledge made him anticipate his fear and exacerbated it. He felt as if the dreadful sequence of events was unfolding according to some preordained scenario that he was powerless to stop.

He was young, about seven or eight, the age of awareness and helplessness. He was in his pajamas in bed in a rambling old New England house with a dozen connecting rooms downstairs and the same upstairs. The two stories were connected by a single flight of creaky wooden steps on one end, which was far from his bedroom. Down below, in the room directly beneath him, was his mother. She was doing something that was dangerous to him. Maybe she was drinking, maybe she was mixing chemicals to make a bomb, maybe she was boiling water to scald him with—he didn't know for certain.

But he had a plan. He would telephone the doctor, who would arrive and make everything all right. Carefully, he dialed the numbers, one by one, on an old rotary phone, releasing the dial each time slowly and softly so that it would make no noise. Still, it sounded very loud to him. A nurse answered and said she would get the doctor. After a long wait, the doctor picked up the line, and

Scott began talking, telling him about the danger. But just then he heard a click, and he knew his mother had picked up the extension downstairs. And she started talking, too, sweetly, slowly, explaining to the doctor in a voice that struck him as unreal that everything was fine, and then she said, "It's all right, Doctor. There's nothing to worry—"

And she was going to say *"about,"* but as she did, the sound exploded, as if in an echo chamber, getting louder and louder until it was a piercing scream. The phone fell to the floor with a smash, and he knew that she had dropped it and that she was running to get him and that the doctor couldn't get there in time. He heard the doors downstairs slamming open one by one and the deadfall of running footsteps. And for a moment he thought of trying to run down the stairs to the front door, but he feared he would meet her halfway on the staircase, which scared him beyond thinking about, so that he merely sunk lower and lower under the blankets with only his head sticking out.

And soon enough the footsteps sounded different, a bit more distant, and he knew she was coming up the stairs. And then they began getting louder again, and more doors opened and closed. Before he knew it, she was in front of *his* door, which flew open as if a great gust of wind had blown it, and there, towering almost to the top of the frame, she turned suddenly into a man with a maniacal grin holding high a meat cleaver dripping with blood. He stepped forward, in one great leap was by the bed, hoisting the cleaver above his head—

Scott awoke, shuddering, drenched in sweat, his heart bouncing in his chest. He was gripping the blankets in terror. He knew instantly that he had been dreaming, that he was okay and wasn't going to be killed. But he had been so frightened that even though the terror began to subside right away, his heart was still pounding minutes later and he was still trembling so much that he looked at his hands and watched them—it was as if they had minds of their own that he couldn't calm.

Before, when he had had the nightmare, he would get out of bed and go straight to the liquor cabinet under the sink and pour himself a stiff scotch, but now, of course, he could not do that. He got up and walked around, feeling his heart return to normal, like an engine that had nearly popped a gasket slowing down. He went to the windows and looked down upon the deserted street. A street lamp sent a funnel of light down onto the sidewalk, and fragments of glass sparkled back.

Here I am, he thought, *thirty-six years old and still dreaming that same nightmare.* He remembered the time he had had it next to Lydia, how she'd sat up and listened to him with her big eyes wide and then had held him and talked to him. He'd told her how disturbed he was that he would dream he was in danger from his mother, whom he loved, and Lydia said she thought it was his reaction to his mother's alcoholism—and the fear that she was out of control. She had promised—her eyes blazing—that someday he would rid himself of it. He wondered about that. All these years later, it still bothered him. *The unconscious knows no time,* a friend of his had once told him, quoting Freud, he said.

For the hell of it—and also because he was wide-awake and feared going back to sleep—he sat before his computer and jiggled the mouse to make the screen saver dissolve. A message was waiting for him, and he knew instantly that it was from Tyler. He held his breath and looked at the words, then read them quickly, then slowly again and again. They were mysterious.

```
DAD COME. TRY 199.6.2.5 "WORDSWORTH"
```

He waited a moment or two to see if there would be more, then tried frantically to answer back, hitting keys quickly, looking for the words that would unlock the mystery or just draw any kind of a response, keep it going.

```
TYLER ARE U THERE?
```

He waited as long as he dared, then typed again:

    TYLER WHAT DO U MEAN? I DON'T UN-
    DERSTAND WHAT IS WORDSWORTH? CAN U
    HEAR ME . . . TYLER ARE U THERE ???

He typed more:

    FOR GODS SAKE TYLER ANSWER

But there was no response on the screen, and he did
not know what else to try.

─────

The next day, Kate checked in the Yellow Pages and
found that there were fourteen ambulance and am-
bulette services in Manhattan, over forty if she counted
the other boroughs. She went on the Internet and, one
by one, called up the Web sites of those that were posted.
Most contained photos of their vehicles. Whenever one
cropped up that was red and white, or anything close, she
copied it and carried it down to show to the porter. Each
time, he solemnly examined it, looking at it from top to
bottom, then shook his head no. Several times he paused
quite a while before responding. In these cases, she
feared that he wasn't really sure and merely wanted to
provide her with a definitive answer, so she made a note
of them. They would merit a follow-up call.

The companies that didn't have Web sites she telephoned directly. She asked them to give a description of
the ambulances. Sometimes they complied; sometimes
they became suspicious and hung up. Only three in all
would agree to look over their logs for the night in
question, and none of these came back with a report
that they had gone to St. Catherine's. A dozen others insisted that the information was confidential.

She was more than halfway through when Saramaggio came to her door and stood there until she looked
up. He told her to come to his office. How strange that

he didn't just telephone or that he didn't tell her what was on his mind right then and there, she thought, trailing him through the corridor. He walked ahead quickly, ducking his head slightly at each doorway.

Once inside his office, he gestured toward the chair with an awkward politeness and sat down behind his desk. He cleared his throat, avoided looking into her eyes, played with a pencil on his blotter, and finally asked how she was doing.

"Fine," she said. "Just fine."

"Good, good," he said, but he didn't sound as if he meant it. His thoughts were elsewhere.

At last, he looked up at her and said, "Look, there's no point in beating around the bush." She nodded her agreement. "Take a look at this," he said, and he opened a drawer, pulled out a document, put it on the desk, and spun it around so that she could read it.

It was some kind of complicated, four-page form that she had never seen before, and at first she was baffled. But as she read on, she felt the anger rising and her cheeks turning red.

"This is outrageous," she declared, turning to the last page.

"I admit, it's a bit difficult," he said.

"Difficult! It's an application for suspension. He's applying to have me suspended! And what are the grounds? What conceivably are the grounds?"

Saramaggio avoided looking her in the eye.

"All that business with the boy," he replied. "You know, how you came in with the father and then there was that unfortunate scene—mostly his fault, I know, but you were there—"

"*His fault.* My God, you were there. You came right afterward. That boy was gone. He was dead and his father just saw that he was dead—you'd expect him to get upset. And after he'd tried so hard to get him taken off life support and been refused— W*ait a minute.* What are these words here? Does this mean to suggest that *we* are responsible for his death, that his father and I—"

"It doesn't say that in so many words, but yes, there is

that implication." He was looking at the wall now. "I mean, the two of you were there, there was a huge ruckus—"

"Now, *come on*. That boy was dead when we got there. None of the monitors, none of *his* monitors, showed any life whatsoever. That's what upset Scott. You know that!"

"Well, that's what you say—"

"That's why we called you."

"Perhaps, yes, but you see, I arrived after it was all over, so how could I reasonably attest that it didn't happen this way?"

"But who says that it did? *Him?* He doesn't even know. He wasn't there."

"Now don't get upset. This doesn't represent any definitive finding. All this is at an early stage; everything will be looked into."

"Don't get upset—how the hell can you say that? You've got the nerve to sit there and tell me I'm suspended for something I didn't even do. And you know that I didn't do anything and you're not backing me up."

"We'll see. I'm not taking any sides at the moment."

"You're afraid of him. That's what's going on."

"I am not. He is, however, a senior doctor here, and he outranks you so that we have to take what he says—"

"You signed that death certificate because he made you do it. And you put down the wrong time of death to implicate us."

Saramaggio gasped. He looked as if the wind had been knocked out of him.

"And that's not all. You signed the autopsy, and you got him to sign it or he got you to. And I don't think any autopsy was ever performed."

Saramaggio stood up. He pointed to the door.

"That's enough. Enough of your accusations. And enough of your snooping around. Leave at once. And you are to consider yourself suspended until further notice."

She left, slamming the door behind her. She was shaking with rage.

On the way back to her office, still trembling, she thought back over the whole episode and to Saramaggio's cowardice and to Cleaver's venality. And one thing that struck her as odd about the accusation was its timing. Why had it been raised now and not weeks ago, when the incident had happened? Why did they want her out of the way now? Was it because she was on the right track?

Chapter 28

By now Scott was familiar enough with the lobby of St. Catherine's to avoid detection. He waited outside until a group of five young people approached—they bore the jaunty aspect of residents—and as they went through the revolving door, he followed. He stuck close to the pack, keeping them between him and the receptionist, until he was past the main desk. He turned the corner into the cul-de-sac of the elevator bank, pushed the button, and stepped quickly into the car when it came. Once on Kate's floor, he walked briskly to her office. The door was closed. He knocked softly, and when there was no reply, tried the handle. Locked.

Somehow he had not expected that. He looked quickly in both directions—no one in sight. He walked down the hallway, trying each doorknob like a hotel thief looking for a lucky break. He got one. Four doors down, the handle turned and opened onto a small office, neatly kept. He slipped inside and locked the door behind him. Thick medical tomes lined two bookshelves, a stack of printed articles rose high over a side table, and on the windowsill was a glazed plaster skull marked off in regions of phrenology, a joke no doubt. And there smack in the center of the desk was what he wanted—a computer.

He sat before it, pulled the chair closer, and switched it on. Out of his pocket he pulled the piece of paper on which he had written the numbers from Tyler. He had memorized them, but he wanted to avoid even the dimmest possibility of mistake.

Now, he thought, *comes the tricky part.*

It had taken him a long time to decipher Tyler's message. He had gone over and over it, parsing the few bits that were there in black and white and looking for the key to unlock them. He'd tried approaching it from his son's point of view, applying what he knew from his instinctive love. Three words and some numbers—that's all there were. He assumed that communication was difficult, that somehow it was an exhaustive labor—that was the impression given when each letter came onto the screen slowly, almost as if it was painful to call them up. And why else was the message so short? It was clearly important—Tyler had begged to be rescued—but he couldn't supply any more details or clues to make finding him any easier. And there was something else that Scott didn't care to linger on—the messages seemed to be getting shorter, almost as if Tyler was disappearing out there somewhere. He had written, "Dad *come*." Not "Dad *help*." The previous message had used the word *help,* so in that sense it was superfluous. But *come* was an active imperative—a command, a supplication—and perhaps it was connected to the second half of the message, to the numbers and then the mysterious single name *Wordsworth*. He racked his memory, back over every conversation they had had about literature and writing and reading; none that he could recall centered on the English poet. Never, so far as he could tell, had the name acquired any special significance in their lives together. There was no one poem that Tyler loved, no quotation that either of them recited, nothing. It was only when he became convinced that the "nothing" was important, that no association provided any linkage, that he was free to look for other explanations. Then he looked upon the puzzle differently and thought that perhaps *Wordsworth* was meaningful to *someone else,* that perhaps it was so meaningful that it had been adopted as a template. Perhaps ... Of course—maybe that was it. A password! Somebody's computer password! And that might explain the numbers—the basic address of a computer system. Now all he had to do was to guess what system and—the trickiest part—the owner of that password. A computer hacker could probably get the information, but he had come up with a shortcut, a guess and nothing more; but it was a good one, because suddenly everything was beginning to fall into place.

And now he had the chance to put his intuition to the test.

He signed on to the hospital's computer and punched in the numbers, a combination that opened a secure subsystem. It responded with a flashing *user name* text box, so he typed in:

    CLEAVER

Then it asked for his password, and he typed:

    WORDSWORTH

Instantly, the screen flickered, an image dipped and tucked, and then there were lines crossing horizontally, rapidly. He realized immediately what they were from his endless hours sitting and watching Tyler in the special ward. They were the tracings of a body's life functions. One line shot up, fell down below zero almost as much, rebounded up half again as much, and quivered off into a flat line and then repeated the same sequence, over and over. It was an EKG. There were also the squiggly lines of an EEG, the monitor of brain activity, and a third line bouncing across the screen that represented blood pressure.

The lines were so regular that he imagined them to be familiar. He thought—but could it be?—that he actually recognized them. They were so invariant that they appeared to come, like Tyler's, from someone in a coma. As he watched, he remembered hearing the leaden sounds from the ward, the steady rasp of breath going in and out like a bellows. He almost could hear the sound now. The more he watched the lines, the more he became convinced that they were the lines from Tyler's monitors. Then the screen flickered some more, and some kind of image seemed to be trying to take shape. It came and went so quickly he couldn't make it out. The lines reappeared, and as he watched they seemed to be fluctuating, at first just a bit and then wildly.

Abruptly, the image cut in again and flickered, like a distant television station trying to break through. The lines reappeared and then disappeared again, and in their place the image materialized. He looked—this time the reception was a little clearer and he could make out shapes. There were long cylindrical objects of some kind running from the top of the screen to the bottom, but it was difficult to say what they were. He looked harder, squinted, stared. They seemed to be—was that it?—some kind of pipes. Yes, they were definitely pipes, like water or steam pipes in an old house—there was a connecting link between two of them, an elbow joint. Long, wide pipes running up and down the length of the screen. But what did it mean? The image disappeared, reassembled itself a moment later—exactly the same. There was no movement, no change. In an odd way, the experience was like watching a video camera trained upon an inert, unchangeable background. The monitor lines came back, and now they were moving rapidly, almost violently. Even the heartbeat was pounding intensely. It had mounted, had become tachycardia. Then suddenly he knew that he was watching a message sent by Tyler. Somehow Tyler had been able to send the electronic signatures of his own vital signs. The image returned, sharper still. Scott tilted his head to one side. It almost looked . . . It could be a view from below. In fact that's what made the most sense, the image of something looked at from underneath—pipes running across a ceiling!

And at that moment, just as the image began flickering again and fading away and the lines reappeared, the realization struck him like a blow on the head and he believed he knew what the image was. He was—just maybe, just conceivably—looking at something through Tyler's eyes. Tyler was probably lying on his back somewhere and was still unable to move, but somehow had managed to communicate through the computer and transmit the image that fell into his field of vision. And that image was an assortment of pipes, large pipes, the sort one would find in the basement of a large building.

That was it! And now as the lines began waving wildly, almost frantically, the image sputtered back and Scott saw something new: a dark spot on the left side of the screen. It grew and at first looked like a mushroom, and then it took shape. And as he stared, he could scarcely believe his eyes—it was someone's head moving into the field, seen from below. A man's head! There was his forehead and broad bald dome and hair over the ears. Was it possible . . . that a man was leaning over Tyler? That would explain why the lines of the monitors were fluctuating so excitedly, and—Scott dreaded to think—so fearfully. Scott hit the *print* button, hoping to capture the image on paper.

No sooner had he done so than the dark shape withdrew and again the picture of pipes came onto the screen. They were fainter now and turning into indistinct shapes, and soon the monitor lines returned and they, too, were fainter. They gradually faded away into nothingness. The screen was blank. He couldn't bring an image back. He turned the machine off and signed in again. The computer accepted his password, but there was no connection this time. Nothing.

Scott felt like wailing at his powerlessness. His son was lying somewhere, helpless, vulnerable, and probably terrified out of his wits. He had had the presence of mind to send an SOS to his father, and what could the father do? Nothing. Nothing for now, anyway—that is, not until he was able to locate him. Then those holding him would learn what he was capable of.

His concentration was so intense that he didn't hear the footsteps coming up the hall, not even when they stopped before the door. A key ring jangled, and a key turned the lock—then Scott looked up and realized that someone was there.

Scott wasn't fazed. He sat back and crossed his arms and waited for the door to open all the way. When it did, he was looking up at the opened mouth of a slight man with cocoa-colored skin in a doctor's smock. The man's eyes were ovals of surprise. He was, Scott realized, one of the doctors who had operated on Tyler.

"What . . . ? What in the name of . . . ?"

"Yes?" said Scott calmly, for all the world as if it were his own office.

"You're Tyler's father . . . Mr. Jessup."

"Yes."

The man remained stupefied.

"I'm Gully. I was one of his surgeons. But what—may I ask—are you doing in my office?"

"I came to visit," replied Scott quickly.

The man looked confused.

"Oh, I see. But how did you get in?"

"The door was unlocked."

"I see, yes. I don't always lock it, that's true."

"So there you are."

"And you came to visit me because . . ."

"I want to talk."

"Most certainly. And about . . . ?"

"About anyone who had anything to do with Tyler's care. I would like to know more about them all. Perhaps now that we've met, you might care to join me for a cup of coffee? Right away."

Gully saw that he was desperate.

"Certainly, I should just pick up some papers."

"No, no time for that now. You could always come back for that."

"Well, if you like."

"I like."

And on the way out, as Scott turned Gully around and ushered him back outside with one arm, he leaned over to the printer and scooped up the page that was resting there. He glimpsed at it to make sure it had reproduced.

It had. There was that same view of pipes in the background, looking a little sharper on paper, and in the foreground, peering down, was the dark shape of a head looking down, the features just barely recognizable. It intruded into the picture like a thumbprint.

Kate set about cleaning her office. After all, she didn't know when she would be coming back. Or—for that matter—*if* she would be coming back.

She hadn't been at St. Cat's long enough to accumulate much stuff, so she used a single cardboard box that had come with a new laptop. She set it on a chair and began filling it. First she put in a six-inch-tall pile of medical records, which were mostly duplicates of current cases. She felt she should keep them at home, just in case. It paid to be safe—she had been badly shaken by the accusations against her, so patently false and clearly intended to deflect blame. Now she would put nothing past them. They might engage in a full-fledged campaign to smear her.

She opened the lower desk drawers and piled in a few supplies, two coffee cups, letters, an address book, odds and ends, computer disks, and various memos on employee benefits and health plans. She pulled out the top drawer and turned it upside down over the box. Out spilled notes, paper clips, business cards, staples, coins, and a pack of mints. She saw a wallet-sized photo of herself and Harry, taken at a restaurant on Fisherman's Wharf, a hokey place but still one that she secretly enjoyed. She held it close and stared at it. Poor, dear Harry. She hadn't thought of him for weeks. And he hadn't called her either—the ardor was probably dying down on his side, too. She felt a tug of regret. The world was so safe when she was with him—safe but predictable. Maybe that had been the problem. She put the picture in the box.

Finally, she cleared off the top of her desk, hurriedly now, sweeping everything into the box, including a framed portrait of her mother.

She carried the box to the other side of her desk, turned out the lights with her elbow, and walked away, pulling the door closed behind her with the tip of one shoe.

Far away down the hall, she saw Gully walking away

and turning a corner in the company of another man.
From the back—for a moment there—she thought he
looked like Scott, but of course that was impossible. They
didn't even know each other.

Riding home in a taxi, the box propped up on the seat
beside her, the injustice of everything that had happened began to press in upon her. Her hands were still
trembling slightly, mostly with anger but also, she knew,
with a general surfeit of emotion. She found it hard to
describe, hard to put words to it. She had given up so
much to come to New York and work under Saramaggio. She had arrived in the big city like any naïve rube
from the West Coast, wide-eyed and full of dreams, and
everything had gone wrong. From the very beginning, it
hadn't clicked. Then came the whole horrible episode
with Tyler, and now she had discovered that the hospital records faked his death and that he had been alive
when he left the hospital. What did that mean? Where
could he have been taken? Was it possible that he was
still alive even now? How could she help Scott find
him? It was even more difficult now that she was suspended. What a vindictive act. Cleaver was behind it.
For some reason, he was striking out, trying to wound
her, and Saramaggio, the lily-livered Milquetoast, was
going along. They had already engineered her suspension from the hospital. What could come next? Possibly
charges of unprofessional conduct—that could derail
her career. And all on fabricated grounds. Who at the
hospital would come to her defense?

As the cab sped down Second Avenue, she looked out
at the people shopping, the deliverymen on bicycles, the
young svelte women dressed to kill. For the first time in
a long while, she felt the New York disease—loneliness.
Maybe she wasn't as strong as she had believed; maybe
she couldn't make it here after all. Maybe she belonged
among the legions who had been lured by Frank Sinatra
crooning the famous lyric and who had failed and had
to turn tail and head home, back to the small towns.
Funny—you never heard about them, only the con-
quering heroes.

She felt a sudden urge to telephone Scott. He needed to know what she had discovered. And maybe at the same time, she thought, feeling guilty for thinking about herself, he could also help her somehow; she needed his strength to shore her up.

She paid the taxi. The elevator operator gallantly carried her box into the elevator and smiled at her as he deposited it at the foot of her door. Inside, she dropped the carton on her dining table, about to go to the kitchen to fix a cup of coffee, when something on top of the pile caught her eye. It was a business card, white with raised blue letters, that read

---

Frederick Butterworth
The Hospital Supply Corporation
Flushing, Queens NY

*From ambulances to X-ray machines,
If we don't have it, we know where to get it.*

She picked up the card, went to the phone, and dialed the number in the lower right-hand corner.

Amazingly, he answered—no secretary, no voice mail, no answering machine. She hadn't expected to get right through and didn't even have time to prepare a spiel. She gave her name and reminded him where they had met. At first he seemed to be casting about for the recollection, but he had the good grace to pretend to remember. Then he clearly did.

"Oh yes," he said. "You're the surgeon. Wasn't that place something? Gave me the creeps!"

They danced around like this for a while, and then she got to the point.

"Mr. Butterworth, I'd like your help with something."

"Just name it. I'm your man."

"Well, I notice on your card that you supply ambulances."

"That's right—ambulances to X-ray machines. Glad you still have it."

"Beg your pardon?"

"The card. I'm glad you still have it."

"Oh, yes. That's how I called you. In any case I thought that since you supply ambulances—"

"We don't actually supply the ambulances ourselves, but we can place your order for you. We operate as middlemen in the transaction."

"I see. Well, what I was wondering was, is there any kind of a directory that would say what kind of ambulances various hospitals have—you know, what models they are and what they look like?"

"You bet."

And so she told him what she was after: the name of every hospital and company in the city whose ambulance had red and white markings. And he said: "I can get that for you in a jiffy. Don't even have to call you back."

He was gone from the phone for a while, though, something like six or seven minutes. And when he returned he said, "Got a pencil? There's quite a list, I'm afraid. It's a popular combination."

"How many?"

"Seven."

He began to read out the names and she scribbled them down, but when he got to one she knew she didn't have to go any further. She let him finish, just for appearances. Then she thanked him very much and hung up. He sounded sorry to hear her go.

Of course, she thought. It had been obvious all along and she should have seen it right away. Perhaps, like Edgar Allan Poe's "Purloined Letter," it was simply too obvious, so much so that it had been overlooked.

She was suddenly certain of where the ambulance that had taken Tyler away had gone on that rainy night. Pinegrove.

Gully was surprised that Scott didn't want to have coffee in the hospital cafeteria and instead insisted on
going outside. He noticed how, as they passed a nurses'
station where Saramaggio was giving instructions to an
orderly, Scott walked on the other side of him, his head
bent as he carried on an animated conversation that
didn't make much sense. In fact, the man seemed so
high-strung and excited that Gully wondered if he was
unbalanced.

In the elevator, he suddenly stopped talking altogether. He crossed the lobby quickly, holding Gully by
the elbow and squeezing so tightly it almost hurt as he
maneuvered him toward the door. The receptionist
seemed to be frowning at them as they passed.

And once outside, Gully's companion seemed to lose
interest in coffee altogether. Instead, he pulled the surgeon urgently to one side of the hospital. He looked in
both directions before he spoke.

"What in the world—where are we going?" asked
Gully.

But Scott ignored the question, turning toward him
with a fierce look in his eyes and inquiring abruptly, "Are
you able to keep a secret?"

Gully thought before responding.

"Well, yes," he said. "But I don't see—"

"Promise me that you will."

Gully hesitated, confused.

"Promise," insisted Scott, with such urgency that
Gully began nodding rapidly and saying, "I will. I will. I
do."

"Good. Now listen carefully. I am going to ask you a
question, and I want you to think long and hard about it
and give me an answer. Right?"

"Yes. Yes." That time, Gully needed no prompting.
And he had to admit that his nervousness was beginning
to give way to curiosity. What could the man possibly
want, and why was he so jittery about it?

"Okay. Here goes. I am going to show you a picture.

It's a picture of some pipes, and I want you to tell me if you've ever seen them before, if they're familiar in any way."

"Right," Gully said uncertainly.

At that, Scott reached into his coat pocket and pulled out a folded sheet of paper, carefully unfolded it, and held it up. Gully's eyes went immediately to the foreground, to the dark head cut off at the mouth.

"Say, who is that? Isn't that—"

"Never mind who that is or isn't," cut in Scott abruptly. "Just look at the pipes in the background. Have you ever seen them before?"

Gully looked at the picture, long and hard, as he had promised. Then he shook his head no.

"Are you sure? Could they be right here? In the basement of St. Cat's?"

The man had such a pleading tone to his voice that Gully wanted to satisfy him, but he could not.

"No, I don't think so. It's hard to say for certain, of course, but I've been to the basement here, and I have to say, I don't recognize them."

"You've never seen them before—there or anywhere?"

"No, I'm almost sure I haven't."

Scott seemed crestfallen, so Gully added, "But you know, one set of pipes looks pretty much like another. It's just that these seem really old, decrepit. See how the paint is peeling off of them? At St. Cat's, the facilities are a bit newer. I don't think we have anything like that down there."

"Okay. Now this man in the foreground here—I think we both know who he is."

Gully nodded. All this was surpassingly strange, he thought. Where had this man gotten this picture, and what significance did he think it carried?

"Now I want you to tell me—doctors sometimes work at a number of hospitals, right?"

"Right."

"Well, does this particular guy work anywhere else?"

"Yes, he does."

"And where is that?"

"Pinegrove."

"Pinegrove. What's that?"

"It's a psychiatric hospital. It's for serious cases—an old place. Say," he added, catching the spirit of the interrogation, "it's really falling down. It could have pipes like that."

"And where is it?"

"Not far at all. Just halfway across the river. On Roosevelt Island."

Scott was gone without another word.

Strange man, strange encounter, thought Gully, feeling a little relieved that Scott had left, but also dissatisfied, since his curiosity was now destined to remain unsatisfied. He watched him rushing up the avenue, waving his arms frantically to flag down a taxi.

Chapter 29

A crowd had gathered at the loading platform for the tramway to Roosevelt Island by the time Scott arrived. It was the beginnings of the rush-hour crunch, a mixed lot of professionals and UN diplomats, mostly from Third World countries. Four handsome and dignified black-as-ebony men were dressed in the flowing, brightly colored robes of West Africa. Scott was breathless—the taxi had moved so slowly that he had finally abandoned it and run the last three blocks—and he pushed his way to the front, close enough to make sure he would be on the next car. One man in a wrinkled blue linen suit seemed about to object, but one look at Scott's urgent expression and he turned away.

The car arrived, slipping neatly into its berth and disgorging its cargo, a fresh-looking crop of people dressed for a night on the town. The doors opened, and the people around Scott surged forward. He moved with the flow and found a place to stand near a window looking south. He wanted to scout the place from the air and choose an isolated path that would lead him to the lower tip of the island. The Queensboro Bridge, next to the tramway line, cut the island in two. To the north was the residential quarter, hulking rectangles of brown and red brick turning gray in the twilight. To the south was a desolate area of scrawny growth and three ancient clusters of concrete and stone—the medical buildings. He knew Pinegrove was at the island's tip.

The doors closed, and the car took off with the stomach-lifting lurch of a ski lift. It rose on its cable at a gentle angle but surprisingly quickly. Scott looked around; the faces that crowded him were passive and bored, masks of beaten-down commuters. Standing, holding on to a bar and feeling a backpack press against his spine, he felt a little wave of claustrophobia rising up. He beat it back by concentrating on the view outside. The car reached a plateau, level and moving fast. The bridge obstructed his view, but for a moment between steel girders, he caught a distant glimpse of steep dark roofs rising up over the treetops, the spires of Pinegrove, he was sure.

He tried to think. He had no strategy and had little time to come up with one—other than to sneak into the place and search it thoroughly and find his son. All he wanted was to rescue him, no matter what condition he was in, and then to make sure that he got everything he needed, for life, or for death, at long last—a death with whatever smidgeon of dignity could still be mustered.

A tramway car leaving the island approached on the adjacent cable. Scott looked in as it passed and saw that it was less than half full, a dozen or so people sitting and standing. And then a particular visage crossed his line of vision. He froze in place; he gripped the rail, unable to move, as he stared at the figure. *There he was,* in the tramway going the other way, sitting quietly, inconspicuously—the same hair around the ears, the broad dome of a forehead, the sharp nose. *Cleaver.* There was no mistaking him. He sat, looking idly ahead, almost as if he were daydreaming, a stationary bust gliding along no more than twenty feet away. The car moved on and Cleaver was gone, a fleeting vision in the half-light whose afterimage burned in Scott's brain.

His heart pounded against his rib cage as if it wanted to break through. He tried to think. What to do? Should he jump on the next car for the return trip? Try to catch Cleaver and force him to admit what he had done with his son? Force him to reveal where Tyler was and lead him to him? Somehow, as Scott had played out the scenario in his mind, he had imagined bursting in on Cleaver at Pinegrove, finding him there with Tyler, and unraveling the whole plot—whatever it was—in one fell swoop. He had been foolish—of course there was always the chance that the man at the center of it all would be absent when he arrived.

His car moved on, began its downward slide. Maybe it was fortuitous that Cleaver was leaving the island; maybe it would be easier to reconnoiter and find out what was going on and locate Tyler. That was his goal, to find him and save him. Everything else could wait— even revenge.

At the terminal, the crowd got off, moving painfully slowly and walking in one direction. Scott broke away, taking a path that led the opposite way. He had to restrain himself from running. The last thing he needed was to attract attention to himself.

He crossed the island and took a walkway along the river's edge on the Queens side. It was deserted. Amid the sounds of the waves lapping at the rocks and the whining of cars over the bridge, he heard his own footsteps. They sounded loud to him. The smell of the river, a bracing combination of brine and fish, struck him full in the face. The sun was sinking over the darkened tops of the buildings of Queens, casting across the sky rays of orange and red that washed against the trees and the mammoth bridge, making it look almost beautiful. Out of nowhere came an unreal, irrelevant feeling: It was like a stage set.

He passed by a cluster of buildings whose windows were mostly dark and continued walking south. After a few minutes, he came to a line of bushes. He stopped behind them and peered through. He saw Pinegrove looming above him, suddenly immense, an apparition out of a Gothic nightmare with its vaulted windows, crenellated towers, and thick stone walls. The only lights were on the lower three floors.

That makes my search easier, thought Scott. He rounded the bushes and crossed a field of weeds that were so thick they tugged at his ankles. In the open, he felt vulnerable, but he hurried and headed straight for an arched doorway at the rear. He gained it and slipped quickly into its shadow. He stopped to listen—nothing.

He took two quick steps forward and grasped the thick door handle, squeezing the brass tongue downward. It would not budge—locked. He rattled the door gingerly, but it did not give. He paused for a moment, then backed away and went to the right, following the contours of the wall. He came to a window, chest high, and looked in. It was dark.

He braced his arms upon the thick stone sill and hoisted himself up. He scraped his knee against the rough-hewn rock, but barely noticed. He stood and leaned against the window, curling his fingertips under the wooden frame and straining to raise it. It wouldn't give. He cupped his hands around his eyes and peered down. The lock was fastened.

He thought quickly but calmly. His mind was clear—no questions or doubts, no hesitations. Time was fluid and moving slowly. He had ample time to consider all options; he focused on each one like a beam of light. He took off his shirt, bundled it around his right hand, and smashed a pane halfway up. The sound of the splintering glass striking the floor inside was enough to make him pause, but only for a second. Balancing easily, he listened for half a moment to see if someone was coming. No one was.

He reached in to turn the lock and raised the window, which shuddered. A triangle of glass in the smashed pane leaned inward in slow motion, then fell to the floor and broke. Quickly, he ducked under the sash and stepped inside and leapt to the floor, landing on the slippery shards. He donned his shirt and looked around—a supply office of some sort, in disarray. No one there. He moved quietly across the floor to the closed door, put one ear against it, and listened. A strange sound met his ear, a muffled burbling, rising and falling. After a few moments, it almost stopped, then started up again. He listened. Voices, many of them. But they sounded strange—a Tower of Babel, many conversations going on simultaneously.

He put one hand on the doorknob and turned slowly. The mechanism was old and gave way slowly, grudg-

ingly. He pushed. The door would not budge. He pulled
it, and it seemed to thrust toward him as if some force
were impelling it backward. Light flowed in along with
a blast of sounds that were unaccountably cacophonous.
He realized what they were—men talking to themselves, some in affectless monotones, others in whispers,
some angry, others giddy. He leaned his head in and
looked down the length of the ward. The sight was striking. The long room was lined on both sides with beds of
white-painted metal frames whose sheets were in disarray, showing blue-and-gray striped mattresses. Lying
upon them, standing in between, walking on the floor
were patients in T-shirts and dressing gowns. A handful
were wearing only pajama bottoms—their bodies thin
or revoltingly fat, pale as candle wax—and one man was
naked, his penis hanging to one side. In the middle of
the ward, now that he looked more closely, a group
walked up and down more or less in line; they carried
themselves with a sense of ritual, like an Italian village
out for the evening promenade, except of course that
some were babbling and others were as impassive as
zombies.

He held his breath and stepped into the room and
was relieved to find that his presence didn't suddenly
rock the place. No alarms sounded to bring attendants
running. One man nearby, twisting a curl of his hair
around a forefinger and discoursing to a wall as if before an audience of ignoramuses, fell silent to examine
him with a modicum of interest.

Scott looked up and down the ward. He could see no
uniforms, no one in charge. He took a deep breath and
stepped out between the beds to join the march. Now
two or three men were looking at him, and one of these
began to whine like a wounded dog and another to utter
a high-pitched keening sound. He stared at Scott and
kept keening, and soon the line was breaking up, men
before him turning to look and those behind retreating
to their beds. They melted away around him. Two men
started shoving each other, and soon the noise level rose
steadily, as if a hand were turning a knob to ratchet up

the volume. Scott hurried past a man who lay curled up on the floor covering his head. The noise was so loud now that Scott was sure it could be heard throughout the building. He ran flat out for the doors of the ward.

Just as he reached them, he looked through their windows and saw two men in light blue uniforms hurrying toward them. He couldn't tell if they'd seen him, but he darted quickly to the right and hid beside the door, his back to the wall. The doors flew open and the attendants hurried in and now the commotion rose to a crescendo. The patients fell away like a flock of pigeons and seemed to forget about Scott. The attendants walked to the center of the room to separate the two fighting men, who were locked in each other's arms and rolling on the floor, and Scott stole through the swinging doors. Out of the corner of his eye, he saw the attendants each pick up a man. He hurried down the corridor, and behind him, as the doors swung open and closed and open again, he heard the pandemonium rising and falling like waves on a nearby shore.

He came to an open office. Inside was the sound of canned laughter—a television set tuned to a stand-up comic who pulled the mike toward his gaping mouth. On a table, tabloid newspapers were scattered about and smoke rose from a large glass ashtray. The smell of marijuana hung in the air.

He passed by, moving quickly now, his eyes scanning everything before him, looking for movement, searching out the door he needed. He found it at the end of the corridor, a thick door with a tiny diamond-shaped window. He opened it and stepped inside. The staircase was dimly lit. He went down.

The stairs turned a corner and he took them quickly, his caution overcome by the sense that he was closing in on his objective. At the bottom was another door, and he opened it and slipped into a basement corridor. It was wide and newly painted, an antiseptic white, which fueled his anticipation further. He looked at the ceiling, and there he saw something that shot into his eyes like

arrows and sent a wave of heat through him—pipes.
They lined the ceiling, thick ones coated with layers of
peeling paint—exactly like those in the image that had
been burned into his brain.

He was there. He was close.

A noise came to him, and he listened closely. A humming, a throbbing. It seemed to emanate from a doorway off to the right. He moved like a shadow down the
corridor, his footsteps soft as a hunter's, and he
reached the doorway. He looked in—a blaze of light,
machines, a curtain of clear plastic hanging down. And
there, just beyond the plastic, slightly distorted by it, a
bed, and lying upon the bed, immobile under a heap of
white sheets, a figure, a familiar figure.

Tyler.

Scott froze. He had wished it, imagined it, dreamed
of it for some time. But now that he was actually confronted with it, he realized that he hadn't ever truly believed it—the shattering possibility, now a reality that
would determine everything to follow in his life, that
his son was alive. Still alive. *There, see, his chest moved
up and down; he is breathing.*

But with the help of machines.

The hated machines. There they were, to one side,
humming and ticking and showing their work in pulsing
lines that skipped across the round screens.

And there was something else. He saw it immediately,
through a window that gave onto an adjacent room.
Movement.

A person.

A man was standing there, a notebook in his hand,
looking back at Scott, his mouth open in amazement.

Kate had tried to call Scott and had left two messages
on his answering machine within ten minutes. Finally
she decided to go there, riding up in the by-now-familiar
freight elevator. She knocked on the door. No answer,
but she could hear Comet inside, whining and sniffing at

the threshold. She tried the door, and as always it was open, so she went inside.

The place was its usual mess. She had learned to read the pattern within it, accustomed as she was by now to Scott's habits, which she had registered with a sharp eye and sharper memory. She fed Comet, who was grateful for company and even more grateful for the can of food, and she snooped. Scott's bed had been slept in, a cup of coffee partially drunk, the remains of a lunch—judging from the crumbs it looked to have been a sandwich—but nothing since. Then she noticed that the computer was on, a screen saver of a Kandinsky painting shimmering. She struck a key. The saver dissolved, but the screen was blank.

Something about the apartment—maybe it was the half-drunk cup of coffee, maybe Comet scratching to go out, which indicated that she hadn't been walked, maybe something else she couldn't put her finger on—suggested that Scott had left quickly. It had the feel of a place abandoned precipitously. But where had he gone? Would he be away long?

She walked Comet, returned, and then resolved not to wait for Scott any longer. She had to go to Pinegrove alone. Maybe she could discover something that would shed light on what had happened to Tyler, if indeed that ambulance had taken him there.

The decrepit asylum had upset her the very first time she'd seen it, months ago now, when the bus had carried her and the others to the depressing tour of its run-down ward. She thought back to Cleaver's brief question-and-answer session and the parade of patients. From the first, she'd been appalled by the institution he ran—it represented everything in the field that she detested, a merciless place that shut its people away like a tomb. But she'd had no idea then of what had become an article of faith for her now—how truly monstrous Cleaver was.

Kate sat at the desk and wrote a quick note to Scott, telling him where she was going. Then she put down a second bowl of water for Comet, patted her, and opened the door, turning back for a last look around. Once again, she spotted that photograph of Scott, Tyler, and Lydia in Nantucket, the one that had filled her with such yearning when she first saw it, the three of them so happy and innocent, unaware of what the future had in store for them. She was glad the photo had captured them that way and frozen them forever in time and space, and gladder still that, for Scott's exhibition, it had been digitized and put on the gallery's Web site for the whole world to see.

She closed the door firmly and stepped into the creaking elevator, trying not to think about the place to which she was going.

Cleaver pressed the button beside the panel that read BRAINTRUST and waited impatiently for the front door to click open. Quincy's little joke name for his enterprise had never struck him as amusing, but now it had acquired an ironic thrust—the man's brain was anything but trustworthy. It had led him down a blind alley. Now everything was going from bad to worse.

He hurried up the three flights, not pausing at the landings. His heart was racing, and he felt a telltale arrow on the left side of his chest that he tried not to think about. It dug in below the breastbone and twisted. He placed the fingers of his right hand upon it and pressed down and continued climbing. That's all he needed now—a heart attack.

When he opened the door, the mastiff was there to greet him, sniffing up and down his pant leg and then leaning his muzzle back and to one side, the attack posture. The tendons on the dog's neck stood out like ropes. Quincy looked up from his workbench, but didn't call him off.

"Hey, c'mon," complained Cleaver.

"He does that with uninvited guests."

The conversation calmed the mastiff, who walked away, turned a small circle, and lay down in a corner.

"I've come for your help," said Cleaver.

"Nothing new in that."

"But this is serious, really serious."

"It always is."

"Damn it—listen to me."

"My, my, strong language for you—*fucking* strong language."

Cleaver walked over and stood behind him. Quincy was attaching a chip to a circuit board, twisting it in the grip of needle-nose pliers. He was taking his sweet time. The back of his neck had little hairs of downy blond. Cleaver had another sudden rush of dislike for the young man—so arrogant, so smart, so vulgar. The neck looked fragile, and he imagined an injury to it, blood spurting from a severed artery, nerve ends looping down like exposed wires.

Quincy finished his task, stood up, and stretched.

"So what's the emergency?" he asked.

"It's Tyler."

As soon as the name escaped, Cleaver realized how odd it sounded. He had never put the name to it before, to the anima that he had unleashed. The more independent it became, the more rebellious it acted, the more it had come to seem like its human progenitor.

Quincy picked up on it.

"What's *he* doing now?"

Cleaver felt his heart, pounding away with little nails sticking into it. Why wouldn't the pain go away?

"It's like some kind of virus. It's in my computer, not all the time. It comes and goes. But when it's there, everything is knocked out. I can't do anything."

The words had come out in a rush.

Quincy peered at him closely for the first time.

"You know, I don't mean to say anything—but you don't look so hot. In fact, you look fucked over."

Cleaver just nodded. He didn't tell him the truth—that he had been getting almost no sleep, because when he did he had horrible nightmares. Things came at him, horrible things, that belonged to a world he never could have imagined.

Quincy didn't admit that he was worried about the project, too.

"Look, if it's a virus, we can fix it up. I've got all kinds of defenses you've never even heard of, a whole fucking arsenal."

He gestured toward a chair. "Now sit down and take a load off. Let me just finish this. Then we'll tackle your little problem."

Cleaver did sit, and he did feel a load shifting. He was not weak, not a sniveler. He was a scientist, a pathfinder, one of the tough breed that didn't shirk from what had to be done. To hell with the nightmares and the doubts and all the rest of it. What was that bromide? Being courageous did not mean not feeling fear—it meant feeling fear and yet pushing on. How true that was. To hell with what he was feeling. He would do what he had to do. Finish this thing that he had started and that meant so much. Quincy was right—it *was* an occasion for strong language. Damn strong. *Fucking* strong.

He felt a little thrill as he mouthed the word, once so illicit. He was not a *fucking* weakling. He was not that little boy standing in the snow in Massachusetts, having heard the news from his mother, waiting for his aching brain to explode. A little boy. Afraid of his father.

The *fucking* snow.

His *fucking* father.

Chapter 30

Scott looked at Felix in the room next door and took his measure correctly—some sort of lab assistant, he deduced. And standing there startled, openmouthed and clutching a clipboard to his chest as if it were some sort of shield, the man didn't appear to be someone to reckon with. Scott waved to throw him off balance, the way some bigwig taking a tour might wave—see, I belong here, just passing through, pay me no mind. He had no idea how rigorous the security was, but he hadn't seen any evidence of it so far.

He lifted his eyes away and turned them on his son. Tyler was lying completely immobile, just as he had during those interminable weeks in the hospital. His bed was made up with light green sheets that looked crisp and clean and offset his lifeless body. An IV drip fed into his right arm, the soft underflesh of which was already blackened from an army of needles. There appeared to be no change whatsoever in his condition—he was still comatose.

But alive.

Scott could see the top sheet rising and falling almost imperceptibly. He could barely stand to look. Emotions flooded in on him from all sides—the relief, a father's relief, that his son was still alive, fed by the thought that if the body was still functioning, then maybe somehow he could be rescued and be made whole again. And contradicting that relief came the opposite thought, the realization that the body was not really alive by any meaningful definition of life—which in turn gave way to a deep sorrow that his boy had not been allowed to die in peace.

To one side sat the bank of machines, throbbing away, doing their work all too well, dispatching meager commands in the form of electronic pulses to keep the pathetic shell of flesh and bone going. Tyler's bandaged head rested upon a pillow, and his eyes were open, though they had a glazed aspect. Looking up, Scott could see that Tyler's line of vision took in the thick pipes on the ceiling above. They were the same pipes as the ones in the picture. Looking down, he could see where Cleaver had stood to lean over him, perhaps to check the bandage. The thought infuriated him—that sadist masquerading as a doctor, the wolf wearing the gowns of a protector. Once again, Scott felt a white heat coursing through his veins like a spiky additive to his blood—pure rage, the kind that is assured, vengeful, careless.

But then another thought took shape, one that carried a glint of hope and that up to now he had not dared let himself give in to. Someone had sent him the password, *Wordsworth,* that had unlocked the image in Cleaver's directory and led him to this place. Who could have done it? And someone had sent him a message saying, *"Dad. Help me."* Was it so inconceivable then that Tyler was there, somewhere, even though his body gave no evidence of him? Or more properly that his spirit, the guiding spark of his intellect, some remnant of him was floating out there, as Cybedon had said? And if that was true, if that spirit was in a sense intact, would it be possible for it to be recaptured and reunited with the body?

He looked again at the man across the way, who appeared flustered, uncertain about what to do. Scott walked with a measured deliberateness into the corridor and from there into the room. The light was bright and seemed to shoot straight into his eyes, but he forced his mouth into an odd half-smile. Felix's lips began to curl as if he were about to speak, to formulate the question for which his brain was vainly searching—something no doubt concerning the identity of this man who approached with such brazen self-confidence that, well, surely he must belong here.

Scott thrust out his right hand and, reflexively, Felix followed suit, proffering his own right hand. Scott grabbed it and held hard, then shook it and continued squeezing it until Felix's eyes widened and a dollop of alarm began to show in the pupils. The idea seemed to be sinking in that the person locking his hand in a viselike embrace might not belong there after all. Of course, he didn't realize that right then that person would like nothing more than to bash his head open on the bedstand.

"My name is Jessup," said Scott, still not releasing the hand. "And I think the time has come for us to have a talk."

He led Felix to a chair and pressed him down, so that he sat upon it roughly. He continued.

"You—what's your name?"

"Felix."

"Okay, Felix. What do you do here?" He was speaking as if to a recalcitrant child.

"I'm an assistant, a lab assistant."

"Who do you work for?"

"Cleaver. Dr. Cleaver."

"Very good."

Scott released his hold and stepped back. Quickly, his eyes cased the room. A pane of thick glass separated them from Tyler's hospital bed. To one side were medical cabinets, a stainless steel table. Close by was a wall, and lying the length of it, dominating everything else, was a large device with a cylinder that could fit a human being. It looked something like an MRI machine, and it contained a stretcher that rested on a track and was crowned with some sort of odd-looking helmet that had two concave metal ovals like eye sockets. Nearby, attached to it, was a computer.

What the hell is that?

He resumed the interrogation.

"Is Dr. Cleaver here now?"

"No, he's gone. He left about half an hour ago."

That the scared imbecile was volunteering extra information was a good sign. He was proving cooperative.

"And do you know where he went?"

"No, I don't. He didn't say."

"I see."

Scott pulled up a chair and sat directly across from the assistant. He reached into his pocket, pulled out a pack of cigarettes, offered one to Felix, who shook his head no, and lit up, inhaling deeply. He dropped the match onto the floor.

"Now, Felix," he began. "Suppose we start with this."

Felix looked up at him, ready to please. Scott gave a nod of his head in the direction of the large window glass and the bed with the motionless figure on the other side. He tried to hold his voice steady. "Why don't you tell me exactly what my son is doing here?"

⌇

Kate's cab began to slow down on Third Avenue around Twenty-eighth Street, and by the time they reached Thirty-second Street, it was crawling. Hemmed in behind a sheet of bulletproof plastic, she felt waves of anxiety sweep over her.

"What's wrong?" she barked at the driver.

An elderly Russian who looked as if he bore the weight of the world on his stooped head, he half turned and shrugged.

"Who knows? Maybe someone in town, a big shot. Maybe an accident."

He leaned down to his right, picked up a Thermos, and poured himself a cup of steaming coffee. He took a sip, then turned back to stare out the windshield, unconcerned.

She suddenly felt a sense of urgency.

"But I'm in a hurry. Isn't there any other way?"

He didn't even turn this time.

"Lady, you want to get to Roosevelt Island, there's only one way. I take the Queensboro and double back. If I go up to the Triborough, it's twice as long. My advice, maybe try some other time."

She felt about in her purse for her cell phone. She pressed the automatic dial for Scott's loft. It rang and rang—exactly what she had expected. Who else to call? The police—that sergeant, Paganelli? Don't be absurd—what do you expect, you'll babble something about ambulances and colors and missing patients and he'll drop everything and pick you up in a police car and take you to Pinegrove and arrest Cleaver? Fat chance. Saramaggio? Don't be a fool. He's the guy who fired you. Not fired, suspended. Big difference. For all you know, he could be in on it—whatever *it* is. And even if he's not, do you expect *him* to believe you, of all people? Who else is there? No one.

She realized, with a pang, that she had never felt so utterly, overwhelmingly alone.

Her pulse began to race and her palms were sweaty. She felt claustrophobic in the cab, no room for her feet, the windows closed. She opened one.

Then she gave herself a lecture, one of her mother's lectures. In a time of crisis, breathe deeply, not once but two, three, four times. Calm down and think clearly. Envision what it is that you want to do and then do it. No nonsense, no delay, no self-pity. That's for the weak ones, not those of us from icy Greenland.

She checked the meter, reached into her purse, and found a five-dollar bill, which she tossed onto the driver's seat.

"Keep the change," she said, getting out. He shrugged and took another sip of coffee.

She walked two blocks and ducked into the subway at Thirty-fourth. She could get out at Fifty-ninth, walk east two blocks, and take the tramway.

Already, outside, walking purposefully, doing something, she felt better. Her mother always knew what to do to get out of a jam.

Scott finished the cigarette by the time Felix finished his story. The narrative had been disjointed but short and concise—in point of fact, the lab assistant didn't appear to know all that much, beyond the fact that

Tyler was "a very special patient," in Cleaver's words, and that the doctor appeared to be willing to bend every rule in the book to keep him alive. He said this in the naïve expectation that Scott might be gratified to hear it.

Felix did admit to his own complicity in bringing Tyler from St. Catherine's. He described how he had gotten a late-night call from Cleaver, how he and a friend had come to Pinegrove to pick up the ambulance and had worn doctors' coats as Cleaver had instructed.

"That didn't strike you as strange? Rushing over in the dead of night? Taking him from a hospital that was better equipped to care for him?"

Felix shrugged, stupidly. In fact, it *had* bothered him at the time—and for those very same reasons, though he had tried not to think too much about it.

"No. I had no reason to think anything was wrong. A lot of strange things go on around here."

"Like what?"

Felix told him about the experiments, the old man who was dying and the woman who had claimed to see him at the precise moment of death, even though they were separated by the full length of a hospital corridor. He explained Cleaver's theory about anima, the seat of the soul, and his belief that it resided in a particular region of the brain where it could be recorded and measured like any other electrical activity.

"And how about that?" asked Scott, gesturing toward the machine and lighting up another cigarette. "What's that?"

Felix turned around to look at it, as if he had no idea what Scott was talking about. But his answer, stiff in tone, suggested that he had been waiting for the question.

"It's a TSR."

"And . . . ?"

"That stands for transcranial stimulator-receiver. It's called that because it interacts with the brain both ways—it can stimulate it to send messages in and receive the messages coming out."

He turned back to face Scott, as if the subject were closed.

"And what's it used for? I see it's made for humans. Did you use it on people?"

The look on Felix's face told him that he had hit it right.

"Patients?" Scott asked, barely credulous.

Again, he knew. He had hit the target, and what a target it was. He could scarcely believe the depths he was plumbing, the monstrous things that Cleaver was capable of. He took a drag on the cigarette, calmly, as if the conversation were about the most natural thing in the world.

Felix hesitated, as if he had been presented with a dilemma, and when he spoke, the words came spilling out as if he had finally reached a decision.

"Yes, we used it on patients. Dr. Cleaver said it was for the advancement of human knowledge, that someday the world would look back on what we were doing and see it for what it really was. Something important, something brave. And he said the patients wouldn't really know the difference anyway, because so many of them were in such bad shape. And he said it wouldn't hurt them, and in any case he got consent forms from them so it was all perfectly legal."

"I see. And tell me, Felix, did the machine work? Were there ever any problems?"

"It worked."

It didn't escape Scott's attention that Felix had only answered the first of his two questions—the man didn't seem to want to talk about the problems—but he decided to let the matter lapse for now. Because a new and stirring idea had begun to take control of him, and there wasn't any room left over for anything else.

Again, he pulled down the curtain of a cool exterior to disguise his thoughts.

"Did you ever work the machine, Felix? Did you ever, say, use it on someone while Dr. Cleaver wasn't here?"

"No."

"But you know how to do it, right? I mean, you assisted him, you were here when he did it."

The reply was a grudging yes.

Scott began pacing around the room, smoking as he walked. He was picking up speed, like a locomotive heading around a downhill curve.

"Now, Felix, the way I look at it—and I hate to be the one to tell you—but the way I see it, you're in way over your head. You're in a lot of trouble. Experimenting on patients, using human beings as guinea pigs. I wonder what that would come under in the criminal statutes—aggravated assault, at the very least. And that's assuming that none of the patients you were experimenting on were permanently injured, but who knows? Negligent manslaughter, maybe, or conspiracy to commit homicide—a clever prosecutor can twist a lot of things, you know. A case like this, it's bound to become political, the mayor gets involved, maybe even the governor. I'd say you're looking at a lot of time behind bars once this goes to the DA, and behind bars is a place where a guy like you isn't going to do too well." He looked into Felix's eyes, casually, as if it didn't really matter to him. "I guess you've heard the stories—I don't have to tell you."

Sitting on the chair, hardly moving, Felix looked as if he were going to be sick. His face was stricken, drained of blood. Scott had known what would get to him. And he wasn't planting any ideas that the poor sucker hadn't already had on his own. He was just stirring up the pot a little.

"You get my meaning?"

Felix nodded and looked at him, a pathetic begging look. As if he were a helpless child. It didn't begin to generate any sympathy from Scott.

"I'm kind of torn," he continued. "I'm duty-bound to hand you over to the authorities. On the other hand, that's my son over there, and I can tell—I can see by the kind of guy you are—that you took care of him. You were kind to him. Right?"

Felix shook his head emphatically.

"Yes," he said. "I was. I did everything for him. I didn't want him to suffer at all."

"Good. I'm grateful, and that reminds me. You said Dr. Cleaver knew how to measure the—what did you call it?—the anima. I assume you can measure it only when it's moving from one place to another. Right?"

"Yes."

"And maybe when it moves from inside the body to outside the body. Right?"

"Yes."

"And did Dr. Cleaver do that to my son—move it outside his body?"

Felix didn't know how to answer.

"Don't worry. I'm just asking," Scott said.

"I don't know."

"You sure?"

"Yes. But I think . . . I know, judging from the things we did, the measurements we took . . . that that had happened, yes."

"And what were you doing?"

"What do you mean?"

"I mean, were you trying to get it back?"

Felix paused to think, and he thought so long he seemed to be trying to come up with a truthful answer.

"I'm not sure, because Dr. Cleaver didn't really tell me what was behind a lot of it, but no, I don't think so. I think he wasn't so much trying to get it back as he was trying to, you know, control it."

Scott took a last drag on the cigarette, threw it to the floor, and stepped on it.

"I see," he said. "And so this machine—I take it that you used it to send people out to the same place where my son is, wherever that is."

Felix nodded yes uncertainly.

Scott walked over to the machine and looked at it, moving the stretcher up and down with one hand.

"What are these things?" He pointed to the eye caps.

"They fit under your eyelids and go over your eyes. That's the way some of the messages are sent in, by electrical impulses that travel through the main optic nerve. That leads right into the brain."

Scott touched the helmet.

"And this picks up the impulses inside?"

"Yes."

Scott pointed to the timer.

"And this?"

"To tell how long you've been inside."

"Why is there a mark here?"

"That's the seven-minute marker. You can't stay in any longer than seven minutes."

"Because . . ."

"Because the computer can't handle any more than that. You stay in for longer than seven minutes and it crashes. Your brain cooks and you die."

"You know that for sure?"

"For sure."

"Felix, something tells me you may be guilty of more than assault."

Felix didn't answer and looked away instead.

"But don't worry, your secret's safe with me. Provided . . ."

"Provided?"

"You do exactly what I tell you."

There was a long silence while Scott crossed the room and looked down at a computer screen. He pulled a chair close and sat in front of it, sliding a keyboard out from underneath, then searching for a switch and turning it on.

Finally, Felix spoke up, in a little boy's voice.

"And what is it you want me to do?" he asked.

"I think you know already, Felix. Come, you're not as stupid as you look."

Scott was taking his time. Once the screen was lit, he put in a password, and then he began carefully tapping at the keys, typing out a message.

"What do you think I want you to do?" Scott asked.

Felix spoke slowly, as if he was reluctant to say the words.

"I think you want me to use the machine. I think you want me to send you out there."

Scott looked up at him and smiled for the first time.

"See—I told you. You're not so stupid after all."

He sent the message, stood up, and walked over to the machine.

⌐⌐⌐⌐⌐

Cleaver had signed on and was waiting for the computer to boot up when he felt restless sitting in the hard-backed chair. The ache on the left side of his chest had not gone away—in fact, it had gotten worse. It now felt like shards of glass sticking up through his breastbone from somewhere deep inside his rib cage. But sitting down hadn't helped. It just made him feel confined.

He stood up and walked around the small room. From the corner, where it was curled up in a large mass of gray fur, the mastiff lifted his head and watched him warily.

Cleaver felt a compulsion to talk. Maybe that would shift his mind from the pain, make it go away.

"I don't get it," he said. "I mean, at first it was okay. I almost felt I could control it. I couldn't make it do whatever I wanted, but it wasn't like this—now the thing seems to be against me. It wrecks everything. I swear it's gotten into my system and ruined my records."

Quincy stopped his work long enough to look up at Cleaver.

"I notice you say *it*," he said. "I would have thought you'd be saying *him*. A moment ago, you called *it* Tyler."

"Well, yes, but that was a slip of the tongue. I still find it a little hard to think of a human intelligence out there. Much less one that's rooting through my files. I mean, with all of cyberspace to roam through."

"But it's not just cyberspace, remember. It's a whole other universe, a netherworld of electrical charges or whatnot crammed full of a lot of things, including everyone who ever died. At least that was your theory, as far as I remember. And don't forget—you were the one who put him out there."

"I know that," Cleaver replied weakly.

"And you're the one who's actually observed the departure of the anima—or whatever the hell you call it—from that old man. And its reappearance before the old lady—right?"

"Yes."

"And you're the one who's been sending the goddamned mental patients into outer space with your fucking machine—*my* fucking machine, actually."

"Yes—well, not exactly outer space. More like inner space."

"Whatever. And you're the one who's keeping that poor fucking boy on life support just so you'll have some control over what happens to his mind."

"What of it?"

"What of it is this. What I'm saying is, who are *you* of all people to be raising doubts at this point?"

Cleaver took his point. But he wanted to keep the conversation going. It was beginning to work—he hadn't paid any attention to his heart for the past several minutes. Though this very thought made him conscious of the ache once again.

His voice assumed an unctuous, self-inflated tone.

"I suppose it's because I'm a scientist. I demand proof, rigorous proof, before I'm willing to subscribe to something that I cannot see with my own eyes. Even if it's something that confirms my own theory and something that I long to be true with all my heart."

The dog rose abruptly and started pacing about nervously.

Quincy called him, and when the dog refused to obey, he sighed and put down the pair of pliers. He stood up, scraping the chair legs against the wooden floor, and walked over to see what was bothering the animal.

As he did so, he passed by the computer screen. He looked at it and whistled.

"Holy shit," he said, in a tone of genuine wonder.

Cleaver stopped in his tracks, suddenly nervous.

"What is it?"

"You better come see this."

Cleaver rushed over to the desk, forgetting for a moment about the sharp pounding in his chest.

There on the screen was written:

    TYLER. I'M COMING. DAD

They were both silent for a moment. Finally, Quincy spoke.

"What do you make of it?"

"A message. From his father. To him."

"Obviously. But from where? How'd he get into the system? How's he gonna come for him, as he says?"

For once, Cleaver was far ahead of Quincy. But he didn't feel like explaining everything—that he had deduced that with the help of that woman Tyler's father knew more or less everything about the experiment, that he had somehow learned the password, that he had gone to his basement laboratory in Pinegrove to try to contact his son, at the site Cleaver had used and that he was about to embark on a journey inside the TSR, probably with Felix's help.

Cleaver didn't want to explain all this because his own mind was already racing ahead down a twisting path. It was a path that was strewn with obstacles and dangers, but it was also one, he admitted to himself as he looked over at the machine, that he had been contemplating for some time.

Chapter 31

Reclining on the stretcher, Scott felt the cold of the metal railing on his shoulders even through his shirt. He lifted his hands and placed them outside, resting them on the sides of the machine. His fingers slid along the glistening surface. He soon felt a gloss of moisture—which was, he realized, his own sweat. It was one more clue to just how frightened he was—frightened of sliding into the machine and the claustrophobia of being confined inside the metal cocoon. And then, of course, there was that other fear that underlay everything else and that he didn't even want to think about, of what might happen to him once his mind was extracted from his body and sent out there into the ether.

He shook it off. In this situation, lying here on the machine and about to enter it, soon to be strapped down and helpless, fear was a useless emotion. And it could only distract him from his mission.

His hands. Where should he place them? Folded calmly across his belly like a corpse in a coffin? That seemed natural.

What was it called, anyway—this place out there? A parallel universe? Mind space? Purgatory—was that it?—the repository of lost souls made famous by poets and seers? He would soon find out just how good they were at divination.

Felix was not good at providing instructions, which did not imbue Scott with confidence. The man was a bungler, that much was clear, and it made everything much more threatening. What would happen if Felix did something wrong, tripped the wrong lever, set the wrong dial? Then

Scott would never travel to the right place; he would never find Tyler and reach him and bring him back—or if not bring him back, then at least be with him and comfort him, wherever he was.

Scott felt the sides of the helmet against his temples. It didn't fit easily. Felix was trying to pull it on, and his fingers were trembling. Scott lifted his hands to the top of the helmet and gave it a vigorous downward tug. It fell neatly into place, like a football helmet, snug against his ears, in the front reaching just above his eyebrows. It carried an odd smell, like a mixture of leather and a tang of some sort of chemicals spilled onto a sheet of metal.

Now Felix was trying to place the eye caps. He pinched the upper lid of Scott's right eye and lifted it, his hand still shaking. It turned the world into a blur, but Scott could see the dark metallic square approaching his eyeball.

"Let me do it," Scott said, brushing his hands away.

He hadn't meant to be abrupt. On one level he was aware of a concern that he had tried to suppress—that in a few minutes' time he would be at the mercy of this frightened lab assistant whom he had just threatened with jail—but there was no other alternative. Only Felix knew how to operate the machine. Still, Scott felt a sense of urgency, and he couldn't allow any delay.

Carefully, he squeezed his eyelash and lifted it, using the other hand to lower the metal contact until it touched his eyeball. It set off a miniature fireball and then darts of red that pierced the darkness. He placed the bottom lid over the metal and he felt the cap expand, covering his eyeball as tightly as an eggcup and sending off another shower of yellow and red sparks that shot across his closed eye like meteors.

In panic, he opened his other eye. Felix was leaning over, peering down, his mouth drawn tight in concentration—Scott could see the dark ovals of his nostrils and even the tiny hairs inside guarding the passages. He smelled his breath—stale, heavy, hot.

"Let's do the other one," Scott said. He gave the directive, which was hardly necessary, to give himself the feeling that he was in control. But his words sounded shaky.

Again, he lifted his eyelid, felt the metal encroach upon his eyeball and expand to cover it and saw the vivid colors—yellows, reds, even, he thought, greens. Now all the world was dark. His arms were strapped to his sides by a thick belt that Felix tightened.

Scott lay there on the stretcher—isolated, alone, exposed, and trapped. He felt as defenseless as a newborn wrapped in a blanket.

He heard Felix moving about, worrying the machine. He wished he would talk, tell him what he was doing and what was going on. At one point, he even thought he heard him humming under his breath. Then he realized it was a noise from the machine.

He heard Felix's footsteps approaching. The lab assistant was standing over him.

"Okay," Felix said. "Here we go."

The stretcher began to move upward, and he knew he was entering the gaping mouth of the machine—he knew it because the sounds of the room suddenly flattened out as if they were coming from far away and he heard the whirl of small sounds echoing in the chamber. His skin tightened in the dead air. He was in a wind tunnel without wind.

"I think it's best if you don't move at all," Felix said. Scott could tell that he was speaking loudly but the words sounded far away, as if he were on a distant hilltop.

"Here goes!"

And suddenly there was a grinding noise that filled his ears, and it seemed to fill his eyes, too, for waves of colors came at him, feeding an illusion that he was the one moving, not they, and that he was gaining speed and heading out through space almost like a rocket ship. He thought he felt the chamber shudder, and the sensation that he was traveling was palpable—it seemed real because it was real.

And as he left the world behind, heading for a tunnel

that twisted before him like the funnel of a tornado or maybe the inside of a hornet's nest, since it was that same gray fibrous texture, he heard a sound from the earthbound world. A familiar ringing sound. And he just had the time and presence of mind to have one final reflexive thought as he headed for the opening of the tunnel, which allowed him to identify the sound outside the machine—it was the ringing of a telephone.

Then a series of shocks smashed into his eyeballs. They jolted him coming out of nowhere, but they didn't hurt. All he saw were balls of light. They turned into waves that seemed to come crashing in upon him, and each pounding wave left behind a void of total darkness. The waves gathered force until a giant wave came cascading toward him and broke apart and separated into fragments like colors of a kaleidoscope. The colors streamed into him and through him and past him. They looked like multicolored meteors of burning rock with tails of yellow and green and orange. Oddly, even when they seemed to be shooting straight through his body, he couldn't feel them.

Quincy's confusion began to lift like a dissipating fog as he sat at his worktable and watched Cleaver. The man seemed filled with new vigor—he appeared to know what he was about, and for the first time in a long time, Quincy felt a kind of respect for him. *Maybe it's no accident that he's a scientist on the verge of a breakthrough,* Quincy thought—*he's got the balls for it, and he seems to know what he's doing.*

Cleaver was punching numbers on a phone—he knew them by heart, and he hit each one with a deliberate intensity.

He waited with the receiver to his ear, then when the connection took, started right in without so much as a hello.

Quincy could hear only his end of the conversation.

"Is he there?" Slight pause. "You know very well who I mean."

A pause.

"I figured as much. Where is he right now?"

Cleaver's eyebrows went up—it was hard to tell whether in surprise or a kind of fettered joy.

"Aha!" he said. He repeated the phrase several times and began pacing in a small circle, as wide as the phone cord would allow. Each time he came around, Quincy could read more excitement in his face.

"And is he in there right now?"

Another pause.

"And how many minutes?"

A short one this time.

"Bravo." The word reserved for opera divas sounded funny addressed to a lab technician, but it was followed by a flood of words that made everything fall into place.

"Here's what you do," said Cleaver. "Simplest thing in the world. You're familiar with the timer—just reach right up there and turn off the override. Let it keep going. He won't even know."

Quincy couldn't believe what he was hearing. Cleaver was quiet, but only for a moment.

"Look, you don't know that. It's not the same as Benchloss. He wants to go out there, he wants to find his kid, you're just giving him more time. I know what I'm talking about, and I'm giving you a direct order. I want you to do it and that's that."

Then came the longest pause of all.

"Right," said Cleaver, and then he hung up with an air of self-satisfaction.

"It pays to have a trustworthy lab assistant," he said.

"Did I just hear what I think I heard?" said Quincy.

"You didn't hear a thing," said Cleaver, taking off his jacket and hanging it on the back of a chair. "And you're not going to see what you're about to see."

He walked over to the TSR machine and touched it gently on top.

"You've never used this one, have you?" he asked.

Quincy shook his head no. He had to admit he felt a

little tremor of excitement building up somewhere in
his gut.

"I bet you've been dying to. Who knows? Play your
cards right and maybe you will. Like right now."

Cleaver smiled an odd lopsided smile, and Quincy was
impressed all over again. *He's really going to do it,* he
thought. *I've got to hand it to the guy. He's not afraid to experiment on himself—and to bet the whole farm on a single shot.*

———

At first, Scott felt giddy from the lights and bright colors streaming past. And the noise—it was like being inside a beer barrel rattling down the highway.

He tried to tamp down his fear. No sooner had he
begun to feel that he could conquer it through an exer-
tion of will than something happened that eclipsed
everything and removed the idea of fear altogether.

It happened like a bolt of lightning, or maybe a clap of
thunder, except that there was no noise, no flash of light.
It was a lifting of himself—a lifting and an unfolding so
that he felt he was being turned inside out. And as his interior was turning outward, it rose up; a fog descended
upon him or he rose to meet it, like a mountain drifting
upward until it disappears in the clouds. And then he had
the sensation that he was expanding, and soon he was
breaking into particles, hundreds of them, thousands, that
began to separate and move gradually apart in slow motion, spreading out horizontally, moving everywhere and
covering everything like a fine mist, moving farther and
farther and yet not diluting, so that they reached the far-
thest corners of the horizon in all directions. They didn't
stop, but kept spreading until they encircled the world,
and then they rose up into the atmosphere and outer
space and through the coldness until they finally reached
the stars and even moved past them, picking up speed.
And that was what he had seen just a moment ago—the
bright lights moving past him, the colors of comet tails.
Still drifting, spreading out, alone in darkness.

*   *   *

Where would I find him? Where would he go?

He was lying in bed, or maybe it was Tyler who was in the bed and he, Scott, was telling him the bedtime story. He couldn't tell the difference between them; the boundaries had dissolved—he was watching the scene from close up, maybe the doorway, and yet he was inside it at the same time. The wallpaper—he recognized it, horses. Or were they monsters?

Suddenly something irritated him, burned and blistered his skin. He turned and tossed and still it was there beneath him eating into his back so that he reached down and felt it and held it, something hard in his hand.

A pebble.

He rubbed it.

He heard his own voice, soothing, soft, comforting, as it had once sounded when he told the nightly story, and as he heard the familiar words, he seemed to enter into the story, living it even as he told it:

And then something very strange happened. At first he felt hot, and then he felt cold. And then he felt warm and then he felt cool. And finally he felt just right.

And suddenly, the mansion rose up before him, grander even than he had envisioned, its antebellum façade centered upon four smooth, tall Corinthian columns extending skyward. Its white skin gleamed with a rosy hue, as if reflecting a setting sun. The steps were taller, too, six of them, so tall that to mount them he needed to use his hands. He looked around. Behind him, porch boards creaked. A hanging swing—where had that come from?—waved gently in the breeze. No one in it.

But Tyler might be here inside. He felt that with a sudden surge of certainty. Surely the mansion, conjured up together at every bedtime, belonged to both of them, to both of their imaginations.

He placed his hand on the thick brass door handle,

and even without turning it, the door flew open as if
someone from the inside had given it a tug and then
whisked away. It was dark inside, and as he glanced
backward over his shoulder, he saw that it was dark outside now also, purplish dark with no trace of the sun,
and the trees, darkened evergreens, swayed violently in
the wind.

Only the stars were out—Orion.

He stepped inside. Candles flickered in sconces to
light his way, so that he could look up the corridor.
There on both sides, stretching as far as he could see,
was door after door after door. Moving slowly down
the corridor, gliding really, he came to the first door,
looked at it, then passed it by in favor of the next and
passed by that one, too.

He stood before the third door and placed his hand
upon the handle, and as he turned it, he knew, with a
mixture of anticipation and dread, that he had chosen
the correct one. It opened effortlessly, as if someone inside was pulling it.

Kate approached Pinegrove with her heart racing, and
she shuddered as she looked up at it. The building that
had so depressed her on that first visit looked scary in
the evening. Most of its windows were darkened, the
steep roof disappeared into blackness, and the doorway
was half hidden in shadows. Charles Addams himself
couldn't have drawn a bleaker picture.

She had been in too much of a hurry to plot out a
strategy and had no idea what she would do if she encountered Cleaver—confront him probably and insist
that he tell her what had happened to Tyler. She didn't
have much ammunition, only the fact that an ambulance from Pinegrove had taken him away from St.
Cat's. Yet she would have to demand an explanation
without revealing where she had gotten her information
or the porter would get in trouble. It was not, she realized, a foolproof plan—it was hardly a plan at all.

Well, she would just have to improvise. Her mother had always told her that she was quick on her feet; now she would find out if she had been right.

She marched up the stairs to the front door. It was sure to be locked. To the right was a doorbell, but she could hardly ring it; it would be difficult to present her case forcefully while standing on the threshold like an Avon saleswoman. And what if she asked for Cleaver and he wasn't there?

She placed one hand on the heavy handle and was about to give it a shove when abruptly the door moved toward her, almost knocking her down. She regained her footing and moved backward with it, pressed almost against the wall, and held on to the handle for a moment. She heard footsteps coming out and treading down the stairs, and peering around the door, she saw the back of a woman walking away into the dusk. She held on to the door handle until she disappeared, then stepped around quickly and entered the building.

She found herself in the same dreary reception area she remembered. The floor was made of tiny hexagonal tiles, but so many were cracked and missing that the mosaic design—some sort of harbor scene—was hard to make out. She looked around nervously. The stairway ahead was empty, and so were the dimly lit corridors leading off to both sides. She remembered that the main offices were to the right and made her way down that corridor, her tread falling quietly upon the floor. She thought she could hear murmurs and sounds of protest coming from the end of the other corridor—the noise, she guessed, of patients being bedded down for the night. It was early, she thought, to be putting them to sleep—the attendants probably just wanted them out of the way.

She came to the administrator's office, which was darkened. She peered through the frosted glass on the door and saw the dim outlines of desks and chairs inside. She moved on. Next door was an office that had a single word stenciled in large block letters on the window glass: RECORDS. That was the one she wanted to enter: If Tyler had been transferred here, then surely there would be a file on him.

She held the doorknob and gave it a turn. Locked, as she had feared. She rattled the door softly and found that there was no give. She turned and retraced her steps, coming back to the main lobby. Cautiously she took the other corridor. Now the noise from the ward sounded louder, an uproar. The patients had clearly been disturbed by something. Maybe the attendants were there—for her that could be a stroke of luck. Sure enough, she came to the nurses' station and found it unoccupied. She looked around furtively—a desk, newspapers, a television set turned on. The smell of marijuana hung in the air. She opened a drawer in the desk and found what she wanted—a ring with five keys. She slipped it into her pocket and stole back down the corridor, through the front lobby, and stood before the records room. When she tried the third key, she felt it turn smoothly as the bolt retracted, and with barely a click the lock unfastened and the door slipped open. Success! Glancing up and down the corridor, she entered stealthily and left the door open a crack behind her.

She had to wait several long minutes until her eyes adjusted to the dark. Then, by the light filtering in from the hall, she spotted the filing cabinets lined against one wall. But the room was too dark to be able to sort through them and read the contents. A green-domed desk lamp stood upon a bulky wooden desk nearby, and she groped until she found a switch on the base and turned it. A sharp funnel of light cut through the room. She took a wastebasket, turned it upside down, and leaned it against the lamp, which directed the glare into a circle on the floor and sent a soft glow over the rest. The room felt almost cozy.

The filing drawers were marked alphabetically in scrawled fountain pen. She followed the letters until she came to *H–M*, then grabbed the handle and pulled. The folders inside gave off a musty smell and dust rose up. There were separators on rusty rails and manila folders written in the same penned hand. Her heart sank—she could see right away that none of the folders appeared new. And none of them bore Tyler's last name. She thumbed through several times just to be sure. She would have to look elsewhere.

She closed the drawer and sat down at the desk, her back to the door, pulling open the drawers and rummaging through the contents. Everything was coated in a thin layer of dust, and there was nothing beyond the usual sort of contents: pencils, paper clips, old sets of keys, a pad with a rubber stamp, index cards, stationery, and other office paraphernalia. She had just opened the second drawer and was lifting out a file of correspondence when she heard something behind her, a little tick like the sound of a door hinge or a high heel upon the floor. She froze.

A voice behind her blustered in confusion.

"What . . . ? Who . . . ? Who are you? What are you doing?"

It was—she noted with a stab of relief—a woman's voice. She turned slowly, both to collect herself and to avoid a sudden movement that could rattle whoever was standing there. She had perhaps ten seconds to come up with a plausible story. Ten seconds—hell, ten minutes wouldn't be enough, she realized.

The woman was young and broad-shouldered, with her hair cut in a bob, not at all the kind of person Kate expected to find here.

They stared at each other for several heartbeats.

"I'm Dr. Willet," said Kate, speaking slowly. She didn't have time to say more.

"I've heard of you," put in the young woman.

Kate was surprised.

"You have? How come?"

"I work for Dr. Cleaver."

Kate bristled at the name and wondered if the woman had noticed. She gave a vague wave of her hand and said, "I was just looking around." And as she gave emphasis to the explanation by actually looking around—and saw the woman glance at the wastepaper basket on top of the lamp—she realized how absurd it was.

"Look, ah—by the way, what's your name?"

"Felicity. Felicity Barrington."

Giving both names made her sound suddenly like a young girl trying to please but she didn't act that way.

"Felicity." Kate pronounced the name roundly and with assurance, seeking the upper hand. "I might as well level with you."

The woman walked over to the desk, retrieved the wastebasket, and placed it on the floor—revealing herself in the rush of light to be quite handsome—and then pulled up a chair and sat down herself, not far away. It seemed to be a gesture of intimacy that Kate found encouraging.

"Yes," she said. "Go ahead."

"Well," continued Kate. "I don't have to tell you—or maybe I do—that some odd things have been going on here. And I think your Dr. Cleaver is at the center of it."

"*My Dr. Cleaver.* He's hardly *my Dr. Cleaver.*"

Kate was stunned.

"Then I take it you don't like him."

"Like him? He's an asshole. Does that answer your question?"

She couldn't believe her good fortune.

"Yes, Felicity, I think it does."

And with very little prompting, Felicity poured out almost everything she knew, which was quite a bit—how Cleaver had used patients to conduct experiments, had imported a special machine to disembody their minds, how one patient had even died in the midst of it. She talked about his crackpot theories, his work habits, even his insomnia. And especially about how obnoxious he was.

"Plus he treats me like a doormat," she said finally, at the end of her recitation. Then she looked Kate in the eye and asked a question of her own.

"I guess you want to get him because he got you fired, huh?"

"No, not exactly. I mean, yes, I would like to get him, but that's not the only reason. You see, I'm trying to help a friend, someone whose son had a horrible accident and was in critical condition and was virtually dead. And I think a couple of weeks ago, his body was taken out of St. Cat's and maybe brought here."

Kate gave Felicity a hopeful look, wondering if she might know anything.

She did.

"You mean Tyler," she said quickly. "He's here—right downstairs in the basement."

Chapter 32

How he got there, he didn't know. The door opened, that much he remembered. Then came a darkness, and a slipping into a kind of a void or maybe a tunnel and here he was. The day, time, year, season—none of that he knew. And none of that mattered. The world he was in was timeless.

But Scott knew *where* he was, and that frightened him, frightened him deeply. He was in bed—*his old bed*—flat on his back, helpless. Was he a child again? An adolescent? He couldn't say, but it didn't matter, for in any case the world about him made him *feel* like a child, defenseless and insignificant. Everything around him appeared large and threatening, inanimate objects like his chest of drawers and the white curtains blowing into the room. They were sinister. And all of them—it seemed exaggerated to think it, but he felt it with a certitude that was alarming—were *conspiring* against him.

The subconscious mind, he had once heard, knows no time. But wait! Maybe recollecting that thought meant he wasn't a child—it was, after all, the kind of thought only an adult would have. *Subconscious mind*—that's not even a concept a child could grasp. Maybe then he *was* a grown-up—not a grown-up, an adult.

But then why do I feel so helpless?

And what bed was this that he was in, felt like he was strapped down into? Was it that same bed long ago where he lay up all night, waiting for the soul-shattering sound of his mother's scream and her rasping breath, holding the cold spoon that he would use to pry apart her teeth? He looked around warily. The room was dim, hard to see through the glaze. The objects were more like shapes—it was impossible to bring them into focus. He tried squinting his eyes. Still no good. They seemed to be in the correct place, the furniture, the dark rectangles of pictures stuck to the walls. There was the bookcase loaded with comics, the old record player that he turned on to blare Tchaikovsky and Beethoven so loud that all thinking was drowned out. But they were indistinct, large dark blots against a gray background.

Long ago, so long ago that he wished he could forget it but could not, when he was fourteen, Scott's mother had stopped drinking abruptly. Scott hadn't known this at the time, or if he had, he didn't register it. All he knew was that she took to her bed in the room next to his. She could barely move. Her toe was broken from a fall down the stairs, and a dirty plaster cast covered her foot, open at the top. A pin had been driven through her middle toe to hold it in suspension, attached to two metal uprights like a goalpost. The toe was black and swollen. It had gotten infected.

It was raining ice outside, a freak storm that covered everything in a slick reflective sheen. It was magical and yet frightening, ominous. The trees crackled and snapped when they waved in the gusts of wind, and their branches tapped and scraped against the window glass like wizened fingers. Roads were frozen rivers, unnavigable.

Scott was downstairs when he heard his mother cry out. It was a long, low moan of pain and fear that mounted to the upper registers and died out into a whine. Something hit the floor, a body. He ran to her room and found her sprawled on the wooden boards in her nightgown, thrashing about wildly, the heavy foot cast pounding upon the floor keeping beat to her convulsions. Her head flew from side to side, her hair electrified, her limbs jerking and flopping. A trail of saliva fell across her cheek. He ran downstairs to phone the doctor, the rings taking forever. Finally, she answered, a severe woman who told him to look outside. He raised his head and saw the ice beating down—no ambulance could possibly get through, she said—and she carefully instructed him: He was to hold a spoon to her mouth downward so that she would not swallow her tongue. That could bring death. He ran back upstairs and now she was quiet, lying there confused, her eyes large, looking at him as if she didn't know him, wondering where she was and what had happened.

She had three more seizures that night, each preceded by that low, anguished cry and followed by those long moments of oblivion in which she asked him where she was and who he was. The next morning rain had washed away the ice. He fixed himself breakfast and went off to school and when he returned at four p.m., she was gone. Later, the doctor called to say she was in the hospital. Four days afterward, she came home again, her eyes now open—he hadn't seen them so open for months—and her toe treated.

When he thought back to it, there was one convulsion that stuck in his memory. When he rushed in, the dog was barking at her, then sank his teeth into her nightgown and tugged at it fiercely so that Scott had to knock him away. He kicked it—hard against the ribs. The dog ran away whining and when he approached it later under the couch, it growled. He returned to his room and lay there in bed, holding the spoon, his eyes open in the dark, listening. He played Tchaikovsky on the old record player, at first soft, then louder, then very loud.

And now he saw himself there, a small pathetic figure lost in the big bed in the darkness and the billowing music. He could look down at himself, his younger self. He didn't feel pity—only, once again, the fear. Fear at what was happening and what might happen. Plus an emotion that he could not name that seemed to be a mixture of repulsion and incredulity—and this is perhaps what saved him, for it imposed a distance and made him able to stand aside and watch what was going on with a remarkable detachment.

And he had to ask himself: Lying there with the spoon in his hand and waiting and listening to the loud music, had he really hurried in to attend to her during each episode? Maybe one time he could have answered that. But by now he had forgotten—if indeed he had ever known.

He heard her again, or thought he heard her, but come to think about it, that was impossible, since she was downstairs, far away in the old rambling house. A sound wouldn't carry all the way from down there. A dozen rooms at least separated them. But he knew she was there; he could feel it. The knowledge filled him with fear that immobilized him. He lay there in bed unable to move, his mind racing, his blood burning throughout his body. She wouldn't come for him, would she? She wouldn't harm him—would she? Her own son? His chest knotted up—he knew she would.

She will.

He picked up the phone and called the doctor. A nurse answered and went to find him, a long time. What was taking so long? Scott could not speak. Finally, he heard the doctor's voice, a strange, slightly accented English, from distant Europe, he had been told. The doctor at last!

"Hello? Hello?"

Scott found his voice. He began to blurt it out, all of it, what was happening, his fear, the danger. Then he heard it: the click. The receiver rising through the air, a rustling. She was on the extension. Her voice came on the line, loud and close, so reasonable, so comforting.

"Doctor, there's nothing to worry about, nothing at all. I'm fine. My son has been having these horrible nightmares, these horrible thoughts. But I wouldn't hurt him. I wouldn't hurt anyone."

He could hear the doctor taking it in, cooing his understanding. *He believes her!*

She continued.

"You see, Doctor, I'm perfectly fineeeee—"

Her voice screeched up, a long, anguished cry with a hint of laughter to it, rising higher and higher, pounding back as if in an echo chamber.

Then she hung up.

Then she started coming after him, room by room, opening the doors and closing them. And he could hear her—feel her—coming closer. Her tread upon the stairs, moving more quickly, a moment of silence as she crossed another room, then another door opening and closing. And another. Loud now. Close.

There was nothing for it; he could not shrink away in bed. He would have to go to the door, to meet her head-on, to stand up to her. It was the only way he could hope to do what he had come to do. He summoned his courage—all of it. For he would need all of it.

Slowly he tossed away the blankets and swung his legs down and got out of bed. He stood and walked carefully to the door, leaning against it. He touched it, feeling her on the other side, imagining her there and almost seeing the flash of something steel in her hand, the cleaver, pointing downward, ready to rise up.

He put his hand on the doorknob and turned it and yanked the door open.

Felicity led the way as she and Kate rushed down the staircase. Halfway to the basement, Kate heard her gasp in surprise: footsteps, someone coming up.

"What? Where are you going?" she heard Felicity ask.

She saw now that she was talking to a tall young man wearing a lab assistant's coat. He looked flustered.

"Nowhere—nothing," he sputtered. "I was just leaving."

"Well, maybe you should stay," Felicity said. "We may need you."

"Can't," he replied quickly. And as he hurried up the steps, he looked into Kate's eyes frantically, then brushed past her so hard she was pushed against the banister. She felt like tackling him, but his air of urgency made her want even more to find Tyler.

Something was wrong.

She raced past Felicity, opened the door, and stepped

into the corridor. What she saw made her stop dead in her tracks. She could scarcely believe it.

There was Tyler, lying in bed just as he had been in St. Cat's. He appeared very much the same. She looked at the monitors and the computer, and she read them quickly with her doctor's eye—not much had changed. He was in a coma, but clearly he was still alive—or still not fully dead. The machines were doing all the work. Her heart went out to him—all this time, weeks now, locked in his own private limbo. As the thought took hold, her heart filled a second time, this time with anger at Cleaver. What a savage he was to do such a thing.

She felt something on her elbow. It was Felicity, touching her lightly, guiding her toward the open door of another room, and as she crossed the threshold she stared in disbelief.

For there was a large machine, something like an MRI, and as she approached, she saw the feet of a person who was in it. She went close and looked inside and saw a man strapped down with a grotesque helmet covering his head and two round devices on his eyes.

In an instant, she knew who it was. She also knew that he was in danger.

She spun around, toward Felicity.

"What is this?" she demanded.

"It's called a TSR, a transcranial stimulator-receiver. It's a way to reach the mind and stimulate it and also, you know, allow it to move—to move outside the body."

Kate stared in disbelief. But in an instant, it all made sense. She knew why Scott was there—that he, like her, had found this place and learned about the machine and now had gone to try to find his son, or his son's mind-spirit, to bring it back to the body. He must have come only a short while ago.

She stared for some time, astonished—astonished that there was such a machine, not that Scott would use it. He would do anything for his son. She looked at his features, what she could see of his face below the goggles. His mouth was twisted down and his jaw clenched, in pain or perhaps in fear. His body, though strapped tightly, seemed to be twitching. She stared until with a force of will she got hold of herself and tried to think what to do. Clearly that young man who had run away had set the machine running. And just as clearly, they would have to figure out how to control it.

She looked up at Felicity again.

"Do you know how to run this thing?"

Felicity, who was also staring at Scott, looked at her with wide eyes.

"Sort of. I've seen them do it, Dr. Cleaver and that guy who ran away, Felix. I've looked in and watched them when they've done it on patients. But I can't say I really know how to do it."

"Is it complicated?"

Felicity looked nervous.

"I can't say for sure," she said.

"Well—I guess we're about to find out."

"What if we do it wrong?"

"He's in there already. So we have to help him anyway—if only to get him out."

"That's true."

Kate stepped over to the control panel and looked at the array of dials and knobs and screens. The image of Scott's face inside was still in her mind.

Cleaver felt no fear, only excitement. Fear was something that he had discarded as soon as he decided to enter the machine—it was a useless emotion. Fortitude, strength, and curiosity—those were the desired companions for a scientist about to journey into the unknown.

Quincy had strapped him in and helped insert the pathfinders over the eyes, a little too eagerly for Cleaver's money. Lying there on the stretcher, he wondered what would happen if something went wrong, what it would feel like, whether it would hurt. And how would Quincy take it—would he help him if he emerged half-dead or a raving lunatic? He worried because he was convinced that his young colleague cared little for him. Only three things would probably matter to Quincy—how to fix the machine, how to get rid of the body, and how to get paid.

But these thoughts were doing no good. Cleaver didn't want to depart on such a negative note, so he gestured to Quincy to come close and asked him to lean down and managed to raise his hand high enough, even strapped to his side, to find his cuff and hold it in his fingers. But then he didn't know what to say.

He tried to think of something noteworthy, a proclamation for history, not something so clearly cooked up in advance as "One small step for man, one giant leap for mankind." Something genuine, spontaneous. Trouble was, nothing spontaneous occurred to him—it never did during the truly important moments.

"So," he said, "you'll be sure to watch for the seven-minute mark?"

"Yes."

"I don't want to come out overcooked. Ha ha."

"Ha ha."

There was, he thought, a slur of irony to Quincy's rejoinder. But there was nothing for it; he could think of nothing else to say.

"Right," he said, letting go of the young man's cuff.

"Right," came the reply.

Cleaver felt the stretcher slide upward and the mouth of the machine engulf him. Then soon he heard the noise of it starting up. He was alarmed that it was so loud; it hadn't sounded that way on the outside. Abruptly, he realized he was experiencing his body in a way he hadn't before. He could feel almost every part of it—his leg, his thigh, his shoulder, the skin on the back of his hand, the hair on his forearm. What a miracle it was, the human body—how the fingers could grip in unison, the muscles contract to raise a leg, how the blood vessels retreated deep inside the skin in times of cold and the sweat glands poured out water to cool it in times of heat. What craftsmanship! What architecture! Why had he never noticed all the tiny intricacies, their ingenuity? Only now that he was about to leave it did he appreciate it, did he pay it any mind. Typical, he thought. And out of nowhere the lyric of an old song flashed through his mind: "You don't miss your water till your well runs dry."

What kind of thought is that to be having? At this moment of all moments, can't I think of something profound, can't I control my mind?

And then, almost as if to prove the point, his mind thought of something that he never would have wanted to, not in a million years. It was the image of the boy Tyler, of his anima, bouncing around in space without respite, like some *Flying Dutchman,* never settling down, never coming home again. What if that happened to him? What if he never came home again? It was, suddenly, a dreadful thought. Why would the mind suddenly toss it up like that, unless the mind was perverse? Maybe that was the explanation. Maybe it was the body—only the body—that was our one true loyal friend. Then why leave it behind?

But stop—the event was happening. Now his body was doing something else, or his mind was—it was hard to tell which. Part of him was staying behind, down below—it must be his body—and another part was lifting and moving up, slowly and then gradually faster and faster still, like a rocket shooting toward a star. He felt stars shooting at him, light coming right into his eyeballs, so powerful it hurt, smashing right into his brain. It came in waves, over and over, more and more powerful.

And then suddenly it stopped.

He was floating aimlessly in space, an astronaut untethered. Spinning round like a leaf in a stream. Mothership Earth was retreating in the distance, though he couldn't see it, only feel it. Then his balance righted itself, and now he wasn't sure where he was. He tried to look down but could not—he couldn't see if his body was there. And as he looked up, he saw darkness slowly lifting, dark figures slowly moving, as in a dream. He tried to focus, but the figures remained indistinct shadows. The light was hazy, heavy with particles, as if he were looking through a cheesecloth. In fact, he was hot, scorching hot. Had the rocket landed on the sun? Maybe that was it. He was on the surface of an alien burning planet or a desert somewhere, and yes, there was a sandstorm coming at him, obscuring his vision, clogging his pores. That would explain it, the inability to see, the figures moving slowly as if weighed down, the sense of oppression from the sun's rays. Somewhere in the Sahara. A caravan of camels, a market in Timbuktu.

But no, he was mistaken. There were no camels, no sandstorms, and those vague figures—he could actually *see through them*. And he was not feeling hot, not at all. Quite the opposite—he was feeling cold, freezing cold. He pulled himself tight into a bundle. Something went into his eyes, on his nose. That was not sand flying through the air—that was snow. He was in a wintry storm. Not Timbuktu—but where?

Cyberia?

His mind laughed at the pun, giggled hysterically. Hysterically because now he was frightened—he knew where he wasn't, but not where he was. His vision cleared somewhat, like a curtain melting away, and he began to recognize some of those shadowy figures in the snowstorm. And he knew where he was. He saw himself, standing ankle-deep outside the dormitory, feeling the dizziness all over again, preparing to faint at the news of his father's death.

~

When Scott yanked the door open, he was amazed to find that there was no ogre on the other side. His mother was not there in her scraggly nightgown, her hair hanging in wet strands on her forehead. There was no cleaver in her hand.

There was nothingness.

His pulse quieted and he took a deep breath, then stepped forward. He was standing in a corridor painted in luminous white. From one end shone a bright light, and the reflection bounced off the walls in a shower of white rays and hurt his eyes. He looked down—it was hard even to see his own feet—but he could tell by some internal gyroscope that he was tall, fully grown, an adult. He looked again at the walls, and there stretching before him, as far as he could see, was door after door after door.

Behind one of them, he knew, was Tyler. But which one?

He had to hurry. He could sense somewhere—he could hear it, maybe—a clock ticking, telling him that time was running out. How could that be in this timeless world?

Which door should I open?

He paused before one, then passed it by for another, then went to a third and a fourth. At the fifth one, he turned the knob, and as he did so, he regretted the choice and wished he could change it, for a dark fog seemed to come from inside. It quickly coated everything around him and blotted out the white light until he was lost in a thick haze. From within he could hear a soft sound, a mumbling or moaning, and once he stepped inside it got louder, though it was still so indistinct he could not place it. Then he looked hard, and suddenly he could make out dim figures moving slowly, as if they were floating, will-o'-the-wisps, slipping through the layers of fog like ghosts.

Souls cast adrift. *Psyche,* the Greek word for "breath," also means "soul," he remembered from a long-distant class in ancient literature. The soul and the spark of life are one and the same. How odd to be thinking of that now, except that something in the look and carriage of these spectral figures reminded him of classic myths—Orpheus crossing the river Styx to visit the forbidding underworld in search of his beloved Eurydice.

They took no notice of him, though now they passed close by, so close that he could reach out and touch them if he wanted. He did not because he quickly saw that he could see through them, which filled him with horror. And he noticed for the first time that there were dozens of them, more than that—scores, hundreds, as far as he could see in all directions.

If he was in hell, where was his Virgil, or his Beatrice?

And indeed, materializing out of the fog, one figure stood out from all the rest; and of them all, she alone appeared to see him. She looked directly at him, and he felt that look like an arrow in his heart, because he knew her well and on one level had been sure he would find her here and maybe even had been looking for her as much as for Tyler.

There was no question about it—it was she, his long-lost Lydia. Her beautiful features were the same—the long nose and high forehead and almond eyes and perfectly sculpted chin—except that they seemed frozen. Even as she looked at him and showed with a dip of her head that she recognized him in turn, they formed a mask, so that he felt a coldness seize him.

She held out her hand, and he took it and it *was* cold, as cold as ice on tree branches. She turned, still holding his hand, and led him—and he had no choice but to follow her meekly, even though he knew in his heart that the destination she was leading him toward was his ruin.

Chapter 33

Again, Kate bent over the entrance to the machine and craned her neck to peer into the chamber where Scott was imprisoned. She tried again to read his expression, which was all but impossible, because his eyes were covered and she was looking at him from below. Still, she feared she could see signs of distress—his cheeks were drawn and his teeth were clenched so tight she could see his jaw muscles bulging.

She did not know what to do. Should she try to extract him from the machine, rescue him from wherever his mind had gone? Or should she let him continue the voyage he'd embarked on to save his son? Which was more dangerous—interrupting him halfway or permitting his mind to travel as far as it wanted? What if his mind went so far away it never returned?

She backed away and looked at the array of machines. There was a timer there—she hadn't noticed that before. How could she have missed it?

She read the clock: three minutes and ten seconds.

The second hand was sweeping down, moving quickly.

"Why is that there?" she asked.

Felicity gave her a blank look, followed her eyes to the clock, and frowned. Clearly she didn't know.

"Is there some kind of limit?" Kate asked.

"Maybe. I don't know. I was never here for the whole thing. All I know is when I saw Dr. Cleaver run it, he always seemed to be in a rush. He was always barking out orders to Felix. You know, do this, do that, hurry up."

"But did they set the clock? Was there a timer? An alarm? Anything—anything at all?"

"I just don't know."

Felicity was getting upset, and her anxiety was contagious.

"Do you know how to stop it?" asked Kate. "How to get him out?"

"Sort of. I think we do it all in reverse—that's basically it."

Kate felt her confidence in the woman ebbing fast.

She looked again at the clock: three minutes and forty seconds.

Kate walked back over to the machine, rested one hand upon it, and then leaned over to reach deep into the chamber. She felt the strap tying Scott down and followed it to one side, where his hand was. She took his hand in her own and squeezed it tightly.

She doubted that he could even feel it, wherever he was. But maybe he could, and just maybe, she thought, it would make him feel a little less alone. For the moment, that was all she could think of to do.

～

Scott followed Lydia. Her hand was weightless, no more than a cloud of smoke in his, but somehow he could feel it or he imagined he could feel it, and that was enough to guide him through the layers of haze. He was feeling numb now, and weightless himself as he followed her.

The terrain changed so quickly he could not keep up with it. One minute it was hot, the next cold, and so on, until he couldn't tell the difference.

They came at last to a small door, and she motioned to him with a graceful sweep of the arm to enter it. He crouched, then crawled, and the door opened noiselessly before him. He went inside and stood up. He was in a room of brilliant white—white marble floor, white tiled walls, white plaster ceiling. It shone as bright as a birthing star, so bright he could hardly see. Slowly, his eyes accustomed themselves and he began to make out something in the corner, a long rectangular object, something familiar. Something important.

He stared at it, focusing his dilated pupils, scarcely daring to believe.

But it was—it was he!

Tyler!

Moving slowly, carefully, as if he were approaching a mirage that might slip away at any moment into a puff of nothingness, Scott walked toward his son. He felt he was moving effortlessly but slowly, as if in a dream. Finally, he reached the bed and he stood over him and looked down at him, lying there motionless. Tyler's head was bandaged; a drip from a stanchion entered his arm. But his eyes were open, wide with fright, and he could move them about. He cast them up at Scott, and the fright lessened and a slow small smile traced itself upon his lips and he seemed suddenly to relax and to breathe out in relief.

When Scott saw this, he could not restrain himself. He lay down next to Tyler and pulled him close and covered him by wrapping his arms around him. He pulled the needles out of his arm and hugged him so tightly that he could feel the boy's heart beating upon his own chest, beating rapidly but steadily. And he realized that the heart was beating in perfect synchronicity with his own. He put his head next to the boy's, and he could feel the pulse there through the bandage, beating out from his temple, so he leaned back and took the bandage off, unwrapping it like a ribbon, and placed his own head next to Tyler's. He imagined he could actually feel what was going on in there, and maybe he wasn't imagining it, because soon he believed he was even thinking the same thoughts.

They looked up out at the total whiteness around them, a blizzard of small white particles that filled the room like bits of ash floating in space. It was almost painful to see, a thick white curtain that fell before them and seemed to seal them off from everything else.

Almost everything. For there in one corner the particles had accumulated and were turning gray and then forming themselves into a long shape, long and tall and dark. They stared harder and the shape transformed itself into a solid rectangle standing on its side. A frame of wood appeared around the edges and then turned into a doorjamb, and right in the center was what he had known would be there—a large wooden door.

And as he looked, knowing and fearing that it would happen, the door opened. He pulled the blanket up under his chin like a bib and sank down lower so that his eyes were peering just over the edge. And still he stared, and what he saw standing there in the doorway, now looking full in flesh and bone and hair, was Lydia. She was wearing a gray suit. And she was looking down at him with an intense expression—it seemed to be a mixture of love and pain. The lower portion of her face was covered in shadow. And as she stood there in the doorway, she shifted a bit to one side and slowly raised her right arm. Her fingers were extended, moving. Was she trying to signal something? Was she waving good-bye to him? Or was she motioning to him to follow her?

All at once, he thought he knew. So the two of them together, as one, began to rise. It was time to go, to follow, to see where she would lead.

Cleaver collapsed in the snow and stared up through the flakes that fell on him like bits of ash. He felt nothing sitting there, absolutely nothing—neither fear nor foreboding nor cold nor suffocation, only tired. Very tired, beyond exhaustion.

He wanted to rest his head on the snowbank, to sleep for just a moment, not long, nothing more. And so he began to nod a bit, then caught himself and raised his head suddenly, for on some level he knew that to do that—to give in—was dangerous, very dangerous. And yet he felt so very sleepy.

No longer did he feel cold, just numb. He couldn't feel his limbs at all—he tried to move them and could not; they were so heavy they felt like they were tied to his sides. And once again he began to nod and then to lean forward with his upper body. He could sleep, just a bit. Then he would awaken, refreshed, and then he would get up and walk some more. But not now.

Slowly his body began to fall to one side, like a tree in the forest. He thought of breaking his fall, but he could not, and his head struck the snow hard, hard enough to rouse him for a moment, so that he was aware, briefly, of the danger. He opened his eyes.

I should not be doing this. I cannot fall asleep here.

But it was, admittedly, restful to just lie here like this, comfortable. What harm was there in a little sleep? It wasn't even that cold. He closed his eyes again and began to drift in the swirling snow.

And then he heard footsteps. Footsteps! Someone come to rescue him!

He knew who it was, the only person it could be. Who else would search for him out here in the dangerous snow? So he opened his eyes and tried to raise an arm to signal where he was, but could not. It did not matter; the footsteps were coming toward him. His father would find him. His father would save him. He would not die here alone.

My father.

And the footsteps stopped right before him. Two feet in front of his face. He summoned up his last reserve of strength and turned his head and looked up. And before he could see, he felt himself being raised up, roughly, back to a sitting position. And he opened his eyes and looked at the face now directly before him.

Not his father, no.

Not my father.

Instead, the face that he saw staring back at him with more than a hint of hatred belonged to Benchloss.

He thought vaguely, as if in a dream, *How did he get here? What is he doing here?* And then, looking up, he saw that Benchloss was doing something: He was reaching down to his midriff, and he unbuckled his belt buckle with his long, slender fingers. And lifting his hand to one side like a preacher in a pulpit pointing the

way to damnation, he pulled the belt through the rings
of his pants so quickly that it seemed to make a hissing
sound, like the sound of a whiplash or the devil breathing. He raised his hand over his head, twirling the belt
around like a lasso, and brought it down with all of his
might. Cleaver tried to protect his face, but he found he
couldn't lift his hands, which were stuck to his sides. He
felt the belt bite into his cheek; he looked up and saw
that it was about to land again, and this time it ripped
into the left side of his chest and pulled away, taking
some skin with it, and it fell on him again and again,
everywhere, on every part of his body, until he felt that
all of his flesh had been torn away and he was nothing
but a poor sagging skeleton. Then Benchloss leaned
down and held him a moment and finally let him go. He
sank back into the snow.

Benchloss, of all people.

He felt sleep come crawling in upon him. He fell back
deeply into the snow, cutting through it like a smoldering ember, so deeply it covered him over in no time, and
he saw just as he disappeared under a tunnel of whiteness that above him it was snowing. The snow fell everywhere on everything. It was like looking through a pair
of long white binoculars, everything far away and small.
Soon he felt a huge weight upon his chest, holding him
down and robbing him of breath. He also felt numb and
then not even that, nothing at all, and the weight lifted,
so that the sensation was as if he were floating upward.
He was going to become a part of everything there,
everything that ever existed, including the snow falling
in tiny flakes everywhere.

Ah—well, time has come to sleep the long, long sleep.

Kate was beginning to get frantic now. She didn't know
what to do, how to run the infernal machine, whether
she should try to get Scott out of there. She looked
again at him—his face seemed to have calmed somewhat, as far as she could tell. She drew back and looked

up at the clock: four minutes and twelve seconds. The second hand seemed to be speeding around.

She sat down at the computer keyboard.

"Does this thing work?" she asked, shooting Felicity a quick look. The woman appeared to be caught off guard by the question, gave back a questioning look. Kate ignored her and hit the space bar. The screen came to life and she hit the keys quickly, one after another:

SCOTT YOU OK?

She waited a moment, unsure whether she should type more. Should she wait or not?

What should I do?

And abruptly she thought of Scott's exhibition and the Web site, and on impulse she connected to the message board. She saw at once that he had not replied. Instead, she saw something else there, one of the photos from the collection. Slowly—ever so slowly—it materialized on the screen, coming in pixilated blotches that took recognizable shape and formed the photo that she remembered: There was the gray shingled fisherman's cottage, the three figures, the small boy in the center with a hand from each parent resting on a shoulder, his beautiful blazing toothy smile, and on the doorway above them the carved figure of a whale.

More keys and another click of the mouse. No reply. She signed off.

The clock read five minutes and fifty seconds.

What should she do?

～

As he moved effortlessly toward Lydia standing in the portal, Scott heard his name. Someone was calling to him sonorously, breathlessly—SCOTT—and the same beautiful voice wanted to know if he was all right. He stopped for a moment, unsure how to respond, for the voice seemed to be coming from behind. He turned—

no one was there. And as he turned back, he saw that Lydia seemed to be beckoning him onward, now with some urgency. He wasn't sure if he should go or not. That voice had stopped him, had raised doubts. He looked down at Tyler, holding his hand. The boy was leaning ahead, straining to pull him forward toward the darkened portal where Lydia was waiting. Scott took another step ahead, then another.

But as he approached he felt himself getting weaker—it was harder to walk, and he felt faint. Lydia seemed to be moving back, disappearing. It was harder to see her, not easier. She was retreating into the shadows beyond the doorway, still motioning with her hand, but now it was clear that she was not beckoning. She was waving him back, urgently, pointing to a small white door that had appeared.

He didn't know what to do. He was losing her, but it was dangerous to follow her.

So he turned to Tyler and pointed him toward the small white door. He saw a look of bewilderment on his beloved face, but he gestured to him clearly: He must go through the white door. His son sadly obeyed, and Scott waited until he was safely gone. Then he turned again to follow Lydia into a long white tunnel with a blinding light, and he heard a loud roaring sound, as if the room behind him was collapsing and everything was being sucked out through the door with him.

~

Kate heard a sound inside the machine and she saw that Scott was struggling, straining against the straps. His mouth was opened wide as if to scream, but instead he groaned slightly, a long low sound that frightened her because it seemed to come from somewhere else, some deep cavernous place.

She snapped upright and turned toward Felicity.

"That's it, turn it off!" she commanded. "Let's get him out of there."

She looked at the clock. Six minutes and forty-five seconds.

But then she heard another sound, one she could hardly believe. It came from Tyler's room, a break in the steady drone and whine of the monitors that had become so monotonous they hardly noticed it. She looked over. The machines were registering a new kind of activity, as if they had encountered resistance, sudden swells and whitecaps in what had been a mirror-calm lake.

She rushed over to him. *He's dying,* she thought. And a surge of hopelessness overwhelmed her—Scott had done so much to try to save him, had risked so much and gone into some unknown netherworld to try to bring him back or at least let him die with some finality, and now that something like that was occurring, and Tyler was finally letting go, she felt nothing but despair. She realized that she had not known how much faith she had invested in Tyler's resurrection.

Then she looked more closely. The machines that were failing were those connected directly to the computer. And the others, the ones monitoring Tyler's direct brain activity, were coughing into life. She looked at the boy lying on the bed, searching for some sign, some confirmation, and sure enough: One side of his face was moving a bit now; his lips were pulling back, like a waxen dummy that cracks alive. One eyelid was twitching a bit, then the other. She looked at his chest—it was rising and falling on its own, inhaling and exhaling more deeply than before. An arm moved slightly, the fingers of a hand contracting and then opening.

"My God," exclaimed Felicity, who was standing beside her, staring at the boy. "I think he's . . . It's a miracle—but I think he's doing that on his own. I think he's coming out of his coma."

For Kate, to see the boy coming alive was unfathomable; she realized with a jolt that for all she had known and thought and felt about him, he had never been a living person for her.

And then, from behind them, they heard yet another

sound: A sob, a gasp—it was hard to tell what it was. But the TSR machine looked odd. All its lights were on, burning as if it had shorted out somehow, and the computer screen spewed out an unending trail of garbled nonsense.

Kate glanced at the clock: seven minutes and thirty-five seconds.

She ran over to look at Scott. His face was drawn, impassive, drained, and his body was immobile. She reached in to touch a hand: It was limp, the fingers still warm but lifeless.

The clock: eight minutes.

She called Felicity over and they pulled the stretcher down and quickly detached Scott from the machine, lifting off the helmet. Kate saw something that she didn't want to think about—as she removed the eye contacts, carefully spreading the lids to pull out the concave metal cups, Scott's eyes looked odd, the pupils wide and still. And as she released the lids, his eyeballs turned up so that she could see only the whites.

She raised him to a sitting position and hooked her arms around his chest and Felicity took his legs, and together they lifted him off the stretcher and lugged him to a metal table. She took his pulse—so frightened that her fingers trembled—and for the first time all her doctorly instincts abandoned her. *Is there a pulse or not?* She couldn't tell, and she was worried—time was going by.

She looked up at Felicity.

"Do you know CPR?" she asked, her voice trembling with urgency as she began pumping his chest.

Felicity nodded. "Yes, yes," she said.

"Good. I want you to use it. But first, help me get this table over there." She pointed to the control panel, then lifted one end of the table while Felicity grabbed the other. Scott's weight made it so hard to move that they couldn't talk until it was in place.

"But why?" asked Felicity.

"Because there's something you have to do at the same time."

And with that, Kate lay down in the stretcher and pulled down the helmet and fitted on the eye contacts. The metal felt unexpectedly hot against the flesh of her eye.

"But what're you doing? I don't get it," said Felicity.

"Reset the machine," ordered Kate.

She pulled up the stretcher herself so that she went into the machine. Her next words echoed back to her from inside it: "If he could go get Tyler, maybe I can go get him.

"And whatever you do, once I'm out there, keep working on him," she added.

The wait seemed endless to her, but eventually she felt something happen: an odd sensation that began in her eyes, the flash of lights and heat going straight into her brain. Then came what looked like a shower of meteors and comets with long tails coming straight at her, so that she would have ducked if she could have moved her head inside the helmet. And finally she felt a lifting, the sensation that everything about her was moving upward, until she realized that *she* was the one moving upward, or at least a part of her was, moving up and out and then spreading out horizontally so that it seemed to take in every part of the world.

And she wasn't frightened. She didn't feel alone—she felt that her mother was somewhere there near her and even her father, which was strange because she hadn't ever known him. But she felt him there, too, somewhere in the background, a presence of him.

She could no longer think. She was a space voyager strapped in for the ride, not knowing where the rocket might take her, what she would see, where she would end up. She tried to close her eyes, but could not. Colors, flashing lights all around, the sense of movement, rapid speed.

And she opened her eyes, and she *did* see her mother. Her mother was smiling at her, the way she always had when she was young; she was not angry with her. Then her mother faded out and the lights stopped and everything cleared, like a fog lifting, and she thought she saw something she recognized.

A beach, the sound of surf, the feel of sand on the

feet. Blue sky overhead, a perfect day with the sun blazing down—it was hard to see in its blurring rays. But the
perspective shifted, like a movie camera swinging to
one side, and there it was, exactly as she had pictured it,
only even more beautiful.

A simple, gray-shingled fisherman's cottage. Its windows were dark; roses crept up a trellis; the roof over-
hanging slightly cast a shadow upon the wall. Below, a
large paving stone on which stood three figures, facing
frontward and smiling, their arms dangled over each
other—man, woman, and child. A trinity—solid, strong,
vigilant, unbreakable. Above them, where she knew it
would be, the carving of a whale.

But who were they? She blinked. Her own mother
and father standing on either side, herself in the middle,
loved, secure? Scott and Lydia and Tyler? She couldn't
tell. The faces were darkened.

She approached and stood before them and reached
out with one hand. The man moved and took her hand.
She felt faint, falling backward, and blacked out.

Scott was at the end of the tunnel. The light burning
ahead was so bright it seemed to coat him with its
warmth, to obliterate him in its embrace. He reached for
Lydia's hand and grasped it. She shook her head. He
stopped for a moment, afraid to go forward. The light
was beckoning, but he did not want to answer its call
without even knowing why.

Lydia turned slowly, gracefully. Her face was expres-
sionless, but as he looked he thought he could read sad-
ness there, a moment before she tilted her head up and
turned back again and let his hand go and drifted
toward the light. *Should I follow?* he wondered.

And then he felt another hand from behind, taking
hold of his—in a firm clasp, a clasp that seemed to say
in its willful strength: I won't let you go.

Felicity did as she was told. She kept applying CPR, pumping air into Scott's lungs, lifting his arms to let it out, long after she felt there was any hope. She did it with all the strength she could muster, even when her arms began to ache and pessimism slowed down the rhythm of her movements.

Imagine, then, her surprise when the inert body below suddenly responded, as if the engine had been kick-started: a small cough, a roll of the head, blood vessels throbbing on the temples. He lay there for some time, breathing on his own, while she stepped back to look at the miracle she had wrought.

She felt proud of herself. She had never brought anyone back from the dead before.

Then she remembered Kate. And she quickly geared down the machine and reached over to pull the stretcher out. She carefully removed the eye contacts and then lifted off the helmet.

It took a while for Kate to come around, almost as if she had been in a deep, deep sleep, except that as she began to surface, she had a broad smile playing upon her face.

Epilogue

Saramaggio caught Scott's eye and gave him a long, hard stare. That in itself was a major advance. For several weeks after Scott had returned from what he called "the land of the dead," the neurosurgeon could barely bring himself to look at him. That's how ashamed he was of his role in the whole affair.

But this was different. This was work, important work. It was crucial that Scott understand the import of what he was saying. And for that, there was no way around it—Saramaggio had to meet his look head-on and drill the lesson into him. Otherwise, he had told himself, he simply would refuse to operate.

"You understand," he said, leaning across the desk in his office, "we have no idea what he'll be like. And when I say *no idea,* that's exactly what I mean. No one's ever undergone anything like this. He'll be different—that's all we know. How different, different in what way—we can't even begin to predict.

"So if somehow you're harboring the hope that we'll be able to return Tyler to you, and bring back the little boy you loved so much exactly as he was ... well, give it up. Please give it up."

He picked up a pencil and drummed the eraser on his desk pad.

"Do you understand?" he asked finally.

Scott nodded yes and gave a little half-smile. He was amazed, as was everyone, at the transformation in Saramaggio. Gone was the arrogant, obnoxious careerist. In his place was a good, practiced, and even at times compassionate healer. Kate had joked that the man had undergone a "personality transplant." So profound was the change that most people believed it would likely last. The hospital bookie was laying two-to-one odds.

"There are some good indications," Saramaggio continued. He had to be careful here, guarded in his optimism, because he didn't want to fan the flames of false hope. "The stem cells are doing well—they've thrived in the colony, so that we have more than enough for implantation. And as far as we can tell, they're healthy. And so is Tyler—as you know."

That part was true and it never ceased to amaze him. Four weeks after returning from wherever he had been—a coma if you wanted to be a stickler, or limbo, the netherworld, some kind of alternate universe if you were given to mystical tendencies—the boy had markedly improved. He was able to move in bed a bit and focus his eyes and even give signs of comprehension. Rehabilitation was going to be lengthy and demanding.

"So do you understand what's at stake in this operation?" Saramaggio asked again, being careful not to use the word *procedure*.

"Yes, I do," Scott replied, sounding strangely formal, like someone taking a wedding vow. And he did understand, too. He knew that he would probably not have Tyler back the way he was before. But he wanted him back so badly that he would accept even a small piece of him. He would accept him—and be grateful for it.

Saramaggio showed him to the door and put an arm around his shoulders. Scott felt the arm tighten in a kind of hug, the most the man could do under the circumstances.

"I guess I'd better suit up," the surgeon said. He smiled at Scott, but the smile was drawn a little too tight. He was nervous.

"You know where to go," he added, and Scott said yes, he did. Scott gave the man's hand a squeeze—*not too hard,* he told himself reflexively, *he has to operate*—and walked out. He took the stairs to the waiting room.

It was fortunate, he thought on the way, that Saramaggio was able to keep his medical license and even to avoid prosecution. Only testimonials by the hospital higher-ups and by Scott and Kate and almost everyone else concerned had convinced the prosecutor not to press criminal charges. Instead, he had struck a private deal to perform community service, an obligation that he fulfilled by working weekends in a clinic in Greenwich—one that was not too far from a golf course. *Oh well,* thought Scott, smiling, *you can't expect everything to change.*

Felix had not been so lucky. He'd pleaded guilty to several charges, including negligent manslaughter and conspiracy to commit negligent manslaughter—the indictment would have been stronger had there only been witnesses to the death of Benchloss in the Pinegrove basement—and received a ten-year sentence and was shipped to a prison upstate. Had the case gone to trial, he would have fared even worse: Four days after he hobbled off in ankle bracelets and handcuffs, the police went to the cemetery where Tyler had supposedly been buried and dug up his coffin. There was a body inside, all right, but some quick supposition and a check of the records revealed it to belong to none other than Benchloss himself. Sergeant Paganelli was red-faced.

Quincy, ever the fast talker, escaped prosecution by the skin of his teeth. All he had done, he explained, was to construct the TSRs, not use them to experiment on patients in a mental asylum. For that—and for all the other sins—Cleaver was deemed responsible. Everyone agreed that Cleaver was guilty dead to rights. But precious little could be done about it, because he wasn't in any shape to stand trial, and he wasn't likely to be for the foreseeable future. His condition had been observable right away, seconds after Quincy had pulled him from the machine. His face was inert, frozen in some kind of grimace. His arms were wrapped around his chest, as if he were cold or hugging himself to ward off some horror. He could move, if he had to, but he didn't seem to want to. In fact, although he was alive, he acted for all intents and purposes as if he had died during his foray into the unknown. Now a patient at Pinegrove, he was the one with the most bizarre of all symptoms. Disheveled and babbling, he was stone-quiet for long periods, periods that were growing, and he had to be restrained much of the time. He was kept inside a straitjacket because otherwise he would rip at his skin with his nails, seemingly convinced that worms were crawling all over him. He also believed he could smell his own flesh rotting. How odd, Pinegrove trustees recounted, that the institution should see two people within a year that had Cotard's syndrome, and that one should have been the person in charge of treating the other.

Scott came to the waiting room. No one else was there. There were those same innocuous paintings on the wall, the battered coffee table, the magazines whose covers were creased with a hundred handlings. It gave him a jolt to see it again, but this time he rapidly adapted and didn't feel so alone in his nervousness. This was true even though Kate wasn't with him. She had wanted to be but he had insisted otherwise—he wanted her in there, in the operating room, to take care of Tyler. Only in her did he have total confidence. She alone would know what to do if things went wrong, what would be best for Tyler.

Kate, too, had been changed by her voyage into the unknown. She had told Scott about how she had treated her mother at the end of her illness and had admitted how guilty she had felt. But the guilt seemed to have gone away, and in its place were nothing but the good memories. She could look at a sparrow and see it for what it was—without thinking of the bird that had lit on her head at her mother's funeral.

As he paced around the waiting room, Scott was strangely sanguine. It wasn't déjà vu. It wasn't that he was so certain that Tyler would emerge whole and unscathed from the operation. He simply felt different, almost fatalistic, as he had ever since he came out of the machine and recovered from his time there. It was hard to describe. When people asked him—as they invariably did—he found himself describing the meteors that bombarded him and the tunnel of light, and he spoke vaguely about believing he saw Tyler. Except, of course, when he and Kate talked it over. After all, the two of them were going to spend the rest of their lives together, no matter what happened.

So to her, he told the truth—that the voyage had been immeasurably more profound, that he and Tyler had traveled together across some Rubicon to the outer limits of the spiritual world and there discovered the spark of creation, and that in that fire from wherever it was—hell or heaven, he couldn't say—their two souls had been fused together. Immutably and forever. So if he didn't have Tyler now, all of him, he knew that he would—sometime, somewhere.

And Kate believed him, and knew that she would be there with them, too.

Still, he paced around the room expectantly.

Scott waited for hours, then heard the door, and turned to see Kate entering the room, her face flushed, and after her, Saramaggio.

They walked toward him, and Scott turned fully to greet them, his breathing suddenly calm, his arms by his side.

Waiting.

Acknowledgments

A number of people helped in the preparation of this book. Among those I would like to thank personally are the following:

Jason Carmel, Howard Hughes Medical Student Fellow at the W. M. Keck Center, Rutgers University, for invaluable research into surgery for epilepsy, the transplantation of stem cells, and a highly theoretical computer system for brain life support.

My nephew, Dr. Daniel Lieberman, neurosurgeon at Neurological Surgeons in Phoenix, Arizona, and research associate professor at Arizona State University, for letting me observe him perform brain surgery and for then wielding an editorial scalpel on my manuscript.

Matt Stallcup, of the University of Southern California, for his fine summary of the work of Stuart Kauffman, and Mr. Kauffman, a visionary thinker, for permission to use his concept of "the adjacent possible."

Dr. Nick Barbaro and staff in the neurosurgery department at the University of California, San Francisco, for their hospitality, which I have poorly repaid by reference to an unnamed and completely fictitious egomaniacal surgeon there.

The Foundation for American Communications for inviting me to a conference on Covering Biotech Advances, where I gathered valuable material from papers by Dr. David Cooper of the Transplantation Biology Research Center at Massachusetts General Hospital East, and John D. Gearhart of the Department of OB-GYN at Johns Hopkins University.

Dr. Donald Reis, who until his death was director of the Weill Cornell Medical College's laboratory of neurobiology at New York Hospital, for a discussion in which he offered the observation that the fastest route into the brain is through the optic nerve.

Dr. Alex Berenstein of Beth Israel for sharing his enthusiasm and information on everything from stem cells to neurosurgery, and his partner, Dr. Fred Epstein, who performed flawless spinal surgery upon me several years ago and who is now showing courage and resilience during his own rehabilitation after a serious accident.

Arthur Ochs Sulzberger, Jr. for sharing his expertise on rock climbing, thankfully done on the ground.

Neil Nyren at Penguin Putnam for his incomparable editing skills and Kathy Robbins, my agent, for her support and insights.

My daughters, Kyra Darnton Grann, for valuable suggestions, and Liza Darnton, for scrupulous, substantive, and line-by-line editing; and Jamie, my model son.

And above all, to my wife, Nina, for her endless hours of work and, not incidentally, her inspiration, love, wit, wisdom, and adventure-making companionship.

ONYX

HUSH

Anne Frasier

"INTENSE...This is far and away the best serial killer story I have read in a very long time."
—Jayne Ann Krentz

"CHILLING...Don't read this book if you are home alone."
—Lisa Gardner

Criminal profiler Ivy Dunlap is an expert at unraveling the psyches of the most dangerous men alive. She understands the killer instinct. But even Ivy has her limits. And the Madonna Murderer will test them...

0-451-41031-9

To order call: 1-800-788-6262

S641/Frasier/Hush

A KISS GONE BAD

Jeff Abbott

"A BREAKTHROUGH NOVEL."
—*New York Times* bestselling author Sharyn McCrumb

"Rocks big time...pure, white-knuckle suspense. I read it in one sitting."
—*New York Times* bestselling author Harlan Coben

A death rocks the Gulf Coast town of Port Leo, Texas. Was it suicide, fueled by a family tragedy? Or did an obsessed killer use the dead man as a pawn in a twisted game? Beach-bum-turned judge Whit Mosley must risk everything to find out.

"Exciting, shrewd and beautifully crafted...A book worth including on any year's best list."
—*Chicago Tribune*

0-451-41010-6

Available wherever books are sold, or
to order call: 1-800-788-6262

ONYX

CHRISTOPHER HYDE

Wisdom of the Bones
A Novel

Master of suspense Christopher Hyde takes us to Dallas in November of 1963, where Homicide Detective Ray Duval is about to collide with history. His girlfriend's mother used to talk about the wisdom of the bones: "When you're close to dying, you can see the truth." Now, with six months left to live, Duval is putting that wisdom to the test. He's trying to save one last life before he loses his own to a terminal heart condition. But the President's assassination has sent shockwaves of panic throughout the city. The killer has kidnapped another girl. And—unless Duval can break the pattern—she'll be dead in forty-eight hours

0-451-41065-3

S630